Of the Past & Eternity

I0744466

Of the Past & Eternity

A Time Travel Novel

Carole Lehr Johnson

INK MAP PRESS

Of the Past and Eternity

© 2023 by Carole Lehr Johnson

Published in Pollock, Louisiana, by Ink Map Press
www.inkmappress.com

Cover Design by Victoria Davies
Cover Photography by Carole Lehr Johnson
Interior Design by Morgan Tarpley Smith
Map by Monica Theiler

Some scripture quotations are from the King James Version of the Bible.

Scripture taken from the New King James Version®. Copyright © 1982 by Thomas Nelson. Used by permission. All rights reserved.

This is a work of fiction. Names, characters, places, and incidents either are the product of the author's imagination or are used fictitiously. Any resemblance to actual persons, living or dead, events, or locales is entirely coincidental.

ISBN 978-1-952928-31-4
ISBN 978-1-952928-30-7 (ebook)

Publisher's Cataloging-in-Publication Data

Names: Johnson, Carole Lehr, author.
Title: Of the past and eternity / Carole Lehr Johnson.
Description: Pollock, LA: Ink Map Press, 2023. | Illus. ; 1 map, 26 b&w photos.|
    Summary: Thrown back in time to 18th-century England with the man she
    despises, the past becomes part of Cora Anderson's present as she struggles
    with faith, love, and her future.
Identifiers: LCCN 2023902332 | ISBN 9781952928314 (paperback) | ISBN
    9781952928307 (ebook)
Subjects: LCSH: Faith—Fiction. | Friendship—Fiction. | Man-woman
    relationships—Fiction. | Time travel—Fiction. | England—18th century—
    Fiction. | BISAC: FICTION / Christian / Historical. | FICTION / Christian /
    Romance / Historical. | FICTION / Romance / Time Travel.
Classification: LCC PS3610.O36 O3 2023 | DDC 813 J640--dc22
LC record available at https://lccn.loc.gov/2023902332

Printed in the United States of America
2023—First Edition

10 9 8 7 6 5 4 3 2 1

To my beta readers, Jennifer, Joellen, Marguerite, Morgan, Nancy, and Sherlyn.

You are the best at keeping me straight. Each of you has different editing strengths, for which I am deeply grateful. God bless you all! Thrive timesheet (May 2-15)

He has made everything beautiful in its time. Also He has put eternity in their hearts, except that no one can find out the work that God does from beginning to end.

Ecclesiastes 3:11 (NKJV)

Books by Carole Lehr Johnson

Permelia Cottage

A Place in Time

The Burning Sands

Of the Past and Eternity

N
Maze
Arch
Herbs
Kitchen Garden
Hedsworth
Orchard
Car Park
W
Lawn
E
Dovecote
Pond
Woods
Chapel
S
River Tamar

Chapter One

Boston, Massachusetts, U.S.A.
April 2023

Springtime held too many painful memories for her.

The aching loss battered her heart while she watched the cherry trees adorning the Boston Public Garden as they swayed in the wind, showering fragile blush petals over the crowded park.

Cora Anderson sat on a bench beneath a gingko tree that had most likely been a sapling during the mid-nineteenth century when the Boston Public Library was founded.

She looked at her phone, noting the time. It was a forty-minute walk from the Isabella Stewart Gardner Museum via Boylston to the park, but her sister should've taken the T or the bus and arrived by now.

Her phone trilled a text message from Selena. She wouldn't be able to make their picnic lunch because of a minor emergency at the museum. Heaving a long sigh, Cora ate a solitary lunch. Halfway through, another message arrived—a picture of an online job application.

C—This is your dream job! Check it out. NOW.

Cora grimaced, packed the remains of lunch, and dropped the phone into her purple bag, which slipped from her fingers, spilling its contents onto the concrete. A small brown Bible stared at her, and she retrieved it, lingering over the feel of the worn cover. She stuffed all the items into the bag, knowing she rarely cracked the book open. Not anymore.

It was time to return to her mundane job at the Minster Hotel. *The* dream job of a managerial position at a historic property was just a wisp on the breeze like the petals floating overhead. Years of applying at the many notable hotels on nearly every Boston street left her disillusioned.

Experience wasn't what she lacked, but it seemed no one wanted a fifty-year-old spinster. They searched for a pretty, bubbly thirty-something. Cora's appearance, both professional and personal, was always important, and she tried to maintain a healthy lifestyle, yet not obsessively so.

History was her passion, and she wanted clients to experience it to the fullest. Employment at a property that existed from times long past held her heart. If only she had the chance. But nothing had worked out yet.

The phone rang just as she reached Kenmore Square. She scanned the exterior of the six-storied hotel where she worked and tapped the phone. "Hi, Selena—"

"Cora, did you look at the job?"

An irritated sigh escaped before she could stop it. The often-sent job prospects from Selena bordered on the fanatical.

"You didn't look—did you?" Impatience tinted Selena's voice.

"No, ma'am." Cora recognized the sarcastic tone in her own words, unable to stifle it.

Someone in the background bandied about her name to Selena.

"Selena, who is that?"

"Oh, it's just Thomas. He said to tell you he knows the current director, and you sound exactly like who she wants as an assistant manager."

"Is this another one of Thomas's cast-off girlfriends?"

"I heard that!" A deep voice commented. "She has you on speaker, love."

Cora couldn't help but snicker. "Let me guess—she's British?"

"You are *good*," Thomas quipped. "Yes, she is."

"Go back to work, you slug," Selena reprimanded him. "I'll take care of my sister's professional life. So, shoo!"

Cora raised her voice. "Bye, Thomas."

"Bye, Cora. Don't let Selena bully you. But this is a brilliant opportunity."

"I give up. I'll look at it tonight. For now, my current employer has probably noticed I'm late."

"Good. I'll come to your place after work, and we'll discuss it. Thomas told me he's been to the property, and it's brilliant."

"That's Thomas's favorite word." Cora cleared her throat. "You're coming all the way to Sommerville?"

"It's only forty-five minutes on the T."

Cora sniffed. "And forty-five minutes back—on a work night."

"You sound like Grandma." She released a loud sigh into the receiver. "I miss her."

Cora's heart squeezed. "Me too."

The grip of shared grief slogged through the space between them. Selena's voice lowered. "I can't believe it's just the two of us now."

Though Cora understood what Selena meant, she said, "We have cousins."

Selena countered, "That's not the same as parents and grandparents."

"Let's not do this again, Selena. God took them from us, and that's that."

"Oh, good grief! God didn't do it to punish us."

Tears never came easily for Cora, but this time they arrived with force, unyielding. She repeated, "Please—let's not do this."

⚭

Cora answered the knock on the apartment door at six-thirty

to find Selena with her overnight case and a large takeout bag from their favorite Italian restaurant.

"That smells delicious, but what's with the sleepover?"

Selena placed the takeout on Cora's kitchen counter and slung her bag onto the sofa with a bounce. "Thought we needed to regress to our teens." She removed two lidded containers and deposited them on the surface.

Cora's eyebrows lifted. "To discuss boys?"

Selena sent Cora a glare that quickly morphed into serious contemplation. "Well . . . I've always wanted to ask you about Bobby Young."

Cora's face heated at the mention of her fourteen-year-old-self's crush. "That was a lifetime and three thousand miles ago."

Selena's phone rang, and she answered with a resigned sigh. "Hi, Thomas—" She helped herself to a bottle of water and steadied the phone between chin and shoulder. "No, I've just arrived. Yes, I'll tell her. Thanks." She stabbed the end button. "That man is more concerned about your career than I am."

The takeout container crackled as Cora popped the lid and lifted it to take a whiff. "What's this?"

"Your favorite." Sarcasm laced Selena's response as she strode to Cora's television. "I thought we'd watch that Hugh Henley movie I gave you for Christmas."

Cora ignored the movie comment and refocused on the dinner. "You mean *your* favorite."

"Don't complain. Open the other one." Selena rummaged through Cora's DVDs.

Cora discovered chicken Alfredo, garlic bread, and spinach salad. She stared at the thoughtful meal, and for the second time that day, tears threatened.

Selena returned to the kitchen and slipped an arm around Cora, noting the tears. "This is unlike you. Tell me what's wrong."

Cora shook her head, snatched a napkin from the counter, and dabbed her eyes.

"I'll get you a bottle of water, and we'll talk." She tugged Cora to the cream-colored sofa, then fetched the water and dropped next to her. "By the way . . ." She held up the Hugh Henley DVD, the cover revealing a Regency man and woman locked in an embrace in front of a grand house. "This has never been opened."

"What would you have done if you hadn't found it?" Cora sighed. "Plus—you know I can't stand that man."

"I brought another one, assuming you'd used this one for target practice." Selena smirked and ignored the slur toward her favorite actor. "Now, tell me what's wrong."

"There's nothing to tell. I'm just out of sorts lately." Cora inhaled a shuddering breath. "A little nostalgic. Spring does that to me."

Selena patted her hand. "Same here. But we can't go on forever crippled by emotion every spring—even if that's when we lost everyone. It was just coincidence."

"There's no such thing as coincidence."

Selena studied her for a moment. "Do you really believe that?"

"I do." Cora sipped the water. "That's scriptural—I think."

She paused. "So, if that's true, then God did *choose* to take our family."

"Cora. Tragedy happens. Grief happens. We trust God in His wisdom to help us navigate it all." Their gazes held for a long while before Selena said, "Let's eat. I'm famished."

They moved to Cora's small dining table and ate in silence, Cora's thoughts tossed scenarios around about the loss of so many family members in such a brief span of years. Selena had been the strong one through it, while Cora had fallen apart.

Though Selena was more than ten years younger, Cora had leaned heavily upon her. So much so it was the final nail in the coffin of Selena's marriage. Her husband couldn't handle the constant choice of Cora's needs over his—or at least, that's what he told Selena word for word at the lawyer's office.

The guilt ate at Cora for her part in their failed marriage, yet Selena's husband, whom she would no longer refer to by name, hadn't exactly been the most attentive to Selena.

Cora had seen how his eyes roamed over her and their female cousins at family events. *Window shopping*, he had joked with Selena if she caught his gaze on another woman.

Selena tapped her arm, and Cora jumped.

"Where were you?" Selena's face paled. "Oh, my gosh—you were beating yourself up again about Randall, weren't you? Cora, I've told you repeatedly it wasn't your fault. If he'd been a proper husband, he'd have understood until you healed."

Cora moved the food around on her plate before letting the fork slip onto the china with a clink. "Yet, here I am—*not* healed. I never will be!" She jumped to her feet.

Selena stood and embraced her. "Let out the anger, but trust God, Cora." Her voice lowered to a whisper. "Please. I'm praying for you."

"I'll try, but I don't think He listens to me right now." Cora pulled away. "I'm off to bed."

"Oh, no, you're not. We haven't discussed the job. Thomas contacted his ex-girlfriend, and she's put in a word for you, so you'll be at the head of the queue." One corner of Selena's mouth lifted. "Leave it to Thomas to use a British term. I wonder what his Swedish ex would've called it?" She led Cora to the sofa and tossed her a throw.

The comment sliced thorough Cora's grief, and she chuckled, her heart warming.

"Now, let's sit, and I'll tell you all Thomas said, then we'll watch the movie." Selena went through Thomas's conversation with his ex-girlfriend about Cora's qualifications and her passion for historical properties.

Before she finished, her thoughts were a confused tangle. "Well, I guess I won't have to fill out an application. Sounds like Thomas has told my life story, plus my resume."

Selena's eyes widened. "I suppose the entire London agency knows about you by now. I'm surprised they hadn't already snatched up someone from the U.K." She waved a hand. "Anyway, first things first, you must go to England in ten days to interview. Thomas said the owner is a bit eccentric and only has his staff conduct interviews on-site. He also said once the manager gave their requirements for the position, she said you seemed a perfect fit. This is your chance, Cora."

Cora snuggled under the green throw, knees drawn to her

chin, as all Selena said sank in.

Could this truly be her chance—or just another dead end?

CAROLE LEHR JOHNSON

Chapter Two

When Cora didn't sleep, her mind churned like the plane carrying passengers thousands of miles from home. What *was* she doing on this flight?

To bolster courage, she read Selena's text message repeatedly.

You're doing the right thing. If it doesn't work out, the worst that could happen is a nice vacation in England. After all, you may meet your own Mr. Darcy.

A winking emoji blinked.

The message made her smile and lifted her spirits. Selena was right. She would make the most of this trip. After all, she'd just spent her savings to travel to the U.K. and had to beggar herself to her boss to have a vacation on short notice.

After customs, Cora made her way to the rail station and settled in for the two-and-a-half-hour train ride to Isley Shafton. Judith Bennett, the hotel manager, said a car would meet the train.

True to her word, a stout middle-aged man with dark hair held a sign with her name printed in large, bold letters.

"Hello, Miss Anderson. I'm Rory." He reached for her bag. "I'll take that, and we'll be on our way. It's but a short drive to the house. Nice scenery and all."

"Thank you, Rory. I appreciate the lift." He bolted like a racehorse down the platform and once in the car served as impromptu tour guide. Lush, rolling countryside sped past until she saw a sign for the village of Isley Shafton.

They crossed an old scenic bridge, and Cora peered down into a slow-moving river.

She tapped the window. "Rory, what river is this?"

"It's the Tamar—a saline and tidal estuary. We've just crossed from Devon into Cornwall." Once over the bridge Rory turned off the main road and onto a narrower one in the middle of a thick forest. "The water supplies some fine salmon in season."

Cora's attention was now on her first sighting of Hedsworth House. It appeared as a quick blur as they drove along the wooded lane, brief glimpses of the structure viewed as if a slideshow panning forward. They glided along a pebbled drive and about fifty feet before the house, it curved into a circle.

At first it appeared to be a rambling Tudor-style building,

its granite front and slate roof glinting in the afternoon sun. Noting the many roofs and chimneys, each era vividly defined, her gaze caressed every section. The scope of its long history sent a chill over her skin.

Her imagination slid backward in time, seeing what might have been, as if the façade whispered her name, calling out to her beyond the centuries. The tires of her *carriage* crunched to a stop, and she half-imagined a footman reaching for her hand to help her alight.

The daydream vanished when a smiling woman whisked Cora through the front entrance, which took them into the massive great hall decorated in the medieval style. Overwhelmed by the sheer size alone, she soaked in the room's ambiance of white-washed plaster and lofty ceiling. The woman's voice barely seeped into Cora's thoughts, saying Judith was in a meeting and would meet her after dinner and led her to her room—actually a suite as it turned out.

The splendid Regency room was done in blue, and she took in every minute detail, including the Mahogany antiques. The warm, brown wood sofa, though upholstered in blue and white striped fabric, did *not* appear to be comfortable.

The entire space, down to the floral print wallpaper, exuded authentic Regency character. She noted the bell-pull next to the fireplace and wondered if it still worked.

While preoccupied with the workings of the long-ago era, a meal arrived with Judith's compliments—herb-roasted chicken, spring vegetables in garlic butter sauce, and sparkling water. Once she'd finished the delicious meal, a knock sounded. The woman who had shown her to her room entered with a magazine she handed to Cora. She said Judith requested she read it to 'get up to speed.' The cover featured Hedsworth House, noting it to be *the* premium period experience for discerning guests.

She flipped through it until a celebrity interview stopped her. A photograph gracing one-third of the page—Hugh Henley. She almost slammed the magazine shut, as much as one *could* slam a magazine closed. Something about the guy pushed her buttons. He came across as an arrogant snob, refusing to leave the U.K., only taking Regency era roles, sounding like he was part of the peerage, nose in the air.

Well, maybe not that high.

Cora and her sister nearly argued over the man, Selena saying he was a dish with his wavy, collar-length brown hair and ice-blue eyes. Being over six feet tall didn't hurt the image either. Selena could go on for days about the *hunky* actor.

Cora shoved the magazine away, and sudden shame gripped her. Why should she feel so strongly about someone she'd never met?

"Stop being ridiculous!" she reprimanded herself as she retrieved her phone to check for messages.

A brief knock and the door opened a crack, bringing her head up with a jerk. A petite blonde with a shoulder-length blunt cut slipped into the room. "Hello, love, did I interrupt a conversation?" Her eyes traveled to the phone Cora held.

Cora's face warmed. She wasn't about to share personal thoughts—verbalized or not. "No, just talking to myself."

"I assume you've guessed I'm Judith." She extended her hand. "A pleasure to meet you."

"It's nice to meet you." Cora clasped her hand in a firm

shake.

Judith motioned to the blue sofa, and they sat as a knock sounded once again. Judith said, "Come in, Lisa."

The woman entered, pushing a small cart laden with a pot of tea, cups, and an assortment of sweets.

"Thought you may like dessert as fortification for a tour of the house." Judith poured tea and dismissed Lisa with a bright smile.

Cora's eyes widened at the spread. "After that dinner, I'm not sure where I'll put it." She patted her stomach.

Judith dug into an enormous piece of carrot cake and rolled her eyes with exaggerated pleasure. "Amanda can certainly bake."

Cora marveled at the tiny woman's hearty appetite. Judith's expression sobered when she caught her watching. "I'm sorry. I meant to inform you we'd need to do the tour today. We have a large group arriving tomorrow, and there's no time then. You must be knackered, but there's nothing for it. Planning the ball for Saturday and such. Gives our guests a bit to settle before the main event."

Cora's head clouded. "Ball?"

"Yes. Didn't you see the article in the magazine I sent up?"

Should she confess she didn't finish reading it? "I . . . um . . . got side-tracked."

"No worries. I'll fill you in when I show you the main ballroom."

"There's more than one?" Cora's cup clinked against the saucer, and she cringed at the thought of chipping the fine china.

"We actually have three. Each accommodates different numbers based on our bookings. If we only have fifteen guests, we ready the smallest ballroom and so on."

Cora said, "I see." But she really didn't. Why would they go to so much trouble and expense for so few?

"Best be getting to it." Judith stood. "We'd do a ball if we had two guests. The owner insists."

"Why?" Cora obediently followed her into the polished, wood-floored corridor.

"He's a stickler for customer service and giving our clientele an authentic Regency experience. No matter what." She emphasized the comment with waggling eyebrows.

Unable to think of anything clever to say, Cora said, "That's commendable."

"Indeed." Judith unlocked an intricately carved door and flipped a switch which lit a faux candle chandelier and sconces that illuminated a spacious room.

Her breath caught at the sight of the magnificent murals on each wall. The Greco Roman artwork covered every inch. Massive in scope, they depicted scenes from ancient times, from warriors fighting battles to lavish feasts. The colors of ochre, blue, red, and black dominated the mixture of tones.

Cora regarded the floor. Someone had stenciled half the room with brightly colored tiles in intricate designs. Puzzled, she asked, "Why is the floor not completed?" She made one step, but Judith seized her arm.

"It's not finished. The artist will complete it before the ball. It's chalk."

"Chalk?" Cora's confusion fueled curiosity.

"Yes. To chalk ballroom floors was all the rage in the Regency era. The idea was born to keep dancers from slipping on the polished floor. They enjoyed the artwork until it was gone."

"This is extraordinary," Cora whispered in awe.

Judith sighed appreciatively. "It should be. HRH has spared no expense recreating all things Regency. He chose everything himself."

"Truly?" Cora asked with astonishment. She wanted to ask why Judith called the owner HRH but thought better of it.

Judith lowered her voice. "I have to confess I doubted his knowledge on the subject and did a bit of research. He was spot on. Down to the last trinket."

Cora's curiosity got the better of her. "How old is he?"

"About fifty."

Cora made no further comment. Though, she wondered how a man barely fifty would have such a great interest in and knowledge of the period. Was he an academic or an amateur historian?

Judith continued the tour, ending at the west side of the car park, near the private garden, a large stone arch prominently facing them. Her gaze swung toward the house, and she noticed a lilac trained to cover a high stone wall, the house roof peeking above.

Continuing their stroll, Cora returned her gaze to the arch. "How lovely." Her fingertips caressed the age-old stone warmed by the waning sun.

"That it is." Judith squinted at the arch. "And for some unknown reason, HRH harbors a bit of an obsession with this pile of rocks. He *claims* it's a remnant of an old abbey that once stood on the estate grounds."

Cora startled at the woman's cynical tone.

"I apologize. That sounded more severe than I intended." She drew a long breath. "It can weary one at times when everything is about this house." She waved a hand to encompass their surroundings. "Being kept as close to its original state and with the Regency refurbishing made from that era. I mean, it was built during medieval times and added on in the Tudor era, *then* they remodeled parts of the interior in the Regency." She shivered. "Makes my head spin."

"Is the upkeep extremely hard to manage?"

Judith tugged Cora through the arch and pointed to a gravel car park. "That was an Olympic-sized swimming pool when HRH purchased the house." She paused for effect. "He immediately had it filled in."

Cora blinked back her confusion. "Whatever for?"

"Said it was not fit for a historic property and to maintain its integrity, he would not allow it. He also had the concrete removed from the drive, paths, etc., and replaced with Regency era elements."

Cora frowned but said nothing. The owner had gone to extremes indeed.

"It shocked us he allowed the indoor plumbing to remain. Thankfully, it didn't take long to convince him how much work it would create for the staff—and the twenty-first century guests would not have been too keen on it either."

The sun slipped behind the thick forest on the west side of the house, and Cora yawned. To think she had only been in the U.S. that very morning.

Judith offered an understanding smile. "I didn't intend to keep you up so late your first day here, but unfortunately it couldn't wait." She guided Cora toward the house. "We'll continue tomorrow morning over breakfast." Their feet crunched across the gravel drive as they approached the house. "Meet me in the red parlor. Any of the staff can direct you. Shall we say half-nine? It'll give us both a little lie in."

Cora exhaled and grinned. "If that means sleep late, I'm okay with that."

Judith nodded with a smile. "Indeed!"

ೞഔ

Cora strolled along the corridor, morning light slanting across the polished floors. She clasped her hands behind her back, fighting the temptation to touch the antique furniture, brush a fingertip on the textured canvas of the portraits, and sit on the elaborate needle-worked bench cushions.

The sounds of movement came and went as she walked. A staff member crossed her path, going from one room to another bearing a tray of breakfast remnants. The aroma of scrambled eggs and ham elicited a growl from her stomach, a reminder she had slept later than usual. She asked the woman where the red parlor was and followed her into a vibrant room, the window looking toward the private garden they'd toured the evening prior.

Judith sat at a small table by the large window, offering her a perfect side view of the walls that formed the garden, the *pile of rocks* partially visible from this angle. She greeted Cora and offered her a seat and tea.

Welcoming the cup of tea with enthusiasm, Cora's gaze traveled to the arch, sunlight reflecting tiny specks off the mica embedded in the stone. The effect made it appear as if it glowed.

"Cora? Are you well, dear? You appear to have seen a fairy?" Judith's cup hovered near her lips.

Collecting her thoughts, Cora blinked, her vision clearing. "I'm fine." She gestured toward the gardens. "It's so lovely. And such a perfect day."

Judith nodded. "If you'd like, we'll tick off the formalities in my office."

Cora's mind whirled, not wanting to voice a question. Was Judith meaning the interview, or did she already have the job?

They finished their breakfast and settled inside a dark-paneled room with a large antique mahogany desk surrounded by floor-to-ceiling bookcases.

Cora's eyes scanned the old books, wondering what treasures lay within.

Judith coughed. "My mum always told me I had a gift for sizing people up. We've known each other less than twenty-four hours, and if it were up to me, I'd say you have the job."

Cora's grip tightened on the chair's arms. "Truly?"

She repeated, "If it were up to me. Yes. I see the reaction to your surroundings is appreciative. I recognize your near reverence for history."

"Am I that obvious?" Cora slackened her hold on the chair. "I've loved history since I was a child. Especially British history." She stared at her clasped hands. "It was a struggle not to study everything I could get my hands on about

Hedsworth.”

Judith opened a file. “What kept you?”

“I hate to confess I didn't want to jinx the possibility, believing I didn't stand a chance.”

Judith's eyes widened. “Why ever would you not? There's nothing in your application that would disqualify you.” She turned toward the computer and pecked on the keyboard, scanning the screen.

“Not on the surface.” Cora grimaced. “Most corporations want younger, recently educated employees.”

“To begin with, your professional record is stellar, and age doesn't factor into our hiring. If you can do the job, nothing else matters.” She continued to peruse Cora's file and slid a manicured nail across the page. “Your previous employers have nothing but good things to say about your work performance.” She peered over the top of purple-rimmed reading glasses. “You've worked at mainly small chain properties?”

Cora met Judith's gaze. “Yes. Modern properties—not historical.”

“Good job performance is just that. It matters not if it be a dog kennel or a posh villa overlooking the Mediterranean.”

Cora's heart squeezed, her already-present regard for this woman increased. “That's very kind of you.”

“No. It's fact.” She relaxed into the desk chair with crossed arms. “I take it you've been passed over before?” The tone was more a statement than a question.

“A few times.” Cora swallowed.

“Then they missed an excellent opportunity.” Judith

briefly studied Cora. "Of course, your portfolio must be gone over by HRH first."

Cora grinned. "Do you call your employer that to his face?"

Without hesitation, Judith said, "Of course." Her phone rang, and she answered it cheerily, "Hallo."

Cora stood and moved away from the desk to give Judith privacy and examined the gold-embossed books, the pull too strong to resist. With hands clutched at her waist to stem the urge to caress the volumes, she lost herself in the book world.

"A little glitch in HRH's schedule."

Cora reclaimed her seat.

"Nothing monumental, a brief business delay for his return. You'll be able to meet him at the ball." She paused. "You can stay that long? Can you not?"

"Well—"

"Oh, come now. We'll pay to change your flight home, and your room and board are already complimentary."

"That's kind of you, but my boss won't be happy."

"Does he know why you're here?" Judith's lips pursed.

"No."

"Then just say you need a few more days of R and R. That's not a lie, after all."

Cora considered for a moment, knowing it was true. She desperately needed some time away, and she hadn't taken a vacation in quite a while. "But I have no formal wear for a ball." She hoped the excuse would release her from attending.

"No worries. We'll get you sorted. We have an on-site costume shop for our guests' use—no charge." Judith stood.

"HRH insists all events be in costume from the Regency era."

Cora bit her lip. It appeared the owner indeed insisted on many things. What if she didn't make the cut?

⚜

Cora stared at the leafy expanse of garden, unsure where she stood according to the grounds map. She frowned, rotating the map to get a better perspective. She hadn't meant to get so turned around on her morning walk.

A house employee appeared around a grove of trees and noted her confusion, likely mistaking her for a guest.

"That's the maze through there, if that's what you're looking for. It's a bit shadowy in places but not too hard to manage."

Cora asked, "Am I likely to get lost and have to be rescued?"

The red-haired girl chuckled. "Not *likely*. It's an easy one. The owner said he'd not want to distress anyone, so he made it simple enough." She scrutinized Cora. "Are you going to give it a go?"

"I believe I will, since there's no danger."

The girl pointed to a lush green doorway. "That's the entrance, but you'll come out on the other end of the private garden. Walls enclose it, the hedges inside are maze-like, and the ceiling is created by crisscrossing wires covered with ivy like an arbor. It's darker than the maze—more *private-like*. But you'll see the exit once you get there." She waved as she strode toward the house.

Cora brushed a hand on the glossy leaves of the hedge and entered the maze with filtered sunlight, revealing the winding, stone path. Peace fell over her as she meandered until a baritone voice drifted through the passageway. She froze, listening to the pleasant singing, searching for a path away from the sound when she noticed a narrow gap in the hedge and ducked into near darkness and strolled a short distance.

Cora slammed into a very real, very masculine body. Shards of light barely illuminated the deeper shadows, revealing a pair of piercing, blue eyes. The man gripped her shoulders and gazed down at her.

"Are you lost?" His voice unmistakably belonged to the singer.

For the first time in a long while, Cora became tongue-tied, staring at a face mostly obscured by the shadows.

"Have I injured you? Please allow me to assist you to the house." He released her, and she stumbled, missing his steadying hands.

She shook from the daze. "That won't be necessary. I'm fine. I'll head back the way I came." She turned and took a step forward when his question stopped her.

"If I may ask, what is your name?"

Without turning, she said, "Cora Anderson."

"It is a pleasure to meet you, Cora Anderson."

At his response, she looked back, but he was gone.

The sound of rustling leaves left her standing inside the small gap by which she'd come. She used the flashlight on her phone to illuminate the circular space, which must've been the center of the private garden. An ornate white iron table and two chairs graced the middle of the area.

Cora noticed a book on the table. She picked up the small bound volume and flipped to the copyright page. It was a seventeenth-century version of *The Book of Common Prayer*. A handwritten inscription graced the inside cover.

To my loving son. May this book remind you that this world is not our eternal home.

Mother

27 April 1776

26

Chapter Three

Cora stared at the green, leather-bound book, the spine lettered in gilt. She flipped the pages and found it contained lovely marbled endpapers. Something so precious should not be left outside. Surely the man was in an extreme rush to leave such a treasure.

Hesitating over what to do—caution won. She gingerly held the small book and searched for the exit. Moments later, Judith met her across the well-manicured lawn, a little breathless.

"There you are." She rested a hand on her chest. "Sandra said she'd seen you go into the maze near gone an hour. I grew concerned."

"I'm fine." Cora presented the book with a flourish. "I found this antique in the maze."

"Oh, that." She took it from Cora. "I'll return it. But that's not part of the maze. It's inside the private garden. You must've entered through a gap from the maze side, which borders the garden."

Cora was about to ask who the man was when Sandra called out to Judith, who offered an apologetic smile.

"Gotta go. Duty calls." She raised the book skyward. "Thanks for this. He would be devastated to have it lost or damaged. It's over two hundred years old."

The man's piercing gaze returned to Cora. Who was he—a guest, a staff member on break? She would be sure to find out.

☙❧

"Cora, you look fabulous!" Judith stepped back so Cora could see her reflection in the mirror. "Especially since you still have jetlag."

She blinked. Was it really *her* in Regency attire, standing in the center of a gorgeous bedroom? This place certainly provided an era immersive experience.

Her light brown hair was swept into an updo, a slender lavender ribbon woven through her tresses. The floor-length ivory dress was adorned with seed pearls, a wide lavender satin ribbon accentuating the high waistline.

Judith cleared her throat and pointed to Cora's feet. "Those tan loafers won't do." She tapped her chin. "Hmm . . . let me check the costume shop for dancing slippers. Be back in a jiff."

Afraid to sit and wrinkle the delicate gown, Cora peered out of the large bow window and saw a tall, dark-haired man in Regency clothing ambling across the lawn toward the maze. He strode with purpose, his bearing proud.

The door flung open, and Cora whirled as Judith entered, a pair of ivory satin slippers dangling from two fingers.

"Eureka!" She dropped them at Cora's feet. "Try them on. I guessed at your size."

Cora slid her feet into the buttery smooth footwear. A perfect fit.

"Splendid!" Judith's eyes lit with satisfaction. "I'll pop by in half an hour, and we'll go down together."

Cora agreed and asked, "May I sit, or would *HRH* be upset if I arrived in a wrinkled state?"

Judith cackled. "That *is* rich. You're catching on quickly, but no. Sitting is fine. See you soon."

The half hour flew by with Cora nervously straightening her gown and hair. She snapped a few pictures of her outfit and sent them to Selena, then received a smile emoji. Cora shrugged, telling herself that her sister was most likely too busy at work to respond.

She slumped onto a chair and began flipping through a magazine when Judith collected her, and they went to the ballroom. A costumed staff member opened the heavily carved doors and announced them by name.

Guests mingled around the room while musicians played softly from the minstrels' gallery above. Cora scanned the room admiring the women's gowns from white muslin to pastel shades. Some wore flowers tucked into their upswept hair, while others had ribbons and pearls secured among the curls.

The question Cora was about to voice to Judith about the women's clothing died on her lips when a grating voice behind them caught her attention.

"I hope they do *not* perform a reel, sister."

The sister answered nasally, "Nor do I. Such barbaric dancing. I cannot abide a display of coarseness."

Cora turned slightly to see the two women, their heads together in covert conversation. The taller one waved her ivory fan in a jerking motion, and said in a lowered tone, "I hear tell there may be a *waltz*." She raised her fan to hide her face, but from Cora's angle she could clearly see her mouth the final word as if it were a curse.

Cora latched onto the dance subject and her insides tightened. She'd not considered the possibility of having to do a period dance.

She grabbed Judith's arm, terror striking her and said between clenched teeth. "Am I expected to dance?"

Judith's eyes widened, smile fading. "You can't dance?"

"Barely. I took a ballroom dancing course in college, but they didn't teach historical dances."

Judith's gaze skittered around the room, lighting on a tall, handsome man approaching. She spoke in a low voice, "Here comes HRH. I hope you can fake a dance with him."

Cora's heart pounded, studying the man in horror. This was HRH? No, he absolutely couldn't be.

His features grew ever more distinct in the candlelight as he stopped in front of them, offering a dashing smile to Cora, and there was no doubt in her mind who he was—the celebrated actor she loathed. Hugh Henley.

CZ80

"Good eve, Miss Bennett, Miss Anderson." The man gave a slight bow and inclined his head, but Cora couldn't utter a word. She'd never been clear-headed around good-looking men.

Judith's lips parted, the line between her eyebrows deepening. "You've met?"

He clasped his hands behind his back. "Not formally. I apologize for the improper greeting."

"You never gave your name," Cora blurted out, "And I didn't recognize you in the dark."

Judith's features shifted from confusion to slow understanding. "Why didn't you introduce yourself?" she asked Hugh.

Without hesitation, he said, "It is not proper for a man to do so."

Cora stifled a snicker while Judith rolled her eyes. So, the man had a sense of humor. His gaze caught hers, and though his smile faded, his eyes brightened. Was it humor—or a challenge?

"May I collect a drink for you?" He aimed the question at Cora, but it was meant for Judith as well.

Judith thanked him and asked for lemonade.

Cora abhorred the drink. "None for me, thank you."

For a fleeting moment, he appeared displeased. "Are you not partial to the refreshment?"

Surprised by his discernment, she nodded. "I don't care for its tartness."

"Lemonade for Miss Bennett and orgeat for Miss Anderson." He presented a half-bow and left them.

Cora leaned toward Judith. "I've read he is a fanatic about keeping Regency protocol, but I didn't believe it. Or is this just for the ball?"

"No. This is Hugh Richard Henley—in all his glory." She waved an arm to encompass the room.

Slow dawning awakened Cora's understanding, and her mouth dropped. "*HRH*. I get it now. I thought you were being sarcastic."

Judith laughed a little too loud and long for the formal atmosphere. "I don't mean to sound disrespectful of my employer—"

Cora's mouth slackened, and she faced Judith. "Your employer?"

"Didn't you know?" Judith's eyes widened. "The paparazzi were all on top of him buying the house."

Cora stammered, "He *owns* the house?" Her head spun with the knowledge. What had she stepped into? "I have to admit, I'm not a fan. My sister is all nut-cake over him. When she talks about him, I shut down."

"May I ask why?"

Cora thought about how to respond without giving offense. "I'll be honest by saying he comes across as arrogant, above others with his demands and insistence."

A throat cleared from behind Cora, and she nearly jumped. It was Hugh. Had he heard her? If so, she had just lost the job.

Judith tapped Hugh's arm. "You scared me witless." She accepted the glass of lemonade and sipped. "That's not gentlemanly."

Hugh had the good grace to appear shamed. "No. It was not." He handed Cora a glass of orgeat, and she carefully tried the drink, which tasted of almond and citrus.

"I beg your apology. There was a crush, and the best path to you lovely ladies was from behind."

Once his gaze found Cora's, she thought she saw a glint of sadness in the ice-blue depths. Though, in the next moment, any trace was gone.

Taking another sip, she savored the drink. It must've shone on her face because Hugh's eyes brightened.

"The drink is to your liking, Miss Anderson?"

Cora nodded "Very much."

He appeared pleased, tiny creases forming around his eyes—eyes that had caught hers in the garden.

The music paused, and Cora looked a question at Judith, but she read her expression and responded, "The dancing will now begin."

Cora nodded, and Hugh leaned closer. "If your card is not filled, may I have the first dance?"

Her chest tightened, horrified at the thought of embarrassing herself. Should she feign a headache? After all, as the employer, he was the one to approve—or disapprove—her likely position at this amazing house. But she also wondered if she could work for such a man.

Cora glanced at him. "Thank you, but I give a warning to your feet. I'm not a particularly good dancer, and—"

Hugh interrupted. "It is of no concern. All shall be well." He flashed a disarming smile and led her away.

She gripped her long-held dislike of him, tossing away the effect of his charm, the intrigue in the way he looked at her. The egocentric celebrity would *not* melt her with his good looks.

Cora Anderson would be all business.

"We'll see how you feel after it's over, Mr. Henley."

Her abrupt manner did nothing to alter his demeanor, nor the formal address, and with a gentle pat to the back of her hand resting on his arm, he said, "My feet shall survive, to be sure."

Once they stood face-to-face, Cora placed a hand on his shoulder, and he tensed. With the clearing of his throat, he loosened his hold on her other hand in his, positioned a hand on her waist, and stared into her eyes.

Unfortunately, the simple action rippled an unexpected wave of pleasure through Cora, and she froze at the precise second the music began. The awkward moment passed as he expertly led them into step. Much too close to fully relax, the flow of the waltz swept her into the moment. He kept his eyes on hers, not once averting them, guiding their movements with experienced ease.

Cora was powerless to pull her gaze from his. Was this almost magnetic pull to the man what Selena and his millions of fans felt too when watching him on the screen?

Except, unlike them, she was actually in his arms like a heroine from his films, and furthermore, she was absolutely *not* counted among his fandom. She shouldn't feel anything concerning him.

"May I share my thoughts?" Hugh's minty breath caressed her face, and his expectant expression begged a response.

"I'm unsure how to answer that."

His laugh had the ring of music. "Then I shall assume that to be yes." He swept them to the doors leading to the terrace, yet not fully out of doors and away from the sight of others.

From what Judith said, he would avoid any hint of impropriety.

Hugh pulled her closer and lowered his voice. "I have not properly interviewed you for the position as Judith's assistant, yet I have read your resume thoroughly and find nothing lacking."

The music, his embrace, the historic atmosphere, and the sense they were floating undid her resolve and, for a moment, she fully understood Selena's fantasy regarding this man.

Cora found it hard to speak but pressed onward. "And your thoughts are?"

His lips parted as if to speak, then he hesitated. "I wonder why someone of your beauty and age should desire to leave your home of such a distance, and—"

Cora sputtered with indignation. "Beauty? Age? What do you mean by that?"

A question flashed across his face before he recovered enough to answer. "Merely that a young woman such as yourself would certainly desire a husband and a family."

Not expecting his answer, she blurted out, "Young? Mr. Henley, I'm fifty years old, and the whole *marriage-and-children* ship has sailed. I want an enjoyable career, and a place like Hedsworth is just what I'm looking for. A place to embrace its history, ancestors, the legacy an old place carries forward. Without loving care, a house like this . . ."

Her gaze took in the nearby guests as they now danced, which was more like a refined version of an American square dance. She returned her gaze to his. It was as if no one existed but the two of them, still in one another's arms, motionless, holding gazes while they spoke.

Cora suddenly felt discomfited as she stared into his eyes.

"I meant no disrespect. It is just that you are so lovely and accomplished. I considered you would have long since been married."

She released him and stepped back, anger rising over his assumptions. "Why must any woman be married, lovely or not? Maybe it's because they either don't wish to be or they have not met the right man."

He frowned. "That is true. They may not wish to marry, or perhaps they have not yet met the man God has set aside for them?"

Her ire rose at such a personal assumption. "Why would you assume so? Furthermore, what about yourself? Why are you unmarried, Mr. Henley? Has God not brought the right woman for you?"

"That is fair. Not everyone is destined to marry." He turned away as if gathering his thoughts. "It is in God's hands for us all, is it not?"

She tried to remain calm. Her eyes stung, memories of her loved ones appearing in her mind's eye. "Yes, God may bring love, but He also allows tragedy."

The music changed to the quadrille, and he cleared his throat, a trace of hurt crossing his features. "I do apologize, for I see my words have caused you pain. It was not my intent. I am certainly not above tragedy and have lost those dear to me."

Cora's anger lessened with the surprise of his sharing about his past. He appeared to be a private man, from what her sister said, always avoiding personal questions in interviews.

A petite, dark-haired woman approached and curtsied. "Lord Hedsworth, I do believe your name is on my card for the next dance." She smiled prettily, showing perfect teeth.

An amused glint of mischief shone in his eyes, making Cora believe Hugh was not in fact on the woman's dance card, but he was too much a gentleman to say so.

He bowed. "I shall collect you before the dance commences."

She giggled, bringing a pink, gloved hand to her mouth, and sashayed away.

Hugh—*Lord* Hedsworth—however she was supposed to address him, returned his attention to Cora. "It seems I apologize to you with regularity. Please accept my apologies, but I must find my next partner after I have a word with Judith." He tilted his chin slightly. "Thank you for the dance. I hope to converse with you again soon."

Cora offered a slight smile, sadness still clinging to her. She watched him go to Judith, whisper in her ear, lifting one finger and then another as if ticking off two tasks to accomplish. Eliciting a cheerful smile, Judith nodded and hurried from the room.

A few minutes later, a fresh glass of orgeat in hand, Cora sat on the sidelines watching a new dance begin.

Hugh led the petite woman to the floor, and they lined up with the others. She surveyed their fluid movement, particularly Hugh. She marveled at the way such a tall, masculine man could move with grace and remain manly. He transformed steps she saw as ridiculous or awkward into almost ballet style precision.

Making a move that brought him facing Cora, her face heated—caught in the act of studying him. Embarrassment faded the moment she realized his smile was genuine and pleased by the obvious attention.

Not knowing what to make of the actor, she rose and located Judith returning from her errands.

Judith gestured to a table in the corner away from the music. "Having a good time, Cora?"

Cora sat opposite, fingers linked on top of the table. "If I excuse myself, will it hurt my chances at the position?"

Mouth agape, Judith asked, "Indeed? Why do you want to leave? Your dance with Hugh was brilliant."

Cora leaned back in her chair. It *had* gone rather well. Much better than expected. She didn't recall stepping on his feet once, but their discussion following the dance was what stayed with her. "I suppose it was okay."

"I watched the entire dance. You and Hugh were in total sync. Any couple who can carry on a conversation and keep the steps so seamlessly is a feat."

Cora stuttered, "I . . . I suppose the discussion sort of

distracted me from my nerves."

Judith crossed her arms. "I think Hugh believes you'd be a great fit for the job based on his reaction to your first meeting."

"Second, actually." Cora recalled.

"Second?"

"The maze. Although I didn't know who he was since it was nearly dark."

"Ah. I forgot." A server passed, and Judith retrieved a cup of punch from him. "Need a refill?" She pointed to Cora's half full glass on the table.

"No. I'm fine. Thank you." She sipped from the forgotten drink. "What do you make of Hugh's reaction to our meeting?"

"He's a polite man, but the attention he gave you is more than I've ever seen him give a candidate." She tapped her cup with a manicured nail. "It's mostly intuition on my part. Let's see how dinner goes, and then we'll talk. Hugh is not much on a behind-the-desk type of interview. He likes to see a prospect in a historical setting—like a ball. How well they fit and adapt. Play a role, so to speak. You must have impressed him."

The announcement of dinner interrupted their talk, and a fair-haired man came to stand beside Judith, his breath huffing as if he'd been running.

"Judith! So sorry I'm late. Trains!"

"Cora, this is Samuel Beckworth, Hugh's agent. Sam, this is Cora Anderson. She's here to apply for my assistant's position."

Sam's bottle-green eyes met hers. "Cora, so nice to meet

you."

Hugh slipped behind Sam and slapped him on the back. "Greetings, old man. I feared you would miss the ball all together."

"No, train was late. Just meeting Cora."

Hugh moved next to her and extended his arm. "We were just going in for supper. May I escort you?"

Cora hesitated. She had wished to retreat to her room, but after an encouraging glance from Judith, she placed her hand on Hugh's arm and allowed him to lead her into a spacious, high-ceilinged room. She expected to be seated next to Judith, but instead he guided her toward the head of the table to the chair at his right where a place card bearing her name etched in flawless script perched beside her place setting.

Each piece was in its proper place with flawless precision. Had she a ruler, she'd most likely find the measurements to be exact. Everything just as it was supposed to be. But after the interaction with her prospective boss, would *she* measure up?

Chapter Four

Dinner conversation hummed around the table, each guest conversing with the person at their side, leaving Cora to speak with Hugh on her left or Sam on her right. Never good with social small talk, she asked general questions about the history of the house and the local area.

Sam was chattier than Hugh, and Cora discovered a few things about why the house operated like a living museum, stopping just shy of forcing the guests to wear period attire for day-to-day activities. Although they were required to dress accordingly for the evening meal.

Cora listened to Sam drone on about some client claiming to have seen the ghost of Lord So-and-So walk the path along the nearby river. Sam mentioned the tale centered on the lord mourning the loss of his parents and sister who died in a tragic carriage accident.

Cora's ears perked. "Really?"

"His portrait is in the gallery alongside many of his ancestors."

"I'd like to see them." Cora was genuinely interested to see the portraits, not hear the ghost tale.

Sam dabbed the corner of his mouth with the snow-white linen napkin. "Judith hasn't shown you yet?"

Cora took another bite of the perfectly seasoned, pan-seared fish and shook her head.

"For shame." Sam glanced across the table at Judith and sent her a cryptic signal, provoking a smug smile from the attractive woman.

Sam's eyes twinkled with humor. "No worries, love. I'll give you the *Sam* tour. Best get on with your training, I say."

Cora's eyebrows lifted. "Pardon me?"

His laughter rang out, and Hugh's head turned in their direction, lips pursed, one eye narrowed.

Sam sent him an apologetic wink, causing Hugh's temple to pulse.

Cora swung her gaze from one to the other, gauging the tension between them, but Sam appeared to shrug it off, and Hugh became all seriousness.

Sam leaned toward Cora, their shoulders brushing. He directed a whisper to Hugh. "Lighten up, man. Isn't a ball supposed to be fun?"

A long pause stretched with the two men staring at one

another, then Hugh's expression softened.

"I'll concede for the moment," he said in a low tone. "But let us keep propriety intact—*man.*"

Sam didn't blink. "Indeed, *HRH.*"

Cora's body tightened, waiting for what she assumed would be a battle, though slight and on the quiet side.

Hugh's face relaxed, and he chuckled. "You are incorrigible, Samuel."

"Of course." Sam sat back and regarded Cora. "Sorry you had to witness that. I won because I know where all the bodies are buried." He winked.

Unable to help herself, Cora peeked at Hugh, now preoccupied with the guest at his left who chatted endlessly about some tree they'd discovered, uncertain what it was.

Hugh's jaw muscle clenched so tight Cora could have sworn she heard his teeth grind. She had to hand it to him. He kept a pleasant half-smile during the entire speech.

After his tablemate turned away, Hugh immediately sought Cora's attention, catching her studying him.

"I hope Samuel is behaving himself."

Cora toyed with the napkin on her lap and glanced at Sam, who spoke with the tall man at his side, both engrossed in a serious subject according to their expressions.

"Yes, he is a perfect gentleman." Cora wished she could have finished questioning Sam about his remark on her training. She didn't have the courage to broach the subject with Hugh. "He said he would give me a tour of the gallery to see the previous owners' portraits?"

Something flashed in Hugh's eyes. "That was kind of him, but Judith will attend to that."

His tone was matter-of-fact, and she didn't respond. The clatter of utensils, the ring of crystal, and the occasional twitter of laughter ebbed and flowed, easing the tension between her shoulders. Allowing the friendly, though Regency-proper, atmosphere to calm her—much like the dance she shared with Hugh. It began as a tense chore and morphed into a soothing, surreal experience she enjoyed. And like the end of the dance, he began questioning her, his clear blue eyes examining her face.

"I apologize if I have forgotten, but have you told me of your family in America?"

"No, we have not spoken of them—or yours."

"Mine are long departed, and I have no remaining immediate family." His eyelids fluttered, and he glanced away briefly. "And yours?"

"My sister Selena and I are the only ones left."

"That, I am sorry to hear. Where does she reside?" He placed his right hand, palm down, on the table and slowly tapped his forefinger. Was this his *tell*? Was she boring him, or was he merely preoccupied?

Cora drank from the crystal water glass and continued viewing his long, well-formed fingers. They were strong and had left heat at the small of her back after their dance.

He cleared his throat.

Her eyes darted up to meet his. "Sorry, just thinking." She collected the question again. "Selena is a junior curator at a small museum in Boston. She's living her dream."

The line between his eyebrows creased momentarily, his tapping increasing, then faded. "And what is *your* dream?" He slanted his body closer as if to show the person on his other side he was fully engaged elsewhere.

Should she allow him to see her honest enthusiasm the way she'd shown Judith? With all the desire inside her?

A peace filled her, and she told him her deepest professional desires about historical properties and the connection she had to them. As soon as she finished, a passion for the past mirrored in his eyes.

His hand inched toward her space, but he withdrew it quickly.

A chair scraped across the tile floor, bringing Hugh's chin up to see Judith notching her chin toward the exit. Naturally, he was the one to give the signal for all to depart, but he had been too engrossed in their conversation so Judith picked up where he had failed.

"It appears it is time for the dancing to resume." He gracefully stepped behind Cora's chair, gripped it, and bent low to whisper, "May I have the first dance—again?"

Cora's courage lagged, afraid her good luck with the other *first* dance wouldn't be repeated. An idea formed in her mind. "Only if it's a slow dance. I'm not well-versed in the fast-paced group dances of the era."

The wide smile deepened the creases around his eyes, possibly making him more attractive, not less. Why did good-looking men only grow more so as they aged, yet women just *aged*? Not fair.

"I'll accept that as a yes."

Maybe he wasn't so arrogant after all.

◌

Embraced in Hugh's arms for the second time, dancing as if the lessons were yesterday, Cora's stunned mind attempted to reconcile all that had brought her to England. Selena wouldn't believe it.

"Where are your thoughts, Miss Anderson?"

Cora started at the question and told a half-lie. "I was thinking of my sister. She'd love it here." She didn't add, 'She'd love *you*.'

"You find her humorous?"

"What?" She faltered, coming dangerously close to his foot.

"Your face near glowed at the mention of your sister." He drew her closer as they swung around the room.

"Yes, I suppose it would. She and I are alike when it comes to history. Hers is more for the artifacts themselves—being on display and such. While I love museums, I prefer the homes and villages and the way our ancestors lived. Their day-to-day existence. Modern times have created busyness—hectic and lacking."

His eyes seemed to search deeper, traveling her face and moving to her lips. Her face warmed under his scrutiny.

Cora sighed with resignation and shrugged a shoulder. "The ship carrying my youth sailed a long time ago, so I live vicariously through my younger sister. She's my life, and I want her to be happy."

They twirled across the floor, and Cora, still amazed at her ease in performing the steps, discovered the dance was over.

Once again, they stood near the terrace doors, now open, the scents of honeysuckle, lilac, and lavender wafting in. She inhaled deeply and allowed the cool spring air to bathe the heat from her face.

Again, he read her mind. "Please step out onto the terrace, and I shall fetch refreshment." He bowed and departed.

Before doing as he said, she glanced at the dancers and saw Judith and Sam involved in a reel, both wearing broad grins. Sam was a nice-looking fellow and most amiable. They were a good match. Or so it seemed. She'd only just met them, and they were, after all, coworkers.

Cora strolled in the peaceful, sweet-smelling breeze. No artificial light shone, only candles in iron sconces on the house's exterior walls and in urns lining the paths. The blue-black velvet sky blinked millions of stars like fairy lights.

Hugh certainly had the right idea of how to evoke Regency ambiance. Something the twenty-first century no longer held dear. Progress and technology had freed mankind of many tiresome, backbreaking jobs, lending more leisure time which seemed to have been swallowed up with other things that lacked truth.

"You look pleased."

Cora's breath caught, and her hand flew to her chest.

"I did not mean to startle you." He extended a glass of her new favorite drink.

She accepted the orgeat and pointed to the gardens and the sky. "This is the past, something our century has lost." She sipped the drink. "We have so many artificial lights, we've lost the stars God created." It was the first time she'd spoken so easily of God's part in the world in a very long while. A miniscule crack formed in her *blame* casket—as Selena called it.

Hugh drew closer, her muslin skirt brushing his carefully polished hessians. It occurred to her he didn't wear the foppish dancing shoes of the era.

"There is a blending of sorrow and awe in that declaration." His eyes creased as he smiled.

He was correct. Cora blamed God for the loss of her family, future, and youth. She would never realize the joy of a large family, a husband, children . . .

She downed the rest of her drink and set the crystal glass on the stone banister and turned away, not wanting him to witness the moisture in her eyes. "Thank you for a lovely evening in the past. Jet lag has caught up with me." Her chin dipped on a sob, but she recovered herself and muttered, "I think I'll turn in now, if you don't mind."

He gently cupped her elbow. "Please allow me to escort you to your room. You are not well. I beg your pardon if my words upset you."

On impulse, she faced him, tears burning, but she no longer cared. "That's unnecessary. I'm really tired, and tomorrow I'll need to schedule my trip home. I thank you for a pleasant evening. It was nice meeting you all."

He gripped her arm just enough to hold her in place and lowered his mouth to be overhead above the music. "Please come to my office once you have risen and broken your fast. Do not make travel plans yet. There is something we must speak of." He waited until she nodded in agreement and released her.

"Sleep well, Miss Cora Anderson." One side of his mouth quirked up into a charismatic smile.

His voice still rang as she reached her room on quivering legs, emotions out of control. What was happening to her? She regarded the plush period room done in shades of blue. A crystal vase now stood on the bedside table containing at least one of every flower she'd seen in the house gardens, including herbs. She buried her nose in the bouquet and imbibed the marvelous mingling of floral and herbal scents and stepped back to admire them. A gilded card with a wax seal leaned against the vase. She opened it with trembling fingers.

> *Cora,*
> *You have graced Hedsworth House with your appreciative love of the past. Please stay and help us keep it alive.*
> *Yours,*
> *Hugh*

Shock weighed on her as she stared at the curving script. She strode to the balcony, opened the French doors, and stepped out to study the silver dotted sky. It looked as if someone had released millions of fireflies. Tears returned with confusion added. Did he really want her to stay because of their shared love of all things past?

She stared at the candlelit garden below and saw Hugh standing where she'd left him, his hands clasped behind his back. He really was the epitome of an elegant Regency earl. A couple joined him, and a few words passed between them. The man shook Hugh's hand and left, but the woman stayed, head bent close to Hugh's. He embraced her for a long while, caressed her arm, then she departed.

Cora's breath held until the woman was through the door and out of sight. So, his interest in her was strictly professional. Her mind stilled, and she was once again on a firm footing. This she could handle.

HRH had no romantic interest in her. He already had someone—Judith.

Chapter Five

Cora lifted her fist to knock on Hugh's office door, pausing a few inches away. This was the moment of reckoning. Before arriving for their meeting, she'd visited Judith to ask details of her duties should she accept the offer.

Judith said Cora would have a small private flat near hers in the northeast wing, and she would give her a tour after meeting with Hugh. Cora stuffed the urge to ask Judith about her relationship with HRH and stored it inside the *none-of-my-business* trunk. She smiled at another of Selena's witticisms. Her sister was clever.

Cora finally knocked, and Hugh answered by opening the door and waving her inside a dark-paneled masculine room. Ever in Regency attire, he fit perfectly with the décor.

"Please have a seat." He moved toward a group of chairs and tables arranged before an over-large black-and-white marble fireplace. A tray laden with tea and a tiered server holding various tea cakes and biscuits—cookies to Cora—sat on the low table in front of the chairs.

He waited for her to sit. "Help yourself."

"Thank you, but only tea. The breakfast was Paul Bunyan-sized."

Hugh chuckled. "Touché." He inclined his head toward the teapot. "Will you pour?"

Cora poured tea into Royal Doulton cups, and he directed he only preferred a touch of milk. She poured hers and dropped a small piece of lemon into the dark brew. They sipped in silence for a moment, surveying each other over the rims of their cups, Cora's rattling when her nervous fingers placed the cup on the saucer, humor dancing in his eyes.

Cora's voice trembled slightly. "I'm afraid I'm going to chip this gorgeous china and be fired before I begin."

"So, you accept?" He held her gaze, expectant.

"I believe I do. Judith filled me in, and the salary and accommodations are beyond what I'd hoped for."

He squared his shoulders. "Excellent."

"When do I start? I'm sure there's much paperwork and such since I'm from the U.S."

"Samuel will attend to that." He continued staring, a constant smile on his nice lips.

Cora internally reprimanded herself for the thought, and besides he belonged to Judith.

"I suppose I'll go home and you—or Sam—will let me know after all the red tape is done?"

His grin flashed wider. "There's no need. You may begin today if you desire. Or settle into your apartment—or flat, as they are now called."

Cora frowned. "*Now*?"

"Take all the time you need to roam the grounds and house. Follow Judith, ask questions—"

Cora placed the cup and saucer on the table. "What about my apartment in Boston? My belongings?"

Hugh's expression sobered. "I appear to be most selfish. Of course, you must attend to your things. Samuel suggested you hire a service that packs and ships all you have, taking the burden from you. The estate will attend to the details and the cost."

Cora absorbed the idea of staying without going home first. She hated the thought of asking Selena to take on the chore of packing her possessions.

"I don't know what to say. It's very generous of you."

"Not at all. Selfish, most likely."

Cora pressed her lips together, unsure how to respond, but she was saved by a knock on the door followed by an ecstatic Judith bursting into the room, bringing both of them to their feet.

"Wonderful news! We can have our wedding in three months. At the end of our busiest season." She bounced to Hugh and gave him a hug, then Cora, whose phone rang out singing Selena's signature tone.

Hugh said, "Please accept your call, then you may give us

your packing decision."

Judith chimed in, "But we'd love it whatever you decide, if you will start no later than three weeks from now. After all," she sent Hugh a wide smile, "we'll need you to fill in once the honeymoon commences." Her sweet laugh filled the room, and Hugh shook his head good-naturedly.

"Pay her no heed. She is one of the silliest women in England."

Judith slapped his arm and danced from the room.

Cora tried to sound light-hearted. "Well . . . I better call my sister back. Perhaps she can help me decide whether or not to return."

"Splendid idea. Please speak with Samuel so he may receive your information for the work visa and such." He walked her to the door. "It is a genuine pleasure to have you with us at Hedsworth House."

Cora managed a nod before slipping from the room, her mind spinning with the realization she had actually taken the job and would finally live her dream. Why did that truth somehow also leave her with a hint of disappointment? Was it simply leaving her sister in Boston or something deeper?

CB80

Tiny wrens twittered their songs above the grape arbor where Cora sat on a secluded bench in one of the many gardens. Two blue-white butterflies flew nearby with their customary erratic flight pattern, and a lone bee buzzed around her head, most likely attracted to her lavender scent, or the blooms.

"Cora, for the third time, I'll take care of your apartment. I have loads of vacation days and would love to visit you in

England. Please let me come. AND—I get to meet Hugh Henley!"

Cora held the phone away from her ear as her sister squealed. When the sound faded, she said, "Selena, he's engaged, and she's also my boss, so lighten up."

The line grew silent except for an occasional giggle. Her sister was the silliest woman in all of *America*. She and Judith would get along famously. Shame revealed she really liked Judith—so why should she resent the relationship with Hugh? Just because he treated her like a lady and showed her a fairy tale world for a brief period, awakening a sense of romance—something she'd never truly experienced.

In the distance, footsteps on gravel averted Cora's attention from Selena.

"Selena, I have to go. I'll call you later this evening—and yes, please come whether or not you pack my things."

Selena squealed again. "Love you! Bye!"

Sam rounded the curve of the pebbled path. "There you are, love. Hugh said he saw you in the vicinity. It's one of his favorite spots." He lifted a shockingly green file folder. "Time to get the ball rolling on your work visa." He dropped onto the bench beside her.

She tapped the folder with the corner of her phone. "Is that why this is green? In conjunction with a green card?"

"Aren't we the comedian?" His smile was indulgent and friendly.

Cora turned serious. "Are you sure they can do this quickly enough?"

"No worries. I have connections." He waggled his eyebrows

and extended the folder. "Just fill in what's left and sign. I've taken the liberty of transferring the information from your resume to save you time."

"Very kind of you."

"I aim to please." He stood and slanted his gaze at her. "After Judith told me about you, I agreed you'd be great here. Hugh and Judith both need someone like you. Judith has especially been a little overwhelmed with the growing popularity of the man. Hugh really is a genius."

"Have you seen his movies?" She raised her eyebrows with a snicker.

Sam chortled, and his face bordered on the irresistible, but he wasn't really her type—blonde, green-eyed, and athletic. Good-looking, to be sure, but more of a brotherly personality in her estimation.

Cora grinned. "He really missed out on being cast in *Austenland.*"

"That's rich. Please don't mention to Hugh you like it." The twinkle in his eye was unmistakable. "Oh, he got passed over for the lead role."

Cora's eyes narrowed. "I could tell him *you* mentioned it to me."

He grew serious if but for a second. "I see you have a mischievous side. We're going to be great friends."

They shared a look. "I hope so, Sam."

"Sam! Where are you?"

"There's the boss. I best hop-to. Just get those forms to Judith soon, love." He sprinted toward Judith's voice.

Cora questioned why Sam would refer to Judith as the boss when he worked for Hugh as his agent. What did he have to do with property business? Again, she crammed the question inside the *none-of-my-business* trunk.

She opened the folder and saw very few areas that needed completing. Sam was as good as his word. She'd return to her room, complete the forms, and go to Judith.

The earlier phone conversation with her employer came to mind and how she gave her remaining two weeks' vacation as notice. Guilt ate at her for resigning in such a way, but she couldn't see another option without returning home for two weeks. The call had ended with him telling her she was fired.

Now it was time to move forward and see her new home.

CB&SO

"This is an amazing flat. I wouldn't have expected it—and Regency period through and through." Cora paused before the large picture window and gasped at the view. From the lovely lavender bedroom, she had a perfect view of the maze, private garden, and the kitchen garden. All were in full growth and lush. She turned toward Judith. "Please tell me there's no chamber pot under the bed."

Judith guffawed. "We're not that Regency-perfect."

She led Cora to another room and presented a gorgeous ensuite bathroom in colors of cream and lavender, then to a small kitchen, and last to a sitting room.

Judith leaned against the door frame and crossed her arms. "I think Hugh would've preferred the chamber pot scenario, but the staff, once again, drew the line."

"Thank goodness." Cora quipped. They returned to the

sitting room, and Cora pointed to the small sofa. "Does that pull out to make a bed?"

"Why?" Judith grimaced.

"My sister is coming for a visit with my belongings." She met Judith's gaze. "I'm sure I can book a room at the local inn." It hit her that Judith would wonder why sisters wouldn't share a bed. "Selena's a bed hog—takes up the whole space."

Judith's face relaxed. "I understand. We'll handle it."

"Please don't go to any trouble."

"This is your new home, and you should be able to have visitors. I'll see to it—no worries."

Judith helped Cora bring the bags to her flat. Afterward, they had tea with three guests in a small parlor, the rest choosing to go to the local pub, Hugh and Sam taking care of some business. By the end of tea, once the three women departed, Cora and Judith whispered over the juvenile exchanges of the women about all the *dishy* men they'd encountered at the previous ball.

Judith groaned. "One would think they came here to snag a husband."

Cora agreed. "Just as in Regency times?"

Judith's cackle filled the space, and she stared at the ceiling. "Most likely." She turned toward the door. "I'm just three doors down on the left." As she reached for the door, a loud knock sounded, and she jerked it open.

"Hello, loves!" Sam's bright smile greeted them from the doorway.

"What are you doing here?" Judith pulled the door wider.

He sauntered into the room as if he owned it. "I'm here to guide Cora on a gallery tour."

Judith's gaze swung from Sam to Cora and back. "Am I invited?"

Sam didn't hesitate. "Of course you are."

Cora clasped her hands. "We don't have to do it today if it's not convenient."

Judith looped her arm through Sam's. "Not at all. Let's do the tour, then have dinner."

Cora walked on Judith's left as Sam guided them through the passageways from the northwest wing, each section taking them to another era, from Tudor times to Regency. Cora peppered them with questions along the way, her mind attempting to absorb it all.

Once in the gallery on the southern side of the grand house, they passed through a narrow hall and inside a long rectangular room. The darkly stained walls held gilt-framed portraits which stood out against the paneled surface. Sam paused at each painting, explained who the subjects were and in which era they lived.

After the third description, Judith told him, "My dear, I do believe Cora can read the brass plaques."

He smirked and lifted his eyes. "Yes, *dear*, but I am the tour guide. Are you trying to nick my job?"

Their gazes held for a moment until the corner of Sam's mouth curved upward. "Cora, please take no notice of our little jest. It's merely who we are."

Judith shook her head and tugged him toward the next painting. Cora's gaze swung to look at it, and she froze. Ice-blue eyes stared down from their lofty perch. Hugh's eyes.

"HRH had his portrait done and placed *here*?" Her tone held more sarcasm than she had intended, but what a pompous diva to hang his own portrait among the historical ones.

Sam faced her. "That's his fifth great grandfather." A glint of humor shone in his eyes, and Cora assumed he was joking.

"Yeah—right."

Judith placed a hand on her shoulder. "It's true. Hugh had his DNA tested before he became famous and discovered the estate had fallen into hands outside the family. This is Richard Henley, 11th Earl of Hedsworth.

Cora stared in disbelief. As superior as she'd believed the actor to be, she never dreamed he'd actually have aristocratic roots. The guest that addressed him as *Lord* Hedsworth made Hugh seem he relished the role. But then again, he was an actor and used to playing parts. Well—Regency parts.

Sam interrupted her internal judgments. "Your face isn't difficult to read. Why do you dislike him?"

Cora sent Judith a disappointed look at sharing her opinion of her fiancé. "It's not that. I'd never met him until I came here." She shifted from one foot to the other, face heating. "My sister thinks he invented romance and is perfect in every way which nauseates me."

Sam's chuckle altered into a horselaugh. "What is she— sixteen?"

It was Cora's turn to laugh. "She's thirty-seven."

Judith shook her head but didn't smile. "What do you find so humorous?"

Sam's head snapped to gaze at Judith. "What is that supposed to mean?"

Judith appeared to have offended Sam in some way. She studied the pair and wondered what had just happened.

Judith turned away and mumbled, "Nothing." She shrugged. "Hugh is a nice chap, and you just have to get to know him before you see that side of him."

"You're right. I didn't mean to take a swing at him by laughing. We are friends, after all." Sam moved to the next portrait. "It's only that Hugh's fans never cease to amaze me with their obsession."

Judith gave a little smirk. "Oh, really?" She paused and tilted her head as if thinking. "Seems like you've been on set plenty of times when *what's-her-name* filmed with Hugh?"

Sam's face flushed, and he shifted quickly to look at the next portrait of an elegant woman.

Some unknown urge surged through Cora, and she snorted, bringing both their gazes to her. "I'm sorry . . ." She slapped a hand over her mouth, taking a few moments to calm before adding, "I didn't mean to do that. My sister's husband used to torment her over the times she dragged him to one of Hugh's movies. So she ferreted out that he had a thing for Julia Arlington, and started encouraging they go to her movies. That shut him up."

Sam met Judith's gaze, and he sighed. "Sorry, love."

Judith responded by patting his arm. "No worries." She lifted her arm and pointed at a woman's visage on the wall. "She was beautiful."

Cora bent to read the inscription. "Isabel Henley, 10th

Countess of Hedsworth, born 1740, died 1776." She straightened. "That's so sad to have died at such a young age—about the age as my sister." Unshed tears stung. She couldn't bear the thought of losing her only sibling and best friend.

Judith squeezed her shoulder. "I feel the same. We have to remind ourselves that these portraits and their belongings hold a past we'll never fully grasp. Only time separates us. We all live our lives as best we can."

Blinking back the moisture, Cora nodded, and as she moved to the next frame, she swung her gaze back once more to the man with the ice-blue eyes.

Chapter Six

A pleasant, but sometimes challenging, routine settled around Cora. She and Judith spent the days, and some evenings, going over schedules, events, and the general operations of the estate. Each evening, Cora fell asleep while reading the history of the house and the village. Though daunting, it thrilled her to be part of something of such antiquity. Now she knew what Selena had been proclaiming about museum life.

The days blended with ease, the staff supportive and welcoming. Whenever she wasn't learning something new, she would take breaks by walking the terraced gardens or occasionally strolling past the dovecote to the west and on to the chapel in the woods. The isolated calm eased her mind about the decision to stay in England rather than return to Boston. Today was one of those days. It was a bright, cool afternoon, almost the dinner hour, and she stole a few moments to go to the chapel.

The path took Cora down the slope, across the gardens toward the river. She paused to enjoy the variety of roses in a considerable range of colors. She bent to smell a vibrant yellow rose when she heard Judith call out, "Hello." She turned to see her boss strolling on the path toward her.

"How goes the work with Amanda? She's an amazing chef, is she not?"

"Amazing is right. I had to taste at least five dishes before she'd let me go." Cora patted her stomach. "At this rate, I'll be ten pounds heavier before Selena gets here."

"*Pfft.*" Judith joined her, and they walked down a few steps of the gardens before she turned to face Cora. "With all the work you're doing, you won't have to worry about gaining a pound."

"Maybe the walk to the chapel will help. Would you like to join me?"

"Thanks, not this time. I'm meeting with HRH to go over some things before he leaves for filming in Cornwall."

Taken aback by the comment, Cora said, "He's leaving?"

"Just for a few weeks. Filming some historical about smuggling and such. A mini-series."

"If I don't see him, say bye for me." Cora made to leave, but Judith held her back.

"Cora. Are you okay? You seem a bit distracted."

Cora pressed her lips together, unsure what Judith meant.

Had she been distracted? "No. I'm fine. Why do you ask?"

"You've seemed a bit . . ."

Cora waited for a moment. "A bit, what?"

Judith studied her through narrowed eyes. "I'm not sure. Just—thoughtful of late."

Cora brushed her fingertips over the soft petals of an orange rose, the shade of a deep sunset, while mulling over Judith's words. She dropped her hand to her side and met Judith's steady gaze. "I will admit I'm nervous about Selena visiting. "You know—with her HRH obsession and all." She hung her head. "I'm ashamed to admit it, but I'm afraid she'll embarrass me."

Judith's lips pursed. "I understand. I have a brother like that. Leave it to him to turn any event into a study in humiliation. Never for him, mind you, but for his family."

Cora sympathized, memories of attending movies with her sister and witnessing the overt displays of adoration at her latest movie-star crush. Oh, how she dreaded the day she arrived and met Hugh.

"How will Hugh handle my sister's behavior?"

"He'll ignore it. He takes it in stride, as if it's another burden to bear." Judith's phone sounded, and she glanced at it. "Gotta run, dear. See you at dinner." She bounced toward the gift shop she'd just left. "Disaster awaits."

Cora watched Judith go and considered how likeable she was, envisioning them becoming friends. She resumed the walk to the chapel, again wondering what drew her to the place—still convinced of God's abandonment long ago.

She strolled past the dovecote and into the thickly wooded

area until she almost reached the river. The tiny chapel, appearing to be only fifteen by twenty feet, built of slate and stone rubble, sat near a small graveyard. She'd been told it dated to the late fifteenth century with a legend attached to its beginnings. The plain interior had whitewashed walls, modest wooden benches, and an altar table. A brass plate hung above the door, detailing the eighteenth-century restoration and the tale of its founding in the fifteenth century. She remembered the evening Hugh had entertained the guests at an elaborate dinner with the story, telling how it came to be.

Cora had sat mesmerized at his commanding performance. Once he finished, she found she'd been so enthralled she hadn't realized she was staring at him until he cleared his throat, which brought her to the present. Their eyes had met, and she blanched at the thought he'd caught her gaping at him and looked away.

She reprimanded herself for acting like her juvenile sister as she eased the chapel door open with a protesting creak. The sound echoed around the small space, followed by the rustle of something moving in the room. Her gaze flew to the source—*Hugh*. He knelt before the small wooden altar, his head twisted toward her.

Cora began backing away, struggling to re-open the door and flee, only widening it to a small crack.

Hugh stood and held out his hand. "Please, do not go."

She halted and stilled where she was. Birds chattered behind her, and a gentle breeze teased her hair. She sucked in a shaky breath.

"I'm sorry to have disturbed you. I thought the chapel was empty."

Hugh made slow, deliberate steps toward her. "There is no need to apologize. God's house is open to all. This is such a peaceful place." He sat on a bench. "Please join me." He patted the space next to him.

Cora hesitated, and their eyes held one another's for a heartbeat before she came to sit beside him.

"Sometimes, I'm drawn to this place."

His confession startled Cora, and she looked around the quaint structure, avoiding his eyes. "I know what you mean. I've had the same sensation."

"In truth?" He asked.

Cora kept her gaze averted. "Does that surprise you?"

It was awhile before he answered, "It is just that you never mention your faith."

Cora's head dipped, and she toyed with the hem of her blouse. "It's taken a beating in the past, and I'm . . ."

Hugh moved his hand as if to brush her arm but drew back. "Yes. I am familiar with the sensation."

She glanced at him and waited for him to finish, but he did not complete his thoughts. The past came rushing to her. Losing so much gave renewed pain. Cora's heart squeezed, and she pulled in an unsteady breath. She could not—*would not*—share past grief with a man she barely knew. She stood abruptly.

"I'm sorry I intruded on your private moment. I think I'll go freshen up before dinner. I'll see you then."

Disappointment flashed in his eyes, and Cora regretted the hasty departure but would not allow him to see her agony. She rushed to the door, and without looking back hurried until she arrived at the dovecote, its conical gray roof peeking above the surrounding beds of brightly blooming flowers. Drawing in an invigorating breath of the fragrant plants, she detected the scent of lavender above them all. As she plucked a few stems, footsteps crunched on the path.

Cora turned to see Hugh walking in her direction, hands clasped behind his back as was his way, eyes downcast. Before he spotted her, she ducked inside the small structure. The nest holes, nearly full of pigeons, fluttered noisily at the abrupt entrance, which made her shriek as she rapidly backed out, still clutching the stems of lavender.

The sound of Hugh's footsteps increased to a run, and she made to dash back to the path before he arrived. In her haste, she lost her balance and teetered toward the small pond near the dovecote.

Attempting to regain her footing, she grasped at a large peony tree and held tight. Staggering on the edge of the pond, the limb cracked, and she scrambled to right herself before it gave way. She looked up to see Hugh, his jacket now gripped in one hand, as he witnessed her struggle.

Just as the tension slackened, his firm hand gripped her wrist, pulling her away from the water. He tossed his jacket to the ground and wrapped his arm around her waist to steady her.

Hugh tugged her closer to him, and she stumbled. Both of her fisted hands landed on his chest, one hand holding the peony limb and the other the lavender sprigs, blooms slapping his face.

Cheeks flaming, she shoved herself away, using his chest as leverage, sending her back toward the pond. Now with both arms, Hugh encircled her waist and rescued her once again.

"Who knew picking flowers could be such a dangerous sport?" He chuckled but did not release her.

Cora's embarrassment surged, and she didn't know whether to burst into tears, run away, or be angry. Another option flashed in her mind—*stay* in his arms. They were strong, and his cologne was pleasant, not a potent overwhelming scent. His smile was affectionate, and his embrace felt so natural.

Like she belonged there.

The thought jolted her to choose option three. She shoved from his grasp, and in doing so, he fell backward, splashing into the water.

Cora screamed, "Hugh!"

He resurfaced, his hair slicked back, wearing a smile. "It is quite refreshing. You should join me." He stood, the water only reaching his waist. As he strode out of the pond, he untucked his white shirt, and Cora's eyes fully grasped the similarities between the scene before her and Mr. Darcy coming out of the lake at Pemberley.

When her gaze returned to his face, he watched her, and his smile grew.

Anger bubbled, and Cora spat out, "What are you smiling at? If I'd fallen in, I could've drowned. I'm not a good swimmer."

Her gaze kept going back to his wet shirt, emphasizing his lean, muscular torso. "Insufferable, conceited man!"

Hugh's eyes twinkled. "You find me insufferable *and* conceited, Cora?" He stepped closer, water dripping from his wavy hair.

Cora's face heated. She said that aloud? She hadn't meant to. She sidestepped him, and he caught her arm, standing shoulder-to-shoulder and whispered, "You unsettle me as well."

With a tremble in her voice, she said haughtily, "Thank you for interrupting my walk. I love picking flowers. The doves startled me is all."

He gave her a knowing look. "That, I see." He nodded. "Then I will leave you to it." He bowed, reclaimed his jacket from the ground, and strode away.

Anger mingled with humiliation boiled inside Cora, and she gritted her teeth, snatching sprigs of lavender and shoving them into her hand one after another. "That man is intolerable, smug, and . . ." She stopped and stared at his retreating back. Why did she dislike him?

She was just beginning to see a different side of him when he had to give that smug, dismissive attitude. She began seizing flowers with vigor. "*Lord* Hedsworth, I'll be glad as soon as you're gone to your next filming!" Despite her anger, his *Darcyesque* scene coming out of the water held firmly in her mind's eye.

☙❧

Cora avoided breakfast so she wouldn't have to spend any time with Hugh before his departure. The evening prior had been excruciating. Forced to share dinner with Hugh and the guests over a formal meal and being carefully attentive to Regency manners had left her drained. The saying *you can't get blood out of a turnip* crept into her thoughts, but in that moment, she felt like she was a turnip and someone had indeed drained her of all she had. Sleep had not come easily, but once it did, she slept fitfully, dreaming of an endless scene taking place at dinner with everyone laughing at her.

She inspected the mantle clock, relieved to find she may get to work and not have to see Hugh Henley for several weeks. Selena's arrival the next day would be a much welcomed distraction.

Grabbing her portfolio, she left the apartment with a fresh outlook on the day ahead. Judith met her in the Great Hall giving instructions to one of the staff preparing it for a large group arriving in a few days. Thankfully, it was only a one-day booking for a family reunion who wanted to experience a Regency dinner in the Tudor Hall.

Judith's brown gaze swung to Cora, one hand still in mid-air, motioning toward the rafters. "Good morning, Cora. Missed you at breakfast." She turned back to the man she was directing and finished the instructions before moving to Cora's side.

"I didn't feel like eating after the meal from last night." Cora opened the portfolio and removed a pen. "So where do we start?"

Judith looked at her, chewing her lower lip. "Cora. You barely ate last night, and I noticed Hugh trying to get your attention several times, and you ignored him." She wagged finger at Cora. "Did you have an argument?"

Cora sighed with strength. "It's not important. We just had a misunderstanding, and when he returns in a few weeks, it'll be forgotten."

"What shall be forgotten?"

Cora whirled around to see Hugh standing at the entrance, both hands on his hips. Her heart lurched in tandem with her stomach. There he was, poised in his Regency attire, like a self-absorbed celebrity. At least he wasn't wet.

Judith chimed in, "I was about to tell Cora about your delayed filming schedule."

Cora turned a confused gaze on Judith, then back at Hugh. It was beyond what she could manage, so she chose the coward's way out. "I forgot something. I'll be back." She sprinted to her office next to Judith's and shut the door. What was it about this man that caused such extreme emotions? She went from experiencing embarrassment to anger in a split second. Did it all go back to her dislike of him prior to their meeting?

A soft knock brought her around. Maybe if she remained quiet, whoever it was would go away. She waited, breath catching. The door inched open, and Judith's head came through and she whispered, "Cora? What's wrong?"

"Are you alone?"

Judith blinked with confusion, entered, closed the door, and whispered, "What in the world is bothering you?"

Cora sat heavily in the desk chair and ran a hand through her hair. "I don't know."

Judith sat in front of the desk. "Hugh's worried. He said you met at the dovecote garden, and you seemed out of sorts."

Cora's head snapped up. "Is that all he said?"

Judith nodded, maintaining eye contact with Cora.

They sat this way for a while until Cora blurted out the

entire story of the walk to the chapel, then the dovecote and so on. When she'd finished, Judith was laughing.

"Why is that so funny?" Cora gripped the arms of her chair and slid forward.

"Oh, Cora. The man is a celebrity, and he makes you nervous. Don't be ashamed. I felt that way for the first few months I worked for him. It'll pass."

Cora's emotions leveled, and she considered the possibility that she may be right, except for . . . "Maybe. But I've had a dislike for him for years."

"You've only just met him. Give it time. He's really a nice chap. Settle in and try to be yourself. Like when you and I are together."

Cora blew out a breath. "I'll try." A question surfaced that she had wondered for some time. "How on earth did you and he—" Her phone rang, and she noted it was Selena. "Sorry, it's my sister."

"Go on." Judith leaned back in the chair and surveyed her day's schedule.

"Hi, Selena." Cora picked up a pen and twirled it as she listened. "You're here?" She bolted from the chair, startling Judith and spilling papers to the floor.

"Selena, why are you arriving early?" Cora paused. "Okay. I'll get Rory to meet your train. I wish you'd let me know before now. Right. See you soon." She stabbed the end call button with more force than intended.

"Your sister's here *now*?" Judith's face pinched.

"Yeah. She said something about being given an extra day off at the last minute. I'm sorry." Cora's irritation grew until she realized the implications of Selena being here while Hugh was in residence.

"Oh my gosh, Judith. Selena will meet Hugh, now that his plans have changed. You don't know the meaning of embarrassment. Selena and Hugh Henley in the same room. This is a disaster on steroids."

The humor twinkling in Judith's eyes was unmistakable. "Let's not panic. I'll send Rory to the station to collect her." She dialed Rory, and after Cora told her the time, she'd passed it on to him and hung up.

Dread rose in Cora until she grasped the desk, staring at Judith. "Quick! We need a plan to keep my sister away from Hugh!"

Chapter Seven

Cora sipped sparkling water and watched as Judith and Selena settled themselves in her sitting room with their own glasses, chatting amiably.

"So, Judith, how long have your worked for hunky Hugh?" Selena flipped a long, dark blonde wave over her shoulder for emphasis.

Cora wanted to roll her eyes but refrained. "*Selena . . .* please let's not do this?"

"You know, Cora, I think that's your most-used phrase for me."

Judith interrupted with a smile. "Long enough. I don't think of him that way. He's a great boss, and we get on well."

Cora's thoughts went elsewhere considering they were engaged.

Selena's forehead furrowed. "But Cora said—"

"Selena, Judith isn't interested in what I have to say. Let's enjoy the evening. Amanda is sending up a wonderful gourmet meal shortly, and since you're wiped out with jetlag, we'll turn in early."

"But I'm not tired." She turned a begging expression to Cora. "I've waited all my life to meet Hugh Henley, so I want to do so asap."

Cora's remorse almost got the better of her until Judith's cough got her attention. "We'll see. He is a busy man, Selena."

Selena's face paled, but she remained quiet, taking a gulp of water.

Judith stood. "I've just remembered I need to see Amanda about something for the group. Cora, I may need you to convince her that this *particular* dish is fine, even though it doesn't fit with her idea of gourmet."

Cora's mouth opened to say she had no idea what she was talking about, but Judith's eyes slanted sideways as a signal to agree. "Oh. Sure." She patted Selena on the knee. "We'll be right back."

Selena shrugged and sighed dramatically. "If you say so. Where else am I going to go?"

Judith whispered as they walked down the hall. "Plan B. I'll get Sam."

Cora agreed, and once at Judith's apartment, she called Sam. "We need your help. I'll explain. Come to my flat, love." Judith blushed. "Funny, Sam. Cora's here."

As soon as the call ended, Cora asked, "What did Sam say?"

Judith turned away. "He's a jokester. Flirts with all the women. Pay him no mind."

Once Sam arrived, they told him how they wanted to keep Selena away from Hugh. "Why?" He scrunched his face comically.

"Sam—" Cora said, "My sister will embarrass herself and anyone present if she and Hugh are together in the same room. She has no shame. He's her one weakness. My sister is a talented, smart woman, but where he's concerned, she's obsessed."

Sam tilted his head back. "*Hm*, I see what you mean. It happens at every film site. The stories I could tell you. And I'm rarely there with him." He crossed his arms. "Frankly, it's nauseating. Although comical at times."

"Will you help us?" Judith pleaded. "Cora is horrified she'll make Hugh angry."

"I will—but how?"

Judith enlightened him. "We want you to keep Hugh away from her. If they are in the same room, put a stop to it as soon as Selena begins to make a fool of herself. You said so yourself that you've seen this happen a lot. You know the signs."

Sam was hesitant, and then agreed. "I think I may be able to pull it off. Are you sure you don't want to forewarn Hugh? He could put a stop to a lot of it himself."

"I'm not sure," Cora said with a frown. "Judith, what do you think?"

"If we do, I think you should be the one to talk to Hugh. She's your sister, and you know how she'll react to any situation.”

Cora's shoulders slumped. “I suppose you're right.” She brought her gaze to Sam's. “Will you still intervene, even if I speak with Hugh? Especially if others are present besides us.”

“Of course. If you think it'll help.” He rose. “Let's go see him now. Judith, you keep the lioness in her cage.”

“Sam!” Judith reprimanded him.

Cora laughed. “She's only a lioness when it comes to Hugh.”

❧

Cora watched as Sam's irritation grew. “I've asked him to keep his mobile with him at all times. It's probably locked away in his desk.”

Sam propped a hand at his waist, his other holding the phone to his ear. He ended the call and shoved the phone into his jeans pocket. “Let's start with the private garden. That's his first choice. Then we'll go down the list of places he likes to hide.”

Cora chuckled. “You sound as if we're looking for a spoiled five-year-old.”

“Exactly.” His face registered only a trace of humor.

They arrived at the center of the private garden, a lantern on the iron table lighting the sheltered space. Hugh sat with one leg crossed over the other, the small book Cora found opened in one hand, and a bottle of mineral water in the other.

Cora's first reaction flew from her lips. “Aren't you the picture of Regency relaxation, sans water bottle?”

Hugh's eyes bored into hers as he politely stood, but his

laugh soon broke the contact. "Again, Miss Cora Anderson—*touché*."

"Hugh, we—well, Cora—needs to have a word with you about her sister. Judith and I bandied it around and decided it's your decision how it should be handled."

His eyes widened a moment before he closed the book and placed it on the table, gesturing toward the vacant chair.

Sam encouraged her to sit. "I'm off to rescue Judith from the lioness." He winked at Cora and left.

"Lioness?" Hugh reclaimed his seat, eyes narrowing.

Cora sat and shifted on the iron chair. "He's teasing about my sister."

"So, she has arrived early?" One side of his mouth curved upward. "Is this her nickname?"

"Not at all. Sam came up with it after our discussion."

"Sounds intriguing."

"I'm not sure how to begin." Judith's words reverberated inside her head, and she accepted them at face value. She squared her shoulders and began telling Hugh about Selena.

His expression shifted several times during the telling, ending with a hint of sympathy in his eyes. She was uncertain if it was for her or Selena—or both. Not once did he interrupt or make comments for which Cora was grateful.

They sat silently for so long, Cora wondered if he would ever respond, his never wavering gaze upon her.

She slid to the edge of the chair, and he stopped her. "Please do not leave. I am thinking on all you have shared. It poses a dilemma if you care what others think of you. Or of her. Is either the case? Perhaps both?"

Cora stammered, "Well . . . I . . . yes, I suppose both." She cleared her throat and shuffled her feet under the chair. "Also . . . I didn't want her behavior to anger you."

He grimaced. "Do I appear to anger easily? I would not have you think it."

She considered the comment, remembering the incident at the dovecote garden, and mentioned it to him.

"You did not anger me. I assumed I angered you with my assistance that kept you from taking an unscheduled swim."

He brought a hand to his forehead and moved a lock of dark hair away from his eye. It was then she noticed he wore a billowy white shirt with the sleeves rolled up, the cord in his muscled forearm tensing with the movement. How had she missed that? He was always meticulously dressed. They had interrupted him in a very casual state.

A very attractive one indeed. She shook her head to clear the thoughts reeling there.

Shame made her face heat, and she was grateful the dimly lit area hid her response. "Yes, I suppose I was. It was wrong of me to react that way. I was surprised, that's all. The birds frightened me, and then you were coming up the path to witness my embarrassment, and . . ."

"At the chapel, you feared me discovering your past wounds and fled." Hugh uncrossed his leg and slid his feet toward Cora, rested his elbows on his knees, allowing his hands to dangle. He was in the most relaxed state she'd ever seen him. It made him seem more *real*, more *human*. Not the cocky, good-looking diva she'd assumed him to be.

"Cora." He brought slender fingers to touch the back of her hand resting on her lap. She kept her eyes on his hand, noting the absence of hard labor. As he placed his hand on the edge of the chair to steady himself, she noticed a scar ran across two knuckles.

Reflexively, she traced the scar with a fingertip and heard his intake of breath. They stilled in the moment until he stood.

"Forgive me." He gathered his belongings and the lantern but did not move to leave. "Please do not concern yourself with your sister's behavior. Thank you for warning me. I will make certain nothing inappropriate occurs. Also I shall speak to Sam and formulate a plan. I would not wish to cause you embarrassment. Rest assured, your sister's embarrassment is all her own. Not for you to bear." He bowed gallantly and held the lantern above. "Allow me to guide you through the dark."

Cora let him lead her, trying her best to push aside the way his touch undid her, and more so the tenderness he exhibited.

 C3℠SO

"Selena, sit still. I'm almost finished. Just a few pins to go." Cora clenched her teeth. Why was her sister so much more irritating since her arrival at Hedsworth House?

She huffed. "I don't understand why I couldn't have the *real* maid dress my hair. We are, after all, in the Regency period."

"I told you. We are booked solid with guests, and they take precedence over my visiting family." She patted the last pin in place and gazed at Selena in the mirror. "You look lovely."

Selena beamed and tugged on a long curl trailing over her shoulder. "Do I need more of these?"

"No. You don't want to overdo it. Your hair looks amazing, even if I was the one who did it."

Her sister twisted on the seat until she faced Cora. "I'm sorry to be so antsy. You did a wonderful job. I just want to look my best before meeting the—"

"Please don't say it again." She grabbed Selena's hands and stared her in the eyes. "You are thirty-seven years old. Grown women don't say *hunky*."

"Why ever not? We're not dead, Cora. Live a little. You're too serious sometimes."

"Hmph! Someone in this family has to be serious and not pant after men they've never met."

Selena crossed her arms. "Can't a girl—woman—be a little ridiculous on occasion?"

"Certainly, around other women. But not in front of the men. Please?"

Selena huffed again. "All right. I'll try to behave. But I'm not responsible for my own actions the first moment I meet—Hugh."

Cora sniggered. "Thank you. But please try really, really hard."

The door opened, and Judith came floating in wearing a lovely pink satin gown with matching pink slippers, her blonde hair pinned up, tendrils lifting as she moved. "Don't you both look wonderful!"

"Judith, you are beautiful!" Selena crooned and peered at Cora. "She has lots more curly strands than I do. You said I had plenty."

Judith howled. "Selena, are you sure you're not seventeen

instead of thirty-seven?"

Selena's face flushed, but she chuckled. "I wish! Now, on to meet the hunk!"

Cora gripped Judith's arm as they followed Selena from the room. "Oh, my word, Judith, please save us."

⊂∙⊃

They stepped into the Great Hall, chosen for this particular dinner because of the number of their guests. It seemed strange to Cora to sit among the polished suits of armor on the walls, animal antlers, swords and shields. A Regency dinner in a Tudor Hall. This was going to be a unique dining experience.

Judith led the women with Cora and Selena at the rear. The men stood in small groups scattered about the massive room. Selena, at Cora's side, gasped at the sight of Hugh, and Cora gently grasped her gloved forearm. "Steady. Remember our chat."

"Yes, *sister*," Selena said meekly but with sarcasm.

Hugh posed—the only word that fit—next to the enormous fireplace in conversation with an elderly man who pointed to the coat of arms hanging above it. Believing him to be involved in deep discussion, Cora eyed every inch of his impeccable attire from his black Wellington boots to his snowy linen cravat. The dark, single-breasted, knee-length frock coat hid most of the white shirt. He really was quite convincing as a Regency gentleman. No wonder he was sought after to portray the time period.

When her gaze lifted from the cravat, his eyes were on her. He dipped his chin and turned back to his companion. Selena grabbed Cora's arm. "Take me to him. Introduce us." She whispered, "*Pleeease*," like a five-year-old begging for candy.

Judith came to their side. "Sam will take you. It was only proper for a man to introduce a single woman in Regency times."

Selena swallowed audibly and nodded, hands wringing at her waist. "I never thought I'd be this nervous."

"Are you really buying all this *proper* Regency etiquette?" Cora asked Judith.

"Are you kidding me? I wouldn't have a job if I didn't." She winked.

Cora chose not to follow, remaining near the serving table, servants standing by to work once everyone sat at the long table centering the hall. She watched the introduction unfold, hands gripped into tight fists at her sides.

Hugh bowed as Sam introduced Selena, Judith standing close, arm linked through Selena's. Cora thought it a good idea. She would spirit her away if she began making a fool of herself. The elderly man focused his attention on Selena, and she appeared to be responding. While this occurred, Hugh said a few words, bowed, and strode toward Cora. Her heart skipped. Was there a problem?

Once he stood in front of her, he extended his elbow away from his side. "Will you allow me to seat you?" He winked and glanced in Selena's direction, who watched them with interest.

Confused, Cora didn't know what to do. She hissed between clenched teeth, "What? Should I? Will it upset Selena?"

He leaned closer and whispered, "It is of no concern. It is my prerogative to seat whomever I choose to accompany to dinner."

Cora wondered if this was part of his and Sam's plan to discomfit Selena into behaving like an adult. After a brief hesitation, she accepted and slid her hand onto his arm and watched Selena shoot daggers at her.

86

# Chapter Eight

Cora avoided eye contact with Selena down the long table. Hugh placed Judith in charge of the place cards and knowingly seated Selena as far away from him as possible. While Cora was thankful, she also felt sorry for her sister. She'd finally gotten to meet her idol, and now he was out of reach. Thankful Judith had given Selena a crash course on Regency table etiquette—only to speak with those to the left or right—*not* across the table, made Cora relax.

Selena's dining companions were Judith and Sam. They sandwiched her between them like a lone book guarded by bookends. Cora noticed her sister's initial discomfort, but she soon relaxed, mostly because of Sam's attention and mild flirting. Judith appeared to take it in stride, smiling as they included her in the conversation.

Cora's attention switched to Hugh's whisper. "She shall be fine. Sam and Judith have all in hand."

She sipped her drink and swung her gaze back to her sister to find Selena glaring, a flash of jealousy slicing the space between them. This was exhausting. Cora wanted to slip away and hide.

"Cora. Please do not fret. We shall not let . . ."

A commotion caught their attention. Selena's chair scraped across the floor, and she stood and leaned toward Judith, but her *whisper* could be heard above the conversations along the table. "I've a headache and am going to my room." She tossed her napkin onto her plate. She left, taking quick strides without a backward glance.

Hugh placed a staying hand on Cora's forearm. "Let her go. She is behaving like a petulant child."

Cora squeezed her eyes shut to staunch the tears, his hand intimate on her arm. "I know. But she's my sister." She opened her eyes and shook her head.

"Please do not leave." He glanced in Judith's direction, who now stood, sending a smile to the guests nearby.

"I'll return shortly." She nodded and left the room.

Cora said between clenched teeth, "I need to go to her and explain. Pray she understands."

"No." His tone was gentle yet firm. "She must learn from this. Judith is superb in these situations."

"How so?" Cora pulled away from his touch. "She doesn't know Selena."

"No. Yet she has handled many women who have tried to become too familiar with me."

Cora shot him a glare. "I don't want her to *handle* my sister. I know her best."

"I am certain you do. Have you had to deal with this particular scenario?"

She fumbled with the napkin on her lap, admitting to herself that she had not. "No." The weak response felt humiliating. "What will Judith do?"

"Attempt to explain that making a scene would only hurt you *and* her."

Cora's eyes widened. "That's it?"

"There are times we are unaware of the consequences of our own actions."

He said nothing further for a while, holding her gaze. "Judith shall convince Selena to return once the dance starts. I shall ask her for one dance—no more. I shall make polite conversation and that shall be that."

Cora tried to consider whether this would mollify her sister for long but doubted it.

Hugh broke into her thoughts. "I shall leave tomorrow before breakfast—without telling anyone—other than you, Judith, and Sam."

"Why?"

"To halt any further possibility of your sister causing a scene. You shall be free to enjoy her company before she returns to America." Hugh glanced at the man placing a dish in front of him and said 'thank you.'

"But I thought filming had been delayed—"

"That is correct. I will arrive a few days early and have a—what is it you say—a mini-vacation?"

Cora laughed. "You say that like a foreigner."

His charming smile nearly stopped her breath. "I am, to you."

True, Cora thought, and smiled, finally calming. "Thank you for that. It's kind of you to do so."

"It is kind of you to treat your sister with such care." He reached for his glass, but before taking a drink, he said, "I wish I had my sister with me to show her the same courtesy." His gaze fell to his plate, silently studying it.

Cora longed to question him about his family but was too timid to do so. Her emotions were already on an uneven plane, and she didn't want to fight back tears for a second time that evening.

⊗⊗⊙

The rest of dinner was pleasant enough. Judith returned when dessert was being served, and she appeared to be in good spirits, chatting and laughing with Sam. They were obviously good friends and got on well.

When they stood to depart to the ballroom, Judith excused herself, and Cora allowed Hugh to escort her. Once inside the cavernous room, the crowd casually scattered around the perimeter. Hugh was showered with young women vying for his attention, Cora being serendipitously shoved to the background, but Hugh kept tugging her back to his side.

The music began, and Hugh immediately seized Cora's

hand and led her to the floor. A few moments into the waltz, Judith and Selena stepped into the room.

Hugh murmured close to her ear. "As soon as this dance is over, I shall ask your sister—once. Then I shall ask each woman in attendance—once. That is all." He nodded, keeping his eyes on hers.

She saw the meaning in his gaze, noting the captivating blue of his eyes were ringed with silver. Cora shivered and looked away. She realized he never asked Judith to dance the first one. Was their engagement a secret? Perhaps they wanted to wait until closer to the wedding before they announced it—keeping their business relationship to the forefront—to avoid the paparazzi.

Hugh's gaze turned to concern. "Are you chilled? I shall have Judith get your wrap."

"No. I'm fine. Really." She looked toward Selena, who watched them closely. "I'm fine," she repeated.

Their dance began and ended much as their first had been the evening she officially met Hugh, leaving her bewildered. Smiling and pretending all was well frayed her nerves. Was she becoming like Selena, allowing a vivid imagination to run free?

Besides . . . Hugh Henley was engaged. The man was off limits. She needed to keep herself in check. He was her boss— and so was his fiancée, who had become a friend.

The music stopped, and Hugh bowed. "I must needs continue my task of dancing, though exhausting it shall be." His lopsided grin teased her.

Cora cocked her head. "Is it really that bad, *Lord*

Hedsworth? But I suppose you can check off the first dance now that it's over." She gave a wobbly curtsy and left him, not understanding her reaction other than her last thoughts of their dance when she reprimanded herself. Why did she care what he thought of her? She only needed to prove to him that she did a good job and got along well with everyone.

A warm hand grasped hers, and she whirled around to meet his startled gaze.

He stepped closer and whispered, "Have I offended you?"

Unbidden tears stung her eyes. She examined the floor and tried to pull her hand from his, but he would not release her.

"No. I . . ." What could she say? Confused, she blurted out the first thing that came to mind. "I think I'm weary from walking on eggshells regarding Selena." She glanced toward Selena and gasped. "Here she comes, Judith on her heels. I guess she escaped."

The comment brought a chuckle from Hugh. "You sound as if she is an errant pup."

"Yes. One who is besotted with you." She slapped a hand over her mouth. "I'm sorry. That was wrong of me. I love my sister, but she can be so—"

Selena appeared at her side and stared at their clasped hands. With pinched lips, she brought her eyes to glare at Cora. There was a brief standoff until Selena turned to Hugh.

"My lord." She curtsied perfectly.

Cora groaned. Leave it to her sister to practice and perform with skill.

Hugh released Cora's hand and watched Selena. "I was about to collect you for a dance, Miss Young. If you are available."

Selena blushed from neck to forehead and stammered, "Yeess. Please."

He performed a half-nod. "Thank you. But I must first complete the conversation your sister and I were having. If you will excuse us a moment, I shall collect you for the next dance."

The music struck up again, which meant Hugh would not be dancing with Selena until the following one. Cora looked from Selena to Hugh and back to gauge the interaction between them. Her sister appeared speechless—for the first time in her entire life, Cora thought. A twinge of satisfaction stabbed, and she immediately repented for it.

Hugh cleared his throat as he placed a hand on Cora's arm. "We shall return presently. There is a matter of business I must discuss with Cora."

Selena could do nothing other than nod and watch them walk away, leaving Cora with some sympathy for her sister.

Hugh escorted Cora to the terrace overlooking the gardens, and they stepped outside. Hesitating, he glanced around, then led Cora into the darkening night and behind a large topiary, blocking them from any prying eyes.

Cora blanched. "Hugh, I thought this would be unseemly in your estimation." She snickered at her own speech, realizing she was sounding just like him.

His eyebrows lifted. "Are you mocking me, Cora?"

Surprised at her audacity, Cora tittered. "I'm as surprised as you are. It wasn't intentional." His hand moved to lie atop hers on his arm, and her gaze swung downward, but he didn't pull away. She twitched her fingers for emphasis. "Isn't this unseemly?"

Cora couldn't see his eyes clearly in the dimness, but she felt the air spark between them. What was happening? Their gazes briefly held, but he still did not move away. Had she imagined it, or had he stepped closer?

Her whisper sounded foreign to her own ears. "Hugh?"

A flash of light from a nearby window faintly lit their space, and she glimpsed his eyes peering deep into her own. He *was* closer. Too close. Hoarsely, she said, "You said you had business to discuss."

He released an annoyed sigh, his minty breath on her cheek. The regret in his voice clear, he said, "Yes. That is true." He gently broke their contact and moved a step away. "Yes." he repeated but kept watching her.

"*Well . . .*" Cora's whisper floundered.

Hugh placed both hands behind his back and paced. "I . . . I do not wish to dance with your sister. Yet I must because I have promised it. What do you believe I should do?"

Cora frowned. "Why are you asking me this?"

"Because I know not what she is capable of. Shall she attempt to . . . *do* something on the dance floor that would be inappropriate?"

It took a moment for the comment to seep into Cora's consciousness. Would Selena do something like that? She had been concerned her sister would make an idiot of herself, but would she make a pass at Hugh while they danced? She crossed her arms and considered it. As crazy as she was about the man, she might just be capable.

He stopped pacing and mimicked her stance with arms crossed over his chest.

After she gazed at him again, she nodded. "She may do that, but I'm not sure—wait!"

Hugh startled. "What?"

Cora's fingers snapped, and she perked up. "Make sure the next dance is a reel or something. *Not* a slow dance."

His eyes brightened. "Yes. And I have already stated one dance per woman." Hugh gripped her shoulders and placed a quick, soft kiss on her lips. "Excellent! Thank you." When he pulled back, Cora swallowed, breathing quicker.

Hugh stilled, a look of pleasure immediately shifting to mortification. "Please accept my apologies. I—I am uncertain what came over me."

"Most—" Her voice came out husky, and she cleared her throat. "Most likely gratitude."

Heated, gentle fingers squeezed her shoulders, causing ripples to tide through her. "Yes, I am most grateful. Now I must speak with the musicians."

Cora placed a hand on his chest. "No. Ask Judith to do it— privately. So no one will assume—"

He dropped his gaze to her hand, and she quickly withdrew it, breaking his connection. "Sorry." She rubbed her hands together, the one that touched him still warm from the contact.

Avoiding each other's eyes, Cora said, "I'll walk around the garden for a few minutes. That will give you time to enter from elsewhere so as not to cause any talk. I'll return, seek Sam, and tell him we need to dance as a diversion."

She heard him swallow before he said, "Yes. Outstanding thought." He backed away. "I shall see you inside—later."

Cora followed his receding back, wondering what had just happened. Was Hugh so used to kissing actresses he had momentarily lost himself in actual reality, or was there something else behind the unexpected and inappropriate gesture?

❧

Cora returned to the ballroom, a reel in full swing. Her embarrassment for Selena was palpable. She obviously didn't know how to dance the reel. Neither did Cora. She refused to join in, even at Sam's prompting, saying he would teach her.

Once the dance was over, Selena's face was flushed. She retrieved a cool drink and came to sit with Cora.

"Are you happy, *sister*? I've been thoroughly humiliated," Selena said between sips of lemonade.

Cora reached over to pat Selena's hand, but she pulled away. "No. Don't attempt to placate me now."

"I don't blame you for being upset, but you must realize that should your defenses drop and you give in to your unhealthy obsession with Hugh, that you may—"

"Hugh? So, you're already on a first name basis?" She placed her glass on the table with a clang, causing heads to turn in their direction, and glared at Cora.

Cora's ire rose. "Selena, it did not humiliate you. There were several unschooled guests attempting the same dance, but with good humor, enjoying themselves even if they misstepped." She clenched the arms of the chair until her knuckles whitened. "I'm sick to death of your girlish behavior over a celebrity. I'm your sister, and I love and care for you. You are such a wonderful, talented woman and I've always admired you, but this has got to stop."

Selena's dark eyes grew large, and her lips formed a surprised *O*. She began to speak, but Cora cut her off.

"Enough, Selena." She hissed between clenched teeth. "You will not cost me this job. And one I'll remind you that you all but forced me to take."

Cora rose and left the room without making eye contact with anyone and went straight to her flat. Her emotions ran wild from her sister's attitude to Hugh's kiss.

She showered and went to bed, praying no one would notice her absence. Not Judith, Sam, Selena, and most definitely not Hugh. Sleep would not come, and she heard Selena arrive, come to her bedroom door and whisper, "Cora, are you awake?"

Cora did not respond, and eventually Selena retired without another word. She slept fitfully until six. She knew her worries wouldn't let her return to sleep, so she dressed and left the flat before Selena rose.

Alone in the staff breakfast room, she picked at scrambled eggs until the door creaked open and there stood Hugh, tall, strong and too handsome for his own good. His smile timid, he surveyed the room with tired eyes.

He hovered in the doorway until he saw Cora. "Are you alone this morning?"

"Yes. I came early so—"

He completed her sentence, "So you would encounter no one?"

Cora nodded and stood. "I'll leave you to your meal so you may depart soon."

He snorted. "You sound more like me each day."

She eased her chair under the table. "I'll take that as a compliment—Lord Hedsworth."

His face drooped. "I am sorry. I did not mean that as an insult."

"None taken." Cora made for the door, but he halted her with a whisper.

"Cora, I am sorry. Yet I am thankful you gave me sound advice about the dance. I do believe it saved us a lot of grief."

"Perhaps. I'm glad I could help." Tears streaked her cheeks, and she continued toward the door so he wouldn't see her sorrow over the fight with Selena.

His quick steps clipped across the room, and he claimed her hand. "I will return in a few weeks. Your sister should be gone by then, and I trust we may renew our friendship without hindrance."

Cora's head snapped up. She read only sincerity in his eyes, and she calmed. "Yes. I would like that."

He gave that dratted knee-weakening smile, and without thinking, she leaned into him and kissed his cheek. "When you return."

The last thing she saw was the startled expression on his face as she sprinted from the room.

ಐ

Cora approached Judith's office and heard raised voices—Judith's and Sam's.

"Selena," Sam said with controlled anger. "Your sister has done nothing wrong other than saving you from shame."

Judith chimed in, "He's right, you know."

She heard shuffling for a moment before Selena's tear-filled voice said, "You're all in on it. She's the cause of my embarrassing steps at the dance. I think she convinced Hugh to not dance the waltz with me. It would have been magical."

Selena sniffed loudly. "And now he's gone, and I'll never get to see him again."

Her crying gasps disgusted Cora. How melodramatic she could be. It was amazing how such an intelligent, successful woman could turn into a teen idol worshiper.

Cora's anger snatched all sense of decorum, and she bolted into the room.

"Selena! I have had enough. This has got to stop. Get a hold of yourself and leave these nice people alone. They are now not only my co-workers but my friends. They don't deserve to be harassed by your childish fixation with their boss. What's gotten into you? I've never seen you this unreasonable. Not even after Randall left you. You kept your wits about you, and I was so proud—"

Selena's head bowed, and tears dotted her dark jeans. She raised a teary gaze to Cora. "But that's just it. Randall wants me back."

Cora's jaw dropped. "He *what*?"

;;

Cora slowly shook her head in dismay. "Now that I know why your emotions are all over the world map, I somewhat understand what's going on."

Cora and Selena sat in Cora's flat with mugs of tea cradled in their hands, peering at one another over the rims.

Selena's mouth curved slightly, but her eyes still shone with tears. "Yeah. My hormones are in overdrive." After taking a sip, she resettled her mug on the table between them.

Cora did the same and touched her sister's shoulder. "Tell me the entire story. When did Randall first contact you?"

Selena began and once the tale was told, they both held tissues and hugged. "So, you see why I'm so out of sorts? I still love him, but I don't want to be hurt again. He sincerely sounds remorseful and says he's had no one in his life since he left me."

"And your fixation on Hugh just grew. Kind of like a psychological escape to make up for Randall's absence. Hugh was a safe zone because you knew you'd never meet him. Until—"

"Yep. Until you got this job, and it all blew up in my face. It was like I was possessed. I convinced myself if I could just meet him, we'd fall for one another, and it would fulfill my ridiculous fantasy."

Cora's stomach tightened, and sympathy for her younger sibling grew. "I really am sorry. I truly wasn't trying to sabotage you."

"I know," Selena said meekly. She brought her gaze to Cora's. "I think he's in love with you though."

Cora jerked herself off the sofa. "Selena! He's engaged to my boss."

Selena cocked her head, a puzzled expression on her face.

"I know. That's what's so awful about it." She pulled in a shaky breath. "Maybe he really is a womanizer like all the magazines paint him to be. I feel sorry for Judith. And you too."

The comment withdrew the wind from Cora's sails, and she dropped to the sofa. "What do you mean?"

"I saw how he looked at you, held you in his arms a little closer than necessary, as he swept you across the dance floor. It drove me batty."

Cora blinked. "I don't understand. He's marrying Judith. She's a wonderful woman and . . ."

Cora almost added that Hugh was a wonderful man. But how could she really know if he truly was? He was an actor. He was engaged. And he had kissed her.

Selena's observation rattled Cora. What was she to do?

Chapter Nine

Cora sat in the garden, pondering the days since her sister's departure. When her possessions arrived, she and Selena spent most of their time unpacking and putting away Cora's belongings. They repaired their relationship and discussed Selena's situation, Cora offering sisterly advice that she prayed would help. When Selena left a week later, they were back to a firm standing as siblings. They parted with tears and agreed they would let nothing come between them again.

The day they'd spent walking through the local village, a favorite place for filming period dramas, Cora thought she'd lose her mind with all of Selena's references to each building. She placed Hugh's character in every doorway, path, and structure, recreating each minute detail of what he'd been doing there. By the end of the tour, Cora was nearly brain dead listening to the inane period pieces filmed there, the most ridiculous title of all being *The Duke Who Loved Me*.

The weeks passed uneventfully until Hugh's return, which caught Cora off guard near the private garden with a boxed lunch, reading a favorite novel. He wasn't due back for another week. She relaxed on the bench beneath the arbor, listening to birds and watching butterflies flutter near the fountain at the end of the path.

The scent of heirloom roses lifted on the breeze, bringing thoughts of her late grandmother, who was an avid gardener.

A noise interrupted her reading, and she lifted her head. A moment later, a tiny meow sounded from the ground. She glanced down to discover a tortoise kitten weaving between her ankles.

"Well, hello there, cutie. Where did you come from?" She petted the mottled brown and gold head with gentle fingertips, and the cat tilted a gaze to peer at Cora. "Aren't you a beautiful addition to the garden?"

"Yes, an accurate description."

Cora jerked, and the startled cat flew onto the bench for safety. Protectively, she cuddled the kitten, and glanced up to meet the source of the comment—Hugh Henley.

"Hugh!" Cora lurched to stand, and the cat tightened against her, claws digging into her chest and arms. She knew better than to force the cat to release her. It would cause more injury than already done.

Hugh reached out to grab the kitten, but Cora stopped him with a whisper. "No. You'll only frighten her if you do that."

She began whispering soothing noises to the cat, gaze held on Hugh.

"I am sorry to have startled you—and the kitten. It was not my intention." He slowly raised his hand to caress the animal's back.

Cora pulled in a shaky breath, her heart calming from the scare, the cat now purring softly inside Cora's protective embrace.

Hugh gasped, "You are bleeding."

"What?" Cora looked at her right forearm to find a trickle of blood there. "Oh. I don't have any tissues with me."

Hugh removed a crisp, white handkerchief from his pocket and placed it over the injury. The pressure brought Cora's gaze to meet his. "Thank you." She shifted to accept the cloth from him, but he stayed her hand.

"Do not move, else the kitten may repeat the offense." His eyes twinkled with regret. "Again, I am most apologetic." He looked at the now docile cat. "My comment was not only for the kitten."

Cora stilled, not quite certain she'd heard the soft words or if she'd imagined them. His hand came near hers, which still held the animal. She ignored the remark, heart quickening, wondering what this man was doing. He was engaged to Judith, and yet here he was making small talk until it changed to something more intimate.

Several moments slid by until he cleared his throat and said weakly, "I bid you good day."

The cat's head popped up, and she meowed. Hugh, turning his gaze toward them, snorted. "At least I received a response from *her*."

"Well, you did call her beautiful," Cora added with a timid smile. He had called her so as well.

◌◈◌

Cora leaned back into the overstuffed chair in Judith's office, intent on what Judith was saying about her new ideas of marketing. Hugh sat next to Sam, though in his agent's capacity, nodding as Judith made an excited explanation on a particular point.

Hugh's expression remained placid, his eyes intent on the presentation. After Judith completed the plan, Sam clapped, and Hugh said, "Your ideas are impressive. May we discuss them further? Perhaps we might have a private dinner tonight—just the four of us."

All agreed they would gather in Hugh's private rooms. Judith excused herself to meet with the chef to arrange their dinner meeting. Hugh stood when she did. As she strode to the door, Sam joined her. "I better go with you. I don't want to be surprised with some strange dish I can't pronounce." He took Judith's arm and pulled her to a stop. "I like eating something I can identify."

Cora asked, "Have you eaten something you couldn't identify?"

"Yes. Judith gave me a lovely dish with glistening, melted cheese on top, and after one bite—which tasted like dirt *fromage*—I discovered it to be snails." His faked a gag and nudged Judith through the door.

"That man is ridiculous," Hugh said with a wide smile.

"He can be. But he's a very nice, polite man. I like Sam,"

Cora said as she rose. "I have to get back to my office and complete the seating arrangements for dinner tomorrow night."

"I'll accompany you as far as the library."

They walked in silence, Hugh's hands joined behind him. When they reached the library, Cora said goodbye and that she would see him at dinner.

"Cora." He took one step closer and looked over his shoulder to see if they were alone. "Please forgive my hasty words this morn. It was not my intention to offend . . . or be inappropriate."

"None taken." She waited, but he remained silent. "Have a good afternoon."

She rushed toward her office and, as she rounded the corner, glanced back to see Hugh watching her. Her face heated, but she offered a smile and entered the room. She rested against the closed door and hugged the notebook to her chest. "What are you doing, Hugh?"

The quintessential English room calmed her overwrought nerves. Judith had asked for her favorite décor, and she had certainly delivered. The plaster walls had been freshened with new whitewash and shaded to a soft golden hue. Chintz fabric covered the chairs, small sofa, and ottoman. The distressed furniture hinted of the shabby chic style with its well-worn edges of gilt.

Cozy was a one-word summary of the ambiance. The cushioned window seat beckoned her to curl up with a book into its comfortable confines. The secluded spot had a marvelous view of the private garden and beyond.

With a sigh, she passed the desk, dropped the notebook onto its surface, and sat in the window. Propping against the wall, she bent her knees and rested her cheek upon them. The landscape, a myriad of colors, mingled with many shades of green, and her tear-filled eyes merged the colors to form an impressionist painting.

A dark figure slowly moved across her line of sight, and she blinked away the moisture. Hugh sauntered across the lawn, hands behind his back. Watching him intently, she thought him a mystery. Mostly, he appeared to have it all together. Then he would say or do something to contradict his persona—like dance in a way that stole her breath, imply he thought her beautiful, and rescue her from falling into the pond.

Her gaze followed him as he navigated around the ancient stone arch and toward the private garden. Once again, she saw the small green book in his hand. The book of prayer.

C8ED

Cora arrived at Hugh's door with Judith. She had gone to Judith's flat well before their appointed time, not wanting to be at Hugh's before anyone else. All the accidental, private meetings with him made her anxious.

A warm, yeasty scent met them at the door. Hugh answered their knock and waved them inside. "Welcome." He gestured toward Sam. "He started without us."

Cora noted Sam's large steaming cup, and the strong, nutty aroma of coffee wafted closer. She adored the smell but hated the taste.

"Would you ladies like one before dinner?" Sam lifted his

108

very modern mug in their direction.

Cora shook her head, but Judith said, "Yes, please."

Sam strode across the room to an antique buffet where a coffee bar had been set up.

Hugh motioned toward the closely arranged furniture by the large window facing the fountain and beyond that the kitchen gardens.

Cora sat and placed her notebook on her lap.

Sam handed a mug to Judith and notched his head toward the notebook. "Why have you brought that?"

"To take notes," Cora said with a hint of sarcastic humor.

Sam sat by Judith and lifted a brow.

Judith playfully tapped him on the knee. "Sam, she's enormously efficient—but not a mind reader."

Cora's face scrunched with confusion, and Sam hooted. "It's a joke, love. If anyone says let's meet over dinner to discuss it further, it really means—have dinner as an excuse to get together socially."

Hugh claimed the chair beside Cora, a mug of tea in one hand. "Do not allow them to trouble you. It is commendable you arrive prepared."

Sam chuckled. "You don't need to coddle her. She's a big girl and can take care of herself."

"Thank you, Sam. I appreciate that." With twitching fingers, Cora slid the notebook between the cushion and the chair arm.

Judith changed the subject by asking about the ball the following night. "We have a pretty good crowd for tomorrow."

She lifted the mug and inhaled the rising, aromatic steam from her cup. "Leonard has an amazing new idea for the chalk design. He saw a sketch in an old book and tweaked it to resemble an ancient ruin—arches and all."

Sam choked and sputtered coffee. Judith patted him on the back. "Did I say something amusing?"

It took a moment for him to regain his voice, and he laughed. "No. It just brought to mind that *old pile of rocks*, as you fondly call it."

Hugh smiled into his tea. "Well, I suppose you may call it *old*. Yet it is not a pile of rocks. It was built during the Roman occupation of England." He squinted in Judith's direction.

She snorted. "Yeah. What's left of it?"

Cora smiled, enjoying their banter about the old arch tucked near the private garden. The evening slipped by with ease, and its eventual end brought a feeling of disappointment to Cora.

Sam and Judith walked Cora to her door, and she went through her evening routine, her thoughts still on the dinner. Lying in bed staring through the window at the night sky, she drifted to sleep filled with a calming reassurance she hadn't felt in quite some time.

CB&SO

Cora gasped as she took in the elaborate chalked floor of the ballroom, hating the thought of it being ruined in a matter of minutes once the dancing began.

"This is extraordinary." Cora scanned the intricate details of the ancient ruins so expertly created they appeared almost three dimensional. It was more amazing than the first one

Judith had shown her before she had begun her position at the estate.

"Isn't it?" Judith beamed and gazed at Cora. "So are you. That dress is smashing."

Cora glanced down at the front of her formal clothing, satin shoes peeking out from under the amber-colored dress. While looking in the mirror, she'd noted how the warm undertones made her eyes appear golden.

Thoughts returning to the floor, she said, "I hope no one trips." She pointed across the room. "Those crumbling stone steps are so realistic, I may try to climb them."

Judith hooted. "Hm. I hadn't thought of that." She shrugged. "They'll be swept away before we complete the first dance though."

"True. But a shame." Cora returned Sam's wave from across the room, but rather than walking straight at them, he skirted the perimeter. "What's Sam doing?"

"Knowing I'll have his head on a platter if he walks on the chalk before everyone arrives."

"Is she talking about me?" Sam halted in front of them, inches inside the border the artist had created before beginning the artwork.

"Naturally." One side of Judith's mouth quirked.

Cora liked their friendly teasing. Everyone had their faults, but these people were easy to work with. And they genuinely cared about one another. Voices filtered from the hall, and within minutes, people encircled the stunning floor, compliments filling the air.

Sam asked, "Where's Hugh? He's never late."

Judith leaned in, lowering her voice. "You may need to rescue him from a chirpy fan. One of the new guests especially fits that profile."

Cora listened with interest until Sam excused himself to locate their boss. He returned shortly with a tall, willowy auburn-haired woman on his arm, Hugh following. Cora nudged Judith, whose attention focused across the room, eyes intent on a man bent over the floor preparing to run his fingers across the chalk.

Before Cora could ask a question, Judith sprinted around the border until she tapped the culprit on the shoulder just as his hand hovered over the chalk. His startled gaze swung up to meet Judith's hard stare.

Hugh's voice at Cora's ear made her jump. "Is Judith playing the Bow Street Runner?"

Cora smirked. "Or constable?"

"Either will suffice." Hugh's eyes remained on Judith and the man even as he spoke to Cora. "I believe you promised me the first dance. Did you not?"

Cora froze, not recalling a discussion where she made the promise.

"Must I ask Sam or Judith to help you summon the conversation they witnessed?" He now watched her.

"I'm sorry I don't remember. But if you say I did."

A waltz started, and Cora wondered if he had anything to do with that choice. Within minutes, she was reliving the previous dances she'd shared with the man. Each one as thrilling as the first.

Hugh wore a slightly different outfit of evening attire, not as somber, but still elegant and well cut in shadowy gray that suited his dark brown hair. He even smelled different.

"What is that scent you're wearing?" Cora breathed deeper to catch its nuances.

"It is called Albany and comes from a London shop." His boyish smile hinted at being caught at some harmless prank. "It is a blend of citrus and lavender."

"Ah." Cora then grasped the scent she couldn't quite identify. "I suppose the citrus mingling with the lavender threw me off. Lavender is my favorite scent, but the citrus mutes it somewhat."

"Most perceptive. I am impressed." He studied her and drew a little closer.

"It's not exactly rocket science, Hugh." She pulled a face, and he snickered in response.

The dance ended, and Hugh left Cora with Judith to locate his next dance partner, and Sam joined them.

"Okay, Sam. Spill it on how you rescued HRH from the model."

Cora's head snapped around to look at Judith. "She's a model?"

Judith nodded, but Sam answered, "Yeah. Cover girl type. She's been on nearly every Brit fashion magazine for the past five years. She has aspirations of acting."

"She's the one you rescued Hugh from?" Cora swallowed hard. "And he *let* you?"

Sam's eyes narrowed. "Why wouldn't he?" His mouth opened. "Oh, I see. Just because she's spectacular looking means he's got to be interested?"

Cora's face heated, and she stumbled over the words. "Well . . . I . . ." She dipped her head in embarrassment.

Sam guffawed. "You're jealous."

Cora lifted her head and stared at him, avoiding Judith's eyes. "Of course I'm not jealous. After all, he's en—"

Judith jabbed him in the ribs, and he yelped, cutting off Cora's words. "Sam. Don't be a git."

Sam patted Judith's arm. "Keep your hair on. She knows I only jest."

Cora sighed, then grinned at them. "I love listening to you two. It lifts my spirits."

Sam put an arm around her shoulders. "Glad to be of service, love. We may take our sketches on the road one day." He waggled his eyebrows, and Judith thumped his shoulder.

"Ow," he hissed.

Cora purposely tried not to watch the dancers, keeping up the chatter with Judith and Sam. After a few minutes, Sam whisked Judith to the dance floor to join the others. Cora refreshed her drink and strode to the terrace to view the candles Hugh always lined the paths with during evening entertainments. She admired his attention to historical detail as she strolled between the romantic lighting, the scent of wisteria and jasmine mixing on the night air.

The serenity enfolded her with a loving embrace, and she thought of God. Was He speaking now? Had she thanked Him for this dream job? Shame flowed at believing He had taken her loved ones and abandoned her. Heart sinking, she stared at the flicker of moonlight reflecting on the river between gaps in the thick forest.

"Cora?" Footsteps approached, and she spun to see Hugh advancing. "Are you well?"

She sipped the orgeat and turned again toward the view. "Yes. Why do you ask?"

"We are to dance soon. I could not find you, and Judith said she saw you step onto the terrace."

"Sorry. It's just so pleasant out here. I wanted to see the lights."

Hugh moved closer, their shoulders touching.

Her mouth dried, and the desire to leave became overwhelming.

"Would you like to walk in the gardens?"

"Thank you, but I've just come through the terraced garden."

"You misunderstand. I mean the private garden where we shall be undisturbed."

Her eyes widened, and she took a step away.

"Please do not misunderstand." His hand came to rest on her arm. "I mean no disrespect. I only desire to talk without interruption. It seems we are always being interrupted."

Cora caught sight of his hand, still upon her arm, and he removed it. "Do you have candles placed there as well?"

His smile weakened her resolve. "I do. The center is no longer in near darkness." He stepped to the side and gestured for her to go ahead of him. They reached the entrance to the terraced gardens, and his long stride brought him to her side, his hands clasped behind him.

She smiled to herself, noting his usual stance.

"You have a striking smile."

Cora glanced his way. She gripped the cup tighter and finished the drink with one gulp. He took the cup and placed it on the terrace's stone railing. They strolled in silence down the steps and around the corner of the house and across the pebbled drive toward the north. When they entered the private garden, small candles lined one side of the walls, far enough away that a lady's skirt was not in danger, although Hugh made a move to have her walk along the opposite side so the candles were to his right.

He was a thoughtful, well-mannered man. A unique find in the twenty-first century. Rarely did a man open a door for her.

Although the silence was eerie, she felt safe with him. They walked for a while, the night's stillness and flickering candlelight their only companions. Reaching the small center of the garden—the place where she'd first met Hugh—the table held candles inside glass pots, a bottle, two glasses, and a napkin-covered plate.

He gripped the back of one chair and pulled it out. "Please be seated."

Cora paused, searched his face questioningly, and sat.

"I hope you like this trivial surprise." He sat opposite her. "I know dinner will be a foray into mindless conversation, and it can be challenging. This is but a brief diversion until we must return."

"Thank you. It's thoughtful of you." She clasped shaking fingers on her lap, wondering what Judith would think about this diversion.

He poured from the bottle. "Judith told me you had a

fondness for sparkling water."

"She did?" Taken aback by the comment, she wondered why Judith would've said such a thing.

"I do." She sipped.

He removed the napkin and slid it toward her. Perfectly made tea cakes beckoned. They looked just like her grandmother's. "Did Judith tell you about these?" She pointed to the treats, not recalling ever telling her new friend this detail about herself.

"Your sister told me."

"Truly?"

"I asked her." He smiled guiltily, claimed one, and tasted it. "Delicious. Your grandmother was a superb cook."

"My grandmother?" Cora froze, a teacake inches from her mouth.

"Selena gave me the recipe."

Cora timidly took a bite, and her surprise must have registered in her expression because Hugh said, "I see I impressed you."

"Immensely. They taste just like my grandmother's."

"I am pleased." He claimed another.

They sat in companionable silence, Cora thankful for the lack of conversation as she meditated over the man's behavior. Once they had emptied the plate and drank the last sip of water, he stood. "I suppose we should appear before the dance ends and dinner begins."

He pulled her chair out as she rose. "I'm not so sure I'll be able to eat after this."

Hugh offered a slight smile. "Please make an effort. I would not have you grow faint." He chuckled. "Nor would I have you unable to wear that lovely dress."

"I'll try to find a happy medium. If I eat too much, I will *not* be able to wear it." A meow interrupted, and Cora looked to the ground and discovered the tortoise cat. She stooped to pet the kitten for a moment, then rose, the animal staying nearby.

Arriving at the exit of the garden, Hugh placed her hand on his arm and stared into her eyes as they strode toward the house. Cora glanced away for a moment, seeing the *pile of rocks* ahead.

A flash of movement gave her pause, and she saw Judith and Sam standing near the garden wall. The dim light must be playing tricks. She squinted to focus on the couple. Yes— they were locked in an intimate embrace. They paused that way a moment, then the embrace became a very passionate kiss.

Cora's breath caught in her throat, but she kept pace with Hugh, who appeared oblivious to their behavior.

Before they passed the arch, blinding twin lights captured their attention, shining in their faces, a motor roaring. A car lurched toward the arch from the car park.

Cora screamed, and Hugh gripped her arm, tugging them through the opening, as the stones tumbled down around them.

Chapter Ten

Cora opened her eyes, head pounding like a drum, to find she was in her own room. One window stood open a fraction, a gentle breeze blowing the lace curtains and filling the space with garden-fresh air. The palest of dawn's light revealed the earliness of the day, her stomach growled in anticipation.

Sitting with care, she dangled her legs over the side of the bed, head pounding in protest. She cradled her face with one palm and moaned, bringing a hand to one temple. A bandage covered that side of her face. When she pressed it, a pain shot across the already aching temple, and dizziness swam through her. Once steadied, she rose and padded slowly toward the bathroom, seeking cool water to splash on her face.

Instead of finding the sink, long dresses hung on pegs on

two walls, and a large black lacquered and gold chinoiserie cabinet stood to one side. A small dressing table and mirror graced the remaining wall with a low stool underneath and beside it a washstand and pitcher.

Cora paused in amazement, wondering if she had a concussion. She swayed and backed from the room, a memory of Hugh snatching her through the arch as a car surged toward them, the smell of exhaust fumes heavy in the air. The last thing she remembered was descending into darkness. Dizziness returned, and she gripped the doorframe.

With deep shaky breaths, she gradually made her way to the bed and knocked a porcelain figurine from its perch on the bedside table, sending it shattering against the floor. Seconds later the bedroom door slammed open, and Hugh stood in the doorway, wavy hair tousled, a bathrobe hanging loose from his tall frame.

"Cora!" He rushed in and helped her sit on the edge of the bed, feet suspended off the floor by several inches.

She gripped her head with both hands. "I'm unwell. What happened?"

A pitiful meow came from the doorway. A small cat's large green-gold eyes scanned the room. When she spotted Cora, she ran and pounced onto the bed, pressing a paw against her thigh. Cora shifted and allowed the kitten to climb onto her lap, using one hand to pet the purring animal, her soft fur and warm body soothing Cora's nerves.

Though the pain did not lessen, Cora cooed at the sweet creature. "How did you get in here?"

Hugh's chuckle lacked sentiment. "She has barely left your

side."

Cora's gaze swung from the cat to him, something in his tone unsettling her. "How long have I been asleep?"

He blew out a breath. "You have not been sleeping. You have been unconscious for these two days past."

"*Unconscious*?" Cora stared at him and blinked. "Two days?"

Hugh nodded. "The doctor said not to worry unless it was for a longer period." He gently removed Cora's hand pressed to her head and sandwiched it between his, sending a shiver through her.

Cora swayed toward him until she rested against his chest. He put an arm around her and stroked her hair.

"I'm sorry, but I'm so weak and dizzy." She closed her eyes. The sensation of being bone weary engulfed her. The cat moved away and curled into a ball, still purring.

"Would you like to sleep for a while longer?" He asked close to her ear.

"Not sleep. Just rest." Breathing seemed tiresome.

Their connection and the gentle purring of the kitten calmed Cora. "I am hungry though."

"Excellent. I will have Mrs. Duckworth send broth, tea, and toast. That should settle well on a long empty stomach."

He stood and scooped her into his arms as though she weighed little. She chuckled weakly, thinking he must be strong to pick up someone as hefty as she.

"Why do you laugh, Cora?" His voice held no humor.

She shared what she'd been thinking, and his voice

softened. "You weigh nothing, my dear."

Cora slurred, "Bet women of the Regency era all weighed about as much as a pillowcase full of feathers." She snickered. The hunger must be affecting her mind. "I've seen the dresses in museums. Selena showed me the ones on temporary loan at her museum. I couldn't get one leg in them." She guffawed and instantly winced, her head swimming again.

"Please do not overexert yourself until your strength returns."

Still standing with Cora cradled in his arms, her hands looped around his neck, their faces much too close. She jolted into awareness. This wasn't right. He was engaged to Judith.

"You may put me down now." She glanced at the bed, and her face burned. This was not good.

He cleared his throat. "Ah, yes. Pardon me." He eased her onto the bed, leaning her against the pillows, then pulled the covers to her chin.

The cat jumped, pouncing onto her lap, and curled into a ball. Both reached to pet the kitten, their fingers grazing one another's.

Hugh backed away and clasped his hands behind him. "I will tell Olive to have your meal sent and attend to your needs."

Before he reached the door, Cora called out to him weakly, "Hugh." He turned and looked at her questioningly.

"Where is my bathroom?" The question pushed past her parched lips, each spoken word a chore.

His face turned ashen. "Gather your strength, then we shall talk." He licked his lips. "Tonight—we shall speak tonight."

He bowed and left the room, leaving Cora with not only a feeling of uncertainty in the pit of her stomach but also another burning question—who were Mrs. Duckworth and Olive?

⁂

Olive, the upstairs maid, or so Cora was told, attended her soon after Hugh left. She bore a tray carrying a pot of tea, a bowl of dark broth, and toast with jam and cream. The food looked tasty, but Cora no longer had an appetite, despite her growling stomach.

Hugh's last words concerned her profoundly, not to mention the young woman dressed in Regency servant's attire. Was this some new rule Hugh had implemented? Cora didn't recognize her. She must be a new hire at the estate while Cora had been unconscious. She still couldn't believe she had been *unconscious* for two days.

The girl's fair complexion was reminiscent of Judith, and Cora wondered why Hugh had not called for Judith? Or Sam?

"Here you go, my lady. Cook does make the best broth in all of England." She placed the tray across Cora's lap, upsetting the kitten.

"What's her name, my lady?" Olive notched her head toward the stretching cat.

Cora's eyebrows lifted. "I don't know. She's a stray I found in the garden."

Olive's face pinched in concentration. "She is a might pretty thing. Got to have a name."

"Yes. I suppose you're right. I'll think about that."

Olive curtsied and pointed to the long needlepoint ribbon hanging beside the bed. "Just pull and I will come."

Before Cora could comment, the girl softly closed the door. Cora stared at the tray and focused on the tea. With great effort, she poured herself a cup and sipped. After a few swallows, her head cleared, and she knew she needed to regain her strength, so she forced down a few bites of dry toast and half of the broth. The effort exhausted her, and she rested against the pillow, the cat now sleeping at her feet.

When she woke, the tray was gone, and the cat rested on the plump cushion in the window seat. A floral-scented breeze drifted through the lace curtains. The urge to find the bathroom returned, and she stood carefully, her heel bumping against something at the edge of the bed. She looked down at the rim of a porcelain chamber pot.

Confusion swept over her for a second before she chuckled. Judith was playing a prank. She remembered the remark she'd made about convincing Hugh that chamber pots were where she drew the line at the Regency experience.

She returned to the bathroom door, but once opened, she found the space had not changed. It was still some sort of dressing room, so she strode to the only other door in the room and discovered it to be the entrance to a small parlor. A flash of recognition hit. This was the door Hugh had entered earlier that day, wearing a robe.

A burst of energy propelled her across the room, and she jerked the opposite door open, surprised by a man not much younger than herself, nor much taller. Hugh was standing shirtless with his back to the man standing nearby inspecting the sleeve of a white linen shirt.

"Cora!" Hugh quickly grabbed the shirt and shoved his arms through the sleeves and yanked it down his torso. He turned to the man and said, "That will be all for now, Crawford. Thank you."

Crawford's face bordered on the treasonous as his forehead wrinkled, his voice no less so. "Yes, my lord." Sarcasm oozed as he dipped his head and left them alone.

Hugh stepped toward Cora and took her hands in his. "I am much pleased you are up and about." He slanted his head and studied her. "Your color has returned. Prettily so."

Cora's face warmed, but her heart did not. "What's going on? All I want is my bathroom, and it seems to have disappeared." She knew she sounded hysterical, but confusion combined with her pounding head made her wonder if she was losing her mind. Her gaze slid to his chest, and the memory of seeing him without a shirt moments before grew unsettling.

He squeezed her hands. "It is almost time for our evening meal. You may not be up to joining me in the dining room, but would you allow me to have a table set in the parlor?" He slanted his head toward the room that separated theirs.

Cora's head spun, and she veered against him. Her hands pulled from his and flew to his chest, his very firm chest. Oh, my. This was *not* good. She twisted away and staggered toward the door, and he caught up with her and took her arm.

"Allow me to assist you to bed—" He coughed. "—I mean to steady you."

She heard him swallow and realized this was just as uncomfortable for him. "Yes, please. I am sorry to be such a bother, but I just want my bathroom." Her eyes stung with tears.

He guided Cora to her bedroom and settled her there, yanked the cord, and pulled the opening of his shirt together as Olive appeared. He strode to the maid and whispered something Cora could not hear.

Hugh returned to Cora's side. "Olive shall see to your needs, and I shall return when dinner has arrived." He sent her an affectionate smile and departed.

Olive was kind as she aided Cora, speaking as if to an injured child about the use of the chamber pot. Cora became convinced she was indeed losing her senses.

After assisting Cora with her personal needs, including washing her face and hands, she helped her put on a high-waisted pale blue dress with tiny sprigs of deep purple pansies woven around the bodice. Olive seated Cora at the table in the parlor, a lap blanket draped over her thighs. Where had the hours gone? She must have slept the entire day since they were about to have dinner.

Olive tucked the blanket around Cora's knees and asked, "My lady, Lord Hedsworth did ask that I be your lady's maid."

Cora's insides swayed. "*My* lady's maid?"

"Yes, ma'am." The girl's face scrunched in worry."

Cora glanced around the room waiting for Judith to jump from behind the furniture and scream, "Gotcha!" Nothing happened while Olive gaped at her, waiting for a response.

"I don't know what to say. I've never had one before." Timidly, she squeaked, "Thank you?"

Olive's face brightened, then faded in confusion.

"What should I call you? Olive?" Cora chewed the inside of her lower lip while she waited.

"Oh, no, my lady." She pursed her lips. "Did you not have a lady's maid in America?"

Slowly shaking her head, Cora replied slowly, "Nooo . . ." The girl's eyes widened, and Cora almost laughed. She changed her approach. "I heard Hugh call you Olive. So why can't I?"

"The maids are addressed in this way, but a lady's maid is addressed by her surname."

"And yours is . . .?

"Cockerham, my lady." She curtsied.

Cora pressed her lips tightly and pressed her fingertips against her temples. What was going on? "That's a nice name and all—but it's a mouthful. I'm calling you Olive and since you're *my* lady's maid, everyone else will have to deal with it." She gave Olive what she hoped was a pleasant smile.

The corners of the maid's mouth curled upwards for a heartbeat but straightened quickly. She curtsied once more. "Thank you, my lady. As you wish." Turning to leave, her eyes met Cora's. "Should you need anything further, just pull the bell, my lady."

Cora nodded, and before the door shut, she processed every memory she had since the accident. Her head no longer ached as much, but there remained a shadow of pain, the memory still fuzzy. She sipped the tea, allowing it to soothe the tension. The door creaked, and two women came bearing heavily laden trays. They addressed her as *my* lady, which further confused her.

She was about to ask what they meant when Hugh entered, dressed as he always did, looking like he just stepped off a film set—in Regency attire.

He thanked the women, told them he would serve, and would no longer be needed for the remainder of the evening.

Cora's nervousness escalated, and found she could not speak, thoughts whirling with unanswered questions.

Hugh placed a small portion of each dish on her plate, the aromas lifting to her nose. "Please let me know if you would like more. Since you have eaten little in the past two days, I assumed you would not require much."

She nodded and forced down the barrage of questions she wanted to fire at him. He chatted about mundane things for a while until she could not hold her concerns from spilling out.

"Hugh. Please tell me what's going on. Am I losing my mind?" She dabbed her eyes with the napkin. "Why can't I remember things? I recall the accident and my life before that, but all of this is so different." She waved a limp hand in the air. "Is this some sort of amnesia or hallucination?"

He blew out an exasperated breath, his eyes dull with expressive pain. "This you shall find difficult to believe." His long fingers gripped his stemmed glass, and he took a long drink. "I awoke from the crash and found you unconscious, a wound upon your head. I grew frantic and carried you to the house seeking help."

He blinked several times, his eyes flitting around the room, his expression sobering. "*Cora*. As hard as this is to believe, we are . . . in the past." He drew in a sharp breath. "The car crashed into the arch just as we walked through it, and somehow we were shoved backward in time."

She shook her head, trying to recall anything after the car lights, but she could not. "Hugh . . . do you honestly expect me to believe that?" She looked around once again expecting to see Judith or Sam. "Is Judith behind this elaborate prank? If so, it's gone on far enough. I'm exhausted."

The wounded expression he wore broke Cora's resolve. "Seriously, Hugh. Just tell me the truth."

Hugh reached across the table and claimed one of her hands. "I am sincere. Upon arrival at the house, the butler, Merriweather, acted as if he recognized me and called me Lord Hedsworth, telling me they had not expected me back from my journey so soon." He cleared his throat. "I assume my strong resemblance to my ancestor is the reason for the butler's confusion."

Cora admitted to herself that he was most convincing. He was an actor, after all. A very attractive, magnetic one. Considering the injury, why would they continue the ruse? Judith had a marvelous sense of humor but not to this extent. Cora's head was truly cut and bruised. When Olive cleaned and redressed it, Cora insisted on seeing it in the mirror for herself.

Hugh squeezed her hand, his eyes holding genuine concern. "Are you ill again? I shall summon the doctor if need be."

Cora pulled her hand away and placed it on her lap. "No— I mean . . ." She stared across the room for a moment and gathered her thoughts. "This must be a bad dream." The kitten appeared at Cora's feet and rubbed against her leg. She looked up at Cora and meowed.

Hugh jumped from his seat. "I near forgot." He retrieved two small dishes from the tray on a table across the room. When he returned, he placed them on the floor near Cora's feet. "I was uncertain which she would prefer, so I asked Mrs. Duckworth to prepare fish and milk. She may have whichever her tiny heart desires."

Cora's chest squeezed at his gentleness toward the small cat. He was a kind man.

He remained on his haunches for a few moments, watching the kitten attack one dish, then the other, purring loudly. He rose and peered down into Cora's eyes—his seeming bluer than she remembered, the silver rings accentuating their clarity.

"We must give her a name." Hugh returned to his chair, still watching Cora.

Cora regarded the cat and her hearty appetite, wishing she could do the same, but food did not appeal very much at the moment. "Lizzy," she said softly.

"Pardon?"

"Her name is Lizzy. After Elizabeth Bennett from *Pride and Prejudice*."

This brought a bright smile from Hugh, his fine-looking features becoming more so. "Perfect."

Cora's head cleared, and she ate a bite of the cold chicken. Thoughts of Hugh carrying her to the house swam in her mind until one particular idea floated there, not wanting to be dismissed. "Hugh? What did you tell the butler when he called you Lord Hedsworth?"

His head shot up, and he stopped chewing. He dipped his

chin, resumed eating, and swallowed hard. "Surprised, I told him I returned early. I then instructed him to contact the doctor."

"And he accepted your explanation without question?"

"He did. I told him we were set upon by highwaymen and they'd stolen the carriage, horses, and our belongings."

"What about the driver?"

Hugh blinked several times before he continued, "It appears the driver was part of the robbery."

Cora nodded, still confused. She ate a few spoonfuls of soup and lay the utensil beside the bowl. "I wonder . . . how did you explain me?"

He peered at the cat, who had cleaned both bowls and was now bathing under the table. "She is a lovely feline and may have the makings of an excellent mouser in the stables." The smile lines around his eyes deepened. "I am uncertain Miss Jane Austen would approve of *her* Lizzy doing something as mundane as catching mice."

Cora agreed, but he was avoiding her question. She cleared her throat. "Hugh?"

His sapphire eyes focused on her. Until now, she described them as ice blue, but their depths seemed perhaps a little darker as tenderness and a hint of understanding shone within them now.

"I told him you are my wife."

Cora could do nothing but stare at him as if he'd lost his mind.

Chapter Eleven

Cora's dizziness returned but not from her injury. "You told him *what*?"

"It was of necessity," Hugh continued to stare, his soulful eyes pleading her to understand.

Understand *what* she did not know. "How so?" She gulped her tea, hands shaking as she gripped the cup with both hands.

"Cora, in Regency times there is social etiquette—"

She cut him off. "Hugh, I don't want to hear your version of what we must do in the name of Regency-proper behavior." Regretting her harsh tone, she said, "I'm sorry. It's just so aggravating to think I'm losing my mind—or this is a nightmare."

Cora propped her elbows on the table and rested her forehead on her palms.

"You must understand. I carried you in my arms late at night when I knocked on the door. How was I to know we were over two hundred years in the past? I thought one of our staff would open the door."

She interrupted. "Well, one of the staff did. But not from . . . from our world." Cora slammed a palm on the table, causing a vibration that rattled the dishes. "I'm sorry, but this is just too much. Do you really expect me to buy this?"

"I expect nothing from you except to keep an open mind."

A quick thought came to her. "What of the dance? Shouldn't that have been still going on?"

He faltered for a moment. "That is what I assumed, but it seems I was unconscious for a period as well. It was very late and the house still." He ran a shaking hand through his thick hair. "It occurred to me the house should be ablaze and the staff searching for us."

"Yes. That's true." Chaos appeared to be closing in on them, and Cora didn't know what to think or do. She met Hugh's gaze and read the same emotion in his eyes. Self-reproach struck her. He was trying to help and gave the impression he genuinely cared about what happened to her.

She breathed deeply, shoulders slumping with defeat. "So . . . as your wife, won't it be a little difficult to explain where you found me?"

One side of his mouth quirked upward. "They inquired where I traveled—it seems *Lord Hedsworth* travels overmuch—so I told them America. That would explain your accent."

"All right. So, you vacationed in America and found a bride. Correct?"

He ran a finger around the rim of his glass, a distant glint in his eyes. "It would appear so." He removed something from his pocket and placed it on the table. With the tip of one finger, he slid it toward her. "I found this while you were sleeping and thought it meet that you wear it—to complete the ruse."

She caught the glint of candlelight on the gold and emerald ring, staring at it with incredulity. "You want me to wear that?"

"Please."

Cora mulled over the implications, blinking in confusion. He was serious. They had to assume the roles of a married couple, actors playing a part. A problem because Hugh was indeed an actor, but Cora nothing of the sort. She had once been demoted from a leading role in her third grade play due to forgetting her lines.

"Okay, let me get this straight. We just happened to be overtaken by highwaymen and all our belongings stolen, along with the carriage, and the driver was involved, but they didn't take the ring?"

Hugh continued circling the glass with his fingertip and nodded. "It was dark, mayhap they did not notice."

"You were protecting my reputation by telling all these lies?"

Without looking up, he said, "I was."

Clearing her throat, she crossed her arms over her middle. "Explain that to me please."

Her statement brought his eyes to meet hers. "Because you are an unmarried woman in the presence of an unmarried man in the middle of the night."

"I was injured." Cora knew a good deal about social strictures from the past. But it shocked her that Hugh would carry it so far. Especially when, at that moment, he did not realize he was in the past, and she told him so.

"Makes no matter. I would not have your reputation ruined and have you ostracized by polite society." He crossed his arms and stared at her. "Someone not employed at Hedsworth answered the door and assumed I was someone else. I could chance nothing. I mean it not as a wedding ring. Any self-respecting Regency husband would give his wife gifts of jewelry."

Cora admitted it was an excellent point. "Okay, I'll give you that."

Hugh's face changed to one of smug satisfaction. "Are you finished questioning me, *Lady* Hedsworth?"

Her jaw dropped. "What did you call me?"

His smile widened. "You heard me well, Cora. We both have a role to play now. I am certain you are up to the task."

Hugh could not be more wrong.

He toyed with her emotions, fragile as they currently were, skipping from amusement to anger and back again. Why would God choose to snatch her away from the career she'd always desired and had only just received, to be stuck somewhere—*somewhen*—with someone she'd disliked for years?

"*Somewhen* is not a word, Cora." Hugh's deep voice rumbled with humor.

Cora cringed. Had she said all of that aloud? "What did I say?"

"You said you were stuck *somewhen*."

"Is that all I said? I'm so distraught I don't know what I'm doing."

"That is all." He shoved his chair back and stood.

She looked at his half-eaten food and then at his face, something unsaid in his gaze. Her stomach growled a protest at not being filled, and he chuckled.

"Don't mock me."

"Why should I not? You are obviously in need of nourishment, yet you insist on picking at your food. If you are still too weak to feed yourself, I will be glad to do so." One side of his mouth lifted in amusement.

Cora shot upward, wobbled, and clutched the table to steady herself. "How dare you!"

Hugh gripped the back of his chair and leaned toward her. "I know not what is running through your mind, but know this, I will try with all my power to get you back to *somewhen* in the future so you may continue your dislike of me. I thought we were growing closer, at times you drew nearer, then removed yourself from me. Why is that, Cora?" He cocked his head.

Unable to answer, Judith's face came to mind, and she opened her mouth to shout that he was engaged to her friend, and how could he flirt with her? When a knock sounded on

Hugh's bedroom door they halted, glaring at one another, his eyes holding a challenge.

Hugh stiffened. "Enter."

Crawford stuck his head through the door's crack and dipped his chin. "My lord, are you in need of assistance? I heard shouting and feared something was amiss with Lady Hedsworth."

Without looking at his valet, Hugh said, "No, Crawford. You may go for the evening. I require nothing further."

Crawford jutted his chin and drew back through the door.

Hugh growled, "That man can be insufferable at times."

"Hm." Cora muttered, "Sounds like someone else I know." She rose slowly, snatched a piece of buttered bread and a napkin, and darted from the room.

ϡϠ

Cora seethed as she bit a chunk from the bread. After one chew, she moaned with culinary pleasure. Mrs. Duckworth was an amazing baker. She'd never tasted bread this good. Wishing she'd taken another piece, she tiptoed to the door and pressed her ear against it. No sound came from their shared parlor.

Lizzy meowed. She put her finger to her lips and shushed the cat. "If you'll be quiet, I'll see what's left that you may like."

Cora slipped the door open a crack and peeped inside. The table had not been cleared, and no one remained in the room. She widened the opening and eased through, her focus on the food. After she'd filled the plate, including bits of fish for Lizzy, she covered it with Hugh's napkin and crept toward her

138

room.

"What's this, Lady Hedsworth stealing from her husband?"

Cora gasped, pressing the plate to her chest and spun around. Hugh stood at the large leaded glass window, hands behind him, peering toward the gardens. He watched her from the reflection in the glass. The first thought was one of gratitude that she'd covered the food with the thick napkin. Her insides trembled, humiliation causing her eyes to sting.

She swallowed a retort, trying to think of something coherent to say. A flash of indignation came over her. "If you hadn't been so insulting, I might have completed my meal." She jerked her chin upward and looked down her nose at him.

He turned and strode toward her with quick steps, hands remaining behind him. "You, my dear, are being haughty."

Cora sucked in an annoyed breath. "How dare you!"

"That's the second time you have said that to me this evening, Cora." He made a step closer until his breath fanned her face. "Proverbs says 'Pride goeth before destruction, and a haughty spirit before a fall.'"

Mouth forming an O-shape, her heartbeat quickened.

His eyes flicked from her lips to her eyes, and they regarded one another. Hugh swallowed so hard she could hear it, eyes again dancing over her face.

Cora sensed the thick tension between them. Did he dislike, or merely tolerate, her? The idea of cutting the tension with a knife curbed her train of thought, giving release to the moment.

"*Lord* Hedsworth, a woman cannot steal from her husband. What's his is hers and vice versa."

His expression softened, and his face drew closer to hers. "My dear, this is the Regency era. What's yours is mine alone. You are entitled only to what I give you." He bent, his mouth near her ear. "That is the law."

His nearness unsettled her. Her throat thickened, and she sniffed. "Is that so?" She stepped toward the table, yanked up a knife, and waved it in his face. "I'm *stealing* this knife." She tapped the plate still hugged to her chest with the tip of the utensil. "And this food."

Cora spun on her heel, flew through the door, and slammed it. Knees weakening, she slid down the door and rested the back of her head against it. Tears formed, but she snickered. She leaned forward until the plate was on her lap. The napkin had protected the dress, for which she was grateful.

Lizzy nuzzled against her side, tiny nose twitching in response to the scent of fish.

"Hold on, girl, we'll have a feast." She rose, collected the saucer from the morning tea, and after adding bits of fish, slid it under the cat's nose. Now somewhat soothed, she carried her plate to the small writing desk by the window and ate.

What a day this had been.

Glad her appetite was returning, she nibbled until sated, then leaned back in the chair and watched the waning sunlight. How would all of this play out? They obviously had somewhat of a like-hate thing going on. How could she allow him to continue acting like this when he had a fiancé? Every time she wanted to point that out, something stopped it. She was confused and angry. Just as she'd gotten settled into life at Hedsworth House, reconciled to her sister, and hopefully taking a step toward healing, she was thrown into the past. It couldn't be true.

"God, I know I've accused you of abandoning Selena and me. I'm sorry about that. Please help me endure wherever this path leads, and please help me survive Hugh Henley."

⊂℈⊃

Cora slept soundly until the creak of the door brought her to sit up with a jolt. Clutching the bed linens to her chest, her throat dry, she croaked, "Who's there?"

The glow of a candle coming through the gap in the door made her gasp, and she opened her mouth to scream but stopped when she recognized who it was.

Hugh filled the doorway, his face half in shadow. "Cora, please forgive me for disturbing your sleep at such a late hour."

Rising, she scurried to stand on the side of the bed near the window, the night breeze sending a chill through her thin gown. Holding the neck of the gown tight against her chest, she swallowed. "Why are you here?"

The candlelight illuminated Hugh's lined face. He bit his lip and ran a hand through his already disheveled hair. He looked most appealing in a tousled state, and she couldn't prevent the smile she felt.

"I was incapable of sleeping knowing how I hurt you. Please forgive me. There is nothing haughty about you." He dipped his head. "It was meant to wound, and God has struggled with me since I said it."

Uncertain what to say, Cora nodded, keeping her vigil by the window. She shivered, the breeze at her back.

"You are cold." He placed the candle on the stand by the bed, removed his dressing gown, and draped the robe over her shoulders.

"You didn't need to do that. I'm fine." She made to remove the robe and return it to him, but he stopped her.

"Keep it until I am finished."

"Aren't you worried about my reputation? You are in my room."

"I am." His tone was low, taking on a deeper cadence. "For all anyone knows, we are married, so my presence here is not inappropriate."

Cora's lips pinched together. "Ah." Her gaze traveled from his eyes to his feet. He was wearing a man's nightshirt that hung to his calves, the neckline cut low into a V. She'd always thought them a silly thing and laughed when she watched historical movies, especially when worn by rugged male actors. She was not laughing now, glad the room was nearly dark, and he couldn't see her heated face.

Eyes downcast, he asked, "Will you accept my apology?"

She studied him for a long while, trying to sort through her heart, longing to ask him about Judith but suddenly not wanting to hear his answer.

"Hugh—" Her arms dropped to her sides, and she closed her eyes to process the raging thoughts.

He moved closer and repeated with a whisper, "Will you accept my apology?"

She heard his erratic breathing but refused to open her eyes. What would Judith say if she knew where he was in the middle of the night—apology or not?

Her stomach clenched, and she tightened the hold of her arms around her chest. His breath fanned her cheek as he raked a kiss there, and her eyes flew open. "What are you doing?"

He abruptly stepped back. "Another thing for me to beg your apology." He bowed and left without another word.

Cora stood, unmoving, for quite some time.

C3&2

The next morning, Cora woke more exhausted than before she'd finally drifted to sleep in the hours after Hugh left her room. Her dreams were strange and disjointed, his face often appearing.

Olive entered, greeting her cheerfully. She came to the bedside and handed Cora a neatly folded paper with a gold seal.

"What's this?"

Olive helped her sit upright, plumping the pillows. "My lord sent it, ma'am." She smiled shyly, cheeks pinked, glancing at Hugh's dressing gown slung over a chair. He'd left without taking it. The girl giggled and strode to Cora's dressing room and returned with a lovely lavender dress over one arm and a pair of matching slippers dangling from her fingers.

"Whose are those?" Cora pointed to the items.

"They belonged to Lord Hedsworth's mother. He said you should have them as your things were stolen by the highwaymen."

Cora had no answer for that because he was right—as far

as the story he'd told. She eyed both the dress and the shoes, wondering if they'd fit. She slid a thumbnail under the wax and broke the seal, unfolding the surprisingly soft paper. The handwriting was similar to perfect calligraphy.

> *Cora,*
>
> *Will you please join me for breakfast? I have instructed Olive to assist you and hope you will not be averse to wearing Lady Hedsworth's things. Crawford assured me they have been well cared for these many years.*
>
> *H*

She didn't know whether to crumple the note or flatly refuse to go when she saw Olive studying her carefully. Cora schooled her features to resemble the happy air she assumed a newly married woman would feel. Her smile was likely a bit overdone, but she was at a loss.

Olive chatted incessantly while she helped Cora dress and then sit at the dressing table. "My lady, you must consider yourself quite the contented bride, what with marrying someone as generous and kind as His Lordship. And we all knew he would end up choosing someone as beautiful as you."

Cora stared at the woman's reflection in the mirror. "Me?"

Olive started at her tone. "Yes, ma'am. You are most lovely. I am sure you shall have lovely children."

The laugh that escaped Cora surprised the young woman, and she jerked back. "I'm sorry, Olive, but we won't be having children."

Her mouth dropped. "Why ever not, ma'am?"

"I'm fifty years old. That's why."

Olive's face paled. "Say it not, ma'am. It is not so."

"That's very kind of you, but it is." She supposed people had not aged well during this era, and considering the poor medical care and diet, it was no wonder a fifty-year-old woman would be considered ancient.

A knock on the parlor door interrupted their conversation, and Olive strode to answer it. Crawford entered and inquired if Lady Hedsworth would join Lord Hedsworth in the breakfast room.

Olive's face reddened, and she dipped her head. "Yes, sir, Mr. Crawford."

It was Crawford's turn to blush, and Cora made note of it. "I'll be down shortly, Crawford. Thank you."

He bowed, his eyes upturned to look at the maid through his lashes. "Thank you, Lady Hedsworth. I shall advise His Lordship."

Olive's hands trembled as she helped Cora into the slippers.

Cora patted her hand. "It's okay, Olive, I'll finish so you may go."

She curtsied. "Thank you, ma'am."

Cora shook her head. What's up with those two? She stepped into the hall and realized she knew nothing about *this* Regency era house, only the present day one, wondering how she'd find the breakfast room. Or was that Hugh's way of telling her it was the same? With nothing to lose, she strolled to the twenty-first century breakfast room and found him sipping tea, reared back in his chair, staring out the window.

Timidness overtook her, and she said quietly, "Good morning, Hugh."

He leaped from his chair, came to her side, and kissed her cheek, whispering, "Please do not slap my face for doing that. It is for appearance's sake."

Heart fluttering, she said, "I understand."

He pulled her chair out and leaned close to her ear. "Yet it was enjoyable."

Cora's face heated, but she had to admit he was right.

Chapter Twelve

Cora acknowledged the breakfast she'd shared with Hugh had been pleasant enough. He behaved, and they chatted about meaningless things while they ate.

Hugh rose from the table and gave Cora a wide smile, his eyes flashing with mischief. "My dear, it is a lovely day. Would you care to take a turn in the gardens with me later?"

She sipped tea and peered at him over the rim of the teacup, pausing before she answered, "That would be nice." Her gaze caught the slight smile of the footman standing by the sideboard.

"Splendid. Now I must see my steward. Will you meet me at the arch within the hour?"

Cora swallowed at the mention of the arch and nodded. When he bent to kiss her cheek, she whispered, "How will you know him?"

He murmured against her face, "I have asked that he come to the library. I shall also inspect the records he brings. He will have signed bills and such." His tender lips brushed her cheek, and her face heated. "I shall see you soon, my dear."

He stood, and Cora looked at him in surprise. He bowed and strode from the room, hands behind his back. It reminded her of a little boy she'd once seen in The Boston Common walking beside his father, mimicking the same stance. Sadness crept through her. She'd never have the privilege of seeing her child next to his father.

The footman cleared his throat. "My lady, may I refresh your tea?"

Not wanting the man to witness the tears, she kept her gaze on the window and nodded. "Thank you." Once his footsteps faded, she heaved a sigh and peered at the table. A neatly folded handkerchief lay where her teacup had been. Cora picked it up and dabbed her eyes. The footman approached the table with a steaming cup and placed it carefully before her.

This time, she met his eyes. "Thank you. You are very kind . . ."

"Alexander, my lady."

"Thank you, Alexander." She tasted the hot liquid and nodded. "Delicious. You have already learned how I like it. It is much appreciated."

The man's face flushed, and he bowed, one arm behind his

back. "You are most welcome, my lady. Should you have need of anything further, please do not hesitate to summon me."

"I will." She gave him her brightest smile to show her appreciation.

He backed away and reclaimed his stance against the wall, which embarrassed Cora. How could she allow servants to stand by to await her beck and call? She knew it was the custom of this era, but she wasn't used to such treatment.

"Alexander?"

He came to her side and bowed. "Yes, my lady."

"Can you tell me where I may purchase books?"

The footman's eyes widened. He opened his mouth and closed it, leaning toward Cora slightly. "Well—my lady . . ." He cleared his throat. "You may venture into the village and seek out the shops there. I am certain they shall assist." He straightened and gave her a kind smile, and added, "You may discover what you are looking for in the library as well, my lady."

"Thank you, Alexander. I will ask Hu—His Lordship, if he will help me."

"Yes, my lady." He returned to his post, lips quivering in a smile.

Cora finished the tea, thinking about the library and what books she might find there. Jane Austen came to mind first. The thought that the author was alive this very year overwhelmed her. She ambled to her room in a daze. Was she really where Hugh said they were, or was this some sort of weird dream? In a dazed state, she found Olive in her room, fussing over the minuscule stain on a dress.

Olive suggested a pelisse in case the air was cool, along with a bonnet. Cora laughed at the ridiculously styled hat and refused to wear it—or the gloves—shocking Olive. Yet she held her ground.

After she'd freshened up and slipped into the pleasant morning air, she resolved to maintain the façade she and Hugh discussed. She would play the dutiful Regency wife until they figured out a way to return home.

A couple of steps along the path revealed Hugh leaning against the aged stone arch, arms crossed over his chest, eyes intent on the *pile of rocks* Judith referred to.

Her shoes crunched upon the gravel beneath her steps, and Hugh's head turned toward the sound. "Ah, you have arrived."

"Yes, *husband*. I have arrived." The teasing tone was unstoppable. This was getting a little easier. At least she convinced herself it had.

With two long strides he stood beside her. Looping her arm through his, he dipped his head to her ear. "I have anticipated this moment. We must begin our perusal of the arch and see if it may be our way home."

Cora narrowed her eyes. "So you believe this brought us here?" She tapped a finger on the stone gateway.

"It seems most likely. Do you not agree?"

Cora thought about the comment, recalling the events of that fateful night. It would seem logical—if logic had anything to do with it. "I suppose."

"Hello there, my lovely."

Cora snapped her head toward him and discovered Hugh bent to pick up Lizzy, her arm still loosely looped through his.

He cradled the cat in his arm like an infant. She lay there, face up, purring loudly as he rubbed under her chin.

"I think you spoil that cat more than I do." Cora turned away and raked fingers along the rough texture of the stone, attempting to understand such a thing capable of transporting them over two hundred years into the past.

She pulled her arm free and rounded the end of the wall, Hugh's voice softly cooing to Lizzy in the background. He was full of surprises. Cora stopped to admire a clump of purple violets tucked between the stones, wishing she had a phone to photograph it. A man's deep voice halted her examination.

"Well, hello. Who might you be?"

As she rose from perusing the flowers, forest green eyes met her gaze. There was something familiar about him. Hesitantly, she made one step away from the stranger, uncertain what to say. The tall, slender man leaned one hip against the stone wall and crossed his arms over his chest, slanting his head and observing her with a furrowed brow.

"Ralph, watch your manners as you are speaking with my wife."

The man straightened and dropped his arms to his sides. "Your *wife*?"

Hugh came to Cora's side, the cat still cradled in his arms. "Yes—my *wife*." The cat purred and twisted until Hugh released her to the ground, and she sauntered away.

"My dear, allow me to introduce my cousin, Ralph Henley." He gently nudged the small of her back.

"It's nice to meet you, Mr. Henley."

"Ralph, please meet my wife, formerly Cora Anderson of

Boston."

The man bowed deeply and smiled. "My pleasure, Your Ladyship." He stepped closer and narrowed his eyes. "It surprises me not that with all my cousin's travels, he should return one day with a bride. Although I must admit, I thought it would be an exotic beauty. You look very English to my eyes, Lady Hedsworth."

The inflection in his voice held a touch of sarcasm, but she didn't know the man and refused to jump to conclusions. She swung her gaze to Hugh and saw his face redden.

"Ralph, that is most rude of you, and I would thank you to apologize to my wife."

Cora placed a hand on Hugh's arm. "Hugh, I'm not offended. I rather like being thought of as English. It is, after all, my home now."

Hugh patted her hand and allowed it to remain while he looked at his cousin. "My wife possesses more manners than you, Ralph. She is most forgiving."

"It was not my intent to offend. If memory serves, you had a liking for an Italian woman of noble birth but a few years ago, therefore one would assume—"

Hugh cut him off with an iron voice. "*Ralph.*"

They held one another in a matching, hard stare for a few moments. Ralph bowed, turned, and strode away without another word.

Hugh blew out a breath. "May we continue our walk and discuss possible solutions to our dilemma?"

Cora nodded, and they strode around and through the arch several times, but neither spoke for a few moments. Lizzy perched on the wall near the gateway, watching them until she grew bored and left.

"Hugh?" Cora watched Lizzy go and halted. "How did you know who Ralph was?"

He peered into her eyes, holding her attention while a wren flew past them and settled on the wall where Lizzy had been perched but moments ago. The bird's bubbling sound spoke as if trying to tell them something important.

He continued to lead her along the path, a long pause stretched before he answered her question, his face solemn. "I discreetly asked Alexander about some of the portraits in the gallery. There was a painting of Lord Hedsworth at a young age with two others. One was Ralph and the other a friend of his acquaintance. *We* apparently spent a lot of time together as boys, Lord Hedsworth being the eldest."

Cora nodded, and they walked on for a while before she thought of something further to ask. "This may make no difference whatsoever, but maybe we should walk through the arch at the same time of day we arrived."

"That is a splendid idea." His sky-blue stare grew more intense, then clouded. "Yes. We should try it, but what if it must be the exact time?"

Cora gasped. "Really? I had not thought of that. Perhaps it's an annual occurrence." She slumped against the wall, breaking their contact and sending the bird fluttering away, a scolding tone in his chirps.

"It is only a theory. We shall walk through every night until we are sent back." He reclaimed her hand, and she straightened, resuming their walk. "I give you my word. We shall return.”

She glanced sideways at the man and allowed herself to hope their return wouldn't be quite so swift.

◌◌◌

Cora claimed a headache so she would not have to share a meal with Hugh's *cousin*, so Olive brought afternoon tea to her room and a headache powder. She told the girl she would take it once she'd eaten. She wasn't about to consume something she knew nothing about, even if she did have a headache.

As Olive laid out the tea things on the small table near the fireplace, Cora asked how she came to be at Hedsworth House.

“His Lordship rescued me from the workhouse.”

Cora looked up from her tea. “He did?” She knew the conditions of the workhouses in England at that time were horrendous, and that children worked the long hours and jobs of adults.

The maid nodded and began tidying the room.

Though she knew the story was about the real Lord Hedsworth, Hugh's ancestor, she wanted to not only know about Olive's story but also glean what she could for Hugh. “How did you come to be working here?”

“My stepfather sent me to work for a dressmaker. She was a cruel one.”

Cora picked up her teacake, trying to offer Olive the space to tell her in her own time, her heart aching for the young woman.

"My stepfather did not want me around once he married my mum. He fooled us all until he got her. Showed me and my mum a different side until after the wedding."

"Why would he do such a thing?" Cora asked between the last bites of teacake.

Olive stopped and turned toward Cora, face pale, eyes misting. "My mum was a lady afore she married my father. When he died, Mr. Blanchard—that be my stepfather—started coming round courting my mum and was nice to me and all." She pressed her lips together tightly for a moment. "After the wedding, whilst we were at the church, he took me off to the side and told me I must leave in three days. Said I was to apprentice to a dressmaker in London."

"London? That's a long way from here." Cora stood and slid the chair under the table.

"Yes, my lady. Was a long way from the village where we lived too." The girl swiped a tear from her cheek. "That man wanted me as far away from my mum as possible."

Cora still didn't understand and told her so.

"Well, as I said, my mum was a lady once, and this man always wanted a noble-bred wife." She paused for a long while. "But I am not like my mum. She tried to teach me to be refined like her, but I was yet a child then."

Aghast, Cora asked, "You've been away from your mother that long?"

"Yes, my lady. My stepfather thought my being five years of age was enough to have learned to be like my mum." She dipped her head. "I do not learn as fast as some girls."

Cora placed a hand on Olive's shoulder. "That doesn't

matter. What kind of monster is your stepfather? Didn't you have family who would've taken you in?"

"He would not allow it. Said I needed to be earning my own way."

"At five!" Cora's voice rose, prompting Crawford to knock and poke his head through the doorway.

"Is all well, my lady?" he asked Cora, but his eyes were on Olive.

"Yes, Crawford. We're fine. I've just been educated to the dangers of this time." Cora slapped a hand across her mouth, and she looked at the valet, who wore a puzzled expression. "We're fine, Crawford," she repeated. "Olive just told me something shocking."

"Yes, my lady. If you are certain." He nodded. "Please let me know should you need anything."

"We will. Thank you."

Cora turned to Olive whose gaze was still on the door, a pleasant look on her face.

"Olive, please continue. So you went to the dressmaker's at five years old? I thought your stepfather would have to pay her to apprentice you. Isn't that correct?"

"Yes, my lady, that is the way it is usually done. But my stepfather used my mother's money to pay for my apprenticeship."

Cora's insides seethed with rage, but she said nothing, allowing Olive to continue the story. They stood toe-to-toe, Olive twisting her apron with shaking fingers.

"I was given little to eat and worked from the rising of the sun to the setting of it. I did not catch on quickly enough, and she beat me." Tears flowed again, and she sputtered, "The only time I got new clothes was when my old ones were too small. She cared not that they were ragged."

"Wasn't she afraid someone would see you and complain?" Cora led Olive to the small sofa and pulled her to sit.

"No, ma'am. She kept me hid in the back room working."

"What about your mother? Was she not allowed to come see you?"

Her eyes flew open. "I never saw my mum again. Was not until many years later that I found she had died the winter after I left."

Cora's eyes filled with tears, and she gripped Olive's hands in hers. "I am so sorry, Olive."

"Thank you, my lady. That is very kind of you. No one has ever asked me to tell my story except His Lordship.

"But how did you come to be here?"

The girl's face brightened. "I was about ten, and I ran away. Lord Hedsworth found me hiding in his carriage. The winter was mighty cold, and I stumbled upon an inn. I only wanted to curl up somewhere warm and die in peace. It was the middle of the night. I saw the inn, and no candle burned, so I figured none would mind if I slept in the barn. There was a very fine carriage there, so I crawled inside and covered underneath the blanket I found there. The comfort of it was too much for me. I never saw such a fine thing before. Sleep overtook me."

Cora inhaled and exhaled slowly, attempting to calm herself.

"When I woke, the carriage was rumbling down the road. I

pushed the blanket aside and saw the finest looking gentleman I ever laid eyes on. He stared at me, and I expected him to toss me from the carriage whilst it moved. I deserved it and all."

"Olive, you most certainly did not deserve that."

"Oh, yes, ma'am, I did. I did wrong by running away. I belonged to the mistress whether she treated me cruel or no."

Cora clutched her hands tighter. "No, Olive."

"I knew by running away I would be bound for the workhouse or hanged."

"Hanged?" Cora screeched.

"Yes, my lady. That is what they do to apprentices what run away. Or the workhouse. Depends on the judge."

"That's horrendous."

Olive coughed and swallowed, choking on her tears. Cora rose and fetched Olive a cup of tea. The girl blanched at the offering. "Oh no, ma'am. I could not allow you to serve me." She jumped from the sofa and stared down at Cora.

"Olive. Sit down and drink this. I *want* you to."

She timidly did as told, and with the last swallow, the delight Cora saw on her face warmed her heart.

"Thank you, my lady. You are most kind."

Cora nodded and returned the cup to the table. "Now, tell me what Hugh did next."

Olive blushed at the use of Hugh's given name but continued, "He asked me some questions while we traveled that bumpy road, but it was heaven to me." Her face shone with fond memories. "He took me to his London townhouse, and the housekeeper treated me most kind, giving me a bath and clean clothes, but not before she fed me until I thought my belly would pop." Her eyes glinted with the memory.

"Lord Hedsworth even gave me my own room upstairs by the maids. It was a tiny room, but it was a palace to me."

"I'm sure it was." Cora smoothed the hair away from Olive's wet cheek.

Olive broke the long silence with a sigh and rose. "Thank you, my lady, for listening to my woeful tale. You are ever so kind."

"I'm glad to be able to help and so happy to hear of Hugh's rescue of a lonely child. Am I to assume you have had a good life here?"

Olive straightened her spine and notched her chin. "Oh, yes, ma'am. So very much." Her mouth twitched. "I have not liked it overmuch the times Lord Hedsworth travels so often, but I no longer feel that way because he found you on one of his many travels. I must be getting selfish, ma'am, because I do hope he will not be traveling so much in the future as I would not like to have the both of you gone."

Cora's insides melted at the kind words. "You are a sweet young woman, Olive. It is a pleasure to have you here. I do believe we are going to be great friends."

Olive curtsied. "Begging my lady's pardon, but it is not proper for a maid to be friends with her mistress."

"Pfft!" Cora huffed. "What a load of hogwash."

Cora burst into laughter, and Olive returned to sit beside her. The door to the parlor opened, and Hugh stood in the space, arms crossed over his chest.

"What goes on here?" The groove between his eyebrows deepened. He strode into the room, his face scrunched into a grimace.

"Olive was telling me how she came to be here." Narrowing her eyes, she sent him a questioning stare. "It is very noble of *you* to help a child in need."

His gaze swung from Cora to Olive. "Why did you feel the need to share this with my wife?"

Olive surged to her feet, wringing her hands. "I am that sorry, my lord."

Cora stood beside Olive and lay a hand on her shoulder. "I asked her how she came to be here."

Hugh glared at her. "Why?"

Cora cleared her throat. "I didn't think I needed to consult with *Parliament* in order to speak with my maid, Lord Hedsworth." She copied his stance and crossed her arms.

Without removing his gaze from hers, he said, "Olive, you may go."

The woman skittered from the room, sending Cora a terrified look over Hugh's shoulder.

"Hugh. What's wrong with you? I was merely having a conversation with my maid."

"It is not your place to do so." A cloud of uncertainly flashed across his face, and he lowered his voice. "What if you had said something about the future—about who you really are?"

She made one step toward him, their shoes almost touching. Tilting her head to look into his face, she punched an index finger into his chest. "You haughty bag of air. Did it not occur to you that the information I collected may help your position here? Anything you can discover about the *real* earl will only help our cause."

The air that left him was almost visible. She'd actually stated her case enough to make him consider the truth.

He closed the gap between them, their faces inches apart. "You called me haughty, Lady Hedsworth." His lips twitched until they curved upward.

"That killer smile will not weaken my knees, *your worship*."

The smile faded. "Do not call me that."

"Why not? Have you not noticed that you've taken on the persona of Lord Hedsworth himself, strutting around like a peacock, telling me how I may and may not act?" She turned, but he seized her arm and swung her to face him. "Don't grab me!"

They held one another's gaze. In an instant, his lips sought hers. She tried to pull away—although with little effort, his kiss continuing. Time slowed, and she returned the kiss, her arms lifting, fingers threading through his thick hair.

Breathless from their contact, they parted, and Cora stepped back. "Hugh. What just happened?"

He gave her a cocky grin. "I suppose my *killer* smile weakened your resolve—as well as your knees."

Cora bristled but calmed instantly. "You really are insufferable."

"True—but you know I l—" He dropped his arms and stepped back.

Cora's heart clinched. What was he struggling to say? The

air between them crackled, both holding their silence for a long while, his penetrating gaze arresting her speech.

The door from Hugh's room opened, and Crawford strode in and removed a cravat draped over the back of a chair. When he veered to leave, he caught sight of the couple and sputtered nervously, "My lord, my lady . . ." He cleared his throat. "Pardon me, I thought the parlor was empty."

Without removing his eyes from Cora's, Hugh said, "That is of no concern, Crawford. Have you taken care of the task I asked you to perform?"

"Yes, sir. I have hid—placed it in your dressing room, my lord." He dipped his chin. "Shall you need me any further?"

"You may leave us." Hugh waved a hand in the air. "Thank you."

"Yes, my lord." Crawford skittered through the door, shamefaced.

Cora hugged her middle. "Would you like to complete your sentence, Hugh?"

He shrugged. "It shall keep for now." His gaze dropped to the floor, and he ran his fingers through his hair. "I must see Ralph." He made to leave but added, "I shall expect you to dine with us this evening."

Cora blinked. "Why?"

His eyes closed momentarily as if impatient with a wayward child. "Because he is my cousin, next in line to inherit, and desires to know you better. You are now his cousin by marriage."

The sarcastic 'ha' left her lips. "I'm sorry. That was rude. You must realize how that sounds. We are not, after all, married." She turned and took one step but spun around to face him. "And he's not really your cousin."

He came to her, ignoring the cousin comment. "We are not married, but we must play the part, *Cora*." The words barely out of his mouth, he swept her into his arms, kissed her, then stepped back. He whispered, "And we shall do that until we return to the future."

In a weak voice, she replied, "Oh really? Why is that?"

"Because I wish it—and so do you." He was out of the room before she could form a coherent reply.

Drat that man! He was unbearable.

164

Chapter Thirteen

Ear pressed to the door, Cora listened to be sure Hugh and his valet had truly left for an overnight meeting at a neighboring estate. Hugh had been secretive about the trip, but Cora planned to use the time away to search his room for any clues. He was hiding something from her, and she was determined to find out what it was.

Once she verified the room was quiet, she moved to the window to see Hugh and Ralph riding down the pebbled drive. She thought about the meal she'd shared with them the night before. Ralph appeared to be a well-mannered man, but he peppered Hugh with questions about his travels and why he left so often. He wanted to know the reasons for Hugh's visits abroad rather than remaining at the estate to care for the tenants, livestock, and crops that funded everything.

Hugh met the challenge with a smile and enlightened him about his steward, Lawrence Dickerson, and how he trusted the man with the operation. Cora had met the man once as she left Hugh's office. The tanned, smoky-haired man was cordial and unassuming, meeting her with a proper Regency greeting.

Ralph was likeable enough, but she didn't fully trust him. There was something oily about the man. He asked too many questions.

Darkness fell, and Olive assisted Cora to prepare for bed. As soon as the maid left, Cora snuck into Hugh's room and started rifling through the wardrobe and a nearby chest, carefully putting things back as she'd found them. She had all night and most likely until the end of the following day to search. By midnight, she had progressed to the dressing room but had yet to find anything to justify her suspicions. She covered her mouth as a yawn escaped and decided to resume her search early the next morning before Olive came to wake her.

Hand on the door to exit the dressing room, Cora froze, a bump alerting her to someone coming through the bedroom door off the hall. A servant would not be entering Hugh's bedroom at this time of night. The house had been quiet for hours.

Crawford's voice was a whisper. "I am certain Lady Hedsworth has long been sleeping, my lord."

"Yes. You are right, Crawford. Let us keep quiet so as not to awaken her."

Cora froze, hand on the door. What were they doing back? Hugh said they would be gone until late the next day.

Hugh cleared his throat. "Speaking of my wife—what do you think of her, Crawford?"

Shuffling sounded and Crawford said, "My lord, you are more ridiculous than Lady Hedsworth."

Hugh huffed. "And why is that, pray tell?" His tone was indulgent and laced with humor.

Cora noted the crack in the door, and curiosity won as she peeped through to see Hugh standing with his arms raised over his head, Crawford tugging the shirt upward. For a moment, Crawford's black head obstructed her view. When he stepped away, she saw Hugh, bare-chested, standing in front of the valet with his hands on his hips, glaring at the man.

Her breath hitched at how masculine he was. Shame filling her, she jumped and turned her back to the door.

"Lord Hedsworth, you heard me. We have always spoken plainly to one another. Is it necessary that I repeat it?"

Cora swept around to peer through the crack to see Hugh's expression. Crawford folded the ivory linen shirt neatly and set it aside.

Hugh squared his shoulders and faced the man. "There is no need to repeat your offense. I merely ask you to explain your response."

Crawford's black eyebrows furrowed. "Both of you are daft."

"What have either of us done to garner that poor opinion?"

The valet ambled around the room, tidying as he went. "Allow me to return these to your dressing room, then I shall explain."

Cora gasped and looked around. Where could she hide?

"State your case." Hugh gritted his teeth. "Spit it out, man!"

Cora watched as the valet faced Hugh and stood akimbo. "The both of you are hopelessly smitten with one another and much too afraid to admit it."

Each gave a hard stare across the room, neither backing down. Hugh deflated first and sank into a nearby chair. "Is it that obvious?"

"Indeed, my lord."

Hugh sighed. "I do not think it mutual, Crawford."

"Then you are blind as well as ridiculous." The valet huffed. "How, pray tell, did you manage to get her to marry you?"

Hugh did not reply.

Hugh stood and reached for the nightshirt Crawford offered, and the valet said, "I do not suppose you need further assistance since you insist upon undressing yourself. I feel as if I am a valet in name only."

"Do not think I recognize not the humor in your tone."

"You have accepted my eccentric behavior for many years." Crawford strode to stand before his employer, looking up into the face of the taller man. "Is there anything you care to tell me, Lord Hedsworth?"

Hugh's expression darkened.

"Sir, you obviously did not marry Lady Hedsworth in order to acquire an heir as her age is near to your own." He lifted one corner of his lips. "So it is to be assumed it was either for love or wealth. And you are already quite wealthy."

Hugh raised an eyebrow. "Are you done?"

Crawford coughed. "There is one thing that disturbs me."

"Yes?" Hugh ground out.

"It is unseemly for my lady to address Olive by her given name." The valet paused for a response.

Hugh blew out an exasperated breath. "My wife has chosen to call her what she wants, and I shall not hinder her decision."

"As you wish, my lord." The valet turned and sauntered from the room, but not before Cora caught his self-satisfied smirk.

Cora silently slid down the door and sat, head in her hands. What was that all about? And how was she going to escape from this room without Hugh discovering her clandestine activity? She contemplated the choices. The first would be to reveal herself and apologize. But that would mean owning up to why she was there. Second, she could wait until Hugh fell asleep and tiptoe to her room.

As she latched onto option two, she heard footsteps growing closer to her hiding place and peeped through the crack again. Crawford had returned and held Hugh's recently shed things and was returning to put them away. Her insides turned to jelly as she frantically searched for a hiding place. There were none. Standing, she forced her back to the wall behind the door, hoping the valet would not close it until he left, which is exactly what he did.

He placed the worn clothing into a wicker basket and left as quickly as he'd arrived. Once the door was firmly closed behind him, Cora released a calming breath. She listened and heard Crawford tell Hugh good night and the outer door closed.

She reclaimed her vigil on the floor and overheard the bed squeaking a protest as Hugh settled for the night. Her ears perked and focused on his breathing. After a long while it slowed and steadied to a peaceful rhythm.

Cora inched the door open and saw Hugh lying on his back, one arm slanted over his head, faced in her direction. Her stomach fluttered at his relaxed features, all worry lines gone. A beam of moonlight caught a strand of wavy hair laying on his forehead, another illuminated his left hand resting on his flat stomach. She saw the scar that ran across his knuckles, appearing more vivid in the moonlight. The intake of her breath caused him to stir, and he mumbled something inaudible, his eyes flying open.

Cora froze, eyes intent on him as he spoke her name. "Cora?" She held her breath, hands clutched at her throat. His eyelids fluttered and closed again, and she used the moment to run to her room, quietly closing the door.

⊂≫⊃

Not wishing to call attention to herself, Cora joined Hugh and Ralph for breakfast, though her face was puffy from not sleeping well. She'd asked Olive for a cold compress before she rose, but it did little good. Troublesome thoughts had kept her from sleeping, Crawford's opinion regarding her, Hugh's feelings toward her, all stirring in her mind.

Ralph sat facing her at the table. "My lady, you do appear weary this morn. Did you not sleep well?"

Cora yawned and told him, "I did not."

The man pulled a face. "It is refreshing to be in the company of someone so forthcoming. Ladies in fashionable society would not be so bold with their declarations."

"Ralph." Hugh growled. "Do not be impolite."

"I was not attempting to be, cousin. I merely noticed her wretched countenance. My apologies." He forked a piece of ham and placed it in his mouth, chewing thoughtfully as he watched Cora.

"None taken, Ralph." Cora nodded politely. She watched Hugh's reaction to their exchange, but his expression gave nothing away. Heaven help her, but she kept visualizing Hugh lying on his bed in the moonlight, all lines smoothed away in his relaxed state. The urge to caress his face had been difficult to fight.

A man with salt and pepper hair walked past the window, a shovel over one shoulder.

"Cora?"

She rotated her gaze to see Hugh staring. "Sorry. I was a thousand miles away." More like two hundred *years* away, she thought. "Who is that man?" She notched her head toward the window.

Without hesitation, Hugh said, "Christopher MacGregor, the gardener." He quickly brought the conversation back to his question. "I was asking if I may speak with you privately after we finish here?" He lifted a corner of his mouth, chin notching upward.

Hugh looked at Ralph. "Cousin, I hope you do not mind, but I must speak with my wife. We shall see you this evening."

"Does it consume an entire day to speak with your wife,

Hugh?" Ralph smirked. "And—cousin—have you not introduced the new lady of the house to her servants?"

"To answer your first question, in this case—yes." Hugh did not elaborate, then answered Ralph's second query. "No, she has not been strong enough to meet all the staff. It will suffice for her to meet them one by one."

Ralph said nothing further, finishing his coffee and excusing himself. "I think I shall avail myself of one of your stallions. Perhaps Mrs. Duckworth will be so kind as to prepare a box for me. A long ride and alfresco dining sounds quite the thing."

Hugh dabbed his mouth with his napkin. "She will be most happy to do so."

Ralph left them with a bow, a cool grin on his lips.

Once the door closed behind him, Hugh addressed Cora. "Would you be so kind as to accompany me on a picnic? We shall be gone the day, so have Olive prepare you for the outing."

Cora studied him for a moment, and thinking of no excuse to deny his request, she agreed. By the time Olive suggested a proper costume for a day away from the house, it was well past breakfast, and the sun's rays peeked over the front entrance, barely settling on the waiting carriage.

Hugh helped her into the equipage and joined her, seating himself opposite.

Cora tried to figure out if his choice of seating was because he wanted to study her expression or to distance himself. They sat in silence for the first half hour of the journey.

She kept her gaze on the countryside flowing past the

window. Bright green pastures full of sheep glided by, the occasional glint of sparkling water in the midday sun revealing itself. The scent of honeysuckle wafted through the windows. The landscape was certainly worth the jarring carriage ride.

"Where are we going?"

Hugh propped his elbows upon his knees and leaned toward her. "Since our evening walks through the arch are not aiding us, I wondered if arches from another ancient abbey might not serve the same purpose."

Cora considered the suggestion and decided anything was worth a try. "That's a good idea." She returned her gaze to the countryside. Hugh's long-suffering sigh sounded in the small space. What had she done now?

"Have I offended you again, Cora?" He pressed back into the squabs and gripped the edge of the seat.

"Not at all." She sent him what she hoped was a confident expression. "Trying anything is better than wringing our hands."

They arrived at the abbey, and after exiting the carriage, the servant drove it to a nearby cropping of cedar trees to set up their picnic. Hugh claimed Cora's arm and looped it through his. "I would not have you stumble on the uneven stone." He inclined a concerned expression toward her.

Cora nodded, throat now dry. He really was a gentleman, an attitude sorely missing from their own time.

The brief walk to the abbey's entrance brought them face to face with an ancient arch that was far from crumbling. She tilted her head back and peered up at the massive archway that rose at least thirty feet above their heads, the cloudless sky an intense pale azure canvas backdrop. The urge to photograph the image swept through her with remorse. Was she going to return to that old habit every instance she encountered something picture-worthy?

"It's fascinating," she whispered with awe. "It's far from falling down though." She swung her gaze around the surrounding abbey and brushed her hand along the curved edge of the opening, wondering how long ago the mason carved such a magnificent entry.

"It is resplendent, is it not?" Hugh's hand trailed the path hers had taken until his fingers touched hers. He tensed, first looking at her hand, then letting his gaze drift to her face.

Her eyes bored into his. She felt, rather than saw, a question in his expression and turned away. She stepped through the arch, praying something would happen, but when she glanced over her shoulder and found him still standing with his hand remaining on the stone, a question rose in her mind. *Would I want to go back without him?* The answer came like a bolt. *No.*

Her face must have revealed her internal struggle because he dropped his hand and marched through the door.

"Are you well? Your face paled." His eyes implored honesty.

She struggled to answer, and it came out raspy. "For a moment, it frightened me. I could have gone back without you." Her head dipped, and the warmth of his hand on her shoulder calmed her.

"Do not concern yourself. Considering the way we arrived,

surely we must return the same way—*together*." His husky voice held more confidence than Cora had ever known in her life.

Eyes widening, she looked deeply into his eyes and saw only conviction. What would it be like to be so self-assured? She doubted she would ever know.

"How can you be so sure?"

"Based upon what we experienced, I see no other option." He took her arm once more. "Let us explore before we rest and eat."

An image formed in Cora's mind of the arch that had brought them to the past. Once they discovered a way back, Hugh would return to marry Judith. Should she tell him of seeing Judith and Sam sharing a passionate kiss? That was a picture she tried to purge from her memory.

As they strolled the magnificent old ruins, passing through every arch, she mulled over his relationship with Judith, yet he flirted with *her*. The flip side was the vision of Judith in Sam's arms. Something didn't add up, and she grew determined to find out what.

After inspecting every stone of the abbey's doorways, they were ready for a break and settled onto the blanket where the servant had laid out a sumptuous lunch. They feasted on cold chicken, cheese, fruit, lemonade, orgeat, and damson tarts. The gentle breeze drifted around them. Her head lolled against the tree they sat under, eyelids fluttering to stay awake. She lost the battle with a contented sigh.

She wakened with a start yet was too comfortable to move other than to swing her arm to rest above her head. The back of her hand slapped against something hard, and she tilted back to see it was Hugh's chest.

Rising to sit, their eyes met. He leaned against the tree, eyes drunk with sleep, a little cocky smirk on his face. "You fell asleep, my dear, and were in need of a pillow."

Had his hands not been relaxed at his side, Cora would have smacked him. Even in sleep, he was the perfect gentleman. She looked around and saw the dozing footman and driver well outside hearing distance.

During her perusal of the surroundings, Hugh had risen and stood above her, hand outstretched. "May I assist you?"

Cora blinked until her thoughts cleared and accepted his hand. Rising, she stumbled and fell against him, eliciting a nervous smile. Her heart leaped in her throat, and she shifted from one foot to the other.

With his fingertips, he brushed a strand of hair from her cheek and whispered, "I would like to ask you something important, Cora."

There was something in his eyes she'd not seen before—yearning. He stooped and rummaged in the basket holding their food and removed a black velvet box. He didn't rise, but pressing a knee to the ground and twisting to look up at her, he took her hand, lips parted, his chest rising and falling with rapid breaths.

"Will you marry me, Cora?" He cleared his throat. "In truth, in this time—marry me?" He lifted the opened box, revealing a slender gold band bearing a topaz at its center, flanked by a small emerald on each side.

Cora gasped, face heating. She licked her lips. "Hugh, how

can you suggest this? You're engaged to Judith." The flash of memory with Judith and Sam in one another's arms replayed.

The blood drained from his face. "Pardon?" He stood and clasped her hand.

A slow anger grew. "Your wedding Judith is planning, remember?" She slid her hand from his and dropped it to her side. She straightened her dress nervously, fingers tugging the ribbon encircling her ribcage, then sat and hugged her tented knees. Her eyes focused across the meadow on two large butterflies flitting from one flower to another and then returned to Hugh.

His frozen form hovered above, his puzzled gaze begging her to explain. The wind rose, tossing his wavy hair, and he combed his hands through the dark mass.

A group of starlings fluttered in a nearby tree, rising to wheel and bank above them like a plume of smoke.

Hugh paced, finally halting a few feet away. "What gave you this idea? Judith and I are business associates and friends only." The crease between his eyes carved deeper.

She snapped her gaze to him. "I saw you on the terrace at the ball. Sam shook your hand, and after he left, you held Judith in your arms for a long while." Cora stood and poked a finger into his chest. "And Judith came into your office and updated you on the wedding plans."

Hugh rubbed his face with both hands, covering his mouth, and his shoulders shook.

Was he sobbing because she'd caught him in his lie? Surely not.

Hugh broke into a mirthless laugh and let his hands drop.

"Cora." He shook his head, smile wide. "Sam and Judith are engaged. Did you once hear her say *our* wedding? She spoke of her upcoming marriage to Sam."

A weight pressed on Cora's chest, and she felt lower than an insect. She sighed. How could she be so stupid? The scene of Judith and Sam together flashed before her. She reeked of shame under his watchful stare.

"Your erratic behavior toward me is now clear." Hugh came to stand before her. "Each time I drew close, you responded in a most encouraging manner—briefly."

She shifted from one foot to another and looked away from his intense stare, the enticing scent of Albany freeing her emotions.

"Moments before the car crashed into the arch, I saw Judith and Sam kissing. I've been pitying you because I thought them disloyal to you." She folded her arms, hoping he would stay away. Confusion wrapped itself around her with this new revelation. She'd spent weeks trying to sort through her feelings and his actions.

His warm breath swept her temple. "What you must think of me—pursuing you while you assumed I was engaged to Judith."

Her eyes met his, and she shook her head. "I think it's the other way around. I've acted so ridiculously. If I'd been more forthcoming with my suspicions—maybe asked questions of Judith rather than assuming so much."

His fingertips grazed her jaw, and her breath caught. "Hugh . . ." Her lips trembled, and she struggled to continue. "May we go home? I'm feeling so tired. There's a lot I must think over."

A flash of disappointment sparked in his blue eyes, but he nodded. "Yes, of course. I understand. It has been a most tiring day. Yet I have enjoyed your company." He lifted the small box, gave her a timid grin, and shoved it into his coat pocket.

"Ditto." She smiled.

His face clouded for a second, then the corners of his mouth curved upward. "Thank you."

Cora knelt, gathering scattered items, and returned them to the basket. Hugh's hand grasped hers. "No, my dear, allow Alexander to tend to this. I shall tell him we are ready to depart. Please rest yourself until then." He took both of her hands and lifted her to stand beside him.

"I think I'll sit in the abbey's courtyard until we leave."

"Very well." He bowed and half-turned to walk away, and she grabbed his arm.

"Hugh, why do you never drop the Regency persona?"

He swallowed and avoided her eyes. "One day I shall tell you." The muscle in his jaw tightened, and the wistful smile he gave sent waves of panic through her stomach.

Cora's suspicions grew. What was he hiding?

Chapter Fourteen

Since the truth of Hugh's and Judith's relationship came to light, Cora didn't know what to think or feel. The attraction to Hugh was still present, but the entire situation teetered on the edge of absurdity. Being thrust back two hundred years with a man she didn't really know was enough to send any woman into fits of hysteria. Attempting to remain calm at all times was tiresome at best.

Creaking brought her gaze up to discover the gardener pushing a wheelbarrow filled with dirt, a droopy-eyed Bloodhound puppy riding atop. Cora tried to recall his name, and it came to her suddenly—Mr. MacGregor. She noted he was a fine-looking man, his forearms well-defined with the exertion. He nodded in her direction, a slight curve to his lips.

Lizzy meowed, and Cora glanced down to see the cat imploring her to resume spinning the blue yarn through the air and trail it along the manicured grass for her entertainment.

"You *are* pampered, you silly cat. I have Hugh to thank for that." Cora's mouth curled into a grin.

"At least I've done something you care to thank me for," Hugh said over her shoulder.

Cora jumped and whirled around to face him, her hand flying to her chest. "Hugh! You scared me." His narrowed eyes were on the gardener.

He waggled his eyebrows. "I have been told I have that effect on women."

Lizzy chose that moment to sail into the air and land in Hugh's ready arms. "See what I mean?" He grinned and rubbed the cat's ears.

Cora lifted her eyes to the sky. "You taught her to do that the first week she graced us with her presence."

He nuzzled the cat with his forehead. "Yes—is she not an intelligent feline?"

Remembering the dog in the gardener's wheelbarrow, she asked. "Why don't you have a dog like most English gentlemen?"

A smile played on his lips, and he whispered, "As you know, I am mostly away on film sets, and the earl here seems to always be away as well."

She titled her head back. "Ah. So true."

Hugh turned at the rapid approach of Olive. She dipped a curtsy. "I am sorry to intrude, my lord, but the modiste has arrived for Lady Hedsworth."

Cora frowned and moved her gaze from Olive to Hugh. "*My modiste?*"

"Thank you, Olive. Show her to the parlor, and Lady Hedsworth will arrive shortly."

"Yes, my lord." She dipped another curtsy and spun around to leave when she caught sight of the gardener. Their eyes met, and the poor girl stumbled. Hugh caught her before she fell into a prickly hedge, and her face reddened.

"Thank you, my lord. I am that sorry. Please forgive my clumsiness." She curtsied again and sprinted off.

Cora pulled a face. "What was that all about?"

Hugh chuckled and lowered his voice. "It seems that Mr. MacGregor has a liking for Olive—as does Crawford. The competition makes her unsettled, and she is constantly in a dither when in their company."

Cora's heart twitched. Years before, she'd lost the only man she assumed ever loved her. Never had she had *two* men vying for her affections. Hugh braced upon one knee, flashed before her eyes. Something they had not brought up since that day. Did Hugh Henley love her? Why else would he have proposed? Her belief was only because they were stuck in a time where propriety reigned supreme, and he had an image to uphold. Yet everyone in this time thought they were already married.

She blew out an annoyed breath. What did it matter? They would—hopefully—be going home soon.

"Does that vex you, Cora?"

"What? Why should it?" She stood and stepped away from

Hugh and Lizzy, intending to return to her room.

"When I arrived, the look upon your face at seeing Mr. MacGregor appeared pleasing."

She kept walking, face heating. "I was not aware of that, Lord Hedsworth."

"Perhaps you will face me, Cora?"

Cora halted and swallowed hard, thinking of what to say. She twirled around to look at him but remained silent for a second. "Hugh, have you ever admired the appearance of a woman with no intention of pursuing her—merely admiring her beauty—never to think on it again?"

The silence grew thick between them, and he coughed. "Touché—*wife*."

She waited for him to leave, but he made no move to do so. He watched the cat rub against Cora's legs.

"It appears the feline agrees with her mistress."

"We have to stick together." She lifted Lizzy, massaging her back, and the cat looked at her adoringly.

Hugh narrowed one eye. "Are you attempting to bribe our pet?"

Cora mimicked his expression. "*Our* pet?"

"Indeed. We are married—are we not?"

Cora was about to bring up the fact that they were not when a piercing, feminine voice tore through the pleasant morning air. "Halloo! Lord Hedsworth."

Hugh's face twisted into a grimace and mouthed to Cora, "*Beware*." She caught his meaning, placed the cat on the ground, and stood next to him.

A tall man with dark blonde hair kept pace with a petite woman, her yellow bonnet's satin ribbons trailing in the air behind. She looked like a bird recently released from its cage. Wondering why she had formed that image in her mind, Cora noticed the woman had a long, sharp nose.

Hugh took Cora's hand and tugged her forward. "My dear, may I present Vicar Sirman and his lovely wife, Eliza."

The vicar removed his hat and bowed. "It is our pleasure, Lady Hedsworth, to finally make your acquaintance." His words came out in a rush and overtook his wife's. "I must apologize for coming unannounced." His sad gaze flickered to Eliza and back.

"Oh, do not be ridiculous, John. They are part of your flock and welcome us at any time. Do you not, Lord Hedsworth?"

Hugh squeezed Cora's hand and released a puff of breath. "Indeed. You are most welcome." He lifted his arm and motioned toward the house. "Let us go to the parlor and have refreshment."

After one step, Cora halted. "Hugh, the modiste is waiting for me in the parlor. I forgot."

The vicar blanched. "You see, Eliza, we should have sent word first."

The tiny woman's head barely came to her husband's shoulder, but the look she sent him made the over tall man appear to shrink. "I shall go with Lady Hedsworth to keep her company, and you men may have a chinwag all to yourselves." She brought her black eyes to Cora. "Would that not be lovely, Lady Hedsworth? We may get to know one another while discussing ladies' garments." She clapped lace-gloved hands together. "How delicious is that, my dear?"

Hugh's hand tightened slightly before releasing Cora. "Yes. That is a splendid idea, Mrs. Sirman." He almost shoved Cora toward the sprite of a woman, forming an overly sincere smile.

Cora's ire rose. He wanted to be rid of the vicar's wife and was using her to accomplish it. With her head cocked, Cora gazed at her husband with a loving expression, fluttering her lashes adoringly.

"But, my dear, I am parched and need refreshment. Could not the modiste join us for tea and when our visit is complete with Mr. and Mrs. Sirman, I can keep my appointment?"

Hugh sputtered and choked back what she knew to be a laugh. He cleared his throat and spoke, but the vicar's wife interrupted.

"Oh, my lady, I would not want to keep you from your tea. We shall merely have it brought to your rooms for the fitting." She grinned, revealing tiny, perfect teeth.

Cora's thoughts forked into separate paths. One being the tiny teeth reminded her of a badger, the other being when had Hugh met this couple?

The vicar's face softened. He shot Hugh an apologetic expression and shrugged. What this poor man's life must be like, Cora wondered, before reluctantly following his badger of a wife.

CB&O

Two hours later, Cora looked up from her book at Hugh's entrance. Exhausted from the visit with the vicar's wife, coupled with the fitting, reading was the only solace she had found at present.

"Where have you been?" She closed the book, holding the place with one finger.

Hugh's longsuffering sigh most likely stretched to the hall. "The vicar is kindly. I enjoyed our visit, but his wife is—"

"Insufferable?" Cora finished for him with a grin.

"Be careful how you use that word." He slumped onto a chair and stretched his legs before him, crossed at the ankle. Dropping his head against the chair's back, he closed his eyes. "Have you seen Crawford? I am in need of a long soak."

"A little early in the day for that, isn't it?"

He opened one eye and found the clock. "Yes. I suppose so." The eye slid shut, and he moaned. "Thank you for attempting to throw me to the wolves."

Cora tittered. "How so?" She knew full well what he meant. "It didn't work after all."

"Oh, but it did. The woman stayed after you finished with the modiste. You claimed a headache—"

"Hugh, she had been here for over two hours and drove the modiste and me insane." She stiffened and glared at him. "I had to do something to escape."

"Well, my dear, she entertained the vicar and myself more than an hour." Sarcasm fueled his voice.

Cora sputtered. "I'm sorry, Hugh. I thought she'd collect her husband and go."

His tone softened. "I know." He opened his eyes and sat upright, elbows dangling from his knees. "That pug-dog of a woman tried to wheedle a dinner invitation from me—for tonight!"

"She didn't?"

"Yes, she did. She reminded me I had invited them on other occasions when they had called unannounced."

Cora's mouth formed an O-shape.

"My reaction precisely." He leaned back again, arms crossed over his broad chest.

"How did you respond?"

One corner of his mouth lifted. "I told her we were preparing to depart for London on the morrow and must be abed early."

"How did she receive this information?" Cora sniffed.

"I did not give her the opportunity to voice an opinion." Hugh's eyes sparkled. "I apprised her that my man of business had contacted me and scheduled a meeting, and we would be away, posthaste."

Cora shook her head. "And how long are we to be gone during this so-called business trip?"

"A fortnight." He reached into his pocket and retrieved a piece of paper. "This came today asking that I come to London to meet with my man of business."

"But you've never met this man. How will you discuss the lord's finances without any knowledge of his affairs?"

"Cora, my dear. I bear a striking resemblance to my ancestor. In all the days we have been here, none have questioned my identity."

"True, but this is more serious." She leaned forward, resting elbows on her knees, gazing into his face.

"Allow me to remind you I am an actor and well-versed in

Regency knowledge." He stood and patted her shoulder. "Have you seen me fail thus far?"

She had to admit to him, and to herself, that he was the perfect man for the role. There were many times it astonished her at his talent to fit into this surreal world. They may not burn witches in this era, but they sure could make life difficult for them. She certainly didn't want to go to the workhouse—or prison.

Cora relaxed, studying his face. He was the most confident man she'd ever met. The moment he'd proposed she noticed the slightest crack in that confidence.

"All right. I'll have Olive pack for the trip. I'm sure she'll know what to take."

"I appreciate your compliance."

Cora rose to stand before him. "I won't do anything that will hinder us from going back. I can't imagine what Judith and Sam think of our disappearance."

He stared, eyes roaming her face, his throat convulsing as he swallowed. Hoarsely, he said, "I promise I shall do all in my power to get you home, Cora." The endearing tone of her name on his lips made her shiver.

Hugh leaned over slightly, his lips grazing her cheek. "I promise."

Cora prayed this was a promise he could keep.

⚬⚬⚬

Cora studied Ralph from across the dining table, his usually calm expression now one of worry. She brought her gaze to the candlelight reflecting on the large windows.

"Cousin?" Ralph addressed Hugh.

Hugh chewed the venison he'd just taken from his fork and dipped his chin in response.

Ralph cleared his throat. "I wonder if we may speak privately after we dine?"

Hugh glanced around the room, looking at Cora first, the footman standing by the serving board, and Merriwether stationed at his post.

"Ralph, I do believe this to be properly *private*. I trust all in attendance."

His cousin's eyes darted nervously around the room, his expression believing otherwise. Ralph licked his lips. "Ah. Indeed." He returned to his meal, obviously uncomfortable in revealing what he had to discuss, and said little else until they rose, Hugh escorting Cora until they passed through the doorway.

"Cora, my dear," Hugh said with all seriousness. "I must prepare papers to carry with us to London. Please excuse me. I shall be up shortly. Perhaps Ralph shall keep you company in the parlor until you choose to retire."

He bowed and left them, but not before Cora noticed Ralph's face brighten as he stepped in to fill Hugh's place. She opened her mouth to say she would go up now, but Ralph smoothly claimed her arm.

"Yes, cousin. I believe my lady and I shall have a pleasant conversation."

Cora craned to see Hugh rounding the corner down the hall, longing to go after him or return to her room. Ralph directed her until they reached the parlor and poured himself a brandy, offering her the same. She shook her head and stood near the window, watching the night sky, wishing she could be home.

"Cora—may I call you Cora when we are alone?"

She watched his reflection in the glass. He leaned against the mantel and glanced down into the cold fireplace. A maid had filled the space with a large bouquet of bright flowers in a white marble vase. She'd seen Judith do the same at their version of this house. How she missed her new life at the *future* Hedsworth House.

"Cousin?" Ralph now stood by her side. "Are you unwell?"

Cora started at his close presence. "I'm sorry. I was— somewhere else."

He tilted his head and looked deep into her eyes. "Yes. I should say so. Are you certain you are quite well?" There was obvious concern in his gaze, which removed some of her trepidation toward the man.

"Yes. I don't mind if you call me Cora when we're alone. But it seems Hugh takes offense at that, so don't press him."

Ralph returned to the mantel and propped himself in a superior posture, appearing to be the master of Hedsworth House, which Cora had no doubt he would've loved.

"You do speak most strangely at times, Cora. Do all Americans speak thus?" He sipped his drink, eyes gleaming with mischief.

The stars sparkled against the coal backdrop, reminding Cora she was not alone. The God who hung every star—all with names—loved her. Though she'd grown up being taught that truth, she had strayed from it far too long. God was faithful and kept His promises. All was in His timing—not hers, and she needed to remind herself of that.

"Yes, Ralph. I suppose so." She left the view, sat by the fireplace, and gazed up at him. "Now. Tell me what it is you want?"

His posture stiffened, and he released a bark of laughter. "You do me injury, Cora."

Cora crossed her arms. "It's just a feeling—but I think you want something, so let's just get it over with. Tell me."

He scrutinized her for a long while. "Very well." He sat across from her and crossed one leg over the other, one foot dangling in the air. "You see—I am in a bit of a fix. Financially speaking. A poor investment, so to speak."

"Hm." Cora bit her lip. So this was it. He wanted money from Hugh.

Ralph's face flushed pink, but he continued, "Just a few sovereigns to hold me until the investment turns around."

"What investment might that be?"

The stare he gave was one of shame. "I would not bore you with the details of which women have no concern nor knowledge."

A spark lit her insides and built into a flame. "So, you believe women do not have the intelligence to understand finances?"

He raised a hand, blinked several times, and gave a closed-lipped grin. "I meant no offense. Women merely have no inclination toward these things. It is for men to sort them out."

She rose and glared down at him. "I'll have you know that

in Boston I was the assistant manager of what was once a very prestigious historic hotel until a manager—a man, I might add—ran it into the ground. Thanks to him, it is no longer well thought of and is a shadow of its former self."

Standing abruptly, Ralph nearly tumbled to the floor. "I apologize, Cora. I meant—"

"*No offense*?" Her voice rose, and heat rushed to her face.

His shoulders curled over his chest, and he peered at the floor. His voice cracked. "I apologize."

As he lifted his head, Cora read true repentance in his gaze. He didn't strike her as a manipulative person, and she dialed back the anger. Regency social customs were out of her understanding, but it seemed women were given very little freedom on many levels, finances included.

Cora's shame welled up inside her. Fear followed on its heels when she realized what she'd said. Her irritation had gotten the better of her, and revealing her professional past could jeopardize their hoax. Before Ralph could comment on her managerial history, she swallowed her pride and placed a hand on his shoulder. "I am sorry. Please forgive me."

He took her hand and patted it. "Let us begin anew as friends."

His smile was so endearing, she agreed and retook her seat, and he did likewise.

"If you do not mind, Cora. I inquire about a small loan to see me through. If you may speak with my cousin on my behalf, I would be ever grateful." His tone now held a touch of warmth and sincerity.

Cora knew what Hugh would say, but she could ask

anyway, hopefully building on their growing, amiable relationship with Ralph. She may need another ally while here, just as Olive had become one.

"Yes, Ralph. I'll ask him."

His smile lit the room, dark green eyes shining, and she thought him a bit more endearing.

"Thank you. I am forever in your debt, cousin."

The door opened with a jerk, and Hugh stood staring at her, eyes hard. "It is late, Cora. Why have you not come to your room?"

Ralph stood, shooting Hugh an apologetic look. "It is my fault. I have kept her chatting overlong. Please excuse me." He bowed to Cora and strode to the door. "We have had a long chat. You have a prize in your wife, Hugh. Do not let her go. Treat her like the jewel she is."

Hugh's gaze followed his cousin from the room, a dazed look in his eyes. He pointed to the door. "What was that about?"

"He was actually quite nice. I'm as shocked as you are."

"That man is up to something." He pointed to the empty doorway.

"Yes. He is. But he revealed something about himself tonight."

Hugh lifted one eyebrow. "Truly?"

"He has a heart and wants people to like him."

"You determined all of that in one evening?"

"Mm. I believe so."

"That's all you have to say?" Hugh narrowed his eyes.

"Enlighten me."

"He made me angry, and I sort of lost my temper and lambasted him."

Hugh's lips widened into a smile. "Bravo!"

"Well, not really. I thought he'd turn on the charm or try to squirm his way out of it, but he did something so out of character."

Hugh leaned toward her, eyes wide with anticipation.

"You're really enjoying this, aren't you? Do you dislike him so much?"

He hunched his shoulders. "Not precisely. He has been but a leech. Seems he has no idea how to do anything with any thought that comes into his head."

"His father never taught him anything?" Cora's confusion grew the more they discussed Hugh's cousin.

"His father died while he was quite young and his much elder brother inherited everything." Hugh ran a hand through his hair before massaging the back of his neck.

"And his mother?" Cora tugged the thin shawl more tightly around her shoulders.

"She died while giving birth to Ralph. An elderly aunt raised him until his father passed. I believe Ralph was but four years of age."

Cora's eyes dampened. "So he was not taught in a loving home?" She bowed her head and whispered, "That's so sad. No wonder he knows no better."

Hugh's hand rested on hers. "I have not considered that before. He spent his life growing up in schools across the country—or so I'm told."

"His older brother didn't take him in?" The heat of anger built again.

"He was too busy marrying and having children. Three of his wives died giving birth to his brood. He tends to choose women with little physical fortitude."

"Hugh! What does that mean?" She clenched his hand.

"It is truth. They always appear to be small, frail women. I know not why that is so." He shrugged.

Cora shook her head and sighed. "What a strange place to be. I don't know how women cope with it all. If I'm forced to stay here, at least my death won't be because of that."

Hugh dropped her hand and stood. "I suppose not."

The sudden sense of loss tore at her. Not as deep as when her family had died one by one but a phantom of mourning. "Hugh—what did I say?"

He paced the room and stopped at the fireplace, resting his forehead on the mantel. "Nothing. It is my fault and my own . . ."

Cora rose and stood behind him, placing a palm against his back. The muscles tensed beneath her hand. "Please tell me."

"It is not your fault nor your problem." He turned, his eyes glistening with moisture.

He gently gripped her upper arms and pulled her into his embrace, resting his chin upon her head and whispered, "Had I but met you two decades past."

Taken aback by the comment, Cora found she too wished it.

Chapter Fifteen

The tension of pain seemed to transfer from Hugh's body to Cora's while holding him so close. If only he would share what that pain was. And what did it have to do with her? What would their meeting twenty years earlier have accomplished? How had the conversation shifted from Ralph's situation to Hugh's?

Hugh moved his chin to her cheek. His tremulous voice murmured, "It has been hurtful that you have not replied to my proposal—whether it be yes or no."

His remark taunted one second and shamed her the next, glad he was unable to see her face. She clung tighter to him and avoided his gaze, not wanting to see the sorrow present. Marry him? How? Cora was so uncertain of her own feelings, the impossible situation they were in, and a niggling impression that something wasn't quite right. She nearly laughed aloud at the thought.

Of course something wasn't right—they were in a different *time*.

Each morning she awoke wondering if this was the day she would wake to find all was as it should be in the twenty-first century. She rested her head on his shoulder, closed her eyes, breathing in the scent of him, relishing the warmth of him.

"Cora?" Her name flowed from his lips like honey.

Weariness overwhelmed her. "Hm?"

He eased back until their eyes met. "Will you marry me?" The pensive glint of his stare nudged her to the present.

She pressed her lips into a firm line, then released them. "Honestly?"

He nodded.

"I would like to say yes."

His features softened briefly. "But?"

"We are in an impossible situation, being over two hundred years in the past. We don't know what will happen tomorrow. We don't know how to get home. How and why would we marry in the middle of all this?" She lifted her hand from his shoulder and waved it to span the room.

A look of confusion swept over his face. "Does it matter that we are not in the future?" His gaze lingered on her eyes, then her lips. He slanted his head placing a soft kiss on her forehead, remaining but a moment before pressing his lips to hers with gentleness, slowly searching the corners, lastly encompassing her mouth fully.

Cora's breath caught at his tender care. This was no lustful, careless action. He truly cherished her.

Memories of lost love crumbled. The man had lusted after her. That was why he abandoned her at the altar—he'd never *loved* her.

Breathless, she broke their contact, eyes caressing one another.

"I love you, Cora." His husky voice held her speechless. "Perhaps since the first words we shared."

She wanted to love him, but fear kept her at bay. Lord, do I love this man? Scripture about love being a choice came to mind, and she sucked in a deep breath, then released it. "I believe I do."

Hugh's face lit with contentment. "So, time has bound us?"

Cora wondered what that meant and said as much.

"Had we not been thrust into the past, would you have taken the time to really see me?" He lifted his chin.

The comment made her pause. "I'm not sure I understand."

"We have been thrust together more since arriving here, thus getting to know one another."

She cocked her head in question. "I thought we were playing roles, so we wouldn't be discovered to be from the future." She cocked her head in question.

"True. Yet do you not know more of me now?" His face lit with affection. "And I of you?"

Her gaze settled on his inviting lips.

His lips neared hers, and she eased him away. "I think we

should stop, Lord Hedsworth, before someone discovers us."

For a long while he studied her face. "You are correct. It is well past the hour all are abed."

Cora shoved him away, her heart racing. "I think it best we part ways for the evening."

Hugh coughed, dropped his arms to his sides, and nodded. "Yes. Pardon me for my thoughtlessness." His cocky smile made her stomach flutter.

"You are forgiven. May we continue our conversation over breakfast?" She lifted one corner of her mouth.

"Of course." He raised his bent arm, and she looped hers through his before exiting the room, sending him an adoring, if not skeptical, look.

What was she doing? Her mind could not—would not—envision a certain future as this man's wife, whether in this time or her own.

❧

Cora followed Lizzy down the hall toward the breakfast room. As they reached the corridor that turned toward the stairs leading to the kitchens, the tortoise cat glanced back at Cora meowing as if to say, 'this is where we part ways.' The kitten pounced down the narrow steps, knowing the kitchen staff would dote on her with tidbits of food. Not only Hugh spoiled her but the entire staff.

Once in the breakfast room, she discovered Hugh and Ralph having a quiet conversation, sipping coffee over their food. She'd never seen them chat amiably. Perhaps Hugh really sought to mentor the young man. Cora hoped it was so.

Their heads lifted upon her entrance, and they bid one another good morning, Hugh's eyes steady upon her. Surveying all the hearty food displayed on luxurious platters, she filled her plate and took a seat.

"My dear, we shall not be going to London. I received word the meeting has been postponed until further notice."

Unable to speak, chewing a bite of toast, Cora nodded.

Hugh stared at Ralph. "Please do not share this information with *anyone* as I do not want to alert the vicar's wife that we shall, indeed, be at home."

She grinned, turning her gaze upon Ralph, who appeared subdued, giving Cora a furtive smile, and she wondered what they discussed before her arrival. All chatted agreeably until Hugh finished his meal and rose.

"I am most sorry to leave you, but the steward needs a word." He placed his napkin beside his plate. "I shall see you later, my dear." He did the unaccustomed and kissed her on the cheek in front of Ralph, whose eyebrows rose comically.

Cora had no option but to nod. Once Hugh departed, Ralph gave her a questioning look before glancing around the room.

He whispered, "Cora, the most extraordinary thing has happened. I must assume it may be because you fulfilled your agreement to speak with Hugh about my financial woes." He gulped his coffee.

When she didn't reply, he continued, "He said he would like to *tutor* me in the ways of running an estate and how to keep proper finances." Excitement lit his face.

Cora smiled. "I'm thrilled for you, Ralph. But I must confess, I didn't mention the money you needed." Ralph's face flushed, and she rushed on before he could speak. "It wasn't necessary since Hugh came up with this idea on his own. Once you explain where you are financially, I'm sure he'll help you."

His features relaxed. "Thank you for being so kind. No one has ever treated me thus." The cup shook as he drank.

Cora's heart clutched with sympathy. The young man needed someone to care by making an effort to teach him. She was glad Hugh had come up with the idea by himself. Perhaps Hugh would use this opportunity to be a spiritual guide to him as well—much like an older sibling. Again, her heart squeezed at the appearance of Selena's face in her mind's eye. She missed her sister. Would they ever meet again?

Ralph asked, "Why do you appear sad, Cora?"

"It has nothing to do with you specifically. Hugh helping you made me think he's being a big brother to you, which reminded me how much I miss my sister. She's so far away."

The man's features seemed to transform. His eyes now glistened, his shoulders straight. She nearly read his mind— he had a cousin who now bore the responsibility of an elder brother—taking the place of his actual brother, who cared little for him. This increased her affection toward Hugh.

"She is in Boston?"

Cora nodded.

"I am certain Hugh would return, so you may visit her." His face brightened. "Perhaps she could come here."

She gave him a thin-lipped smile, nodding again. "That would be nice."

Ralph reared back in his seat, hands pressed against the edge of the table, looking very pleased with himself for thinking of it. He stood and bowed. "I am away to attend to business for Hugh. Have a good day. I shall see you later."

Cora watched him go, a sprint in his step he had not held before. Sipping tea while gazing out the window, she saw the gardener stroll past, the brown puppy following on his heels, tail wagging wildly. The door to the breakfast room creaked open, and Olive strode to Cora's side.

"Hello, Olive. Do you need something?" Cora returned her gaze to Mr. MacGregor.

Olive sputtered, "Ah . . . yes, my lady. I . . . um . . ."

Cora regarded the maid briefly, but her eyes traveled back to the gardener, her face red. "Does he make you nervous, Olive?" She pointed to the chair next to her. "Please sit."

Olive's mouth dropped, hand flying to her chest. "Oh, no, my lady. It would be improper."

"Oh, for Pete's sake. Sit down."

With mouth gaping, she sat, wringing her hands.

"I didn't mean to sound harsh. I understand the protocol of this—" Cora pursed her lips. "I mean, if I ask you to sit with me, how can anyone object? It's not like you did it of your own accord to be disrespectful."

The maid's gaze inched toward the man and his dog again.

"Relax. I only want to have a talk." Cora notched her head toward the scene outside the window. "I've seen how you behave around him, Crawford, and their regard for you. It seems there's a love triangle going on here."

Large hazel eyes stared at Cora in shock, confusion flashed for a moment before she understood Cora's meaning. "Oh, no, my lady. I would allow nothing improper in my behavior. I promise." Her hands slid to the chair's arms, white-knuckled.

An irritated breath escaped Cora. "I know you wouldn't. I meant that these two men are taken with you, and I'm wondering if you are partial to one of them or neither?"

The question seemed to calm the girl. A corner of her lips moved upward slightly. "They are both agreeable men."

Cora wouldn't have tagged that description particularly on Crawford—although he was what a twenty-first century woman would call *cute*. Mr. MacGregor was another story. Although ruggedly good-looking, he really didn't appeal to her overmuch.

"Which do you prefer, Olive?"

The maid startled as if she'd never been asked anything so personal. She resumed twisting her hands. "I do not know, my lady. The ways of—" Olive cleared her throat. "—attraction are foreign to me."

Cora pinched her lips together to halt her amusement. "Hm. Let me try another tack here." She rose and brought the teapot to the table, having sent the servants away after Ralph's departure. She poured Olive a cup of tea and refreshed her own cup. When she slid the milk and sugar toward her, Olive stared at Cora as if she'd taken leave of her senses.

"Please help yourself." She returned to the sideboard and came back with a platter of pastries. "Try these. They're amazing."

The expression she wore was one of wonder that a *lady* would treat her so kindly.

"Olive. Please join me. It's nice to have the company of another woman."

After a few moments, the girl warmed to the attention and did as prompted. They sat in companionable silence until she said, "Since you are a married woman, please tell me how you knew Lord Hedsworth was the proper man for you and how he proposed, my lady."

Cora thought about how she may embellish the details to fit this period. She couldn't very well say they traveled through time, and she hardly knew the man—and they weren't married at all.

Beginning with truths would be a good way to start. "Hugh—Lord Hedsworth—has shown uncommon kindness to many people. Not only to friends, but to staff. He's generous."

Chewing on a pastry, Olive finished and swallowed. "Where did you make his acquaintance?"

Leaving out the meeting in the private garden, before she knew who he was, Cora told her they met at a ball.

"How romantic, my lady," Olive crooned.

The comment brought back their first dance. It had been like a fairy tale. One she'd never forget.

"Yes, it was romantic. It was a waltz."

Olive sucked in a shocked gasp. "Truly?"

Cora chuckled. "Yes."

"Is that when you knew it would be a love match?" Olive's hands clasped at her throat.

"A love match?" Cora winced. "Why would you say that?"

"It is your appearance as you look at one another." The maid's face beamed proudly.

Cora cleared her throat, chin dipping. "He proposed to me

during a picnic in the Boston Public Garden. He dropped to one knee and . . ." She could practically see him, the nervous look on his face and the topaz ring.

She brought her head up, Hugh's gaze on hers. His expression weakened her knees.

Olive surged to stand and bowed. "My lord, I—"

"No need to explain, Olive. I know my wife well. She most likely badgered you to keep her company. I am unconcerned." He strode to Cora and bent to kiss her temple.

He sat on Cora's other side and motioned for Olive to retake her chair. Hesitantly, the girl did so, glancing nervously around the room.

Hugh put his hand on Cora's shoulder, heat emanating from his hand. "So, my wife is regaling you with my proposal. To what do I owe this retelling?"

"*Dear*, most women are interested in hearing of romance." Cora lowered her voice. "Olive has two admirers and needs a little guidance."

The maid coughed and fidgeted.

"I'm sorry, Olive. I didn't mean to embarrass you. Perhaps Lord Hedsworth can shed some light from the male perspective." She waggled her eyebrows at Hugh.

He crossed his arms over his chest. "I entered romance rather late in life, so I may not be the best to share advice in that arena."

Olive released a sigh. "Thank you, Lord Hedsworth. Yet if there is any advice you may offer, I shall be most grateful."

He cocked his head in thought. "Very well. I have observed the men on this estate who hold you in high regard. You are a lovely young woman with fine qualities." Hugh smiled. "Much like my wife."

The maid twirled a strand of auburn hair that had escaped the pins and peered with admiration at her employers. When Hugh leaned toward Cora and caught her hand, something spilled from his pocket and tumbled to the floor. The black velvet box lay between their chairs. Their eyes met, and an unspoken message passed across the space separating them. He scooped the box up and tucked it into his pocket.

"Now, regarding your predicament of how to choose a husband with prudence, I am certain my wife has given you wise advice. Heed it."

"I believe she wants an opinion from a man." Cora bit her lip to staunch a smirk. She'd put him on the spot.

Hugh's eyes glinted playfully. "I see. Would the men in question be our gardener and my valet?"

The poor girl's mouth slackened.

"Hugh—don't tease her. She's already beside herself with worry." Cora patted Olive's hand. "Not to worry. He's only baiting you to see your reaction."

"Yes, my lord, you are correct. Yet I know not how to—what to—" She paled.

He moved to the edge of his chair and rested his elbows on the table, cupping his hands under his chin. "They have both shown they have a regard for you, yet you are uncertain how to ascertain their worth as a likely husband. Is that not correct?"

Olive nearly came out of the chair. "Yes, sir! Precisely." She almost glowed with the knowledge that Hugh expressed what she thought. "It is most difficult to understand how to really know someone properly."

"So true. Have you searched your heart?"

"My lord?"

Cora's gaze swung from one to the other, knowing what Hugh was aiming for.

"How do you *feel* about these men? Are your affections stronger toward one more so than the other?"

Olive blushed, and she wrung her napkin with shaking fingers. "I am uncertain, my lord. Both are comely men and most kind to me." Her eyes misted. "How do I know they shall always treat me kindly, my lord?"

Hugh's face scrunched into a frown. "Why would they not?"

She sniffed, and her gaze came to Cora. "My stepfather was most kind to my mother *afore* they married."

Hugh nodded and sucked in an angry breath. "I see," he said between clenched teeth. He stood and began pacing the room. "Men of that sort should be horse-whipped."

Cora understood his rage. Cruelty of any kind was something she'd never been able to wrap her mind around. *To treat others as you wish to be treated* reverberated in her mind. It seemed such a common-sense sentiment to be understood by anyone with half a brain.

"I agree. Let's get back to the subject. How do you really get to know a man and how he'll behave toward you in the future? I've wondered the same, Olive." Cora swallowed an uncomplimentary thought about her ex-fiancé.

The maid sent Cora a startled expression. "Yet you have

chosen most wisely by marrying His Lordship. All can see you have a love match."

Hugh halted his pacing and stared at Cora. Her face flushed, heating with a combination of humiliation and exposure, much like standing before a crowd in her slip. Had her feelings for Hugh been so transparent to the staff?

He returned to his seat beside Cora, gathered her hand, and her chest heaved rapidly. Hugh's gaze pierced hers, and she stiffened.

Without taking his eyes from her, he addressed Olive. "Yes, Olive, I do believe you are quite right. For myself, it was love at first sight." He leaned close and placed a feathery kiss on Cora's lips. Her breath hitched at the contact. It seemed the man had the ability to elicit a completely different excitement each time he kissed her.

Olive gasped, and Cora, breaking the interaction, looked at the maid who held clasped hands under her chin, a dreamy expression on her youthful face. "I have never seen a lord and lady *kissing*." She whispered the last word in awe.

The young woman deserved happiness. The real earl had begun by liberating her from a life of hard servitude, but Cora wanted her to have the love of a good man. She would make it a mission to discover which man would deserve Olive.

Hugh's lips hovered over Cora's, expecting to repeat the accomplishment.

"Hugh, I think Olive has had enough of our PDA."

His brow furrowed.

"Public displays of affection," Cora reminded him.

He tilted his head back. "Ah. Indeed. How improper of

me." He winked.

"Olive, perhaps Lady Hedsworth may instruct you on discovering your true feelings toward these men." He rose. "I shall leave you in her most capable hands." Bowing his way from the room, he sent Cora a heart-stopping smile.

Once the door clicked shut, Olive asked Cora, "Oh, my lady, you are a most fortunate woman."

Until that moment, Cora had not realized how true that statement was. "I believe you are correct, Olive."

Chapter Sixteen

Cora's gaze came up to see servants arriving in the dining room to set out the midday meal, and she led Olive to her room where they continued their discussion.

"My lady, how did you come to know you *loved* Lord Hedsworth?" The poor girl's voice grew desperate.

When *did* she know that? Did she even now?

"I don't really know what to say. I'm not sure at what moment I realized it." Cora looked out the window. The sun had topped Hedsworth House, long shadows stretching across the gardens.

"Olive, which man makes your heart skitter?"

Cora slanted a look at the young woman, seeing her

features tighten with deep thought.

"Why don't you think and pray on it for a day or so? Examine your feelings while in their presence. Pay close attention to their behavior and your reactions." Cora hesitated before saying, "And pray."

Olive nodded, making no move to leave, confusion etched on her face.

Cora stood and placed a comforting hand on her shoulder. "I tell you what—I'll keep a close eye on both of those men and determine what I see. Okay?"

Olive's face clouded until Cora added, "All right?"

The maid smiled and rose. "Thank you, my lady. You are too kind." She curtsied and left the room.

Cora sighed with relief. Exhausted, she fell onto the bed, telling herself she'd only rest for a few minutes then go down for lunch. Eyelids fluttered and closed, the pure ecstasy of relaxation taking over.

A sound startled her to waken, but lack of energy held her lids firmly closed, and she moaned. "Olive, I'm not hungry. Please let me sleep."

The bed shifted, but she still did not open her eyes. "Please." She lolled her head away from the maid followed by her body and slung an arm over a pillow, hugging it close. Unable to remember the last time she'd slept so soundly, she released a contented sigh. A gentle touch cupped her shoulder and slowly slid along her arm, a hard chest resting against her back. Eyes flying open, she stiffened.

"I meant not to disturb you. You look so serene while sleeping."

She could not easily rise with his weight against her, so she slid to the other side of the bed, rose, and faced him.

"Hugh. It's not proper for you to be here," she hissed, hands on her hips.

His laughing eyes met hers. "Tsk, tsk. Cora, it is so easy for you to forget that we are married in the eyes of the staff."

"Yet we're not—Hugh." she whispered while her heart raced.

"I suppose not. Yet I do not come for any nefarious reason, only to speak with you."

"Then why not knock?" she asked indignantly.

He held his chin high. "I did."

Cora searched for a sarcastic comeback, yet none came. "Oh."

"Are you unwell?" Hugh's smug expression changed to one of alarm.

Cora strode around the bed, giving him a wide berth, and sat on a chair near the fireplace. "I'm fine. My conversation with Olive probably wore me out. I didn't know counseling someone could be so exhausting." She yawned.

He sat across from her. "You do look well-rested."

"I am. I must've been tired. I slept through lunch, and I rarely miss a meal." She grinned more to herself than at him.

Her eyes widened. "Now—back to your groping me in my sleep, *sir*."

The look of horror on his face was priceless. "I beg your pardon." Hugh puffed out his chest.

"Don't get your cravat in a twist, Hugh. I am right."

"I merely touched your arm."

"And pressed your chest against my back." She lifted her brow.

"Ah, well, I suppose I did that." He hung his head for a moment, then peered back at her. "Cora, you must know my regards for you, and we are playing a role, and . . . and . . ."

"I've actually made you speechless?" Her lips pursed. "It feels good to know I have that power over the great Lord Hedsworth."

He jerked to his feet, made two long strides, and drew her to stand. Lowering his voice, he spoke against her ear, "Cora. You must face that I love you and want you to marry me. Please consider my proposal from the picnic and let me know your decision. I should like to make you my wife before we go to the future, whenever—*if*—that happens. Either way." His features reflected determination mingled with a nervous twitch near his right eye. He bowed and departed.

She stood frozen, mouth agape, staring at the door. Within seconds, a knock came, and the door opened, Hugh's white knuckled hand on the door latch. He closed it, his face subdued, came, and cupped her face in his palms. "Cora, I am weary of these games. The subtle innuendos, the stolen kisses, pretending to be married. I would that it be true."

Her gaze caressed his face, sapphire eyes, and the kindness she saw there. Barely a whisper, she murmured, "Hugh, I cannot marry you. I am too old to have children. Face it, men can have children even in old age—not women." A hot tear escaped and skimmed her face. He wiped it away with a fingertip.

"It matters not. I may be *able* to have children, but nonetheless, I am too old as well. My final years should be spent with a woman I love and cherish. That woman is you."

Her heart betrayed her head, and she licked her lips, bringing his gaze to them. This time, *she* kissed him. They drew closer, his hands cradled her face while her hands cupped his shoulders.

The door opened, and Olive's shocked stare met theirs. "Oh, my lady, my lord. I am that sorry to interrupt." She backed from the room, then paused. "I simply want what you have. A truly passionate marriage." She curtsied and shut the door.

They laughed, clinging to one another. Cora said, "I suppose we should help her decide which man she should marry."

Hugh's long fingers stroked her face, hungry eyes searching. "I think it best to allow God to guide her, not us."

Cora ran her hands through his thick hair and nodded. "Perhaps you're right. You may give me one additional kiss before leaving my room as it is unseemly." She whispered into his ear, "Because we are not married, Lord Hedsworth."

"Yes, my love."

She drew back, hands on his chest, pushing him away. "If we marry, how are we to explain it to everyone?"

His face seized a wicked expression. "That, my dear, is something I have already considered."

She cocked her head and narrowed her eyes. "Oh, really?"

"I would like a wedding ceremony in my own home." He proudly twitched his chin upward.

Cora met his self-satisfied stance and crossed her arms, fear washing over her. Would a wedding in this time mean they were legally married? What about a return to the future? What would happen to them then?

❦

Cora's hands gripped the edges of the dressing table's stool, mulling over the conversation and the kisses she'd shared with Hugh as Olive brushed her hair and began pinning it into an upswept style. What had she been thinking? The staff believed them married, but guilt at their intimacy—though just kissing wasn't wrong—still plagued her. She was so weak. Hadn't she learned her lesson with—?

"My lady?"

Cora jumped, thoughts of Hugh fading into a mist. "Sorry, Olive. I was daydreaming."

"There's no wonder there, my lady. Not after the kiss my lord did give you." The maid giggled. "Your dreamy expression does give it away."

Cora's face heated, but she met Olive's gaze in the mirror. "You've never been kissed?"

Olive's fair complexion turned pink. "Just on the cheek, my lady."

"And which gentleman gave it to you?" Cora couldn't help teasing the girl.

She leaned over and spoke into Cora's ear. "Crawford."

"*Crawford*?" The answer was more shock than surprise. Whenever the valet looked at Olive, his face flushed. Cora wondered how he'd worked up the courage to do so. "Good for him."

Olive chuckled. "It scared the life out of me, my lady. I was folding the bed linens below stairs, and he came to collect clean ones for His Lordship's bed. I turned to see who had entered, and he placed his lips on my cheek and scurried out."

Cora grinned, enjoying the pleasure in the maid's large hazel eyes.

"He forgot what he came for and returned a bit later, but he would not meet my eyes."

"At least you know how much he likes you."

She shrugged. "If he would only *say* so."

When Olive finished with Cora's hair, she turned to the maid and took her hands. "Just take your time and be sure which man is the right one for you. Don't rush into anything." Cora pursed her lips then said, "Promise me?"

Olive's eyes glowed with affection. "I shall, my lady. No one has cared enough before to guide me." Her face collapsed. "Except for Lord Hedsworth of course . . ."

Cora squeezed her hands. "I know what you mean. Men aren't usually good with women's emotions. Lord Hedsworth helped you escape a life of drudgery in a terrible place, but he wouldn't know where to start with instructing you on finding a husband." She winked. "I bet he could size up Crawford and Mr. MacGregor's characters. I think we should seek his counsel on that. Don't you?"

Olive brightened. "Oh, yes, my lady. That would be most welcome."

"What would be most welcome?" Hugh glanced at Cora, and he said, "I did knock, yet there was no answer. You must pay attention to your surroundings."

She huffed. "While I'm in my own room, I shouldn't have to."

Olive released a tiny gasp, gaze swinging from one to the other.

Cora released her hands and rose. "Not to worry. He's only teasing." Hugh's eyes roamed her from head to toe. "Hugh, maybe next time you could knock louder?"

He continued to ogle her, and she ignored him. "Hugh? Are you listening?"

Olive tittered, bringing Hugh's gaze to her. "I apologize. It is just that you look so beautiful. Olive has outdone herself. Every man at the ball shall envy me."

"Ball?"

His face shuttered. "Yes. That is why I asked you to dress more formally this evening, my dear. Did you not know?"

"Olive, would you excuse us please? And thank you for taking care of my hair. You did a splendid job."

Without a word, Olive curtsied, leaving them.

Cora crossed her arms and fixed him with a stony stare.

Without exchanging words, he crumpled into a chair. "For the second time upon entering your room, I must apologize. I did not intend to be deceitful, but it is imperative I attend this ball with you on my arm."

"All you had to do is ask," she said icily. "Why is it so important I attend?"

He clasped his knees and rocked back to gaze at her. "There is a web of valet intelligence that supersedes the best of

English intrigue." At this, one corner of his mouth lifted. "It is quite amazing really. One valet may pass on information to forewarn a comrade, so His Lordship may not be put on the spot as it were."

"Oh, Hugh, just tell me what time it is without *how* to make the watch." She released an irritated sigh.

His laughter tempered the frustration, and she raked her gaze over him, only now taking in his formal attire.

Hugh looked like he'd just stepped off the cover of GQ—had it existed in this era. He caught the nature of her inspection and rose, taking one tentative step toward her.

"Hugh, do not come any closer. By now, I know that look. You are *not* going to kiss me." She gave him a hard stare. "You haven't answered my question."

"Very well. There is rumor surrounding *my* frequent travels and to come home so abruptly with a bride on my arm has tongues wagging. If I sequester myself in my estate and rarely appear, there could be serious talk and grave consequences. We do not need any undue attention to reveal who we really are—do we? Should someone discover our duplicity, we should be out on the street with nowhere to go."

A hard truth sped up her heartbeat. "How could we be so oblivious? There is something very serious we have not considered."

He cocked his head, eyes narrowed. "Yes?"

Cora swallowed hard, fighting the lightheadedness washing over her.

"How do we know the real Lord Hedsworth won't return as abruptly as we arrived? What are we going to do if he shows up and we are found out?”

❦

Cora gripped Hugh's arm, eyes scanning the massive ballroom. The crowd intimidated her beyond what she had relayed to Hugh on the carriage ride, further worrying her since he had not answered her plea for what they should do if the real earl returned soon. She swallowed, sighed heavily, and gripped him tighter.

He bent to murmur in her ear. “If you continue to clutch my arm with further strength, bruises will ensue.”

“And who would see them other than Crawford?” She gave him a pointed glare edged with jealousy.

“Very well.” He placed his hand over hers and held her gaze. “I shall not leave your side.”

“What if someone asks me to dance? That terrifies me.” She bit her lip. “You know I’m not good at this era’s dances.”

His expression softened. “You did splendidly when last we danced.”

“That was the waltz. The only ballroom dance I feel confident doing.” Cora looked away for a moment and saw a gangly man approaching. Between her teeth she said, “Hugh, here comes a man.”

He snorted. “Fear not. I shall protect you.”

She discreetly pinched his arm, eliciting a small groan of pain.

“Lord Hedsworth, so nice to see you returned from one of your many travels.” He bowed in Cora’s direction. “And this must be your lovely new bride. Good job, old man.”

Cora smiled and hugged Hugh closer.

"Yes, Lord Elliot. Allow me to present the Countess of Hedsworth. And Cora may I present Branston Fitzgerald, the Earl of Elliott.

Cora dipped her head, refusing to release Hugh's arm to curtsy. Neither man's face registered disapproval, so she assumed it was acceptable. "It's nice to meet you, Lord Elliot."

"It is my pleasure, my lady." He bowed gracefully, then addressed Hugh.

She surveyed the young man as he and Hugh spoke, certain the wavy-haired lord was already breaking hearts at such a young age. He appeared to be about twenty and wore his hair a bit longer than she thought Regency era gentlemen were allowed.

Lord Elliot's dark ethereal eyes turned to her. "May I have this dance, Lady Hedsworth?"

This young man, young enough to be her son, dared to use his charms on *her*? Seriously? "I—"

Hugh cut her off. "My wife dances with none but I, sir."

Lord Elliot tilted his head back slightly. "Yes. Of course. You are newly married. It is to be expected." He flirtatiously lifted one corner of his lips. "I quite understand you would care not to share such a lovely wife so soon after the bridal tour."

The humor of the situation almost undid Cora. She wanted to laugh at the ridiculousness of this man, half her age, flattering her. Hugh, apparently, found no humor there.

"Thank you, Lord Elliot. I believe a waltz is to begin shortly, and I would like to escort my wife onto the floor." He bowed and eased Cora out of the man's range, brow furrowed.

Cora nodded at Lord Elliot. "A pleasure to meet you."

His smile would have melted her knees twenty years ago. She chuckled, bringing a scowl from Hugh. "Why the frown?" Her heart constricted. "Are you *jealous*?"

Hugh stiffened and harrumphed. "I dare say not!" The shadow in his eyes gave him away.

"This is so rich. I've never had a man jealous of me." She sighed dramatically. "It feels rather good."

The music struck up the cords to a waltz, and he turned, taking her in his arms. "Surely you jest?"

He pulled her close, and all thoughts of Lord Elliot vanished. The memory of their first dance crashed into her emotions, and she was back in the ballroom at *their* grand house.

Once he looked into her eyes and caught her reaction, he smiled. "I did fear he had captured you."

Her smile grew slowly, and she brought fingertips to his cheek. "How could you think that?"

She saw his throat constrict on a swallow, and he twirled them about the floor.

"He is a most agreeable young man. Wealthy and charming." He inched closer. "And he has enchanted women much older than himself."

She pulled a face. "Really?"

"Do you doubt it?"

Cora shrugged, knowing it most likely to be true.

"Hugh?"

"Yes, my love."

"He's not *you*."

His expression shifted. Cora wasn't sure to what, but it was most certain to one of pleasure. She'd said the right thing. Not that she hadn't meant it. Lord Elliot was very pleasing to the eye, but youth was fleeting. If he had a godly character, one day he would be like Hugh. Nice-looking *and* an upright man.

Once the dance ended, Cora excused herself to the ladies retiring room while Hugh retrieved them something to drink. On her return journey, she wove through the crowd to find Hugh, one conversation catching her attention.

A petite, fair complected girl who looked no more than eighteen spoke to an older woman twice her size. "I hear she is either a widow or a woman on the shelf, but most wealthy either way. Perhaps Lord Hedsworth is in dire financial straits and *had* to marry."

The elder woman lifted a black lace fan and swept the air quickly, sending springy, gray tendrils to bounce around ruddy cheeks. "Truly? One thing is most certain—he did not marry her to give him an heir." Their shrill giggles pricked Cora's ears, and her face heated.

Shoulders tensed, she forced herself to keep moving, eyes scanning the room for Hugh. A different voice snagged her attention this time.

Several young women gathered around a tall, statuesque woman with flaming hair. "I tell you he did not marry for love. Just look at her. She is much too plain for Lord Hedsworth." She tittered. "And just look at that gown. It is several seasons out of fashion."

They all laughed as Cora made a step toward them.

She speared them with a glare. Stopping two feet from the group of crows, she said with a low, menacing voice, "It's no wonder Hugh did seek a wife far from here. Why would he want to marry gossiping, cruel-tongued vipers?" She twirled away, head held high.

She caught sight of Hugh holding two glasses, eyes searching. The closer she got, the more his face turned into a frown.

"What is wrong?" His gaze was not on her but the crowd beyond. She turned and saw the women she'd just insulted, faces red with rage.

"What did you say to them?" He handed her a drink.

Cora gulped the orgeat and told him. His face paled, and gripping her arm, they strode to the balcony. The cool evening air invigorated her a small bit, the scents of the coming night heavy.

He said through gritted teeth, "Why did you do that? There shall now be a scandal."

His words caused her chest to tighten, guilt growing. She should have held her tongue, but the anger elevated with such force it was as if she couldn't have stopped if she'd tried—and she hadn't tried.

"I'm sorry." To buy a moment, she sipped the orgeat. With tear-filled eyes, she met his gaze. "Do you want me to apologize to them?"

His jaw slackened. "You would do that for me?"

With a swallow, she nodded. "I messed up, and I own it."

He stared at her for a long moment. "What did they say to

anger you so?"

She tugged in a painful breath and relayed every cruel word they said, leaving nothing out.

The longer she spoke, the more his face colored. When she'd finished, he placed his glass on the stone railing and all but dragged her into the ballroom.

"Hugh—what are you doing? If you want me to apologize, you don't need to go with me."

He stopped once he reached the gaggle of women. "Pardon me—*ladies*." He paused and met each one's eyes. "My wife said she would apologize to you for words spoken in haste."

Each woman put on a smug expression and lifted their chins.

"But I will not allow it." His voice rose so all in the room could witness what he had to say. "My wife is neither plain, nor unfashionably dressed. And—I *did* marry her for love. I do not find her plain in the least, no matter her age. None of you who spoke such cruelty shall ever measure up to her beauty, wisdom, or kindness. I am uncertain if any of you holds a single one of these attributes. Beautiful clothing does not create a *lady*. Only God does."

There seemed to be a collective gasp around the entire ballroom. Hugh pulled Cora's hand to his lips and kissed it. "Come, my dear. This gathering has grown dull."

Voices murmured loudly as they crossed the room, Lord Elliot meeting them at the door. He bowed, both hands clasped behind his back. "Lord and Lady Hedsworth. May I say I admire your courage and your fortitude? You make a formidable couple." He gave them a sincere grin with a slight dip of his head.

"Thank you, Elliot. That is most generous of you. It is high time that bunch of vipers had a proper set-down."

Lord Elliot brought his hands in front of him and clapped. "Bravo!"

So, Lord Elliot was more like Hugh than she thought. She was glad to see it. If they were stuck in this era, perhaps he may be an ally. Reality struck again, *what if* the real Lord Hedsworth returned before they went home?

Relief met Cora at seeing the carriage, exhaustion having triumphed with all the stilted conversations, introductions, accepting plans for outings, teas, endless social events, and ending with the drama of her disgrace.

The rocking carriage lulled her, and she dropped her head onto Hugh's shoulder, eyes closing as she inhaled his cologne. His hand wrapped around hers, and he placed a tender kiss against her hair. Contentment filled her, and the thought of never returning to their future time wasn't as much of a concern at the moment.

03&80

All was quiet at breakfast following the ball, Cora barely speaking to Hugh. Fatigue from the late night kept her yawning repeatedly, even after two cups of strong tea. She blinked at the sunlit room and attempted to strike up a conversation.

"Hugh, tell me what you've learned about Lord Elliot."

His head shot up from peering at the paper before him. "What?"

"Oh, Hugh, give it a rest. I'm just curious. I have no interest in a twenty-year-old man, for Pete's sake."

He had the audacity to roll his eyes but relaxed immediately. "I apologize." He drank a gulp of coffee and scrunched his face in concentration. "His father died a year gone, and his mother retired to a nearby country estate. He is visiting her at present but shall return to London soon."

"Hm." Cora nibbled on a bite of toast, holding his gaze.

Ralph rushed into the room, shaking a piece of paper above his head. "Cousin Hugh, you shall not believe what I hold in my hand."

Hugh's mouth quirked. "A *letter*?"

The poor man's face crumpled, causing sympathy to wrap around Cora. "Ignore him, Ralph. Please tell us your news. By your grin it appears to be something good." Her heart went to Hugh whose face reflected lines of fatigue from the previous night's incident.

Ralph gave her a thankful nod. "Yes, my lady. That it is."

Hugh puffed out an impatient sigh. "Well, out with it, man."

He sat and lay the letter on the table, smoothing it fondly. "It appears an investment I did make last year has come about." Ralph beamed. "The coal mines of Yorkshire are highly profitable, but the one I invested in had a collapse, and I thought my funds depleted. This—" He tapped the letter with force. "—requests merely fifty sovereigns to further my speculation and reap me double what my original investment was."

His gaze swayed from Cora to Hugh, expectant approval

written on his face. Finding none, he asked, "Is that not excellent?"

Cora met Hugh's eyes with a question.

"Ralph, I fear to tell you this, but it must be so. This is a ruse. They desire more to line their pockets, not yours."

Cora's heart melted at the sight of his crestfallen expression. "Hugh, are you sure? Is there not some possibility their request is true?" From the sorrowful look on his face, she knew it was hopeless.

"I fear not."

She directed her gaze at Ralph. "I am so sorry, Ralph."

The man visibly shrank. She had to give him credit for his attempts at trying to please Hugh. None had ever believed in him, and he was trying to earn approval from his cousin.

Hugh cleared his throat. "I must tell you that the suggestions you made on the north fields will surely improve the crop yield. Not by much, nevertheless, it is improvement."

Ralph appeared to brighten at this small gift. "Thank you, cousin. That is something."

Cora gave Hugh an appreciative tilt of her head. "Ralph, please have some breakfast."

Though timid, his smile touched her.

They ate, mostly in silence, and Ralph left to pen a letter to the would-be coal investment to tell them he would no longer send them a farthing.

When Hugh came to pull Cora's chair out, she asked, "Was that true about the coal mine?"

"Yes. Ralph reminded me that I *had* tried to sway him the

first time he sent funds for their ill-advised scheme.”

"Ah."

He kissed her neck. She whispered, so the footman couldn't hear, "Hugh, you pride yourself on only acting like a Regency gentleman, yet you are increasingly behaving like a twenty-first century man, what with all the kissing going on."

His grin held a hint of mischief. "And you, my dear, do not mind one bit."

Cora whirled to meet his grin, but she could not refute the claim. What had she gotten herself into by falling in love with such a man?

Chapter Seventeen

Cora and Hugh strode arm in arm through the arch. Watching her feet move one step after the other, Cora's thoughts returned to the ball.

She brought her gaze to Hugh. "You do know I saved you from hordes of silly, title-seeking young ladies at the ball?"

"Indeed. I am most grateful." His step faltered, and he broke their contact, facing her. "Have you considered my proposal further?"

A rush of anticipation curled inside her stomach. Did she want to accept? She had concluded she was in love with him, but was she ready for such a commitment so late in life? Any life they shared in the twenty-first century would also include harassment by the paparazzi and all the pressures of being a celebrity's significant other. Could she handle that lifestyle?

"Cora? Are you listening?" His voice held an emotional bite.

"*Ye . . .* yes," she stammered. "I'm listening, and I've thought about it often. Hugh, I—"

His head swung around at the sound of steps approaching.

Lord Elliot's lips quirked into a wide smile. "Good morn, Lord and Lady Hedsworth." Once within a few feet, he bowed, one arm behind his back.

Cora saw a flicker of irritation pass over Hugh's eyes. "Good morning, Lord Elliot. What brings you to us?"

An uncomfortable tone edged his voice. "I came to inquire how the land lies after the ballroom misfortune."

Cora glanced at Hugh, then Lord Elliot. "We are well. Thank you for asking." She gripped Hugh's hand. "I am thankful my . . . husband . . . stood up for me."

Hugh's face transformed from sullen to tender.

"It does my heart joy to find there are true love matches possible in our condescending society." His posture stiffened. "Perhaps there is hope for me. Or is it akin to fetching water with a knife?"

Hugh's laughter roared. "Much the same, my friend."

Cora sensed the two men had bonded, similar to Hugh and Ralph. She was glad for them. Reality slapped her with the knowledge the friendships would be severed once they returned to the future, which saddened her.

Selena's dark blue eyes stared at her, long blonde hair

swinging. Tears formed at the fear her sister must be experiencing by not knowing why she had disappeared.

The two men carried on a conversation Cora did not follow, and when she grew cognizant of the amiable tone, she observed them more closely. In appearance, they were much alike. They could have been brothers. She then thought of Ralph, who also fit the profile. This may well be a band of brothers that would disappear once they left.

Lord Elliot responded to something Hugh said, "Yes, Lord Hedsworth, I should be honored to dine with you and Lady Hedsworth this evening."

Cora's lips parted into a smile toward Hugh. "Perhaps Ralph could join us?"

"Of course." A grin creased his face.

Cora focused on Lord Elliot. "Please remind me of your given name?"

His face clouded for an instant. "Branston, my lady."

She lowered her voice and glanced at each man in turn. "Is it totally inappropriate for me to call you that except in a private setting?"

Lord Elliot beamed and bent toward her. "It shall be a secret between the three of us."

Hugh clapped him on the shoulder, sending a flock of sparrows into the gray-white mottled sky. "Splendid."

A flash of lightning lit the world white, followed by thunder, and Cora gasped. Hugh placed a comforting arm around her shoulders. "I believe we should move indoors."

Branston bowed. "I shall depart as I am on horseback and shall return by carriage this eve should we have rain. Thank you for your kind invitation."

Once he was out of sight, Hugh resumed his questioning while they quickened their pace to the house.

"Will you answer me, or must I badger you repeatedly?" he asked without humor.

With short, nervous strokes, she smoothed her dress and drew a shallow breath. "There is so much to consider." She held up a finger. "If the real Lord Hedsworth comes home, we have nowhere to go." A second finger lifted. "I'm uncertain I'm cut out to be the wife of a celebrity." Before she lifted another finger, he gently took her hand and kissed it.

"Hugh." Her voice hitched. "And I miss my sister."

A fitful wind swirled leaves and dirt around them, and another clash of thunder struck. He took her arm, and they sprinted for the door as a throbbing pulse of rain arrived.

Once the door closed behind them, Cora shivered, and Hugh briskly rubbed her upper arms. "May we discuss this further once you have changed into dry clothes?"

She lost herself with his closeness, the scent of his skin, and the warmth of his body. Her mind was a muddle of so many emotions entangled like a ball of yarn.

"Yes. I suppose so. A cup of scalding tea would be nice." She backed away from him on unsteady legs, wondering how to approach what was to come.

CB&SO

Cora arrived in the parlor refreshed but still indecisive about how to handle the marriage proposal. Olive had prepared a hot bath, and she'd lain there soaking in the lavender-scented water, her anxiety still present regarding the three points she'd told Hugh.

She straightened her back, wanting to run away, then drew a sharp breath, forged ahead, and strode toward him.

Hugh rose from his seat and went to her, bending to kiss her cheek. "I trust you are restored."

"Yes. I'm much better."

He seated her, poured a cup of dark tea, and placed a small lemon cake on her plate. "To fortify you until Branston arrives."

She noted the time on the mantel. "That's hours from now, so I may need a little more than a bite-sized cake."

The corners of his lips lifted into a slight smirk, and he reclaimed his seat.

Before he spoke, she dove in with all honesty. "Hugh. I believe I'm in love with you." She lifted her hand with the palm out. "But—I don't yet know my own mind where marriage comes into it for the first two reasons I mentioned earlier."

He propped his elbows on the table. "Which of the two came first?"

Cora lowered her voice. "What will happen if the real earl returns?" She twisted the napkin on her lap. "That frightens me."

An unreadable expression clouded his face, and he crossed his arms. Not meeting her eyes, he said, "I see."

While Cora drank tea and nibbled on the cake, she studied his face. Not sure what she'd said that upset him, she saw the turmoil churning inside him. His expression depicted agony.

What could she have said to produce such a reaction? He knew her struggles with their situation.

Hugh rose and clasped his hands behind him. "I must attend to a tenant." He bowed. "I shall see you at dinner." He turned on his heel and took long, purposeful strides toward the door.

Slack-jawed, Cora stared at his retreating back. She'd never seen him so unsettled. A deep sigh escaped just as Ralph entered the room.

"What ails cousin Hugh?" He used his thumb to point over his shoulder. "He looked blacker than the cloud that just moved over the meadow. It appears he is bound for the stables. Upon his return, he shall be as drenched as a pilchard."

Cora grinned at Ralph's attempt at humor. "I don't know what I said to upset him. It was obviously my fault."

Ralph's eyebrows rose at her confession. "I dare say he is merely in the dudgeon and shall soon recover."

Cora's brow knitted, and Ralph laughed. "Dudgeon means he is in a dark mood."

"Ah." Cora tilted her head back. "Is he prone to being in the dudgeon?"

"Yes. I fear on occasion. But not often. It passes soon enough."

She lifted the cup, peering into the rippling liquid. Strange that this was something Hugh shared with his ancestor. Yet she knew one could inherit most any trait. She prayed it would end soon since Branston was coming in a few hours.

Ralph poured himself a cup and sat beside her, shooting a

curious glance over the rim of his cup. "Does his disposition pain you?"

Cora pursed her lips. "Yes, I suppose it does. Especially if I'm the cause." She would, of course, not share the reason with Ralph.

A clap of thunder and lashing rain brought both of their gazes to the storm building outside the window where sheets of water poured in rivulets down the glass.

She lifted her eyes to the ceiling. "It appears your cousin will be soaked indeed."

Ralph chuckled. "Serves him right. Perhaps the drenching will cool his black mood."

Cora nodded. "I hope so since we have a guest for dinner."

Ralph bit his lower lip. "Indeed? And who might that be?"

"Lord Elliot."

"Splendid. I have only had the pleasure of meeting him once or twice and enjoyed his conversation immensely. I believe we are of an age."

"That's exactly what I thought. You two should get along great."

Sometimes by Ralph's expression, Cora thought she spoke a foreign language, then his features would clear as he understood her strange way of speaking.

"Yes, cousin. Just as I thought."

After a few minutes of idle discussion, Cora excused herself and went to her room to read. After an hour of reading the book she'd been shocked to discover in the library—a first edition of *Sense and Sensibility*—she mused over Hugh's behavior, no closer to understanding what she'd said wrong.

Olive came and held a dress in front of Cora, asking if it would suffice for their evening guest.

Cora scanned the sage green garment shimmering in the light. "That's pretty. I'm sure it'll do just fine." She touched the fabric, finding it to be silk, the movement causing it to ripple into shades of green in the glow of the candles. The modiste had done a fine job.

The maid dressed her and created a lovely hairstyle that framed Cora's face with tendrils of hair flowing at just the right places.

When she entered the parlor, Hugh, Ralph, and Branston stood talking by the fireplace. Their gazes met hers, Ralph and Branston smiling, Hugh scanning her from head to toe with a sullen expression.

Ralph came to her and bowed. "You look exquisite, cousin Cora." He caught her hands, kissed the back of each, and led her to the others.

Lord Elliot repeated Ralph's movements with a similar smile of approval.

Cora chewed her lower lip and met Hugh's eyes. He wasn't exactly angry—but sad. What did he have to be sad about? Other than he was stuck in a time not his own, was playing the role of his life, living with fear that the man he portrayed would show up at any moment and the dirt would hit the fan.

The thought came to her that he had the added stress of covertly finding out all of the real Lord Hedsworth's personal life and history. So far, he had done a splendid job of playing the spy. *And* he felt responsible for her since they would both be out on the street—or somewhere she'd not thought of until now. They would be sent to jail.

She flinched at the thought of a dark, damp flea-ridden room, most likely crawling with vermin. Clasping her hands until her knuckles shone white, she looked down at them. The toes of a pair of gleaming black hessians appeared near her feet.

"*Cora.*"

Without looking up, she knew Hugh would ask what was wrong, and she didn't want to answer, especially with Ralph and Branston present.

Head still bent, she said, "I'm fine, Hugh. Just a small headache."

"Touch her face, Hugh. She does appear a bit peaked."

She looked up to see Ralph leaning closer, eyes narrowed.

Hugh placed his palm on her cheek, cocking his head. "She does not feel over warm."

Cora sniffed and stepped back. "I'm fine." She peered at Lord Elliot and marched to his side. "Branston. I'm so glad you could join us."

"Lady Hedsworth, it is my pleasure."

Merriweather entered the room and announced that dinner was served.

Hugh immediately came to her and lifted his bent arm, signaling for her to take it.

The absurdity of it all almost made Cora laugh. She stifled it and positioned a hand on his arm like a proper English wife, admitting to herself that the antiquated manners of this period were far from the rudeness of the twenty-first century. Although women were little more than chattel, they were treated with politeness. At least in public.

They had yet to attend church and knew they should, but fear kept them from going because of *her* fear of being caught in their deceit. Hugh wasn't the least bit concerned. He was an excellent actor. She was not.

They dined on mock turtle soup, baked fish, fried beefsteaks, chicken curry, and a variety of vegetables. Cora attempted to eat a few bites of each item presented, but it was too much. She wondered how the entire Regency era population—of the aristocracy at least—weren't obese. Dessert was also over the top with an assortment of orange pudding, blancmange, trifle, apple dumplings, syllabub, and a variety of cakes. The excess bordered on the obscene.

With the expression Hugh shot her, she knew he read her mind and sent a feeble smile. She was over trying to figure out what she'd done and would not let the night end without discovering what it was.

Cora cleared her throat and joined the conversation. It had something to do with the river that ran near the house. "Did you say something about mining across the river?"

"Yes. They mine silver and lead just across the river from Hedsworth Quay. Mining flourishes in the valley."

Hugh's frown deepened. "And lives are lost."

"Really?" Cora ate one last bite of trifle and eased the plate away. "Why?"

Branston opened his mouth, but Hugh raised a hand. "Because it is a dangerous venture and until someone makes it safer, it should stop." His voice was hard and unyielding.

"That is correct, unfortunate though it may be," said Branston. "Yet many owe their livelihood upon working in the mines."

Ralph nodded. "Yes, yet I do believe children should not be allowed to work there. It is dangerous enough for grown men, but children are not mature enough in mind to make a split-second decision should danger strike."

Branston slapped Ralph on the back. "Well said, man."

Pleased by the praise, Ralph squared his shoulders and notched his chin toward Lord Elliot.

Cora noticed how Hugh observed the interaction, his face softening at the camaraderie between the young men. When he saw Cora watching him, his face darkened.

She stood abruptly and tossed the napkin onto the table. "Good evening, gentlemen. I'll leave you to your port and whatever else it is you men do once women are not present. I enjoyed your company." Her glance was for Ralph and Branston alone. She avoided Hugh's eyes.

The men jumped to their feet and bowed. Before they could voice their agreement, Cora was out of the room.

Unable to hold back the tears any longer, Cora slipped into the parlor. She sat on the settee and dropped her head into her hands. How could she continue to cope in this insane situation? She'd done something—*said* something—to upset him to the point of him not wanting to be near her or meet her gaze.

"I want to go home, Lord. Please send me home."

"I am sorry my presence is so unbearable to you, Cora."

She started, but rather than looking at him, she said with a sob, "Go away, Hugh."

A tentative hand cupped her shoulder. "Please forgive me."

Her breath caught. She wanted nothing more than to fling herself into his arms, yet she fought the urge and continued crying. His hand moved, sliding across her back, tugging her toward him. She shoved him away and stood, tears streaming.

"No! You have treated me like I have the plague and won't tell me what I've done wrong, so don't try to cozy up to me now."

His face registered hurt. He nodded. "I understand." With one step, he drew closer, kissed her wet cheek and left her standing in bemusement.

Cora's anger cooled. He'd not even put up a fight, leaving her with the feeling she stood on a remote island—alone.

CB&D

Cora woke with a raging headache and told Olive she'd like to stay in bed a while.

She waited until she felt certain Hugh and Ralph had eaten breakfast and left to tour the fields and see the tenants as they'd now grown accustomed to.

Cora dressed and strolled down the hall, feet like dead weights, as she trudged to the breakfast room.

Hugh and Ralph still sat at the table, cups in their hands. Their plates were gone, and they were obviously at their leisure.

Clearing her throat, she nodded and backed up a step. "I'm sorry to have interrupted. I thought you'd be in the fields by

242

now." She turned to leave, but Hugh's voice halted her mid-step.

"Cora. Today is Sunday. The carriage is ready to depart for church. Do you not remember?"

She gritted her teeth, not turning to look at them. "I'm sorry. I woke with a headache, and I forgot what day it is."

A chair scraped across the floor, sending dread through her. Footsteps sounded. She gulped down an impatient sigh.

He whispered, "If you are *truly* unwell, Ralph and I shall go alone, and I shall make your excuses to the vicar."

The emphasis he placed on her infirmity made indignation rise, but she tamped that down as well.

With dripping sarcasm, she said, "I do feel unwell, but I'll go anyway. I wouldn't want to upset anyone." She pulled her gaze to his with a scathing glare.

His startled expression triggered shame. Just because he'd been distant and rude was no reason for her to do the same. She pressed her lips together and looked over his shoulder at Ralph, whose questioning face appeared in agony.

"I'm sorry, Ralph. I hope you are doing well today."

He nodded. "I am sorry to hear you are ailing. If you would like, I shall fetch the doctor."

Cora held up a shaking hand. "No. I'll grab my things and meet you two at the carriage."

Ralph stood. "You have not broken your fast." His voice cracked with concern.

"Not to worry. I've gone without breakfast before." Her traitorous stomach chose that moment to growl loudly. She hurried from the room before poor Ralph could protest.

In moments, Olive had retrieved a pelisse, gloves, bonnet, and a small Bible. After Hugh helped Cora into the carriage, Ralph seated across from them, she relaxed a little, keeping her gaze on the green countryside outside the small window.

The church was only a five-minute ride, or so she'd been told, yet she dreaded the journey with Hugh so close.

Ralph reached into his pocket and retrieved a small cloth-wrapped package. He extended it to Cora. "It is unbearable that you should go without something to break your fast before church."

Her gaze held his for a moment, a kind glint in his eyes. She accepted his offering. "Thank you, Ralph. You are very sweet." Hugh shifted in his seat and grunted something inaudible under his breath.

Cora unwrapped the parcel to discover a thick slice of bread with a layer of cheese folded between it. She sent him a sincere smile and took a bite. Ralph reached into his other pocket and pulled out a small silver flask.

Hugh reached and snatched it from his hand. "I think spirits should not be consumed on the journey to church, Ralph."

Cora grasped the vessel from him, removed the top, and carefully sipped the drink. "That is the most delicious tea I think I've ever had, Ralph. Thank you." She smirked at Hugh and lifted a haughty brow, then handed him the flask. "Have some." It was not a question.

Shame-faced, Hugh took a sip and swallowed. "A little too sweet for my taste." He turned and watched the hills go by.

Cora's lips tightened, fighting the urge to punch him on the arm.

CB&O

The church service revived Cora to a degree, but guilt regarding her behavior poured over her, and in the quiet church with only the vicar speaking, she begged God to forgive her. She asked God what she should do. Hugh's demeanor of late was exasperating. They hadn't tried the arch for several days, and she wondered why. If the real Lord Hedsworth made an appearance, their trouble would truly just begin.

Her mind replayed the supposed scene that would happen if he did.

If he were a violent man, he may do harm to Hugh. There was no way he could prove he was an ancestor by the same name—despite their remarkable resemblance. But still . . .

As they filed from the church, Cora attempted to distract her troubling thoughts by surveying the old building. Though not large, the lovely interior with dark beams high above sent chills along her spine. She imagined the long-ago services in the Tudor-era structure. The history of the church was captivating. Stepping into the past was stepping backward in *history*. How would she have coped had they been sent to an earlier century?

They reached the doors, and the vicar shook hands with the men and briefly chatted. Cora nodded when Hugh and Ralph escorted her past, but not before the vicar and his wife invited them to afternoon tea. Hugh made their excuses because of Cora's headache. The vicar's wife insisted on walking next door to retrieve her homemade remedy for megrims.

When she returned, she placed the dark glass bottle in Cora's hand. "This is most kind of you." Cora clasped it with both hands and hugged it to her chest.

The elder woman beamed with pleasure, and she patted Cora's shoulder. "It will do you good, my child."

The carriage ride home was much the same as the one taking them to the church. Cora's prayers in church had brought the realization she must apologize to Hugh once they were alone. Sitting across from Ralph, she watched as the swaying carriage lulled him until his fluttering eyelids finally closed and his head rested on the squabs.

She leaned toward Hugh until their shoulders touched, and she whispered, "Hugh, I want to apologize."

His sapphire eyes moved to examine every inch of her face, making her cheeks heat.

Cora swallowed hard. "What did I say or do to upset you?"

Hugh's expression held until the carriage stopped at Hedsworth House. He glanced at the sleeping Ralph. "Now is not the time. I must needs consider—" The carriage door opened, and the footman held it. "Tomorrow. We shall speak tomorrow."

Cora narrowed her eyes, and before he stepped out, she swore his eyes held the moisture of unshed tears.

Chapter Eighteen

Cora woke to the sound of rain pattering against the window and the low rumble of thunder in the distance. Rolling to her side, she snuggled deeper into the comfort of the bed, indifferent about rising for breakfast. Before she returned to blissful slumber, Olive stood over her.

"My lady, breakfast has been laid, and I have chosen a morning dress for you."

"Olive . . ." She lifted an arm from beneath the covers and swiped the air. ". . . please, let me sleep. It's my only escape."

"Escape from what, my lady?" The maid chortled. "Escape from a husband what loves you, a pleasing home and gardens to roam, and plentiful food?"

Cora groaned. "A guilt trip this early is not my idea of a joke, Olive." She opened one eye to look at the girl whose brow was knitted.

"What is a *guilt trip*, my lady?"

She sat up in bed and hugged a pillow. "It's when someone is trying to say you should feel bad for complaining because you have more than you deserve."

Olive nodded with understanding, and the frown line disappeared. "I did not intend to make you feel bad, my lady."

"Now the guilt has returned." She slid her feet to the floor. "I love sleeping when it's raining, waking up now and again to listen to the soothing rhythm."

Olive stared out the window with a forlorn expression. "The rain makes me sad. Especially so when there is no one to talk to."

Cora read the sadness in her eyes. "I'm sorry."

"My lady, please pardon me for being so bold, but what is it like to lie within Lord Hedsworth's arms abed and listen to the rain?" The maid's gaze fell to the floor, and her cheeks reddened.

Cora coughed. "Well—I . . ." She cleared her throat. "With all honesty, that hasn't happened yet."

Olive's eyes widened. "Did it not rain in America after you married—and before you came to England?"

Cora wanted to laugh at the strange comment, biting her lip. "Yes, it did."

"And has it not rained over much since you arrived?" Her face grew hopeful she would receive the answer she sought.

Wishing to accommodate the girl, Cora smiled. "I'm sorry. I don't have the answer you want." She changed the subject before she thought too much about what it would be like to lie abed in Hugh's arms. "Have you given much consideration to our last discussion about Mr. MacGregor and Crawford? Are you now leaning toward one in particular?"

Olive's hazel eyes widened. "Oh . . . no, m . . . my lady. I fear what to do. Should I choose wrongly—" She burst into tears and buried her face against the shawl she held for Cora.

Cora stood, wrapped an arm around her shoulders, and led her to the settee, sobs now close to becoming wails.

"It's going to be okay," Cora crooned.

A knock sounded, and before Cora rose to answer it, the door opened slightly, and Crawford's voice called out. "My lady, Lord Hedsworth asked that I enquire if all is well."

"Yes, Crawford—" She stopped. "No, it's not well. Please tell him to come here at once."

Olive shot to her feet. "My lady!" She wrung the shawl into a wrinkled knot. Cora took it from her and replaced it with a handkerchief.

"It's all right, Olive. We should get his opinion."

The maid backed away, face etched with fear. "Please do not worry my lord with my problems." She sniffled. "I beg of you."

Hugh strode through the door, his expression tight with concern. "What is this caterwauling about?" He stood, hands on his hips. His gaze swung from woman to woman and halted on Cora.

Olive curtsied. "I am that sorry, my lord. All is well. I would not like to be a bother with my worries. My lady said you may help but please do not concern—"

Cora tapped her shoulder, halting the nervous discourse. "Hugh, you are the master here, and one of your staff is in distress and needs male guidance. In this ti—place, you can intercede. Two men vie for her attention, and she doesn't know how to choose." She crossed her arms and met his eyes.

The twinkle she found there gave the impression he was going to laugh. She made an imperceptible shake of her head, hoping he would read the communication. Laughing at Olive at this point would send the girl into additional hysteria.

He crossed his arms over his chest and cleared his throat, causing the twinkle to dissipate. "I see." He stared at Olive intently for a while. "Olive, has either man proposed marriage to you?"

The girl's face turned as white as the sheets on the unmade bed. "No, my lord." Cora heard the nervous swallow that followed.

"At last, we get to the heart of the matter." Hugh lifted his eyes to the ceiling. "Then how do you know either of them *wants* to marry you?"

The maid opened her mouth and closed it. She looked at Cora, then back at Hugh.

Hugh pursed his lips and pointed to the settee. "Have a seat."

Olive did so without delay and aimed large eyes at him, a near worshipful expression present on her features.

He paced back and forth while Cora watched until Hugh's eyes raked over her. She still wore the modest nightgown.

Heat flared from neck to hairline, and she strode to the bed and hastily put on her wrap.

Hugh paused his pacing and looked intently at Olive. "Do nothing until one of them makes a declaration of marriage. If, in that moment, you find your heart engaged with that man, you shall have your answer. When this occurs, I shall have a word with the man and attempt to seek out his intentions and determine if he will suit."

With the admiring gaze Olive gave Hugh, she thought the girl would drop to her knees before him. Cora sat beside her. "Does that make you feel better? I think Lord Hedsworth's advice is wise, don't you?"

Olive dabbed at her tears and nodded vigorously. "Thank you, my lord. That is most helpful."

Hugh bowed and departed, closing the door gently behind him.

Cora's heart swelled at how well he handled the situation. He really did fit into this world. It was no wonder he was such a successful actor. His historical research on this era was precise to the point of obsession. But she supposed it had paid off for him.

Olive appeared to have brightened, and Cora added a few additional words to Hugh's advice. "I think you should relax and try not to be so timid. Make yourself more attractive by wearing your hair up like you arrange mine. Smile more and always have a ready 'good morning' or 'good evening' for both men."

Concentration creased Olive's features before she agreed. "Yes, my lady. I shall try to do so." Determination flashed across her face, then darkened. "I fear I shall not be allowed to do my hair like yours. The other servants shall say I am putting on airs." She dipped her chin.

Annoyance ran through Cora, though she realized the girl was correct. "I'll have a word with Mrs. Muse. I may have a solution that will please all the women in this house."

Cora watched as Olive's eyebrows rose, but she said nothing.

⸻

Cora's curiosity grew as she strode to the library where Hugh had asked her to meet him. When she arrived, he sat in a brown leather chair near the window, rain pecking against the glass. He closed the book he'd been reading, using an index finger as a bookmark.

"You wanted to see me?" Cora stood facing him, hands clasped at her waist.

He looked up. "Please sit—you look like they have roused you for the firing squad." Hugh pointed toward the chair across from him.

She sat and attempted to look the proper Regency woman.

"Mrs. Muse came to me."

Cora stiffened, dread building. What had she done now?

Hugh's blue-eyed gaze fixed upon the rain-drenched window, his chest heaving in a deep sigh. "She tells me you would like to have Olive *practice* her hair arranging on all the female staff so she may hone her skills." The corners of his mouth twitched slightly, schooling his features quickly into a slight frown.

"I did." She jutted her chin and stared at his reflection in the window. "Is that a problem?"

"Not necessarily. The request seemed to confuse Mrs. Muse. She was also concerned it would take them away from their work."

"Not at all. I was thinking one woman per day for a few weeks." Cora bit her lip and cocked her head as if concentrating on the matter.

Hugh moved his regard from the window to her. "What are you up to, Cora?"

"Nothing of importance." She rose. "Just leave this part of Olive's courtship to me."

The light in Hugh's eyes brightened with understanding. "Very well. I shall tell Mrs. Muse to allow it." He opened his book as if dismissing her.

Cora strode toward the door.

"Where are you away to?"

She twisted around to look at him. "I'm going for a walk. We haven't been through the arch in a while, so I thought I'd give it a go—as you say."

His head snapped in her direction and gestured toward the window with the book. "In this?"

Cora shrugged with a smirk. "Why not?" She bounced out of the room so she wouldn't have to hear his admonishment.

The walk was a spur of the moment thought just to irk him. As she considered it, the better the idea sounded. They did after all have umbrellas in this time.

She changed into suitable attire and had Olive retrieve an

umbrella. The gear weighed more than the twenty-first century version, so she held it with both hands and marched into the downpour. After only a minute, she came face to face with Mr. MacGregor. They'd never been this close before, but she greeted him as if it were a lovely spring day, sun shining and all well with the world.

He gave her a questioning glance. "Good day, Lady Hedsworth." He tipped his hat, sending a stream of water down his back.

"Good day, Mr. MacGregor." She watched his dog, soaking wet tail wagging, looking up at his master as if questioning whether to approach their visitor or not. The gardener pointed his finger down, and the dog sat at his feet.

"May I pet him?" Cora lifted her eyebrows.

"If you would like, my lady." The corner of his mouth half lifted, a chuckle perching on his lips.

Cora stooped and patted the dog's head, and he smiled at her. Hugh would call her demented that she thought a dog able to smile. She laughed. "He is a wonderful dog, Mr. MacGregor."

"That he is, my lady." He patted the dog's head, and a flash of affection crossed his rugged features.

As much as Cora had grown fond of Hugh's valet, she wasn't so sure Crawford was the man for Olive. Any man or woman who loved animals and treated them kindly may generally be trusted.

The urge to discover more about the man spurred her to speak. "Mr. MacGregor?"

"Yes, my lady." His light brown eyes met hers.

They were unusual, rimmed with forest green. She saw why Olive was drawn to him. Having second thoughts about the question burning in her head, she adjusted the umbrella nervously before she blurted awkwardly, "What are your intentions toward Olive?"

His hand stilled on the dog. "I beg your pardon, my lady?" He boldly met her gaze.

She swallowed. "I apologize. I don't mean to meddle—"

He interrupted, "Yet you have, my lady."

The statement rankled her more than she wanted to admit. "Olive is a sweet, impressionable young woman. I just don't want her to be hurt."

"I would never do such. She *is* sweet—and lovely."

Cora's gaze traveled to his salt-and-pepper hair. She noted he had few wrinkles around his eyes and mouth and tried to determine his age. "You are of an age, Mr. MacGregor. . ."

"Yes, my lady. I am of *an age* to be sure. Old enough to be a father to Olive." He looked down at his dog. "I have never married, desiring a love match and not one of convenience. I can care for myself. I need not a wife to be a maid and such." His jaw tightened, and his eyes met hers. Concern marred his face, and he said, "Love her, I do."

Cora had no words to offer as she read his pain.

"Olive was but ten years of age when Lord Hedsworth rescued her. She followed me 'round the gardens most days. Said she wanted to help me plant beautiful things."

"She didn't work in the house?"

"Lord Hedsworth said she was too young to work. Though many girls her age do."

"That was kind of him." Cora's attention focused on his reaction to her responses.

"Yes. He told Mrs. Muse to train her a few hours each day so she may attend to her studies."

Tears stung Cora's eyes. "Very commendable."

"Yes." A revelation hit. "Do you think your affection for Olive is like that of a father?" She quickly laid her hand on his arm. "I mean no disrespect."

His gaze dropped to her hand on his arm. "None taken, my lady."

She jerked it back.

"Cora, what do we have here?" Hugh barked, his voice hard.

Cora jumped and turned toward him. "Nothing. We were just talking."

He came to her side and addressed the gardener. "Do you not have tasks to attend to?"

"Hugh, I stopped him to ask a question. That's all." She hated herself for sounding so groveling.

"With your hand on his sleeve?" Hugh ground out. "Explain yourself."

Cora looked at the gardener. "I'm sorry, Mr. MacGregor. I wouldn't have asked you that question if I'd known my *husband* would be so offended."

"What question?" Hugh sent the man a nasty expression.

Cora blew out an exasperated breath. "Oh, good grief, Hugh." She addressed Mr. MacGregor, "Thank you for sharing your feelings with me. Again, I apologize for intruding. Please go on with your duties, and I'm sorry for interrupting."

He dipped his chin and motioned for the dog to follow him.

"Cora, it is not appropriate for you to dismiss a servant in my presence. I am to do that."

"You really are insufferable, Hugh." She flounced away through the rain, which had begun to come down harder. Not wanting to give him the satisfaction, she walked toward the arch. As she approached the opening, she heard quick footsteps on the gravel path growing faster the closer she got to the arch. His hand on her upper arm pulled her to a stop.

He hissed through clenched teeth, "I thought we agreed we would not go through this alone."

All she wanted to do was step through and be home. She swung to face him. "What are you afraid of?" She tugged free from his grasp. "And what are you not telling me? You said we'd talk today."

He drew a long breath, eyes darting toward the arch. "I am afraid of nothing. There are things you do not understand about this time. I only try to protect you." He took two steps away, then turned abruptly and returned. "What feelings did MacGregor share with you?"

The change of subject startled her. "*What . . .?*" She put her hand flat on his chest and tried to shove him away. "I merely asked him what his intentions were toward Olive."

His eyes widened, and he blinked in confusion. "I know not what to say. How did he respond?"

She marveled at how quickly he calmed and anchored her attention on him. "So it doesn't bother you at all? That I asked him that question? No 'how dare you break protocol with a servant?'"

"It is unseemly," he said meekly.

Before he could stop her, she bolted through the arch, hearing him growl, "Cora!"

Reaching the other side, she turned to face him. "I'm still here." Tears burned, and she blinked them away.

He made long strides until he stood before her, water dripping off his dark hair. "Don't ever do that again. We must do it together."

"Why must we, Hugh?"

He cupped her shoulders and pulled her into a tight embrace for a moment, then easing away said, "Because of this." He brought his mouth to hers.

She pushed him. "Everything cannot be solved with a kiss. You're keeping something from me, and I want to know what it is."

He dropped his arms, eyes reflecting sorrow and taking long strides, walked the path through the woods, rain pelting him like sleet, wind whipping into a frenzy.

Cora stood with mouth ajar as he left her soaking in the rain. She watched until he was out of sight. He was going toward the chapel. She remembered the day she'd found him there praying. Later, he'd found her at the dovecote. She smiled at the memory of him falling into the lake and coming up like Mr. Darcy, and her heart thawed. Annoyed at the situation and how it had gotten out of hand, she lowered the umbrella closer to her head for additional protection and ambled along the path after him.

The walk was a far cry from the pleasant, sunny stroll she'd taken in the present day. Blowing rain soaked her, and she moaned at the lack of sense she had in making the journey.

Cora entered the chapel. A burning candle illuminated Hugh kneeling at the altar. Her heart constricted. Had she been too hard on him?

God, please forgive me if I've hurt him.

The need to kneel in prayer and penitence urged her forward. Stooping beside him, he didn't look up, yet he reached for her hand and squeezed. She closed her eyes and prayed. They remained there until her knees burned with pain, and she shifted slightly.

Hugh lifted his head and drew her to stand before him. "Let us sit." He walked them to the first pew, and they sat.

"Have you ever heard the story of the young lord who used to live here?" His serious eyes met hers, questions lingering there.

"I have not. Tell me." Cora sandwiched his hand between hers, warmth emanating from their contact.

Hugh began to tell the tale of a sunny spring day in 1777 when a Vis-à-vis town coach rumbled along the rocky road, a young man's gray horse keeping abreast and the constant chatter from the girl inside lifting on the breeze, her parents releasing an occasional chuckle.

Nearing their destination, imagining fishing on such a fine day made the young man spur his horse on to make the narrow curve in the road before the coach, eager to make his vision come to fruition, but as he pushed his horse onward, narrowly missing the carriage's team of horses, the driver called out, '*Master—*'

Hugh's eyes focused on the front of the chapel, a haunted edge to their blue depths. "The young man's horse sailed over the fallen tree blocking the road. His gaze swung to look over his shoulder in time to see the horses rearing. A broken limb protruded, and his hand caught on it, dragging the fractured wood like a knife. Blood flowed from the slash, but he ignored it as the carriage tilted sideways. The girl screamed, and wood cracked before it tumbled over the edge of the road and into the rushing river."

Cora gasped, her eyes welling with tears. "How awful!"

Hugh pulled his free hand to lie atop hers. "It is a short story yet tells much."

"That's very sad." Cora sniffed, her thoughts on what a horrible scene for someone to witness. "Who were those people, Hugh?"

He licked his lips, his gaze rising to meet hers, his eyes filled with tears. "That foolish young man on the horse was me."

Chapter Nineteen

Cora stifled a laugh—one of hysteria, not of mirth. She blinked in confusion. Had she heard him correctly? Had the slip to the past addled his mind? "What do you mean, Hugh?"

Hugh pulled in a deep breath. "It is true. My selfishness cost my family their lives."

The anguish in his features gripped Cora. The man radiated pain and sorrow. Was he that good of an actor?

Her sister would have said yes, but Cora would have to disagree, which meant he told the truth.

The more she sat in stunned silence running everything through her mind, the more she realized if they were able to travel backward in time what would prevent someone from going forward?

Cora gasped, tears stinging her eyes, heart racing. "You're from the past," she pushed out through gritted teeth.

Betrayal seeped into her, and she sprang to her feet. The agony in his eyes did nothing to quell the swirl of anger and disbelief within her.

"You lied to me."

Hugh tried to take her hand, but she jerked away and rushed toward the door.

He'd lied by concealing his true identity. He was the *real* earl. All of it had been a lie.

"Please allow me to explain." Hugh called after her, his pleading voice cracked with emotion. He rushed on, words flowing fast. "After my family died, my uncle took me in, sent me to school, and managed the estate until I was of age—"

She no longer wanted to hear excuses from a man again. Not from her ex-fiancé, Selena's ex-husband, or anyone. Head aching, she sprinted through the door, his last words trailing behind like the lying snake in the garden.

"I felt lost until I met you."

As she reached the dovecote, hot tears mingled with the cool rain, the umbrella long forgotten at the chapel. She crept inside the dark, stone bird sanctuary, unconcerned about the smell. Frozen in place, she clasped her hands together beneath her chin. "Oh, God, please help me understand."

The furious flapping of birds' wings escaping their intruder halted her prayer, and she rushed into the squall, lightning flashing across the murky sky. The storm inside her heart erupted in much the same way.

Becoming soaked no longer a concern, Cora slowed her pace until she reached the arbor-covered bench in the garden. It provided some shelter, and she sat.

Hugh's words echoed through her mind, although she'd heard all he said. The ones that stung the most were, "Until I met you."

Self-loathing saturated her more than the downpour at having trusted another man. With a bitter voice, she shouted, "I told you so. Why did you trust him and give him your heart?"

Mr. McGregor's dog crawled from underneath a nearby lilac bush, propped his head on her knee with sad eyes, and released a whimper. Within seconds, Lizzy sprang onto her lap, shivering.

Cora flinched, then settled. "Hello, are you frightened of the storm and taken refuge together as friends?" She patted each simultaneously. A crack of thunder sent both animals huddling closer. "It's nice to be needed." She cuddled the cat and stooped, gripping the dog's collar and leading him away.

"Come on. We're going to the stable where it's snug and dry. I'll go to the kitchen and ask Mrs. Duckworth if she has some scraps to share."

Lizzy purred, and the dog wagged his tail enthusiastically. Her heart warmed at caring for these sweet creatures, getting her mind off the barrage of trouble she found herself in. At least, they wouldn't lie.

ℭℨ℘

Cora removed her sodden clothes with Olive's assistance, peeling off the garments clinging to her wet skin.

"My lady, you must have a hot bath. It shall not take long to have one brought up."

"Olive, I'm fine, really. I just want dry clothes and a hot cup of tea."

The young woman sighed painfully, giving in. "Very well, my lady. Yet I shall bring a bite or two as you have eaten little this day."

There was no need to argue, so Cora agreed. If she could choke down any food, it would be an effort. When Olive had gone to order the tea, Cora sat by the window, the Austen novel unopened on her lap. The rain still peppered the window as she stared through it toward the sky, which looked angrier than before.

Out of habit, she reached for her phone to check the weather app to see how long it would last. What was she to do? More than ever she knew she didn't belong here. He did—but not her.

A fresh wave of tears threatened, and she heard the door open. "Olive, I'll have my tea here. I don't have the energy to go to the table."

Hugh cleared his throat, and Cora surged to stand, bracing herself on the wall. "Leave, Hugh! I don't want to see you." She dropped to the chair and turned her head to the window, not wanting him to see the tears.

"Please, Cora," he rasped. "Allow me to explain."

"Why should I? It will most likely be another lie." Cora knew her words were harsh as she sucked back the bitter taste of past rejections.

She heard his feet shuffle and peeped from her peripheral

vision to be sure he wasn't coming closer. His throaty groan reached her, and the taste of his kiss returned. Her fingertips came to her lips at the memory, and she twisted to look at him. She had to somehow forget him, forget everything between them, forget she loved him.

His low, quavering voice called to her, "Cora. I am sorry. There are many reasons I did not tell you. Perhaps that was not wise, but I knew not what to do."

Cora scowled, her anger rising again. "Hugh, I'm just your woman *du jour*. Nothing more than that. A Regency earl in this century and a good-looking actor in the twenty-first century that women fawn over." She choked out the words, believing each one.

His face flinched at each stabbing word. The silence hung in the room like a dark mist, and he clasped his hands behind his back, opening up as if a target. "I shall leave you for now and give you time to calm. I know you to be a fair-minded woman and will eventually allow me to share what I have to say." He rubbed his eyes with the base of his palms, blood draining from his face. He turned and left the room.

Cora felt lower than dirt. She may have had a right to question his reasoning, but she had no right to speak to him so cruelly. God sent the word *forgiveness* through her mind, and she recoiled.

Still watching the rain when Olive arrived a few minutes later, the girl placed the tray on the small table beside Cora's chair and shot her mistress a grave look. "My lady, shall I fetch the doctor? You look quite pale. Perhaps the soaking did you harm."

"It's my heart that's sick, not my body," she said, nearly

choking on the words.

Olive's hands went to her throat. "Oh no, my lady. What ails you?"

"Hugh ails me, Cora. Please never trust a man again. I gave you terrible advice. They will always disappoint."

Olive gasped and plopped into the seat across from Cora. "No, my lady. That must not be so."

"I can't go into detail, but he lied to me about something very important." The burn of unshed tears grated on her nerves. She was tired of mourning him.

She heard Olive swallow and watched her. What more was there to say?

"Mayhap it was a misunderstanding, my lady?"

"Not likely." Cora's gaze focused on the tiny mole beside Olive's lips, and Mr. MacGregor's declaration of love returned. "Have you come any closer to knowing what your feelings are toward the two men who hover around you?" She smiled at her own description. Cora had never had men hover around her. She wasn't jealous, just miserable. Miserable that the man she'd come to love could deceive her. The revelation of his lies hit her harder—no wonder he knew everything about Lord Hedsworth and didn't seem overly concerned for his eventual return. He *was* Lord Hedsworth.

Olive's voice snapped her out of her reflections. The maid's gaze dropped to watch her fingers pluck at the fabric of her dress. "Mr. MacGregor stopped me as I went to the henhouse to gather eggs for Mrs. Duckworth. Mary, the new kitchen maid, is feeling poorly and could not attend to the task."

"It was kind of you to do that." Cora waited for her to

continue as a hush fell over the room, the coursing rain the only sound. "What did he say?"

The maid peered up at Cora through her lashes, a spark of light shining in them. "He asked when the rain stops, would I like to walk with him through the gardens?" She released a tiny cough. "Once our chores are done for the day."

Despite Cora saying to never trust a man again, her heart leaped, and she allowed herself a grin.

"My lady, do you think I should refuse?" Olive's cheeks blushed, a hushed tone in her question.

"No . . . I mean yes . . ." Cora's throat became dry. "I don't know what I mean, Olive. Love is so complicated." Her eyes closed, and she pressed the back of her head into the chair, wishing to be three thousand miles and two centuries away from this place.

"My lady," Olive whispered, "shall I fetch the doctor?"

Cora's eyes snapped open. "I'm just weary of—everything right now." She reached for the tea and took a long drink.

A knock on the door brought Olive to her feet to scamper across the room. Cora kept her gaze averted in case it was Hugh. She returned with a large crystal vase containing roses, sprigs of fern filling the spaces between the long stems.

"Are they not lovely, my lady?" Olive buried her nose in one of the red blooms. "And there is a message." She placed the vase on the tea tray and handed Cora the card.

Knowing they were from Hugh, she motioned for the maid to put the card on the tray. "I don't want to receive anything from him right now."

"The card may be an apology since the flowers are red."

Her voice lifted a pitch. "*And* they are Provence roses."

Cora frowned. "What does the color or type of rose have anything to do with the message?"

"Oh, my lady. It is ever so romantic. Flowers—and their colors—have meaning." Olive's face took on a wistful expression.

Meaning? Yes, she knew a little about that but not enough to decipher these. Voice quivering, she said, "It doesn't matter. I don't want to know." She sat back in her chair, focusing on the never-ending rain. The weather fit her mood, and she couldn't be bothered with a cryptic note from Hugh.

"Very well, my lady." Olive ambled around the room, unnecessarily straightening bric-à-brac and humming.

After a few minutes, Cora sighed, "Oh for Pete's sake, Olive. I can tell from the look on your face you won't let me rest until you reveal what the flowers mean."

The maid scurried to return to the chair across from Cora and snatched up the note. "Well . . . first, a red flower means the gentleman is passionately in love." She beamed at Cora as if expecting a response.

"And?" Cora lifted one brow.

Olive shifted uncomfortably. "The Provence rose means my heart is in flames."

Cora stared at the poor girl for what seemed an eternity. Olive held her gaze for a long while until she lifted the card.

Heaving a sigh, Cora nodded, and Olive rose and strode to the writing desk, retrieving a letter opener. She sat, carefully opened the wax seal, and unfolded the paper.

"Olive, was that really necessary?"

"What, my lady?" Her pinched eyebrows nearly making Cora laugh.

"To go to all that trouble just to break the seal." She pointed at the object.

Olive shot her a curious look. "To keep it pristine so you may have it as a keepsake."

She extended the note to Cora, but she waved it away. "You read it."

Her eyes widened. "It is most private. I should not be privy to such a declaration from your husband."

Cora considered the remark, then dismissed it. "You read it so you may see how men manipulate women with their deceitful words."

A still, small voice whispered, '*Do not judge.*'" She straightened her spine. "What did you say, Olive?"

"Nothing, my lady." Olive held the paper, poised to read.

"Go on. Read it please." Cora relaxed, the soft words humming through her head.

Olive read in a low, sweet voice, as if reciting poetry.

Cora, my love,

I know I have wronged you, yet I had no excuse to do what I've done except for your protection. Please allow me to explain all. It is not a short tale and deserves to be shared so you may fully understand my predicament.

My love for you is most real. I know not how to express what my heart reveals.

What I have broken, determined I am to heal.

My eternal love,

Hugh

Cora breathed deeply, trying to block the softening of her heart toward Hugh. He had a way with words. Didn't all actors?

Olive sniffed as she folded the letter and placed it next to the vase with shaking fingers. "My lord loves you. Please allow him to explain himself."

"Oh, Olive. It's not so simple."

"I understand not." She slowly shook her head. "Do not all err, my lady, and desire forgiveness?"

As if the still, small voice spoke once more, now coming from Olive. Cora's unease bred guilt.

⚜

The next morning, pink roses arrived. Cora lifted her gaze. "Okay. Tell me what these mean and read the goofy note."

Olive presented them to Cora with a questioning expression, shifting from foot to foot, her expression clouding. "Goofy means ridiculous."

The maid sagged, eyes dimming with sadness.

Cora squeezed her hand. "It's okay, Olive. The wound is still fresh."

She dipped her chin and sat, opening the note with extreme care, not bothering to retrieve the letter opener.

Scanning the note briefly, her hand flew to her chest. She

looked at Cora, eyes holding unshed tears.

"My lady, I shall tell you the meaning of the flowers before I read to you." Her lips parted slightly before beginning. "The dog rose means pleasure mixed with pain, and pink is for the beginning of a relationship."

No cord or cable can draw so forcibly, or bind so fast, as love can do with a single thread.
Robert Burton

My dear Cora,
I pray we may begin anew with our relationship.
Always yours,
Hugh

Her disloyal stomach fluttered. How could she fall for such nonsense? And who was Robert Burton? It must have been some obscure poet she'd never heard of. Then why had the line melted her hardened spirit?

"Is that not lovely?"

Cora harrumphed. "Just words to con me."

"What does that mean, my lady?"

"It's a scam, a rip-off, ploy, swindle, cheat, trick, mislead . . ." Her dictionary shut down. She could go on, but by Olive's expression, she'd delivered the meaning.

Olive pressed her lips into a thin line, a pained stare aimed at Cora. Saying no more, she removed the tea tray and left Cora to her conflicting thoughts. Scenes played in her mind of all the times he'd said things that made little sense until now. The fact that Hugh knew tremendous details about everyone they met. He introduced them to Cora without pause.

Another item on her list glared. What was this camaraderie he had with his valet? Their relationship was well in place, and she hadn't noticed it until now. Did he know about Hugh's time-travel experiences? Had she been duped by more than just Hugh?

CB&ED

A third bouquet arrived the following morning before Cora rose from bed. The sound of the door opening and closing brought her head around to peer at Olive placing the customary cut-glass vase on the bedside table.

Through sleepy eyes, Cora viewed the purple hyacinth, breathing their sweet, powerful scent. It brought memories of her grandmother's spring garden. She had the most wonderful hyacinths in every color. Spring? How had Hugh come upon these during the summer? She sat against the pillows and fondly brushed the blooms with her fingertips.

Olive stood over her, note in hand. Without speaking, she popped the seal and read without prompting.

> *We never live so intensely as when we love strongly.*
> *We never realize ourselves so vividly as when we*
> *are in the full glow of love for others.*
>
> *Walter Rauschenbusch*

The note was unsigned, and Cora frowned. "He only quotes

someone? He writes nothing else?"

"No, my lady. The meaning of the purple hyacinth is one of apology, asking forgiveness, and deep sorrow."

Cora's eyes swam with tears, and the small voice returned. *'I forgave you.'*

274

Chapter Twenty

While the quiet forest surrounded Cora with the occasional chirp of birds or the rustle of a small creature in the underbrush, she observed the stream's lazy ripples from atop the stone bridge, the gurgling soothing her troubled spirit. She had walked for some time before arriving at the bridge that crossed the narrow tributary, spilling into the river.

Her heart led her to the chapel, but she stayed far away, afraid Hugh would be there and not wanting to see anyone. She preferred to be alone.

Forgiveness, heavy upon Cora's heart, burdened her. What should she do? It was as if by forgiving Hugh, she was condoning his behavior. Her gaze swung to the thick trees, and the thought of finding a hiding place there to collect her thoughts and pray called to her.

With a tentative step, she backed away from the stone guardrail to amble toward the tree line but froze as Hugh stepped out of the dimness of the forest into the light, exposing the varying shades of brown in his hair. His hands were clasped before him, and Cora caught the movement of his left thumb, nervously rubbing the scar on his right hand.

Silence hung between them like a heavy tapestry, and she longed to rip it in half and allow it to settle at their feet. Her hand came up, and she shoved away a disobedient strand of hair.

"I've been to the chapel searching for you." Making a half step toward her, eyes looking to the ground, he brought his gaze to her face.

"Hugh. I apologize," she said, her voice laced with emotion. "I had no right to treat you so harshly. I forgive you for lying to me, and I would like to hear your story—your *entire* story." Heat spread through her, the words rushing out, her eyes not leaving his.

He stared, his gaze appraising her. He closed the distance between them with a few long strides, grabbed her hand, and brought it to his mouth, pressing a soft kiss to her knuckles.

A low and pleasant hum warmed her blood as he next brushed his hand across her cheek.

"Hugh . . ." His name was cool and sweet on her tongue. She licked her lips as if to savor it.

"Cora." He placed her hand flat against his chest and brought his mouth within the same breathing space as hers. "May I kiss you before I tell my story?"

She nodded. With painfully slow, deliberate progress, the inches between them disappeared, and his lips met hers. When he pulled away, Cora sought to draw him back to her.

Against her ear, he asked, "Shall we go to the chapel?"

Cora nodded again, accepting his offered hand, relishing the warmth.

Traveling across the bridge, Cora thought in two hundred years, would she walk across this bridge again? Or would it be only in this time?

The old door of the chapel squeaked a protest as Hugh opened and closed it, and then escorted Cora to a pew at the front of the antiquated structure. She wondered if the story of the Earl of Hedsworth building the chapel in the fifteenth century to commemorate his escape from capture by King Richard III's men was actually true.

Hugh sat slanted on the pew to face Cora, keeping her hand in his. "I have told you of the carriage accident and the great loss at my own folly." He held his hand up, the scar prominent in the sunlight radiating through the windows. "This is the physical recompense with which I must live with daily." He fisted his hand, pounded it against his chest, and pulled in a long, deep breath. "The remainder of that reward is the pain I carry here."

Cora eased her hand from his and brought it to cup his stubbled cheek. "You were only a boy."

"I was a headstrong young man determined to seek his own pleasure." The firm finality in his voice brooked no discussion. "You are the first woman I have met that has eased the memory."

"I know about the accident, but please tell me the rest."

He stood and paced, hands behind his back. Cora noticed he mostly did so when deep in thought or troubled.

"It all began when I came home from school for the last time. My uncle had seen to my education, and I traveled the continent extensively. He said it was time to take my rightful place as earl. It pained me a great deal, knowing it was my fault that my father was not still here to do so."

He paused in front of the altar and looked at the cross hanging behind it. "Until I turned my life over to Christ, I was truly a lost soul among the living." He returned his gaze to Cora. "My uncle led me there. It is to him I owe my sanity. Well, rather, to God. My uncle was the catalyst."

Hugh stood there, face fading from one emotion to another before resuming. "I had been home a few months, seeing to the tenants, crops, and so on. Taking a walk one afternoon in the gardens, I stepped through the arch, and my world changed."

"What met me was unthinkable. I shudder even now." Before he turned away from Cora, she saw a flush creep across his cheeks. "Only now do I know how to describe such debauchery. Men and woman wearing scantily attired swimwear cavorting in a large pool of water. Some reclined along its edge upon cushions, holding large vessels of spirits. They laughed as if taking part . . . I cannot speak it. It is not for a lady's ears." He winced. "I turned and fled back through the arch, back into the civilized world."

The desire to laugh came and went before it could take root. She understood what he meant. "You're right. It's shameful."

"Indeed. And it appears the world grows more so by the day as I have witnessed during my time in the future."

"What year did you—arrive?"

"It was my twentieth year that I stumbled upon the scene. In the beginning, I assumed I was in the throes of a hideous nightmare. I avoided the arch for some time, but weeks later, I was deep in thought and walked through the arch again. On this day, I was thrust into a ball where I met Samuel." A corner of his mouth lifted, and the softening of his expression revealed how much he missed his friend.

"How did he handle that?"

"Oh, it was friendship at once. I shall have him tell you. He was scouting for period actors for Regency productions."

Cora snorted. "And as they say, 'the rest is history.'"

"Yes, something of that nature." He smiled awkwardly. "He said he saw in me the perfect Regency actor."

Hugh shared more of what happened, and she grew enthralled at all he told her.

"Now I return to the arch. Samuel knows the truth about everything. I trust him with my life, and as the only one to know of my time travel, I charged him with special instructions. If I were to go back to my time and something should happen to the arch in the present time, he should have it rebuilt immediately and to the exact specifications, so I should be able to return."

Cora leaped from the bench. "So he's working on it as we speak? Oh, Hugh, that's marvelous." She grabbed him into a tight embrace. "You are a wonder!"

He continued to hold her, pulling a fraction away to peer

into her face. "I shall always strive to be such to you." He swallowed. "If you shall have me."

She cocked her head, lifting one corner of her mouth. "I'll think on it."

Growing serious, he narrowed his eyes. "Will you be able to handle my career as an actor *or* as Lord Hedsworth?"

"How about both?" She waggled her eyebrows.

"Both?" He questioned her with a sidelong glance.

"I've had a lot of time to consider our options—what with me quarantined in my room receiving flowers from secret admirers and all."

He straightened his back. "Secret—"

She cut him off, remembering the quotes. "I received a lovely note from Walter somebody. I can't recall his last name."

He smirked. "That was cruel, Cora. You put fear into me, and I wanted to know the rogue's name."

"Hm. Are you not a rogue, sir?" She attempted a British accent. "You have kissed me countless times, and that is *not* a seemly thing to do in the Regency period."

"True." He pursed his lips. "I believe I shall do it again." He flattened his hand against her back, drew her closer, and kissed her until her knees weakened.

She pulled away and released a breathless sigh. "Oh, my. Yes. I suppose you may be allowed to do that again. Yet only at our wedding."

His lips parted, his eyes registering surprise and did she dare say *joy*?

"Indeed? You accept?"

"Yes, Hugh. I believe I do." She hugged him. "I'm not sure in which century yet, but I do."

ଔଚ୍ଚ

Cora reclined on the chaise lounge in the library while Hugh sat at the desk writing a letter, his voice breaking through the quiet. "If we stay here—pardon me—if we are *forced* to stay here, would you care to live here on the estate or go to London?"

Cora snapped her head up from the book she'd been reading—a first edition of *Pride and Prejudice.* "What? Where?"

They had spent the past few days discussing the possibility of being able to return to Cora's time, but Hugh's question was the first occasion he had suggested a plan that involved them staying here.

He looked at the library ceiling and sighed. "My dear, you do have a choice."

"I don't want to live in London in this century or the one we came from. I like it here." She caught herself. "I like Hedsworth House in either time, but I do want to go back."

The expression he wore was one of confusion. "Why can we not do both? The way I have been living for decades."

"Coming and going as we please? How do we know it'll work that way for *both* of us? What if I never see my sister again?" As soon as the words were out of her mouth, she regretted saying them. "I'm sorry. I know you miss your sister and parents too."

In a low voice he said, "I do."

Cora mulled over their strange situation for which she had no simple explanation. "Have you been able to go back and forth as you wished? I mean, you planned each visit and the arch never failed you?" She shifted, suddenly restless.

"I confess it never occurred to me that the arch would reject me. Henceforth, I strode through whenever I *chose* to travel . . . away."

"So you avoided it unless you needed to go?"

"Yes." The one word was voiced with conviction, and his arms dropped at his sides. "Mayhap it is the need within me that causes me to travel thus."

Not thoroughly convinced, Cora said, "Well . . . the first time you came through was not of your desire."

This did not seem to concern him. "Oh, I believe I did—subconsciously. I was in turmoil over the future without my family. A life spent running this estate and all the holdings my father left. It was overwhelming. My uncle was old and fading quickly, so it would not be long before I no longer had him to rely upon." A flash of sadness covered his face. Quickly rebounding, he gave her an impish grin.

Cora sent him a sideways look. "I'm not sure I like the way you're smiling. It appears as if you may be up to no good."

He beamed. "Trust your instincts, my dear. I am most certainly up to something." He came to kneel beside her, seized the book, and closed it. "We are going to have a ball."

She scrunched her face into a frown. "A ball? Why?"

"Perhaps since we came here during a ball, we may return the same way." He quirked a smile. "What do you think?"

"Hm. It sounds intriguing." She wilted. "And if it doesn't work?"

He grunted and tapped his chin with a forefinger. "Let me see. What is the saying from your time . . . do not be a Debbie Downer?"

Cora flung her arms around his neck. "You never cease to amaze me, HRH."

He released a guffaw that echoed throughout the room. "I shall strive to always do so."

"Please," she murmured. "I never want us to grow apart."

Hugh pulled her to arm's length and peered into her eyes. "There, there, I assure you, it shall never happen. Quite the contrary. The relationship of a time-traveling couple shall never grow stale."

She briefly touched her lips to his. "Is that what we'll be? Living the back and forth travel kind of life?"

He inclined his head. "If we plan carefully, I believe we may make a success of it. It has worked thus for me all these past years."

Puzzled, she asked, "How do we plan?"

As he rose, he pulled her to stand. "Of late, I have given it much consideration. I would like to take Ralph and Branston into our confidence and elicit their aid."

Cora made a half-step back to fully read his features. "Honestly? Is that wise?"

"I trust both men. We shall come up with a reasonable last will and testament, so if we do not appear—say within one year—Ralph inherits all, and Branston shall be his mentor. This way, they will be certain to care for everything on this side of time."

Cora's pride over his careful consideration of their predicament increased her trust in him and her faith in God for bringing them together despite their unusual situation. God truly was in control of all things.

"That's a good idea. Perhaps we need to pick apart every scenario and make notes until we speak with them."

"Indeed. There is much to consider." His sapphire eyes bore into hers, searching. "I would that you marry me in this time."

"Hugh. We've talked about it. Everyone would wonder why."

"I have thought on it overmuch. We shall say that though we married in America we desire a ceremony here." Satisfaction gleamed in his eyes.

Cora played with a tendril of his dark hair. "Yes. I see how that may work. What about the ball though?"

He stared at her lips, and she put her palm against his mouth. "We are not doing that again. This is a serious discussion."

"It is rather difficult to have one with my arms about you." He nuzzled his face into her neck.

Cora sighed and pushed him away, returning to sit. "Until we marry, there will be no more of that."

He bowed and strode toward the door.

"Where are you going?"

"To find Mr. Sirman."

"The vicar?"

"Yes, my dear." He paused and said over his shoulder, "*I have a wedding to plan.*"

Cora didn't know whether to be happy he was so focused on the task, or fearful of it finally coming to fruition. Was she sure it was a good decision to marry Hugh Henley at all, no matter the time or place?

ೞೞ

Cora kept to the tall Chesterfield chair in the library, reading long after Hugh had gone. At least she tried to read. She rested her temple against one of the wings, the supple leather smooth against her skin, her mind returning to Hugh saying he would seek the vicar. Did she want to marry him here? Once she'd come to the realization she truly loved him and wanted to be his wife, she'd imagined a lovely wedding at the present-day Hedsworth House with Selena as maid of honor, Judith as bridesmaid.

After a long while, she drifted to sleep, her head lolling against one side of the high-backed chair. The crack of a slamming door in the distance wakened her followed by the staccato of boot steps growing closer. The door opened, and blinking away the sleep, she saw Hugh's formidable figure standing in the opening.

A roguish grin played on his lips. "Did I waken you?"

She closed the book and nodded. When Hugh stepped further into the room, more footsteps sounded, and Ralph and Branston entered behind him.

"I met these rogues on the road, and they followed me home." Hugh sat in the chair next to her and waved a hand for the two men to join them.

Ralph greeted Cora with a bow. "Good day, cousin Cora. I trust you are well."

"I'm fine, Ralph."

Branston gave a bow, took her hand, and kissed it. "You are looking most lovely today, Cora."

Hugh's head reared back and sent the young man a glare.

"Hugh, don't be such a stickler for etiquette. I've asked Branston to call me Cora."

Ralph hooted. "Hugh, I would give a sovereign to have a painting of your face just now."

Branston guffawed. "Merely a sovereign, my good man? You have come a long way. But a few weeks ago, you would have said one hundred pounds."

Hugh still watched Branston through narrowed eyes, but with another glare from Cora, he softened and smiled at the man.

Branston said cheerfully, "Hugh does tell us you are to be married again. What a lark. We are most pleased he has invited us."

Ralph agreed and slapped Hugh on the shoulder. "It shall be a day for merriment. Are all the plans in place?"

Cora brought her gaze to Hugh and chewed her lip, sending him a questioning look.

"The vicar shall advise the best date he has available and shall come and take tea with us on the morrow."

Ralph's eyes widened. "I suppose he shall bring his wife?"

Hugh swallowed. "Yes. I assume so."

"She is a rather . . . disagreeable woman." Branston lifted

one eyebrow in mock horror.

Ralph gave his opinion, and the three men entered a conversation, Cora shutting it out. Her thoughts were on a wedding in this place. Was it selfish to want one in the twenty-first century with Selena in attendance? She supposed they may do another then. What about their honeymoon? They wouldn't be able to go anywhere since they needed to stay near the arch in case Sam repaired it on his end. They needed to be ready.

A tap on the arm brought Cora back to the present, and she met Hugh's imploring gaze.

"You were not listening, my dear. Since the wedding is for our closest friends, Ralph suggested we have it at the chapel in the woods. What say you?"

She cleared her mind of the previous thoughts. "I suppose that would be nice. It's also a good excuse not to invite many guests."

Branston slapped his palms on his thighs and notched his chin. "Splendid, and I say we get on with planning the ball. What shall be the theme?"

Cora sent Hugh a questioning look. He'd already told them about the ball?

Hugh sighed impatiently. "Thank you, Branston, for bringing it up. I had not as yet informed my wife I shared it with you."

"Well, if you told him, why shouldn't he bring it up?" The bite in her voice made her wince. "I'm sorry. I didn't intend to sound so irritable. This ball has me a bit on edge."

She turned her gaze to Ralph and Branston. "Enormous

crowds make me nervous."

They both voiced their skepticism, saying she was much too lovely and refined to warrant such anxiety.

Again Hugh's face flashed with jealousy, and Cora's suspicions grew. If his green-eyed streaks persisted, she would have to rethink their upcoming nuptials. A jealous man had no place in a marriage.

Chapter Twenty-One

At Cora's insistence, Ralph and Branston joined in the discussion of possible themes for the ball, and the young men departed Hedsworth House in a cheerful manner, chatting about the upcoming event.

After they left, Cora turned her thoughts to Hugh's outward displays of jealousy. She wouldn't tolerate such behavior. He had nothing to worry about.

Hugh stood by the window, his back to Cora. Before she could voice her concerns, he addressed her. "Why did you allow them to enter the plans for the ball?"

She pursed her lips in thought, keeping silent until he turned and came to sit.

"Well, Cora?"

Instead of answering, she sniffed and picked up the book she'd been reading before the solitude ended at the men's arrival. Though she saw Hugh from the corner of her eye, she ignored him until she could collect her wits.

Hugh crossed his arms over his chest, continuing to study her.

"Hugh, we have a problem." She slammed the book closed. "Answer my question with total honesty."

He turned to face her nodded and scowled.

"I see the looks you send to any man who compliments me out of politeness. Are you jealous?"

He had the good graces to appear ashamed. A flush crept across his cheeks, and he turned away.

The scent of his cologne wafted toward her and brought to mind what a masculine man he was. Though, he still maintained the manners of a perfect gentleman, well dressed and impeccable in every way. Cora bit the inside of her cheek to ward off the rising desire to kiss him.

"I would not have you think me a suspicious man." He paced within her periphery but never met her eyes. "Yes, I confess I experience a touch of jealousy when a man compliments you." He paused in front of her and held out his hand. "Allow me to finish."

Cora's amazement that he knew she was about to interrupt him galled her. The fact that they were getting to know each other so well offered her a sense of belonging, building a stronger connection between them.

"Yet I am never angry nor do I mistrust you." He halted, his blue eyes rapt on her. "I have attempted to examine why jealousy gallops through me as these situations occur. The true reason I have only just realized. It is because we are not yet united in marriage, belonging solely to one another."

His revealing words took her by surprise. There was some truth to it, she must concede. Oh, good grief! Her very thoughts were beginning to sound like a Regency woman. Hugh was rubbing off on her—in many ways.

Without thinking, she rose and placed her hands on his shoulders. "If you sincerely believe that, can you assure me once we're married, there will be no more suspicious glances or hard looks? I cannot abide jealousy." She slid her hands down his biceps and stopped when her palms lay on his forearms. "Although I've never experienced it before, and a tiny bit might not hurt. I may see you speaking with a beautiful woman at the ball and not like it very much."

His lips brushed her ear, raising goose bumps across her skin. "I shall never give you reason to believe me unfaithful."

"Good." She pecked him on the cheek and returned to the chair. "Now that we've got that settled, may I please read?"

"Yes, my dear. I must speak with MacGregor about preparing the chapel and the grounds for our wedding." He bent and kissed her forehead and made to leave.

"Hugh?"

He paused at the door. "Yes, love."

"Would it be proper to have our wedding in the morning and the ball that evening? Sort of a celebration party. That way we may have a small, private ceremony, and the ball would be for everyone else."

The slow grin building on his lips pleased her. "That

sounds excellent. As soon as the vicar has a date, we shall prepare." He rubbed his hands together as if longing to dig in to a sumptuous feast, then left the room.

After reading for hours, Cora walked in the garden. Perhaps later, she'd go to the stable to see the new kittens. She told Olive where she was off to, taking the parasol to shield her from the sun. As she walked, a darkness fell over her emotions, thinking of Selena and how she wished her here for the wedding. The only thought that comforted was the idea of another ceremony in the future. The longing to text Selena was so strong a sudden wave of wretchedness gripped her.

After a long stroll, she sat under the arbor where several minutes later Hugh found her there crying. He approached in long, confident strides, face gleaming with joy. She stood at his advance, and he halted when he got close enough to see the tears and lengthened his strides.

"Cora . . . what is wrong?" His hands cupped her cheeks, and he brushed away the tears with his thumbs.

"I miss Selena." She buried her face against his neck.

He tightened his hold. "I know. You shall see her soon. Of that I am confident. And we shall have a large wedding, and she shall take her place beside you."

Her chest squeezed at his words, but they didn't register in her head. All she could think of was her misery. "Hugh, I feel like I'm stuck in one of your corny films, and you're just acting out a scene. I want to text Selena and ask her the title of one of those ridiculous movies." She pulled away from him and saw his hurt expression.

Hugh gripped the edges of the columns supporting the

arbor, hemming her in. "Is that what you truly think of me? Of my work?"

Her throat dried, and she struggled to speak.

"Why suddenly, do you feel thus? A few hours ago, all was well."

She tried to duck under his arm, but he was quicker than she and stepped closer, pushing her further under the arbor, the backs of her knees against the bench. "Let me go, Hugh."

"I shall not until I understand the sway of your moods." His shoulders drooped. "This is exhausting. I know not what may come next between us. I want you, Cora, for the past and eternity. No matter where time places us. Yet you either long to marry me or not. Which is it?" He opened his mouth to continue, then stopped.

The color drained from his face when she did not answer. He dropped his arms and stepped back, shaking his head slowly from side to side. "Which is it, Cora?"

A long, paralyzing moment passed before Cora flung herself into his arms. "I'm sorry," she mumbled against his chest.

He did not lift his arms to embrace her, his breaths coming nearly as fast as his heartbeats.

Time seemed to stop, and Cora's tears subsided. What was she doing to this man—to herself? Her emotions had ridden on highs and lows since they'd appeared in the past. His heartbeat slowed beneath her ear, his arms still hanging at his sides. Had she stepped over the line one too many times? Had she passed the point of no return?

Uncertain whether to continue clinging to him or let him

go, she took one tentative step back and looked at him. His eyes were closed, skin pale. Cora surveyed him from head to foot, his stance stiff, hands fisted at his sides. A shiver of fear—not one of physical harm but one of loss passed through her.

Pride goes before a fall.

Cora clenched her teeth and breathed deeply. The small voice again. The words pressed on with intensity. Cold seeped into her bones, limbs shaking as she touched his hands. He flinched but did not relax. She lifted one fist and molded her hands around it, trying to send her warmth to the hurting young man that was still inside him.

With trembling lips, she said, "Hugh, I love you. I do want to marry you."

She heard his hard swallow, yet he said nothing.

"I am mortified that you will stop loving me. That you will leave me." She held back the tears. "I'm afraid I will not be able to be a good enough wife in this century considering all the social restrictions, and I'm afraid I will also fail in my time because of your career. All the gorgeous women clamoring for your attention. I can never measure up to their beauty and talent, constantly vying for your attention."

Cora continued holding his hand for a long moment. When he did not respond, she slowly dropped his arm and rushed to the solace of her room, wishing with all of her might that it was instead a portal to her home.

CB&ED

Cora looked up from her bed at Olive's frowning face. She wanted to hide from the world and embrace her misery.

"My lady, what is the matter? It do seem Lord Hedsworth

is always hurting you." Olive tucked the bed covers around Cora's shoulders. "I shall fetch you a cup of tea."

"No, Olive. I don't want tea. I want to sleep for a week, and maybe it will all be over by then."

Olive halted in the middle of folding one of Cora's chemises. "What shall be over?"

Cora sniffed. "Never mind." She rolled to her side and faced the window, bright beams of sun slanting between the half-drawn curtains. How was she going to live here with him if they were unable to go back? Misery multiplied, and she groaned.

"I shall fetch the doctor, my lady."

Cora bolted to sit upright. "You will not. And I forbid you to tell Hugh I am unwell. I don't want to see him."

Olive blanched at the tone in Cora's voice, and she bobbed a curtsy, eyes wide. "Yes, my lady." She backed toward the dressing room, folded clothes hugged to her chest.

"I'm sorry, Olive. I don't mean to be cross. I'm in turmoil. It's not your fault, and I apologize."

The woman's expression softened. "If marriage is such a distressing carriage ride, I shall not want to have one."

The analogy brought a smile to Cora's lips. "That just about sums it up. A *very* bumpy carriage ride."

A knock sounded, and Olive strode to the door. Cora dropped to her side and tugged the covers over her head. She would fake sleep if it would get rid of Hugh.

Cora couldn't hear the whole exchange from under the covers, but she could hear Olive saying she was not well.

"I shall not leave until I see her."

This raised voice was not Hugh's. Cora inched the covers just low enough to glimpse Ralph standing at the door, one booted foot keeping Olive from closing it.

"I am her cousin and wish to see how she fares. Hugh will not speak of her. I must assume they have quarreled." He raised his voice, "Cora, I insist on speaking with you—now!"

She blinked at his unaccustomed sharp tone. Through the covers, her muffled response was almost comical. "Go away, Ralph. Your cousin is insufferable, and I do not want to talk to him or anyone else."

Olive released a small squeak of surprise, and Cora moved the barricade to see Ralph shoving the door and slipping through. He hurried across the room and fisted his hands, placing them on his slender hips. Dark green eyes smoldered as his gaze surveyed hers.

"Why are you still abed? Hugh shall not say what is wrong. Branston and I need you to discuss the ball preparations." He aimed his gaze at Olive. "Will you please gather what Lady Hedsworth needs to dress?"

The maid's eyes flickered from Ralph to Cora, fearful of whom to obey.

Ralph came close to the bed and fisted the bed linens. "Am I to resort to drastic measures, my lady?" He grimaced, humor absent from his expression.

Cora gasped. "You wouldn't dare!"

"Care to try me, *my lady*?" His arrogant smirk expressed just how serious he was.

Cora steamed but agreed. "Oh, very well," she barked.

"Olive, do as he says." She redirected her remarks to Ralph. "Go on and leave, you, you . . ." Her voice shook. ". . . *traitor.*"

He collapsed into laughter. "Whatever it takes to bring the two of you together again. It is painful to see him so crushed. I dare not imagine what you did to cause him such pain. He has been a nasty bear all day."

Ralph's expression sobered. "Cora, I do not wish to take sides, for he is my cousin by blood. If he wronged you in some way, please share it, and I shall see to his punishment."

"You would take sides against him?"

"Only if he hurt you." He turned and rushed from the room, sending Olive an apologetic lift of one brow. "I believe the gardener is strolling as we speak, Olive. I'm sure once Lady Hedsworth is dressed she will have no need of you until well after dinner."

Cora caught the slight teasing of his tone and watched crimson spread across Olive's face. The Henley men had no equal—that was for certain.

⊂⧓⊃

Cora arrived at the dining room to find Hugh at his customary place at the head of the table, Ralph and Branston about to be seated. Their heads came around to meet her gaze, and she nodded a greeting, unable to form coherent words.

Hugh stood politely yet refused to look in her direction. She thought she saw a fleeting expression of remorse there. At least she hoped so. Regretting her part in the upheaval of their relationship, she still had trouble forgetting his refusal to accept her apology and explanation. It had fallen on deaf ears. And maybe she shouldn't have insulted his work.

Branston rushed to pull her chair out, and she glanced at Hugh to see if he wore the jealous expression she hated. Although he did witness Branston's attention, there was no sign of jealousy.

"Thank you, Branston." The footman placed the napkin on her lap, and she took longer than necessary to arrange it to avoid Hugh's gaze. She then peered at the sparkling chandelier, focusing on the perfectly formed tear-shaped drops of crystals shimmering overhead. Anything to keep her mind off the situation boiling in the room.

Ralph attempted to discuss the ball with only Branston joining him. They bantered back and forth through the first two courses of the meal while Cora and Hugh ate in silence. Once the main course arrived, Ralph and Branston's impatience was palpable.

When dessert arrived, Ralph jumped to his feet and tossed his napkin onto the table. "What in blue blazes has passed between you?" He looked at Cora, then at Hugh. "Until yesterday, your obvious affection for one another was nauseating."

Branston, taking a sip from his glass, snorted and had to bring his napkin to his mouth to stem the flow of liquid. He coughed until able to speak. "Here, here. Ralph is most accurate. Please mend this tear in your relationship. The wedding and ball are a fortnight hence."

Cora hung her head and watched the napkin absorb her tears. She wouldn't allow them to witness the flow. Her chair shook as she kept her head down until she composed herself.

"Cora, please rise." Ralph lowered his voice. "*Please.*"

She quickly blotted her tears with the wet napkin and stood, her eyes on the floor.

Ralph seized her hand and led her around the long table. When he halted, she saw Hugh's hand clutching the edge of his chair's arm.

"Hugh," Ralph said in a commanding tone, "Here is your wife. Branston and I are leaving. We shall return in one hour. If she remains at your side, and you remain in your seat, we shall give up our quest to reunite you, and you may live the rest of your lives in a miserable marriage full of discord. We do not wish this for you. And neither does God."

Cora halted, guilt surging for her behavior in the garden. Yet she had confessed and apologized, Hugh choosing not to reply. He was as an iceberg, his true feelings buried deep. She didn't know whether to run or stay put. Hugh's deep breaths held her in place. She watched his strong hand grip the arm of his chair tighter, knuckles tensed with the effort. Every hair on her head tingled. She wanted reconciliation, but hadn't the attempts been all she could do? If he wanted it also, should he not have responded to her pleas?

On impulse, she dropped to her knees next to his chair, not touching him, keeping her head bowed. She closed her eyes and prayed for God to intervene.

Your will be done, Lord. Show me what to do now.

It seemed an eternity. Legs growing numb, she swayed, nothing to hold on to unless she gripped his arm or the chair. She would never touch him again unless he made the first move. Just as she was about to give up and leave, a hand rested on her shoulder. Had Ralph returned before the hour had passed to release her from this torture?

Soft lips against the back of her neck immediately released the pain she possessed. Hugh's chair rasped against the elaborate rug, and he knelt beside her.

"Cora, my dear, dear, Cora. Please rise. I can bear it no longer. I love you. My stubborn pride held me from you because of all you said." He caressed her back and dropped his voice. "My acting has been my salvation all these years. It has kept my mind occupied whilst I grieved my family. I have been running since that day."

How many misunderstandings would they have before their relationship collapsed? The turmoil was unbearable.

Keeping his voice low, he continued, "I confess it wounded me when you spoke so critically of my career. Please understand, I have no say over the titles of my films. To be truthful, I do find them to be most ridiculous."

Cora brought her tear-stained face up to read his expression and saw only honesty. "Then why were you so angry when I said it?"

His eyes scanned her face for a moment. "I deemed I was not high enough in your estimation. That you saw me as less than I should be."

She slapped a hand over her mouth to smother a sob of revulsion at what she'd said. How had she not known the words would have cut him so harshly? Had someone told her working at a historic property was a ludicrous job, she would've been heartbroken.

"Hugh, I know I've apologized, but please allow me to do so again. It was heartless of me to say that. I was lost in my own pity and didn't consider your feelings. Just because I don't like your movie titles is no cause to judge them."

He shot up an eyebrow. "You have not seen them?"

Cora wilted and shook her head. "Selena has tried to make me watch them." She sniffled. "Now it's my turn to confess. I *wanted* to hate them."

He grunted, and she dropped her gaze.

"My sister is obsessed with you as you know, and I was sick of hearing her prattle on about you, so when she played one of your movies I'd pretend to watch, my mind planning out job search scenarios for the following day. It got to the point I'd shut out Selena too . . . whenever she talked about your latest tabloid story."

Hugh shifted his weight to a sitting position and pulled her to do the same, holding both of her hands. "My dear, you were jealous before you even met me."

Cora stared at him, about to retort what an absurd statement it was. She closed her mouth and puzzled over the comment, then realized he was right. It must have shown on her face because he laughed.

"I'm not sure if that's an entirely *accurate* word for my reaction to Selena's preoccupation with you. It leans a little more toward her focus on you despite the . . . titles."

"So you are judging a book by its cover, so to speak?" He grinned.

She pinched her lips. "I suppose you're right. Because I *do* judge books by their covers. A silly cover sends me scurrying to find a different book. It's hard to take them seriously."

"I grant you that, yet had it not occurred that you could at least view one of my movies before making the assumption they are ridiculous?"

Cora squeezed his hands. "If we had the ability, I'd watch one with you today."

"Small consolation as it is not possible."

"As soon as we return, I promise we'll do so." She tugged her hands from his and scooted to his side, then lay her head upon his shoulder. "We need to try harder to communicate better from now on."

"Agreed."

The door opened, and Ralph stuck his head through. When he saw them on the floor, he chuckled and said, "Come along, Branston. All is well."

When neither of them made a move to rise, the men swaggered toward them, wearing superior expressions.

Hugh reclaimed Cora's hands and lifted her with him as he rose.

Cora's gaze wandered over the men's faces. "You each look like the cat that ate the canary."

They frowned, looked at one another, and shrugged.

Cora and Hugh shared a laugh that puzzled the men further, Ralph asking, "Why is that so humorous?"

Hugh answered, "Perhaps I shall enlighten you one day."

Cora shot Hugh a knowing smile.

Chapter Twenty-Two

As the day drew closer, Cora's anxiety about the wedding and the ball following on its heels increased. The reconciliation with Hugh had healed her misgivings about marrying him, though the fear of never returning to her time was ever present.

Cora surveyed the large ballroom, memories of the first time she'd seen it when Judith had said the grand house actually had three. The one in which she now stood was the largest. The sense of being here just weeks prior brought back the yearning to be in her own century. Hugh had copied every minute detail of this room at the present-day Hedsworth House. He had outdone himself recreating the house as it was in the Regency era.

Once she and Hugh returned to her time, every room would still have the ability to bring back memories of their stay in this time—their arrival, getting to know one another, their chapel wedding, even their honeymoon. She blushed at the thought. At her age, she would soon be a bride, something she never thought would happen.

Her eyes caressed the sparkling crystal chandelier, holding dozens of candles. She remembered how the faux fixture had lit the room when she'd danced with Hugh. So much had happened since that night.

Approaching voices and echoing footsteps on the wooden hall floor brought Cora from her reminiscences. Hugh stepped in, Ralph and Branston behind him.

"You two shall have to convince my wife that a masked ball is the thing." Hugh placed an arm around Cora's waist. "Is that not so, my dear?" The hint of a smirk appeared on his face.

Cora glanced at the men, air stalling in her lungs. "I . . . I'm not sure."

Hugh hugged her closer. "I am aware of your aversion to crowds, though perhaps hiding behind a mask may provide courage."

She considered it and finally relented. "I suppose you have a point."

Hugh nodded and looked at the men. "Well, you have it. We leave you to manage all the arrangements as we must plan our wedding, gentlemen."

Ralph and Branston smiled broadly, bowed, and excused themselves to attend to their task.

Cora's brow creased. "Isn't it unusual for men to be in charge of giving a ball?"

Hugh chuckled. "Perhaps, but I have placed the housekeeper over them with Merriweather and Mrs. Duckworth as their assistants. They shall keep the lads in check."

It was Cora's turn to laugh. "I'm not sure those *lads* are very pliable."

"Trust me, my dear. Mrs. Muse will brook no mischief taking place." Keeping his arm around her, he led her outside where Mrs. Duckworth had the footman set up an afternoon tea for the two of them. Hugh had arranged paper and writing utensils by each place setting.

"I see you've already prepared our wedding planning session." Cora poured their tea and took a steadying sip, her hand trembling.

Hugh placed a hand on her shoulder. "Please do not fret. It shall be a simple ceremony with close friends in attendance."

She smiled over the teacup, courage rising. "So, where do we start?"

He presented a piece of paper holding the list of guests' names. After skimming it, her eyes widened, and she looked at him intently. "Hugh, the only people invited who don't live on the estate are Branston, the vicar, and his wife. And Ralph is only visiting."

"Precisely. As it is a small chapel and all the persons to be invited are closest to me except for the vicar's wife, I thought it meet they should be the ones to share our joy."

Cora grinned. "*Except* for the vicar's wife?"

"I am ashamed of myself but yes. As you have witnessed, she is not an amiable person. Our poor vicar must live with that, and I do not intend to exclude him from an enjoyable meal and some jollity."

"*And* he's marrying us." Cora stated with amused sarcasm.

"There is that."

"I suppose the lavish ball that evening will more than make up for those not invited to the wedding." Cora bit into a piece of decadent lemon cake.

Hugh chuckled. "As long as Ralph and Branston take their task seriously enough. I fear they may come up with some outlandish theme. All they have revealed is as it should be at a masked ball."

Cora poured herself another cup of tea, and as nonchalantly as possible, she said, "I wish we could have a honeymoon here. What other woman in my time can say they had a genuine Regency honeymoon on the continent?"

He gave her an indulgent smile and patted her hand. "I wish it were so, but we must stay near the arch."

"I understand. That doesn't mean I have to like it." She leaned forward and kissed his cheek. "That is not an invitation for further kissing."

He compressed a hand over his heart. "You wound me." The corner of his mouth twitched, and she traced a finger over the groove on one side.

"That, my dear, is no way to *discourage* my intentions."

Disrupting the silence that ensued, voices came from the other side of the hedge bordering the patio.

A woman spoke in a shaky voice. "I know not what to say,

Mr. MacGregor."

The deep tone of the gardener's voice was difficult to distinguish.

Hugh whispered, "Is that Olive?"

Cora nodded and made to rise from her chair, but Hugh placed a staying hand on her arm. "Hugh, they need their privacy. We need to leave."

He murmured, "It pleases me not to eavesdrop, yet I must know his intentions and do not trust her to tell us. She is a timid young woman. I would not that she be hurt."

Torn between agreeing with him or not, Cora settled on her seat, ears perking.

The couple's conversation continued, soon moving away from them, pebbles crunching on the path taking them further from the patio.

Hugh sighed impatiently and sat back in his chair. "I grow weary of worrying about her. Mr. MacGregor would make a suitable husband, though there are a few years between them."

"How many—exactly?"

"It is a great number." He rubbed his jaw, eyes distant.

"Wouldn't Crawford be a better match since they are much closer in age?"

"Age matters not. Sharing common things joins people more so than age," he stated with confidence.

"Do you really believe that?" She bit her lip, mulling over his self-assured tone.

"I do. One must have more in common than not if there is

to be a successful relationship.”

“You sound as if you speak from experience.” Cora waited to see how he reacted, but he schooled his features, and she saw nothing revealed there. “What is the age gap between Olive and Crawford?”

“Near on twenty years.”

Cora started. “Really? So, *both* are old enough to be her father?”

“Yes, so it would appear.”

Her mind grew unsettled at the sweet, innocent girl’s—young woman’s—future. This era of history was not so very different from her own. Certainly, older men married younger women, but it was such a wide chasm. She longed for Olive to have a long, happy marriage.

“Hugh?”

“Yes, my dear. What troubles you?”

“Olive’s future. It’s so hard to find marriages that are actually happy. I want that for her.”

He didn’t speak at first and instead studied her for a moment. “Tell me why you believe this way.”

Cora’s gaze swung to the hedge that separated them and the couple they’d just overheard. “I speak from experience and from shared experiences of others. Too many relationships begin with one person not revealing their true selves. Once they marry, their genuine nature comes out, and the marriage is not a pleasant one. I don’t understand why people can’t just be themselves. Wouldn’t they save everyone a lot of grief by doing so?”

Tears burned at the memories of past relationships.

Hugh extended a hand toward hers and gently stroked it with his fingertips. "You speak truth, yet all are not honest with themselves or others. I know not why they have no ability to be truthful."

Cora's gaze caressed his face. "I'm glad we've had our difficulties and revealed them so we may move forward with openness."

Hugh whispered, "And I."

They sat in comfortable silence, Cora considering Olive's future and her own. A slight breeze ruffled the papers in front of them. She lay a hand upon them, then placed a teacup on top as a paperweight, her mind going back to the same question that unsettled her. "What if we can't go back?"

Hugh flinched in surprise. "Pardon? Why do you ask that now?"

"I was just thinking of Olive. She has so few choices. Scarcely does a woman have a career that supports them. I hate to think of Olive being a maid all her life. How lonely would that be?" Cora realized she'd not answered his question. "I asked because it is a real possibility."

"Regarding Olive, I trust she shall find happiness with either man." He didn't comment on their possible inability to return.

"She's fortunate to have a choice, but discovering the right path to choose is a challenge." Cora toyed with the edge of a paper.

"Not if I interview them." Hugh stood and looked down at her.

"What?" Cora's stomach filled with dread. "Would that be

proper?"

"I employ them. Olive is under my protection, and I must look out for her best interest."

Cora realized he was correct. Why had she not thought of it earlier? "I like that idea. What will you say?"

Hugh reclaimed his seat and picked up a fresh sheet of paper. "Why not assist me with a list of questions? From a woman's standpoint, I would think them invaluable."

She released a long sigh. "Now I know why I love you so much."

☙❧

Cora and Hugh compiled a list of interview questions for the gardener and the valet. She hurried to her chamber to ask some questions of her own of Olive. Without giving away what she and Hugh were doing, she questioned Olive in a conversational tone about what expectations she held for a husband.

Once the maid left Cora put the comments on paper, went to the library, and gave them to Hugh, who accepted them with a smile. "Thank you, my dear. I shall add these to the list we created. Will you please advise Mrs. Duckworth to send up coffee, tea, and cake? I shall summon MacGregor and Crawford, so I may commence with the interrogation." He waggled his eyebrows.

"Oh, Hugh. I know you don't mean to speak with them together." She cocked her head, suspicion growing. "Do you?"

He had the nerve to roll his eyes toward the ceiling. "Do I appear daft, my dear?"

Cora stepped within arm's length of him and rested her palms on his face. "You may be fine to look upon, but even I would not marry a daft man."

He released a loud guffaw. "I shall take that as a compliment."

"As you should." She spun around to leave, but he caught her arm and drew her to his chest.

"Cora, my dear, Cora." His blue gaze roamed her face. "We shall have a wondrous marriage for we are of a like mind."

Breathless, Cora melted against him for a second, then forced herself out of his grasp. "None of that. You must behave"

He straightened as if at attention. "Aye, aye."

She crossed her arms with a mock frown. "That's better. You must take care of Olive. That will take your mind off of me."

He strode toward her, hands clasped behind his back, raking his gaze over her form. "That shall never happen." He lifted his chin and returned to his desk.

Cora chuckled, pleasure flowing through her, as she left to go to the kitchen.

CB&O

A few days later, Cora and Hugh strolled through the gardens, discussing the turn of events regarding Olive's future.

Cora shook her head vehemently. "That girl doesn't have a clue. Even after I explained what you'd discovered about both men, she is still undecided."

Hugh squeezed her arm against his side and patted her

hand. "I know not what advice to give now. She appears a bacon-brained . . ."

"Hugh! That's unkind. She's a sweet girl but has no experience regarding men. Olive has seen so many unhappy marriages, not to mention her mother's. She's at odds about deciding."

Cora spoke further on the topic and then asked, "If you were forced to choose which man she should marry, who would it be?"

He stopped short, and she stumbled against him. Peering down into her face, he said, "I shall not reveal that thought."

"Why not?" Cora pleaded.

He wore a doleful expression. "What if I am incorrect?"

"I'll concede that. Let's just say *if* you had to choose, which man would suit her best?"

"That is a trick question."

"My, aren't you the modern man suddenly?" She narrowed her eyes.

"I aim to please."

"Enough, Hugh. Which man?"

"Very well. I suppose . . ."

"Hi, ho!" Ralph bounded in their direction along the path. "We have secured all we need for the ball."

"Are we never to have any privacy?" Hugh muttered under his breath.

Cora snuggled closer to him and whispered, "In two weeks." She directed her gaze to Ralph. "That's exciting, but shouldn't you tell us what the theme is so we may dress properly?"

Ralph stopped and sent them a roguish grin. "I shall never mislead you. Trust me. As you shall be the newly wedded couple, you shall not require costumes."

Cora and Hugh shared suspicious glances, then turned their attention to Ralph.

Cora shrugged a shoulder. "I'm okay with that."

Hugh wasn't so easily put off. "I think it unseemly our guests should participate, and we shall not. Tell us your theme, and we shall prepare." He sent his cousin a stern look.

Ralph appeared undeterred. "Very well. Allow me to consult Branston. He shall be the deciding voice." He turned and sprinted away like a small boy itching for trouble.

Disapproval gleamed in Hugh's eyes. "Why do I sense impending doom?"

"Don't worry. I'm sure they wouldn't do anything to embarrass us." She tugged his arm to continue walking. "Answer my question."

He looked at her with feigned innocence.

"Don't do that. Tell me which man you believe would suit Olive best."

"You shall not like it," he said it with a straight face.

She crossed her arms. "Hugh!"

"Very well. Christopher MacGregor."

This declaration surprised Cora. As close as he and Crawford appeared to be, with their uncommon camaraderie between servant and master, she'd assumed he would be Hugh's choice.

He studied her briefly. "Does that concern you?"

She shrugged. "Not *concern* . . ."

Gingerly, he took her hand and held it. "Then what?"

"I understand the gardener is very nice and all." She paused.

A wry smile passed over his face, and he lifted a brow.

"Hugh—he's just too old for her. Don't you see that?"

"I do not. Crawford is much older than she is as well." Hugh dropped her hand and stretched his arms over his head, intertwining his hands behind his neck.

"Yet not as much as Mr. MacGregor."

Hugh narrowed his eyes. "Cora, love, you *are* marrying someone two hundred years older than yourself. You are aware of that, correct?"

She sent him a glare. "Hugh, do be serious. I think we should bow out and let them settle things. Olive has her own decision to make, and it seems those are her only choices. After all, how is she to meet anyone else?"

Hugh drew closer to her. "Excellent point. Let us focus on our own marriage." He leaned down, his lips close to hers.

Cora placed one finger against his mouth. "I'll allow one kiss, and then we must settle the rest of the wedding plans."

He captured her hand and brought it to his lips. "This kiss does not count toward my allowance." As his lips skimmed hers, footfalls sounded down the path.

They turned their irritated gazes toward Ralph and Branston, and Hugh exclaimed, "My word! Can you two not leave us in peace for a moment?"

The men's steps faltered, faces falling.

Cora told them, "Don't let this grouch get you down. He just thinks too highly of kissing."

Slack-jawed, the two men recovered quickly and burst into laughter.

Branston stepped forward and bowed. "It may be improper for me to say, but if I had such a lovely bride, I should lose no time in kissing her at every chance." He lifted Cora's hand and kissed the back of her fingers.

"Here, here!" Ralph shouted.

Hugh sent him a scathing expression, which did nothing to deter his cousin.

Cora tucked her arm through Hugh's. "We appreciate all you're doing to make the ball a success. Now please tell us what the theme is."

Branston returned to Ralph's side, and they bowed, each wearing wide, prideful grins.

"As I am not of the family," Branston said, "I shall allow Ralph to announce our scheme." He gave an exaggerated bow, one arm behind his back slanting toward the sky.

Hugh's lips thinned, holding his silence.

Ralph strode forward. "It is to be a masked wedding ball— every man shall don wedding apparel and each lady shall be a bride—all wearing masks." He beamed, full of his own brilliance.

Hugh's laugh grew. "You jest, surely?"

Uncertain how to take in the strange suggestion, Cora thought she'd never heard of such a thing and said so.

Branston asked, "Do you not see how utterly unique it shall be?"

Cora looked between the two young men. "Whose idea was this?"

"It sort of altered when Branston said all the women should come as a bride, and I took the bait and suggested the men should be the grooms." His proud smirk accentuated his puffed-out chest.

Hugh placed an arm around Cora's waist. "Do you agree to this—lark?"

She peered into his eyes and nodded. "I don't think we should do it unless *both* of us agree."

He looked at her for a long while. "Very well. You two wastrels may go forward. The invitations should go out as soon as is expedient, so our guests shall have time to prepare."

They cheered, sending the birds shooting skyward to escape the silly men.

Cora thought if she could fly, she should have followed them. She glanced at the arch, not too far away, and longed for home.

CB&SO

Cora perched in a corner as maids and footmen scurried around the former great hall, cleaning and rearranging furniture. This room being the largest required a great deal of preparation. They polished, brought more crystal than she'd ever seen, and arranged mirrors throughout. Hugh explained it would increase the candlelight along with the crystal.

When he came into the cavernous room and caught sight

of her, he came to her side. "Well, my dear, how goes the planning?"

Cora linked arms with him. "It appears to be going well." She pointed to the myriad of crystal vases. "Why so many? And where will we get enough flowers to fill them?"

The corners of his eyes crinkled, and he squeezed her hand resting on his arm. "Where do you believe all the flowers with which I romanced you came?" His thumb caressed the back of her hand. "The estate does not have a greenhouse, yet Branston's does."

A footman approached and extended a silver tray holding a piece of folded paper. "For you, my lord."

"Thank you, Alexander." He broke the seal on the message, reading slowly. His lips pressed into a tight line, and he folded the paper and tucked it into his coat pocket. "I shall see you later, my dear. I have business to attend to." He kissed her briefly and taking long strides left her to continue her perusal of the decorations.

It pleased her to see that he acknowledged each servant by name—and kindly so. He treated them very well. The concern in his eyes while reading the letter gave her pause. She hoped it wasn't bad news.

Chapter Twenty-Three

Cora attempted to stifle a yawn as she entered the breakfast room the next morning. Hugh reclined in his customary chair, a cup of coffee in one hand, the other holding the newspaper. He looked up at her approach and rose.

"After a yawn such as that, I dare not inquire as to the quality of your sleep." He went to the sideboard, prepared a cup of tea, and brought it to her.

Cora dropped onto the padded Chippendale chair. "Thank you." She sipped while she admired the dining table. The mahogany revealed reddish tones from meticulous care, its fine even grain shining with careful polishing. Judith's description of the antique furniture returned to Cora, reminding her that the popular wood was a symbol of strength.

"Shall I fetch your breakfast as well?" He asked with a lopsided grin that she found most attractive.

"I'll serve myself in a moment. I want caffeine for now." She watched him over the cup. "Were you able to resolve the reason for yesterday's message?"

"Ah, indeed. It is all taken care of." The glint in his eyes did not go unnoticed by Cora, a secretive look if she'd ever seen one.

Hugh folded his paper and resumed drinking coffee, the strong, pungent scent of the brew permeating the air.

"I noticed you only drink coffee in the morning and tea in the afternoon."

He thoughtfully chewed a bite of toast and nodded. After swallowing, he said, "Yes. Coffee gives me an extra lift. Although I must confess, I am not overly fond of the flavor."

"That's exactly what Selena says." Her mood dampened at the thought of her sister.

"I am sorry. We shall endeavor to do all possible to reunite you with your sister." He stood and came to her side, kissed the top of her head, and said, "I must be away to handle a matter. I shall see you at dinner."

A flush of apprehension hit her. "You'll be gone all day?"

He must have read the unease because he cradled her cheek in his palm. "It is of no concern. I merely have a task to attend to, and it shall consume the better part of the day. It is nothing for you to worry over."

The truth in his tone eased her somewhat, and she relaxed. "All right. I'm sure there's plenty to do for the wedding plans." She rose and stretched her arms to encompass him into a hug, inhaling his scent. The more they were together, she realized she'd made the right decision to marry him.

'Whither thou goest . . .'

The moment they shared appeared to engulf them in a flash of isolation as if they were the only two people who existed in a perfect place where nothing could reach them. An intimacy on a spiritual level.

A sudden revelation overcame Cora. Was that what God wanted with her? To know her on a deeper spiritual level, caring and guiding her come what may?

She slipped a few inches from Hugh and met his eyes. Is that what God was trying to show her through this entire experience, through Hugh himself and her love for him?

Just as she had done with Hugh, she judged God outwardly, what she saw, and in her bitterness, made Him out to be the one who stole everything from her. Had she been wrong?

God had given her Hugh. She did not doubt He brought them together, and she would be forever grateful. Perhaps she was beginning to truly see God in a different light.

She smiled up at the actor she had loathed not so long ago and whose eyes looked on her adoringly. In a voice laced with emotion, she said, "I love you, Hugh."

His eyes flickered across her every feature, his hand rose to cup her chin. "And I love you for all eternity." Hugh's lips parted, and gently, he pressed them to hers for a moment. He pulled back and said, "Nothing shall ever part us. Not even time itself."

A cough sounded. "I beg your pardon, my lord. Your horse

is ready." Alexander bowed and departed.

His cheek against hers, he whispered into her ear, "Remind me to throttle that man upon my return."

Cora laughed. "I'll help you."

CঙEO

That evening at dinner, Cora entered an empty dining room. She checked the ruddy-brown rosewood mantel clock just as it chimed the hour. Where was Hugh?

The footman asked if she would like to be seated or wait in the parlor with a drink of some sort.

"No, Alexander. I'll wait here. Bring me a glass of lemon water please."

"Yes, my lady."

Candles flickered down the long table, the room exuding a romantic aura bringing back the goodbye she and Hugh shared that morning. The shift in their relationship was beyond what she could explain. It was mysterious —as if he was truly a part of her now. They no longer argued but discussed and worked out whatever misunderstandings may have caused a rift between them.

By the time Cora sat, the footman had returned with her drink. She settled into the chair, comfortable but worried why Hugh had not arrived for dinner. She sighed deeply and considered returning to her room when she heard a commotion at the front door.

Fast footsteps pounded toward the dining room, and she stood. The door opened abruptly, and Hugh bolted through, hair wet, mud marring his hessians.

Cora hurried to him. "Are you okay?"

He grasped her upper arms. "I am well. In my haste to come to you for dinner, I had to travel through a cruel storm."

She brushed the rain from his forehead. "I began to worry. You always keep your word."

He trailed his fingertips along her neck. "I am here now. Please allow me to change into dry clothes, and I shall return soon."

She nodded and watched his tall, lean figure leave the room, then went to her seat and breathed a sigh of relief.

When he returned, he appeared unscathed and sat smiling at her like the cat that *wanted* to eat the canary.

As if on cue, the servants began bringing the meal. The pleasant smell wafted toward them like a mist carried by a breeze. Savory aromas of meat mingled with vegetables followed by ambrosial scents of sweets.

Cora couldn't remember a meal she had enjoyed more. By the time they had completed all the courses, relaxation coursed through her entire body. She wanted to melt into her soft bed and sleep. She dreamed of falling asleep in Hugh's arms and smiled.

"And to what may I credit that smile?" He teased and reclined in his chair.

Cora pulled in a long, gratifying breath through her nose. "You, my dear, *you*."

He narrowed his eyes. "Me?"

"Yes. I don't think I've ever been so relieved to see you come through that door." She pointed toward the opening.

"I am sorry to have worried you needlessly." He dropped his chin to his chest. "Yet I assure you the surprise I have brought will be worth the concern."

Cora perked. "Surprise?"

"Ah. I have your attention now." The pleasure etched on his face delighted Cora.

"You do, sir."

He rose and came to pull her chair out. She stood, and he wrapped her into a hug, making her feel desired, protected, and cherished in a way she'd never experienced before she met him.

Timidly, she asked, "And when will I receive the surprise?"

The vibration of his chuckle triggered her heart to race. Only three days and he belonged to her.

 C3 80

The eve of their wedding came upon Cora with a rush of emotions. Not of indecision but concern about her being a good wife to him. She was not a young bride, yet he was not a young groom either. They had much to learn. Would she be all he wanted in a wife?

When she'd told him she wanted to be alone at the chapel to pray, his face altered into concern. "Shall I attend you there? We may pray together." His face made her think of a small boy, afraid he's done something wrong but unable to figure out what it may be.

"I merely want to have some alone time with God. You have helped me strengthen my faith. I needed that. I'd blamed God long enough for taking my family from me. Now I have to thank Him for you."

She gently patted his chest. "God put me on this path that led to you, and whatever the future holds here or in my time, we will be in it together with Him guiding our steps."

He claimed her hand and pressed a kiss to her palm.

Cora strolled to the chapel, a light mist engulfing her, but it was of no concern. Birds still sang above, and the colors of the flowers lining the path shone brightly. She was truly, fully happy for the first time in her life. He loved her as she was—shortcomings and all.

She knelt before the altar and spoke to God, thanking Him, asking Him to forgive her for her unbelief and for blaming Him all those years.

Selena's face flashed before her just as she made a move to leave. Doubt crumbled her resolve, and she fought it. What if she never saw her sister again? Further what ifs crashed against her. Knowing the enemy was attacking, crippled by the emotion and unable to pray any longer, with tears falling, she whispered into the silent chapel, "Jesus, help me."

A calm washed over her while she also knew the attacks would come again. She had to be ready. She needed God to stand against what she couldn't. "I trust You, God. Please strengthen me."

Feeling calmer still, she rose, strolled through the mist, and went to her room. A long bath would help soothe her. Olive was waiting, the bath already prepared.

"Olive, thank you. How did you know this is just what I needed?"

The maid blushed. "This is the eve afore your wedding, my

lady. What else should I do?" She smiled sweetly.

Cora turned toward the bed where Olive had laid out the nightclothes and halted. An enormous basket sat upon the bed, overflowing with bottles, boxes, and luxuries. "What's this?"

Olive beamed. "Lord Hedsworth said to tell you to read the message."

Tentatively, Cora went to the basket and broke the seal.

My dearest love,

From the moment we met, your sweet lavender scent captured me. These luxuries are for you to indulge yourself prior to our wedding. You deserve to be pampered.

Shakespeare says beauty lives with kindness. In you, his words prove truth, for you, my love, are both.

Throughout time, I am yours,

Hugh

Cora's eyes fixed on the romantic words in his bold writing. Her heart pounded, and the scent of lavender filled the chamber. With trembling fingers, she touched each item, not believing she used products from the exact same company in her own time. The basket held soap, cologne, powder, a lace bag containing dried lavender buds, and lavender toothpaste.

Selena didn't understand Cora's borderline obsession with everything lavender, one time declaring if she crammed another lavender product into their bathroom cabinets she would disown her. Her sister was dramatic that was certain, perhaps Hugh should get her into acting.

Thinking of Selena, Cora realized if it were not for her sister, she'd gladly stay in this era with Hugh. The unexpected disclosure came as a shock. If only they could come and go as Hugh had done all these years. The idea brought a pleasant sensation, and she shivered.

"My lady?" Olive said softly. "Would you care for me to put the lavender in the water now?"

Hugh *liked* her lavender scent. She picked up the small alabaster jar containing the toothpaste, her name elegantly printed on the lid. So Hugh had her own personal blend created. He really had thought of everything.

Olive came to stand beside Cora and placed a hand on her arm. "My lady?"

"Hm?" Cora brought her gaze to Olive. "Oh, I'm sorry. Yes. That would be very nice. Thank you."

The maid smiled knowingly. "Are you a tad nervous, my lady? I know you do not enjoy large gatherings. But his Lordship made the wedding a small affair for you."

"Yes?" She considered Olive's words and realized she was nervous. "I suppose so."

"Your dress arrived while you were out. Would you care to try it on one last time to be certain all is well?"

Cora inhaled and slowly released a shaky breath, her focus moving from the bed to the snowy white dress hanging over the paneled dressing screen across the room.

The Brussels lace overlay cradled tiny pearls shimmering in the candlelight. Her breath hitched at the sight. She was finally to be married.

At her age, she'd never thought it possible. Why had she not trusted God that if it were to happen then it would?

Taking a deep breath, she steadied herself as Olive supported the dress tenderly across her extended arms. A rush of butterflies fluttered in her stomach. Tomorrow was her wedding day. Nausea replaced the flutter, and she rushed to the chamber pot.

"My lady!" Olive hurried to her side.

Cora gulped as she watched the maid and held up one hand. "I'm fine, Olive. Really. I thought I would be sick, but it has passed."

Olive retrieved a damp cloth and came to kneel by her, patting Cora's face.

A knock sounded, and the door to the parlor eased open. "Am I allowed to see my bride the eve before?" Hugh's cheerful voice echoed through the chamber.

His eyes met Cora's, and he bounded toward her and dropped to his knees. "Olive, what is the meaning of this?"

The maid looked at Cora before she answered, "We were about to try on the dress, and she became ill. Her face paled, and she ran to the chamber pot."

Hugh's face blanched, and he took the cloth from Olive. "I shall care for her. Please get the doctor."

Cora sat back. "I'm fine." Cold sweat dampened her skin, and Hugh began to stroke her face and neck.

Olive twisted her hands shakily. After a moment, she looked at Cora. "Pardon me, my lady, may it be that you are with child?"

Hugh's head shot up, staring at Olive, then at Cora, mouth hanging open.

Cora's heart raced, and she gripped his arm forcefully. "No! I am not." The incredulous expression on Hugh's face frightened her, and she almost read his thoughts. Discounting her age, she could practically see him counting the weeks they'd been here. She gripped the front of his shirt, pulled him toward her, and whispered something in his ear.

His face brightened, and he looked at Olive. "She is not, Olive." He wrapped an arm around Cora and pulled her up with him. "I still believe we should summon the doctor. Something caused your sickness, and we must establish what it is."

He helped her to the settee, and once seated, draped a blanket over her knees. She grabbed his arm. "Please don't call the doctor. I know what caused my nausea." A look passed between them, and Hugh dismissed Olive and sat beside Cora.

He placed his palm on her forehead. "You have no fever. That is good."

She closed her eyes and leaned against the back of the settee. "Hugh . . ." She became disoriented and pushed her fingers against her forehead, a headache forming. "I am sorry to upset you. I really will be fine. The full realization that at fifty I am to be married hit me full on when I saw the dress. I honestly don't know why I reacted that way."

Cora blew out a tired breath. The fact that it is white might be the reason. Unable to look at him, she swallowed and swung her gaze toward the garment, once again hanging on the screen.

Hugh remained quiet for a long while, then held her hand. "I believe I understand." He cleared his throat. "I am aware that things are different in your time, Cora. All fall short of God's desire for us. Please understand that I want you, no matter your past."

Cora blinked. Her lips parted, then closed. He thought—?

"Hugh, I think you misunderstand." Unable to broach such a personal subject, she considered how to say it and suddenly understood the implications to what he alluded.

"Wait. Let me get this straight. You grew up in the Regency period when men thought it was okay to . . . dally . . . with women but women weren't supposed to do the same? Correct?" Her ire grew the more she thought about it. He was giving *her* a pass?

He stiffened and dropped her hand. "Pardon?"

"Oh, don't *pardon* me! You're willing to forgive my past indiscretions, but what about your own?"

He rose and ran a hand through his thick hair. "I am confused. Did you not grow upset upon seeing the white dress because of your past?"

Cora jumped to her feet and stood before him. "No! You idiot! It's because I'm fifty years old and *never* been with a man." She swallowed. "I'm nervous."

He appeared as if someone had struck him. She glared at him until she could stand it no longer. "What do you have to say for yourself?"

His face lit like a candle. "Are you upset because you believe you have no experience and I have?"

The foolishness of the situation washed over her. Believing

him a man of the Regency, she allowed herself to accuse him of being . . . What? She thought herself akin to a young woman fresh out of school with no knowledge of anything. Maybe it was just embarrassment at being so simple-minded.

Without touching her, he stepped into her personal space and muttered, "We are equally matched. Neither of us has *any* experience in the sense of matrimony. Is that not a good beginning?"

Cora shamefully cupped her face in both hands. "Oh, Hugh." Her shoulders quaked.

He pulled her into his arms. "My dear. We are so well-suited."

Rather than tears, Cora chuckled, and he held her tighter. "I am such an idiot. I apologize for calling you one."

"Indeed. I think it most appropriate. Perhaps we both are." He laughed. "After all, I was most concerned when Olive made mention that you were perhaps with child."

"Surely you knew that to be an impossibility?"

"Hm. Perhaps. Yet I have heard of situations—"

"Oh, please." Cora waved her hand in the air dismissively. "Once again, we've had a misunderstanding and a reconciliation. Let's pray these occurrences are far and few between in the years to come."

"Indeed." He encased her in his arms and said into her hair with much emotion, "Whether in this time or the future."

Cora's mind traveled to the future. A future with Hugh whether in his century or her own.

Chapter Twenty-Four

After Hugh left Cora's bedroom, she relished the lavender-scented soak, sighing in contentment while Olive bustled around the room on the other side of the privacy screen. The girl chatted away excitedly at being asked to attend Cora at the wedding as her maid of honor.

Hugh had accepted her request with a raised eyebrow and asked, "You know you are flying in the face of convention . . . correct?"

She'd responded by telling him she didn't care who thought what, and Olive was the closest woman she had to a friend here. He'd agreed with a curt nod, and that was that. Her maid would now be a maid of honor.

Cora emerged from the screen, freshly bathed and donning

her nightclothes. She watched Olive as she poised in front of the long mirror, the new dress Cora ordered for her held against her form, admiring the reflection.

"Olive, you look lovely. You'll make a splendid maid of honor."

The young woman twirled around, mouth agape. "My lady, I am that sorry for preening so. I have never worn such a handsome gown."

Cora crossed the room to her dressing table and removed a small box from the drawer, then turned toward Olive. "In my ti . . . Where I come from, it is customary for the bride to gift the maid of honor with a token of their friendship and appreciation." She extended the little box.

Olive's mouth dropped, and her skin turned pink. "It is too much. You have given me this lovely dress which is most kind of you and my lord."

Cora stepped closer and picked up the maid's hand, placing the gift into her palm. "Please accept it. I owe you much. You have given me your friendship and served me above and beyond what I deserve."

The incredulous expression on Olive's face caused Cora to be ashamed. She'd held so many pity parties for herself and now saw this person who had nothing. If not for Hugh's Christian kindness, this poor girl would be in the workhouse. Humbled by her reaction, she grew more determined to help her find a truly good man to love.

"Open it."

Olive untied the satin ribbon, fingers trembling, and removed the lid of the box. She gasped when her eyes held the contents. "Oh, my lady. It is so . . ." Tears streamed down her cheeks, and she grabbed Cora into a tight hug but released her immediately. "I am that sorry, my lady. It was improper for me to act so."

"Olive, that's not true. You did exactly as I would have done, so do not be ashamed."

Gulping a breath, the girl nodded and clutched the petite topaz cross to her chest.

Cora removed the necklace from her grasp. "Turn around, and I'll put it on for you. There's no reason to wait for the wedding."

Olive closed her eyes as if with pleasure and nodded. When she turned to look in the mirror, Cora almost cried at the young woman's elated expression.

The room dimmed, and they turned to see that a draft had extinguished some of the candles lighting the room. They both laughed, and Cora said, "I suppose we both are in need of a good night's sleep. Tomorrow will be a tiring day, what with the wedding in the morning, a wedding breakfast and then the ball."

Olive's smile grew so wide Cora thought her face may crack and chuckled. She gave Olive a brief hug. "Now, off to bed. I'll see you in the morning."

Olive curtsied, a hand pressing the necklace against her chest. "Thank you, my lady."

Cora sat on the edge of the bed, her head surging like the nor'easter winds that raged across the Boston area from time to time. Elated and nervous about the following day, she prayed for peace and calm. God had revealed she was making the right decision to marry Hugh but that didn't stop her from the insecurity of their first day as husband and wife.

☙❧

The morning light stretched across the counterpane of Cora's bed, and she blinked, lazily stretching arms above her head, fully rested. A relaxed sensation washed over her until she realized it was her wedding day.

She sat upright, eyes scanning the room. Where was Olive? She needed her presence as a supporting anchor. Before she bounded from the bed, Olive darted in and slammed the door closed. She pressed her body against the door, eyes wide with fear.

"My lady." Her breathing came in quick gasps. "His Lordship is in the hall and desires to see you."

Cora's face crumpled. "Why?"

"He says he wanted to come to you afore the day ended last eve, but Master Ralph and Lord Elliot kept him too late."

Still seated, Cora placed her hands on her hips. "Tell him it's too late now. A bride should not see her intended on the day of the wedding until the ceremony."

Olive swallowed hard and cracked the door. "My lord, Lady Hedsworth says she is not allowed to see you until the ceremony."

Hugh spoke loud enough for Cora to hear. "Tell Lady Hedsworth that as we are already married, I want to see her now."

Cora heard the quiver of a laugh in his voice but responded with all seriousness. "Tell Lord Hedsworth that he must

336

remember his place and recall their *previous* acquaintance and hold to this tradition." She knew he would catch on to her reference, meaning they weren't actually married yet. A long silence ensued, and she waited for his reply.

In a lower tone, he said, "Very well. I shall close my eyes, and you bring my bride to the door, and I shall speak to her without looking upon her face."

Well, that was creative. She had to give him that.

As she rose from the bed, he said loudly, "She must close her eyes as well. Else it would not be fair."

Cora stopped in the middle of the room and tittered. "Yes, my dear." At the door, she told Olive, "Stand guard and do not allow this door to be opened any wider."

"Yes, my lady." The maid's eyes glinted with humor.

Stepping to the door, Cora squeezed her eyes shut. "Hugh, are your eyes closed too?"

"Yes, love."

Olive whispered in her ear. "He has placed his hand through the opening, my lady."

Cora reached out and fumbled until their hands met. His relieved sigh was audible, and he tugged her hand through the crack.

"Cora, give me a kiss before we part."

She moved closer to the door, feeling foolish. His lips found hers with ease while Olive stifled a giggle. Cora fought the oncoming laugh and brought a hand to caress his face. His lips curved upward against her own.

He chuckled. "This is not what I envisioned."

"Maybe if you'd come to see me last night it could've been avoided." A hint of sarcasm laced her words.

"Indeed, I do apologize. My cousin and my friend are most entertaining."

Cora lay her head upon his shoulder. "Don't let it happen again." She placed a hand on his chest and pushed him away. "I shall see you later."

He sighed. "Soon."

Olive closed the door, and Cora looked at her, thinking the girl would swoon. "Olive, don't be so silly."

The woman grinned playfully. "Oh, that a man would treat me so, my lady."

Cora touched her shoulder. "Does Mr. MacGregor or Crawford not treat you so?"

She stared at the ceiling. "Not like that. They compliment and say sweet things, yet not as my lord does with you."

"Well, we'll see about all that once I'm married and settled."

She shot Cora a questioning glance.

They prepared for the ceremony, beginning with Olive, then she helped Cora dress in the lace gown sprinkled with pearls. They stared at one another nervously—for entirely different reasons.

Olive, along with Mrs. Duckworth and Mrs. Muse, escorted Cora to the chapel, all the men and guests already in place. Branston stood by the door and the glance he gave Olive was unmistakable. Cora then realized they'd never met. There had been no need as a Regency lady's maid kept to herself, rarely meeting their guests. The slackened expression and softness in his eyes betrayed his admiration of the girl. She had a few moments to ponder the incident, waiting for him to open the door.

As soon as they gave the signal the bride had arrived, the rich, lyrical music of the violin began. The sweet strains of the smooth, emotional tones gripped Cora's spirit, and she floated into the church. The fluttering in her stomach increased, and her mouth dried.

The walk down the aisle was dreamlike. Cora pictured her family sitting on the first pew, their faces alight with pride as they watched her approach her future husband. She shook off the ghostly image and her gaze met Hugh's. All fear fled at the expression of contentment he wore.

He truly loved her.

She barely noticed Ralph as the best man by Hugh's side, and she claimed her place. The words the vicar spoke sounded as if in the background, murmurs of sacred lines. The remainder of the ceremony blurred until Hugh placed the topaz ring upon her finger and lifted the veil, his blue eyes caressing her face. Before their vows were sealed with a kiss, he whispered close to her ear, his breath tickling her skin.

"You are the most beautiful bride I have ever seen, Lady Hedsworth."

Her eyes moistened at the sincerity of his tone, his eyes, and when he kissed her, she knew it held everything she'd hoped for. It was as if it were the first kiss they'd ever shared.

They moved to the vestry where Crawford and Ralph witnessed the marriage by entering the marriage lines into the parish register book as well as the vicar, parish clerk, and the newly married couple.

Hugh and Cora stepped outside ahead of the guests into the cool morning light. Cora closed her eyes and breathed in the scents of flowers, earth, and unpolluted air. The ethereal vision of her family surrounding them surprised her. It differed from what she'd imagined in the church. The grief of them not attending her wedding was suddenly like a great weight upon her shoulders, a grief in physical form. The air left her lungs, and she gasped to catch a breath.

Not a panic attack! No, please not now, Lord.

She gripped Hugh's arm tightly, and his head snapped around. The instant their eyes met, his neck stiffened, and he gave a pained stare. His smile fell away. "What's wrong? You appear ill."

Cora painted on a cheerful expression, stretched toward him, and murmured, "I think I'm having a panic attack. I . . ." She didn't want to tell him what she'd imagined about her family's presence. "I'll tell you later. Just please don't leave my side."

Hugh rested his hand on top of hers, and she slackened her grip, looking at the scar on his hand. She realized she had not seen him toy with it in a long while, something he did when difficulty plagued him. If he remained calm after what he'd been through as a boy and the trauma of traveling into the future, then she could as well.

Cora said a silent prayer for strength, and the peace she'd sensed with each prayer returned. After she looked at him again, the genuine smile she sent him caused his face to relax. She lifted his hand placed on hers and tenderly kissed the scar.

He shivered and bent. "Are we now able to share kisses in public, wife?"

A low, pleasant hum coursed through her limbs. "You are the Regency expert, husband. So is it proper for married couples to share PDA?" She peaked her eyebrows.

His face wore confusion for a moment, and then the confusion cleared, understanding the reference. He tilted his head back a fraction. "Propriety has many facets in this time."

The guests' chatter and laughter surrounded them on the walk to the house, bringing added comfort to Cora than she would've predicted. She hung onto Hugh's arm like a lifeline. Other than Selena, he was her only family now.

For a second, her mind focused on her sister, but she quickly shoved it away. How was she? Were she and Randall reconciling at this very moment? With Cora's absence, Selena may have gone to him out of grief for her missing sister. Stillness crept into her heart, saying not to agonize over something she had no control over.

Hugh stopped their procession and addressed Ralph. "Please escort everyone inside, and we shall be with you in a moment."

Ralph's wide, knowing smile met each of theirs. "Ah. A little while alone?" His eyes moved skyward, then he bowed and backed away from them, herding everyone inside.

Hugh held Cora's hand, and they strode to the arbor-covered bench. Once out of sight, he wrapped her in a loving embrace, silent, just holding her close. Birds warbled, and a meow announced Lizzy. They dropped their gazes to the bench where the mottled cat perched, looking up at them expectantly, green eyes wide. She lifted a paw and stretched it, her *toes* separating as if to say she wanted to be included in the affection.

Hugh chuckled. "Not today, my girl. Today is for us. We shall spend time with you later."

Cora positioned her fingers on his chin and rotated his face back to her. "She came with us, and we must take her back home."

He sent her a cocky grin. "Are you commanding me so soon after our nuptials?"

"I'm glad you're smiling. I want no misunderstandings between us. My ex . . ."

His smile dropped. "Yes?"

Cora puffed out an annoyed breath. "Sorry. Old wounds. I'll tell you all about it sometime."

His fingers meandered around her neck and paused at the nape, holding her in place. "I am giving you fair warning. I am about to kiss you now, and there are no witnesses."

Their eyes flickered over one another's face, and she nodded. "Indeed."

He stroked a strand of hair away from her face, allowing his fingertips to caress her temple and trail to her lips.

She sucked in an unstable breath, waiting expectantly, but when he made no move, she frowned. "I thought you were going to kiss me?" She wrapped her arms around his waist.

"All in good time. I'm enjoying your lovely face."

A pleasurable sigh escaped. Apparently, she *had* to come to the Regency era to find a truly romantic man. And she thanked God for being so generous, proof that He loved her even with all her failings.

ೞ

Cora and Hugh wandered, arm in arm on the garden path, speaking softly when Ralph and Branston found them. Cora saw them first and smiled a greeting.

"Hi, ho!" Ralph sang out. "We have come to bring you to your wedding breakfast."

Branston stepped behind the couple and prodded them forward. "Off you go."

The breakfast room had been prepared for the occasion since there were so few guests, and the great hall was nearly ready for the ball that evening. Cora watched the small group already partaking of the meal. The wedding cake looked like a giant fruitcake, but she said nothing as it was the tradition of the era as Hugh had told her.

Tantalizing aromas of tea, coffee, and hot chocolate perfumed the air. The sideboard groaned with an assortment of yeasty-scented breads, toast, ham, eggs, and fruit. Cora had forbidden boiled tongue being served and nearly gagged at the thought.

Cora, thankful Hugh never left her side, tried to relax with all the well-wishing guests and ate a tolerable amount of breakfast, though her stomach wasn't all that interested. The last guest departed, and all she wanted was a soft bed to sleep in until the ball. If only she and Hugh could return to the future.

Under the table, his hand lay upon her knee, and she brought her gaze to Hugh. She squeezed his hand, giving him a feeble smile. Fatigue washed over her, and guilt swelled. She shouldn't feel like this on her wedding day.

Hugh leaned closer. "You appear weary."

Cora inspected his blue gaze, getting lost in the affection glistening there. "I am. I'm really sorry. We have hours until the ball, and all I want to do is sleep." She looked away, not wanting to see his disappointment. They wanted the same thing, but she did not have the strength for anything except slumber. "I'm sorry." She repeated. "This has been so stressful, and my only coping skill is that of my bed."

"Alone, I fear." There was no anger in his tone, merely sadness. "I do understand. I should merely like to hold you in my arms until your sorrow passes. Which I know it shall."

Cora saw the truth fixed on his face. She was a very fortunate woman to have a husband who was kind, understanding—a man who held all the biblical traits of love. She cradled his face in her hands and kissed him, uncaring who watched. Tears burned, and she blinked them away.

"Wait here for a moment." He crossed the room and pulled the bell for a servant. When Alexander arrived, he spoke low.

Hugh came to her, pulled her up, and led her to her chamber. "You shall have your much-needed rest, my dear." She noticed they made the very long way through the house before arriving at their adjoining rooms.

They had set aside the privacy screen, and servants were filling the tub with steaming water. The scent of lavender hung heavy, and she happily breathed it in and glanced at her new husband.

As if sensing her stare, he looked up and beamed with

satisfaction. "I promise I shall not intrude on your privacy. I shall retire to the library and read."

Cora sighed languidly. "I know you wouldn't. I'm already realizing you are a most thoughtful husband. I think that trait is mostly foreign in the twenty-first century."

He chuckled, and his indulgent look sent warmth through her very spirit. As he left she slid into the tub and lay back soaking away the unsettling thoughts she'd been fighting.

346

Chapter Twenty-Five

Cora woke with a start. Soft snoring brought a sense of unease. Turning to her side, she watched Hugh's tranquil face as he slept on his back, his muscular chest rising and falling gently.

Moonlight crept between the heavy curtains, and a beam lit his face. He appeared much younger in the pastel light.

She longed to glide her fingers over his face, yet she was afraid she'd waken him. What time was it? The ball was to begin at ten. Though she'd rested well, she bore the strain of putting on the proper face for an event that would last until dawn. A thought slammed into her. They would be going home tonight. She'd convinced herself since they arrived during a ball, they would return the same way. Excitement filled her, and she sat upright.

Cora sidled next to Hugh and whispered into his ear. "My love, I think we need to rise."

His breathing paused, and his head tilted toward her, eyes blinking. His groggy gaze brought a quiet laugh.

She pressed her lips to his and sat back. His eyes widened.

"Good morn, my sweetness." His fingers lifted to her cheek, and she heated at his touch.

She shoved his shoulder. "No, Hugh. It must be nearly time for the ball. It's still nighttime."

His gaze went to the window, and he shot up. "Surely Olive would have wakened us at the appropriate hour?"

Cora snatched the robe from the end of the bed and put it on.

"I'm sure she would. I'll check the clock." She went to the mantel and noted—just after nine. "We have less than an hour to be ready."

Hugh rose, stretched his long body, and groaned. "I believe I could have slept many hours more." He made his way toward her, arms outstretched, a look of mischief on his face. "We have slept together as man and wife now."

The shelter of his arms brought Cora to a place of protection. "Yes. And you were the perfect gentleman."

"Of course." He smirked. "Yet later I may not be so."

She chortled and hugged him close. "We may spend our night in *my* time."

His expression faltered for a second, then brightened. "Certainly."

Their affection halted by a knock, and Hugh ground out, "Blasted, Crawford."

Cora moved to stand beside him, and Hugh put an arm around her shoulders. With obvious irritation in his voice, he said, "Enter."

Olive strode into the room, Crawford on her heels. They curtsied and bowed, respectively and began preparing their lord and lady's garments. Hugh followed Crawford to his dressing room, leaving Olive to attend to her mistress.

As Cora put on her wedding dress for the second time that day, she remembered the appraisal Branston had given Olive.

"What did you think of Lord Elliot?"

Olive jerked, the ornate mask trembling in her hand, feathers shimmering as if in flight.

Cora allowed the maid to place the mask securely over her eyes. "I noticed how he stared at you."

"*Me*, my lady?" Olive's face blushed, and her hands trembled.

"Yes, *you*," Cora said with irony. "I know you noticed him too. He is a very charming young man."

Olive's eyes misted. "No, my lady. I am but a maid, and he is an earl. There could be no attachment as my station is much below his." Her voice shook with emotion.

Cora gave her a motherly hug. "Olive, you are more than a maid. Every woman is beyond what they do to survive. Lord Elliot is an honorable man."

She retrieved a handkerchief for Olive and pulled her to sit upon the settee. "Hugh would agree. After all, I'm a nobody but Lord Hedsworth fell in love with me, and nothing has stopped him from marrying me."

Olive's eyes rounded as she wiped her nose and stuttered, "I am not like you, my lady . . . you . . . are refined as a lady should be."

"That's kind of you to say." Cora brushed a loose strand of hair from her forehead." You are lovely, Olive, accept it. And you can learn as I have to be more refined. It is not your beauty alone that has Crawford and Mr. MacGregor following you around like puppies. You are sweet, kind-hearted, and intelligent."

The maid tittered and stroked her eyes with the handkerchief. "Truly?"

"Yes, truly." Cora patted her shoulder. "All will be well." She stood to meet Hugh, then paused. "Olive . . ." She bit her lip. "Do we happened to have a spare mask?"

The maid nodded.

"Good." Cora crossed the room and found one of her prettiest dresses she'd not worn and brought it to Olive. "Put this on with the mask and come to the ball."

Olive stepped back rapidly, shock registering on her face. "It would not be proper."

Cora placed her hands on her hips and attempted a stern glare. "Am I not your mistress?"

Olive nodded.

"Then I order you to do as I say." She raised her chin.

Hugh came into the room, and his gaze rotated from one woman to the other, his eyes narrowing. "Have I interrupted something?"

"No, my dear." Cora caught his arm and slanted a look at Olive. "I shall see you soon?"

Olive dipped a curtsy and nodded, swallowing hard.

"Good." Cora's gaze settled on her husband. "I'm ready."

Hugh peered into Cora's eyes, his eyes clouding with suspicion. "You are plotting something."

"Yes, dear. You are correct. And I do believe it is an excellent idea." She heaved him toward the door and glanced back to Olive.

Once in the hall, Hugh's low voice asked, "What was that about?"

Cora notched her chin and in a cool tone said, "Didn't you see how Branston surveyed Olive at the wedding?"

He laughed. "Seriously, my dear? I had eyes only for you. The entire Spanish Armada could have sailed up the river, and I would not have noticed."

"That's very poetic of you. I believe my plan will get things rolling for Olive. One of these men must make a stand for her, or she'll never decide. She's much too young to waste away if she truly wants a husband and children. If she doesn't, that's fine too."

He patted her hand atop his arm. "Wise words. In this time, she has not much of a future without a husband."

"Sad but true." Cora sighed. "Yet she could have a very happy life with a man like Branston."

Hugh stopped her. "You do realize that society frowns on a titled gentleman who marries far beneath him?"

Cora looked into his intense blue eyes. "I'm very aware of

that, but you know it does happen?" She cocked her head. "After all, you married me?"

☙❧

Cora's breath hitched at the sight of the ballroom teaming with couples, some dressed in outlandish wedding apparel, though most wore traditional attire. As she and Hugh's entrance became known, all clapped at their arrival. Hundreds of candles illuminated the great hall, shining from the highest rafters of the Tudor Hall—the oldest section of the impressive house.

Candlelight seemed to soak into the white plastered walls, emitting a glow. To Cora's romantic mind, it was like a fairyland, the genteel men and women moving gracefully around the room dressed in their finest.

How far society had sunk into public displays of depravity in her own time. She knew all eras had hidden scandal, but in the twenty-first century, it seemed nearly any type of behavior was acceptable. How easy it would be to live in this place compared to her own. The verdict came as a shock because she dearly missed Selena, her only family until now. She now had a husband.

Hugh asked, "Shall we dance?"

The scent of lavender and roses perfumed the smoky air, and she suddenly had a problem taking in a full breath. She drank in Hugh's charismatic presence, pushing aside the anxiety. *Lord, what was happening to her*? She'd prayed and believed this emotion was a thing of the past, but it kept resurfacing.

In his arms, she felt protected and cared for like she never had been with any other man. So, what was there to be afraid of? More importantly, God was with her and supplied all her needs. Her emotions immediately calmed at the thought.

Yes, God would always be with her.

"You wear a lovely expression. Would you care to enlighten your husband as to the source?" Hugh's tone teased, eyes intent on hers.

"We agreed to have no secrets?"

He guided her effortlessly around the room with the flow and enchantment of the music's notes and slanted his head. His face briefly hardened, worry written on the creases of his forehead. "Yes, we agreed."

Cora chuckled. "It's not dire. My thoughts were of Selena, and my mind strolled to that dark place where I think of my family from time to time—well, their absence." She gave a tightlipped grin. "Then I thought of how you make me feel. And . . . my thoughts went to God, my ultimate protector."

Hugh's bright countenance created warmth to spread through her. "That is the way it should be. God first. All others next." His lips brushed a quick kiss across her cheek as the dance continued.

Tired from dancing, they stood near the wall where a long refreshment table was loaded with drinks and tidbits to carry them through until the late supper. They watched the dancing and sipped on iced punch.

A woman wearing a brilliant red lace dress, a red-feathered mask, all embellished with pearls, glittered in the candlelight, danced past them. Cora's eyes bugged, unable to keep herself from gaping. She elbowed Hugh's ribs and hissed, "Who is that woman wearing red?" She immediately caught her mistake. "Sorry. I guess you wouldn't know since she wears a mask."

Hugh broke into a mirthless laugh. "My dear, other than you, everyone attending well knows who is behind that mask."

Cora's curiosity piqued. "Do tell."

He leaned over and whispered, "She is a notorious actress visiting a near relation we invited to the ball. They did not inform me of her attendance and to avoid scandal, I chose to look the other way." His face altered. "Have I done you a disservice? I do apologize. I should have consulted you."

Cora lifted a brow and shook her head. "It doesn't matter. As long as she doesn't do anything too outlandish."

"I shall make certain of that." Hugh grasped her hand. "Another dance?"

Though a bit fatigued, she couldn't refuse. By the end of the dance, they carried their punch to the garden. Cora's nerves hummed. "Hugh. May we please try the arch?"

Upon their exit, she saw Olive enter the room, and as if drawn by some magnetic force, Branston headed straight for the maid. She watched as Olive's timid smile emerged. Branston had recognized Olive, though she wore a mask.

Hugh followed her line of sight and gazed at the same scene. "Should we intervene?"

Cora placed a hand on his arm. "Let God handle it. To quote Regency vernacular, 'they will suit quite well.'"

He laughed, nodded, and led her to the terrace.

"I forgot to ask if you'd placed the letters where Ralph would find them."

He began to speak, huffing out a breath first. "I have."

Cora understood about the letters to Ralph and Branston, which detailed what they should do if they disappeared. He would leave the estate and all his holdings to Ralph and ask that Branston mentor his cousin.

"And yours to Olive?"

She nodded, emotion gripping her. She'd miss Olive—her friend. She prayed God would give her a man that would cherish her.

Arm in arm, they strolled the path toward the arch. Cora halted, her gaze roaming the garden. "Lizzy!"

Hugh patted her hand like a scared child who needed soothing. "She will be fine. If she does not return with us, everyone will continue to spoil and pamper her. They know how you adore the cat and will continue as you would."

A tear slipped from her eye. "I know."

He blotted the tear with his finger. "Whatever the outcome, we have one another always."

She knew he was right. Then why the melancholy? Her chin trembled as they walked on.

The sliver of moon barely lit their path, which illuminated the arch in an otherworldly aura that made her shiver. She clung closer to Hugh, who must have sensed her unease and put an arm around her shoulders.

He paused briefly as the arch was within their reach. "Are you ready?"

Cora sniffed and heaved in a long breath of the pungent air. They strode cautiously through the portal and once they reached the other side stopped. Hugh turned them to peer at the arch, Hedsworth House lying beyond, sounds of the ball filling the night.

They shared a look, and Cora said, "Should we see if it's . . ." She didn't know how to express what lay in her mind.

"Yes. We must find out if it worked."

With listless steps, they returned to the ballroom and found it just as it was. Merry music played, couples danced, candlelight cloaked the room in romantic light. Though the sight was delightful, Cora's joy faltered. Would she ever go home again?

෫෩

Cora scanned the room. Ralph stood near the fireplace, punch in hand, speaking with a short, balding man of middle years. Branston and Olive sat on a settee against one wall, a barely proper distance between them. Though they wore masks, both smiled with happiness she'd never seen on either of their faces. Though sadness washed through her, she touched Hugh's hand, got his attention, and jerked her head in the couple's direction.

His eyes widened in obvious surprise, then quirked a brow and heaved an exasperated sigh. "Touché my dear, touché."

"You can't fight romance you know?"

"Do I not know it?"

Cora fought mounting anger and sought a diversion, failing to keep the acerbity from her voice. "Do you really oppose Olive and Branston to have a relationship?"

Hugh twitched, his eyes curious. "Cora. I do not care for the sound of your voice. You concern me."

She wilted against him. "I'm so tired." The sensation of panic obsessed her. "Hugh . . . God has abandoned me. First my family, then Selena, now this. I feel like I'm in a coffin and someone's nailing it shut. I was convinced we'd go back tonight." She grabbed his upper arms and squeezed with all the strength she possessed. "I have to see Selena. She can't go back to Randall. He's wrong for her. He'll hurt her again." Her voice rose with each declaration.

Cora watched Hugh glance around the room. Thankfully, the music drowned out her voice. What was she doing? To Hugh, herself . . . Why did she give in to fear so easily?

Looking up again, she saw Branston and Olive approach, wearing anxious expressions. Olive took Cora's arm while Cora watched Hugh's face, horrified at her outburst. "My lord, allow me to escort my lady to her chamber."

Branston skirted around the women and murmured to Hugh, "We shall follow behind." He dipped his chin, eyes holding a question.

Hugh agreed, and as the four left the ballroom, the party surged onward.

While Olive quietened Cora, the men gathered in the private parlor.

Once Olive dressed Cora in a nightgown and tucked her into bed, Olive sat on the edge and held her hand. "My lady, may I get you a drink?"

Cora shook her head against the pillow. Shame washed over her. "I'm sorry, Olive."

"It is nothing to be shamed about, my lady. You have had a very long day." She wiped a lavender-scented cloth over

Cora's face. "You rest for a while and mayhap you and Lord Hedsworth shall return to the ball before the unmasking. It shall be hours yet."

The comfort of the bed and Olive's kind ministrations soothed Cora, and she sighed deeply. "That sounds wonderful. I'll just rest my eyes for a little while. Not long." She closed her eyes, and the bed moved as Olive left. The door to the parlor opened and shut and the room filled with silence.

Cora didn't sleep, but she felt better away from the crowd. The door creaked again, and she squeezed her eyes shut, only wanting to be left alone. Soft footsteps approached, and the bed gave way as someone sat.

"Cora?"

Hugh's low voice pierced her heart. She'd disappointed him again.

She cleared her throat, not lifting her lids. "Yes?"

"Please tell me why this keeps occurring. I fear you may be ill."

Turning her head away from him, she allowed hot tears to slip through her tightened eyelids. Her chest heaved as she tried to hold back the flow.

Hugh shifted on the bed and the press of his long body against hers caused the sobs to increase. "I . . . I've failed you— again."

He pressed a handkerchief against her cheek, she claimed it and dabbed her eyes.

"You could never disappoint me." His breath brushed her ear, and he pressed his mouth against her temple.

Quiet entered the room and hung like the morning mist

over the garden.

"Will you please share your feelings? Why do you believe you react this way?"

A lump caught in her throat, and she swallowed it away. "I failed my sister by my dependency on her after our parents died. So much so that her husband grew tired of my frequent presence, and he left."

A few sobs escaped before she continued, "And now I've left Selena, and he wants her back, and I'm not there to help." She curled into a ball and buried her head in the pillow. Her voice muffled, she cried, "Selena will think I've abandoned her." Her shoulders quaking, Cora hugged the pillow tighter.

Hugh encased her into a firm embrace and mumbled into her ear. "I believe this has been what you have struggled to discover until now. Mayhap the healing has begun."

Still holding Cora in his arms, he continued, "God is bigger than all of this. He brought you here for a reason. He brought *us* here for a reason." His hesitation was like a thousand words shifting in the air. "God brought you to the past so you may embrace *our* future together. The same way He did in sending me to the future."

Sobs racked her body. His words seeped into her heart and mind. Memories of how Selena coped when Randall departed. Her sister was a strong woman and supported and pulled Cora through her own periods of grief. She would manage again—with or without Cora.

Hugh's comforting arms around her, Cora slowly relaxed, muscles releasing their tension. His words echoed in her head.

He was right—God brought them together. Whatever time He chose for them would be where He wanted them, and she must accept it and find joy in it.

Chapter Twenty-Six

"Hugh, I know we don't have to wear the masks any longer. It's not as if they don't already know who *we* are, *but* I'd rather keep mine on to hide my puffy, red eyes." She slipped the ornate mask on, and Olive secured it.

He laughed. "Whatever your heart desires, my love."

"Thank you, Olive." Cora stood from the dressing table and faced her maid. "Now, you go back to the ball—" Her words were cut off by a knock.

Hugh crossed the room and opened the door to Branston filling the space wearing a sheepish grin. His eyes traveled straight to Olive. "I came to see if all is well."

"Sure, you did." Cora pressed her lips tightly for a moment, then eased Olive toward Lord Elliot. "We'll follow you. We do not want a scandal by your arrival without chaperones."

Hugh sent her a smug look, and they departed for the rest of the ball, following behind Branston and Olive.

Cora's gaze surveyed the way Branston kept his hand on top of Olive's as he guided her to the hall. His eyes returned to her profile repeatedly as they chatted quietly. Olive appeared poised, but Cora knew the maid's heart lurched at being noticed by someone far above her station. The young woman was educated and poised thanks to Hugh—and had a heart of gold.

Moments before their arrival at the great hall, Crawford met them in the passage, and his sad gaze as she passed Olive squeezed Cora's heart. She shook off the emotion. He'd had his chance for some time, and it looked like he'd waited too late. The gardener would soon experience the same regret. If for no other reason, the evening might help Olive decide once and for all which of the men she genuinely loved.

Branston immediately escorted Olive to the floor and into a waltz. Cora whispered to Hugh, "I believe Branston may have found himself a wife. You've schooled her well."

"Are you not a bit premature?" One side of Hugh's mouth lifted into a teasing grin.

"Hm. We'll see." She placed a hand on his shoulder. "Are you not going to ask your wife to dance the waltz?"

"Indeed. Is that not when you first fell in love with me?"

"I believe it was the other way around." She grinned. "Let's just say it was probably mutual, though I didn't realize it then. I was quarrelsome with every breath."

He spread his arms wide and cocked his head. "Let us agree

it was mutual whether we were aware of it or not."

She lifted her chin. "I suppose that'll have to do for now."

They assumed the waltz position and danced onto the floor, reliving their first waltz so many months prior. Cora examined his face—that night fresh in her mind. How their contact made her feel as he'd swept them onto the terrace. And his mention of God.

Ardent lips met her cheek, and she started at the touch.

"A pound for your thoughts."

She smiled. "They're not worth that much."

Hugh widened his blue eyes. "A pence?"

The waltz ended, and the clock chimed midnight. Time for the mask reveal followed by an elaborate supper. Laughter rang out, and a strange costume of the most hideous shade of green and pink speckled with yellow paste gems was revealed to be worn by none other than the vicar's wife.

Hugh and Cora led the party into the dining room, and he glanced around as if searching for someone.

"Who are you looking for?"

"Ralph. I have not seen him lately."

"I saw him dance a few times. Come to think of it that was a while ago." Cora frowned, her arm on her husband's. "Why are you concerned?"

"I could not say. I did speak with him, and he appeared distracted. As if his mind was elsewhere."

"Let's not overthink it. He'll turn up. In fact, he may already be in the dining room. That man has the appetite of someone twice his size."

Hugh laughed. "Well said."

The dining room glowed much like the great hall. Wall sconces glittered against the mirrored backdrops. Candles flickered from chandeliers, shards of radiant light beaming down. The swing of cut-glass crystals on the candelabras trailed the center of the table sparkling like diamonds.

A melody of voices carried on cheerful discussions mingled with the tinkle of china as the procession of food in front of the guests grew more astonishing by the minute. Cora wondered how they ate this much food so late at night? It began with white soup, continuing with so many dishes she lost count.

Soon, the aroma of food, beeswax, and countless perfumes overwhelmed Cora's senses. Nausea rose, and she tapped Hugh's thigh under the table. His gaze shot to hers. Once he looked at her, his features grew serious.

Cora mouthed, "I'm not well."

He slid his hand onto hers and leaned toward her to whisper. "Smile as if all is well. We shall step outside into the fresh air."

They stood, and several guests peered at them curiously. "Not to worry. We shall return shortly. A bit of fresh air is all we desire."

Cora leaned against him, lightheaded, and lay her head on his shoulder. The cool night air hung heavy with floral scents, and she inhaled the soothing fragrance. "I'm sorry. All the smells seemed to choke me. I think the catalyst was the candle smoke."

Hugh rested his cheek on top of her head as they strolled

the gardens. "Does the air help?"

She nodded. "Very much. I'm already revived. May we walk for a while before we return?"

"As you wish. I rather like being alone with you after all the festivities." He sighed heavily. "Though you know we must return and stay until the end of the ball."

"I know." Cora's tone held regret. "I don't mean to be ungrateful. It's all been wonderful. Just a little overwhelming." She squeezed her eyes shut, then opened them again. "Of course, if I had not allowed my insecurities and fears to cripple me, things would be much better."

"We all struggle at times. You have no need to apologize—least of all to me."

Peaceful companionship settled around them like a welcoming blanket on a cold night. Stars glistened, a million pricks of light among the ebony.

"Hugh?"

"Yes, my love." A light breeze ruffled his dark locks.

Cora reached up and pushed back a strand of his hair. "Thank you for showing me how to fully trust God again. God spoke to me through your actions and words. I'm okay with whatever happens. His will be done."

Hugh halted their progress along the pebbled path and faced her, pressing his lips to hers. She felt his smile and returned the kiss. Without words, he looped her arm through his and resumed their pace, both satisfied with whatever God's plans revealed.

The tranquil night enveloped them as they ambled through the garden, not paying close attention to their surroundings but only each other.

A shriek rent the night, and they turned to see Ralph running toward them, waving a paper wildly over his head.

His form blurred, the cloudy haze of dawn framing him in orange, bronze, and yellow.

"Wait! Do not go, Hugh. I've read your letter—"

Cora strained to hear his words, but he seemed to be farther away with each hurried step, his words echoing.

A glance at Hugh revealed a knowing look, one of regret and relief. Cora understood when she spied the familiar edge of stone behind his shoulder. *The arch.*

൦ॐ൭

Cora blinked, and Ralph disappeared as well as the night. She clutched Hugh's arm tighter and squinted toward the path where Ralph had rushed toward them.

He was gone, and the path revealed daylight. She swallowed the lump in her throat and turned to Hugh, his eyes on the house.

He pressed a hand to his forehead. "Cora . . . we have returned." He murmured the words, barely above a whisper.

Cora leaned into him, a wave of relief surging through her, as she took in the car park and scanned the arch to see it had indeed been repaired. Something brushed her leg, and she glanced down to see Lizzy rubbing against her. The slight gesture warmed her heart.

She licked her lips, surprised to taste the salt from her tears. She would dearly miss Olive and Ralph and the others, but she breathed in deeply and nearly pinched herself to ensure it wasn't a dream.

Hugh put his arm around her shoulders. "We are home, love. Truly."

"Cora! Hugh!" Two voices melded together as Sam and Judith rushed from the car park toward them.

Judith grabbed Cora from Hugh's embrace and squeezed her into a fierce hug, then released her. "We've been so worried!" They stared at one another for a moment, and Judith hugged her again. "We thought the past had claimed you both."

Sam hugged Hugh, shoved him away, and slapped him on the back. "I thought we'd lost you and Cora forever, old man."

Hugh laughed and reclaimed Cora to his side. "So did we." He sobered and narrowed his eyes at Judith. "Wait, what did you say?"

Cora's ears perked. "Yes, Judith, what *did* you say?"

Judith's face paled. Sam stepped closer and laced his fingers with hers. "I had to tell her, Hugh. She was ready to call the police, and we couldn't stand the publicity. I worked as fast as I could to repair the arch." He kissed Judith's cheek. "She near drove me to Bedlam, telling me the arch was not important as long as you and Cora were missing and for me to leave it be."

Hugh's brow lifted.

"We only just finished today." Judith blew out a shaky breath. "If Sam had not told me the truth, I think I would've gone mad."

Cora's mind whirled, and she remembered her sister. "Have you spoken to Selena? She must be in agony over where

I am."

"Not to worry," Sam chimed in. "Judith covered very well—once I told her the truth. She texted her from your phone."

Cora's mouth dropped. "You pretended to be me?"

Judith's chin met her chest. "I'm sorry. Sam told me what had happened, and I couldn't very well tell your sister. She would've thought me insane."

"I suppose you're right." Cora *knew* she was. "Thank you for that."

Cora shifted her attention to Sam. "Please tell me how and why you believed Hugh's time travel thing in the first place, Sam? I was there, and it still took me days to believe."

Sam's cocky grin delighted Cora. "That's what family is for, my dear."

Cora frowned. "Family?"

"Ah," Hugh said. "Did I forget to tell you Samuel is my cousin?"

Cora and Judith's voices rose simultaneously. "Cousin!"

Both men looked at the women and wore nearly identical grins.

Sam held his arm high. "I confess. I'm the one who discovered the arch while visiting Hedsworth House. After several *trips,* I attended a present-day Regency ball, and Hugh stumbled into the garden and joined the festivities. We met, and I explained I had been here many times and had a newfound profession that excited me. I must confess it was some time before I became acclimated to the culture, but once settled, I rather enjoyed the challenge. Since I am a second son, I had to earn a living. Who would've thought it would be so many years in the future?"

Cora whispered, "A talent scout?"

"Yes," Judith said, starry-eyed. She pressed Sam's hand between hers. "It was love at first sight for me." She nudged him with her shoulder.

Sam shrugged. "Hm. It took me a little longer."

Hugh laughed loud and long. "My cousin has always been a bit of a scoundrel." He looked at Judith. "Since you came to work here, you are all he has talked about. A little while longer *indeed*."

Sam's face reddened, and he observed his shoes.

Judith's face softened. "Thank you, Hugh. I've always wondered."

Sam put an arm around her shoulder and cuddled her against his side. He grunted with a shrug.

Cora stretched her neck. "I am sooo ready for a shower."

Hugh cleared his throat. "Um, Cora, do you not think we should tell them?"

She sent him a puzzled look, and he brought his mouth to her ear. "Our marriage."

Her mouth formed an O-shape. "Sorry. Yes. I think so."

Judith and Sam stared at the couple. Judith bit her lip, and Sam's eyes squinted.

Hugh blew out a breath. "We are wed."

Silence hung in the early morning light, the hum of a car in the distance and the muffle of daily chores performed on the estate.

Judith dropped Sam's hand, and she squealed, gripping

Cora into another hug. "You and Hugh? Oh, my gosh! I cannot believe it. I thought you loathed him."

Cora released a nervous titter. "I did."

Sam stood frozen, his expression almost comical. A series of emotions crossed his face, and a slow realization of what this meant spurred him on. "Hugh, I never thought I'd see the day when you found a woman perfect for you. I'm glad it's Cora. I wish you all the best."

"Thank you, Sam. I am the happiest of men."

Cora's gaze beamed at Hugh. "I think we shall get on quite well for a while."

Hugh's eyes roamed his wife's face. "I think we shall get on well forever, my love."

Cora's heart soared. Yes, they would, indeed—with the God of the past and eternity watching over them.

Epilogue

One year later . . .

"Cora, I told you I'm fine. Randall is pampering me beyond normal."

In the background, Selena's husband asked her where his keys were, and his cheerful humming eased Cora's thoughts about the man.

"Selena, you are thirty-eight, and this is your first child. Of course I'm concerned." The shadow of disquiet over her sister re-marrying Randall lurked in the back of her mind, but so far, he seemed a changed man. His encounter with God appeared genuine. They married secretly and shared the news with Cora the week after she and Hugh returned.

Keeping the secret of Cora's and Hugh's covert absence from Selena had not been difficult for Judith as her sister's preoccupation with Randall kept her busy.

"I'm glad you and Randall are happy. Perhaps had I not been such a basket case years ago, it may have worked out then."

Selena's voice dropped, sorrow edging her tone. "That's where you're wrong. It took something drastic to get Randall's attention and steer him to God. He'd been miserable until he realized God is at the center of any successful relationship."

A melodic baritone invaded their conversation. "Hi, Cora, sorry for the interruption, but we must leave for the doctor's office for the ultrasound, so we can see Aiden for the first time."

Cora chuckled. "Aiden? You don't know if it's a boy yet."

"My husband is determined. That's the name he's settled on."

"Well, sister, you're about to find out. Let me know as soon as you do. Have you chosen a girl's name yet?"

Selena whispered into the phone, "He won't allow me to think it." Her voice lowered, and Cora strained to hear. "My choice for a girl is Portia."

Cora shook her head. Her sister always made the most unconventional choices.

"I know what you're thinking, so I'll move on. How's life with hunky Hugh?"

"Selena!" Cora huffed. "That's my husband."

"Oh, lighten up, Cora. I'm only joking. I have my own hunky husband, so we're even." Selena laughed. "Is he still the ever-present Regency gentleman? Or have you converted him?"

Cora beamed as she watched Hugh's approach down the path from the private garden.

The stride of his tall, trim form every bit a gentleman. She'd never want him to be anything else. "I want him just as he is—*my* perfect Mr. Darcy."

THE END

374

Author's Note

This is my first time delving into the Regency period as a writer. I've been reading Regency era books and watching Regency movies for many years, yet I've never written about the period. What historical fiction reader can pass up a good Regency story? Which brought me to write my own.

The location of Hedsworth House is just over the Devon border into Cornwall. After visiting Cotehele, located in the Tamar Valley, I knew this had to be the inspiration for *Of the Past and Eternity*. While not modeled exactly after the historic house, it was a great location. I actually met one of the garden volunteers on the train to Cornwall. We had a long discussion about books and the historical properties of Cornwall. She invited me to tour the house—which I did. It was a wonderful afternoon walking the rooms and gardens that mostly dated to the Tudor era. To see the property, visit: www.nationaltrust.org.uk/visit/cornwall/cotehele

Several notorious swindles marked the nineteenth century, including one involving a fictitious country, one connected to the transcontinental railroad, and a number of bank and stock market frauds. For Ralph, Hugh's cousin, I tweaked a common coal mining scam to match my timeline, so the specifics are not exactly to that era.

The language of flowers flowed from the Regency era into the Victorian, the Victorians finessing the tradition. I have taken liberties with the fine details of floriography to suit my story, so if you see something amiss, please disregard as I used poetic license—again.

The items that Hugh gifts to Cora for their wedding are based on actual Yardley products, which have been produced since the 1770s. Research reveals they fashioned small pots of toothpaste during this era, and I created a lavender option. I've enjoyed their lavender-scented products for most of my life and still use them.

Chalked ballroom floors were something new to me when I began research for this novel. I cannot remember a Regency novel or movie where it was mentioned. The artistic element fascinated me, so I slipped it into the story.

I didn't want to get too caught up in Regency attire, so I kept it simple, rather than walk my reader through the tedium of the many layers, changes of clothing, etc.

Regarding wedding rings, I chose to slip in the use although it was not a customary thing during the Regency era. I mean, what is a wedding without the bride's ring? Men did not normally wear them until the mid-twentieth century.

I hope you enjoyed Cora and Hugh's story, and that God has spoken to your own heart—as He did mine—regarding the past and eternity. Thank you for taking time out of your busy life to read my novel.

God bless,
Carole

Enjoy *Of the Past & Eternity?*

Here's a preview of another time travel novel by the author

A Place in Time

Chapter One

Stanton Wake, England
March 2021

Adela Jenks rummaged through a dusty crate, from time-to-time glancing across the room at her friends, Kellie Welles and Leanne Harcourt.

The pungent scent of incense nearly choked her, a thread of smoke drifting from the counter next to the cash register. Ever the optimist, she searched for what she hoped would be a memorable keepsake of this trip with her two closest friends.

The shopkeeper had told her the charity shop began as a

meat market five hundred years before, developing into many businesses through the centuries, and was reborn in the late twentieth century as Charity's Charity Shop. Not a clever name, to be sure, but one you wouldn't forget along with its history.

Everything was so much older, more historic in England—one reason Adela had longed to come.

She heard robust laughter and looked up to see Leanne plowing through a rack of vintage garments.

Leanne met her eyes. "Kellie, what's Adela doing in the corner? She sounds like a humongous pack rat."

Kellie held a long flowing silk robe up against her tall, curvaceous figure. "I have no idea . . . how does this look on me?" She twirled and tilted her head from side to side. "Hmm?"

"The two of you do *know* this is not a large shop," Adela said matter-of-factly. "I can hear everything you say about me. But—" She paused to sneeze.

"All you're doing is stirring up dust and aggravating your allergies," Leanne quipped.

"I'm determined to—" Adela sneezed again. "—find a keepsake that won't take up half of my carry-on."

Another sneeze. The potent incense had to be the cause. With a moment of reprieve, she looked at Kellie. "That silk thingy is beautiful. Don't you think so, Leanne?"

Leanne turned to Kellie. "Yes, the emerald complements your blonde hair, and the size of the print suits your height. You should get it."

"Really? I do like it, and it will please Adela since it doesn't take up much room in my bag." Kellie grinned and flung the garment over her shoulder.

Adela stood, dusting off her hands, and approached them. "I heard that." But she grinned and held up a small item in triumph. "I found the perfect keepsake."

Kellie and Leanne exchanged questioning looks, probably thinking of her penchant for *unusual* purchases.

"Don't give me *the* look," Adela admonished them. "It's something truly unique."

"What is it? A seventeenth-century fork for your cookbook project?" Leanne teased. "Whatcha gonna do? Pose with it for a picture?"

"Droll, very droll." Adela smirked at Leanne while Kellie chuckled.

Opening what appeared to be a small, thin antique book, Adela's lips curved into a smile as she took in the first page. "Oh, yes. This is exactly what I wanted."

A vintage passport.

❧

Seated in Lady Margaret's Tea House in the village of Stanton Wake, Adela chatted with Kellie and Leanne about their day over afternoon tea. Adela took out her new purchase and examined it. A ripple of brightly colored fabric slid over the page as Leanne flung her Celtic scarf around her neck. She glanced up. "What *are* you doing?"

Kellie answered, "Being ridiculous, as usual." She pulled the robe from her bag. "Not fair. I can't wear this around my neck."

383

Adela ignored their banter and jotted down a few notes in her journal of all they'd done since breakfast.

Leanne huffed. "I can't find my lip gloss." She plowed through her purse, piling things on the table.

Kellie pointed to the passport. "Why don't we have a look-see? Find out whose past you're delving into."

Adela tugged the leather tab from a tiny slit. The passport was close in size to a contemporary one, but when she opened the cover, the paper was blank, yellowed, and musty.

She noted Kellie and Leanne's disappointed expressions and smiled. They thought she'd purchased something of no value.

Adela gradually unfolded the paper to reveal one sizeable piece folded into ten sections. Two revealed faded black and white photos—one of a man and the other of a woman and a small child.

Leanne squealed with delight, and Kellie grinned.

Adela fixed them with a mock glare. "You both always seem so surprised when I find something of worth."

By the time their second pot of tea arrived, they'd learned the passport belonged to a man from Southampton and his wife and young son. They discussed the places the family had traveled to, then their conversation moved to the upcoming festival.

"I don't know what to expect." Kellie's expression clouded. "I hope it won't be a letdown."

"No worries, Kellie," Leanne said. "We'll have a great time. Just dressing up in those costumes Adela made will get us in seventeenth-century mode. Remember how hard we laughed when we tried them on the first time? All those layers. I thought I'd ache for days at how funny you looked when you got your arms stuck in that chemise, wriggling like trying to escape a cocoon."

"The least you could've done was stop laughing and helped me out of it. Adela had to rescue me while you lay on the floor laughing your fool head off."

Leanne's face lit up. "It *was* fun." She grew thoughtful. "With all those layers, we might need a two-hour start on dressing."

Kellie munched on her scone and nodded.

Adela studied the passport absentmindedly. Her thoughts went to the costume patterns ordered a year before their trip, and the time taken to sew the period garments. She'd been meticulous about the right fabric, colors, and patterns related to the era.

Taking a sip of tea, she glanced at her friends over the rim of her cup.

"Let's finish our shopping before dinner, go back to the cottage and crash," Leanne offered. She stifled a yawn. "Jet lag's still got me."

Adela signaled the waitress to pay and asked her to bag up the remaining scones. She tucked the paper bag in her tote, and they stepped out into the uncommonly warm March afternoon.

She closed her eyes and inhaled the sweet fragrance of wildflowers and foliage. The fresh country scents invigorated her as they strolled the lane toward their cottage.

Her gaze fixed on a pasture full of sheep, little ones running back to their mothers for safety.

Adela froze.

Beyond the field, the perfect example of a seventeenth century manor house stood at the end of a tree-lined gravel drive. Enough of the house was visible to glimpse its splendor.

Something about the house called to her, inexplicably. She longed to rush up the drive. Foolish, she knew, but the urge was there nonetheless.

"Adela," Leanne called out. "You'll become a sheep if you stand there any longer."

Adela shook her head, awakening from a trance, but the connection, the pull of the house, stayed with her.

Èž

The tiny tourist office stood at the center of Stanton Wake in a building dating back over three hundred years. Beryl, the short white-haired woman answering their questions, was most knowledgeable about the area. Having lived in Stanton Wake all her life, there wasn't a thing she didn't know about the village. Many of her ancestors had been born in the area.

Leanne whispered, "Let's find out about the Adela Jenks Manor House, so we can get some lunch."

Kellie elbowed her.

Adela ignored them. She had told them about the house and what she experienced, but she didn't expect them to understand.

She didn't even understand.

But maybe learning more about the place would somehow jog her memory about the connection to the house, perhaps one of her ancestors had lived there.

Beryl told them Maximus DeGrey built Dunbar Park about 1600. His father had bequeathed him one thousand acres. "He had no siblings—at least there is no evidence he did. His son, Henry, inherited. After his death in London, his son, Marcus, took charge of the house and brought his young daughter to live at Stanton Wake. The manor has never been out of the family's ownership."

"Do you think there's a possibility for a tour?" Adela's stomach clenched.

"Not likely. They only do tours during the festival and are probably booked. The family is protective of their privacy."

Leanne jumped in. "How can we find out? We *really* would like a tour." She placed a hand on Adela's shoulder. "Adela is a gourmet chef and history enthusiast and would love a tour of the house and its kitchen as research for her cookbook. Would you be so kind as to help us?" She turned on her winsome personality, which had amassed an enormous social media following and a career as an influencer along the way.

Beryl tapped her chin. "Let me see what I can do." She picked up the phone and dialed.

Leanne whispered to Adela, "That's a good sign."

Beryl stepped out of earshot and spoke quietly into the phone. Nodding, she walked back to the counter where they waited.

Adela held her breath.

The woman's mouth stretched into a wide grin. "You, dear American ladies, have an appointment to tour Dunbar Park tomorrow afternoon."

Adela gently took the woman's hand. "Wonderful! I don't know how to thank you."

"My pleasure, dear, my pleasure. It's nice for someone to take an interest in our local history. Everyone seems bent on tearing things down to put up something modern. Such a disgrace. I prefer visiting places that own morsels of history, not places where everything was built last week."

Adela laughed and bid her goodbye.

Walking along the cobblestone street, Adela marveled at their good fortune to tour the house, and she hoped it would reveal some of its secrets to her.

About the Author

Carole Lehr Johnson is a veteran travel consultant of more than 30 years and has served as head of genealogy at her local library.

Her love of tea and scones, castles and cottages, and all things British has led her to immerse her writing in the United Kingdom whether in the genre of historical or contemporary fiction.

Carole is the author of four inspirational novels set in England as well as a novella collection. Her second novel, *A Place in Time*, was a Notable Book Award finalist for the Southern Christian Writers Conference.

She is a member of the American Christian Fiction Writers (ACFW) and served as the past president of her local chapter. She and her husband live in Louisiana with their goofy cats.

For more information, visit
www.carolelehrjohnson.com

Sign up for Carole's newsletter on her website for updates on her next release, U.K. travel features, recipes, book recommendations, and more.

Books by Carole Lehr Johnson

Permelia Cottage

A Place in Time

The Burning Sands

Of the Past and Eternity